# THE
# FLEET
## IN THE
# WINDOW

## DAVID BERGAMINI

POPULAR LIBRARY · NEW YORK

Copyright © 1961 by David Bergamini
Library of Congress Catalog Card Number: 60-12581

Published by arrangement with Simon & Schuster, Inc.
Simon & Schuster edition published in January, 1961

**DEDICATION:** To Pic, Alec and Jack, my three sons,
as yet illiterate, who nightly counted
the pages in the growing "story of Peter"
and were mightily impressed.

## CHAPTER 1

Peter Baldwin sat on the edge of the blanket stirring his big toe in the sand and keeping watch down the beach toward the promontory where the other school children would appear if they came looking. A flash breeze rattled and flapped in the palm leaves overhead, but for Peter it was as if the afternoon in its listless fever had only yawned. He turned back crossly to Enid and Norman. They were still at it.

"Come on, Norm, it's my turn," said Peter. Enid rolled Norman off the top of her and sat up.

"I'm tired of kissing." Each syllable Enid spoke had a separate musical pitch which she attacked without sliding or slurring. Her parents were Scandinavian—that is, her father was Scandinavian. Her mother was dead.

"But it's my turn," said Peter again.

"I don't care. I want to swim. Norman does it better anyway. Your lips are too thin."

She got up, dusting sand into Peter's eyes. Norman jumped up after her and the two of them ran down through the breakers and started water fighting on the sand bar beyond. Peter watched them stonily, then threw himself back beyond the blanket and rolled his cheek into the sand. He was hurt and humiliated but also shocked. She thought and spoke too literally, too physically. Good people, if they talked about lips at all, admired thin ones. Thin ones were more sensitive. Not that Peter spent much time considering appearances—his own or anyone else's. But his mother had often warned him that pouting could permanently thicken his lips, a possibility which she seemed to contemplate with

5

real loathing. And so Peter had learned to be conscious of his mouth, and sometimes felt himself readjusting it to be tight and ready for expressing kindness or intelligence. The trouble was Enid didn't value kindness or intelligence. She didn't seem to care much about good and evil. No one did in her world. No one in her world even went to church. People said her father was a Nazi. He sold German machinery to the sugar refineries.

Peter pictured Enid to himself in two ways. In the beautiful way she was only a face: hair as fine and yellow and straight as Jeanne d'Arc's should have been; a thin straight nose; sunny blue eyes; a high forehead, tanned and glowing; and a quick, timid smile which hinted at inward thoughtfulness and contentment. Peter wanted so much to make friends with her—real friends who could talk easily. But in the ugly way Enid was more than a face. And her body was arched with evil energy. Her hair was fresh out of curlers. Her nose tilted upward foolishly. Her eyes were shifty and teasing and her mouth twisted in a smirk of mischief. He heard her laughter blown in to shore and he knew that she was looking like that now, splashing about and pretending to Norman that she couldn't swim well. Soon they would have to rejoin the other children at the bus. The school's long-awaited seashore picnic would be over without his having talked to her alone and asked her the questions he had planned. If she said she was innocent, would he believe her? Or if she admitted that she knew? He heard her laugh again and felt she was jerking him to hell by a cruel, snaky leash made of reflections on moving water.

"For God's sake, you are drowning me," she shouted.

Please God, thought Peter, please God, if you can still hear me—please, if she is wicked, help me to put her out of my mind. Help me to purify my thoughts. Help me not to go on playing the Game with them.

The Game had started last summer vacation as Truth or Consequences. The players took turns asking one another embarrassing questions. The person questioned could choose either to answer with the sworn truth or perform a dare, a consequence, imposed by the questioner. Enid always preferred to take the "consequence." At first they made her climb trees or handle beetles or carve their names on her desk. Later they made her expose part of herself. But she was already fifteen, two years older than Peter, a year older than

Norman. And they found her body disturbing, especially revealed piecemeal as it was. Calendars and post cards had prepared them to think a nude girl should look prettily artificial and abstract, like an advertisement for candy or for strawberry shortcake and whipped cream.

One afternoon after school while they waited for Enid in their secret place in the woods they talked the situation over and agreed not to set her any more undressing consequences. They reasoned that she could not be so unembarrassed if she knew anything, and if she didn't know anything they had no right to take advantage of her. With this restriction on it the Game might have staled and died, but Enid re-enlivened it the same afternoon by making Peter kiss her. He brushed her cheek in the way of greetings within his family, but she would not accept it. She meant on the mouth. Shamefacedly Peter did his best, but no, a peck was not enough either. Enid had to show him. And he found that the silly sissy ceremony filled his young senses more vividly than the most abandoned sick daydream he had ever devised.

In the following weeks Enid's innovation came to dominate the Game. They dropped all pretense of asking questions. They reduced the rules to one: that Norman and Peter should kiss Enid an equal number of times. One kept watch while the other took his turn with her. The boys felt guilty and secret and dramatized their sentry duty. Enid insisted it was only part of the Game. And in fact there was little likelihood of their being discovered. Their hiding place was an island in the bed of a gully half a mile through the woods from school. After the floods of the last rainy season the side slopes of the island had been freshly overgrown with jungle. It was so thick that they had been able to cut a tunnel through it and curtain the entrance with vines. But on the top of the island six domineering pine trees suppressed all undergrowth and carpeted the ground with needles. Even from the banks of the gully on either side no one could see through the fringe of vegetation into the room within.

If the children did hear anyone walking in the woods nearby, or if it rained, they could still retire to the cave. Not much of a cave really. More just a shelf of rock sticking out over a bed of clay. But it was secret. A cascade of vines and crawlers hung down over the ledge and let in only a little dappled sunlight. Also, the cave had its own approach tunnel, a crawlway through the bushes which began at the clear-

7

ing and was completely separate from the tunnel leading into the clearing from the outside world. This meant that an intruder penetrating to the Inner Keep, as Peter called it, would have to discover two separate secret passageways. In case of siege—a picnic in the gully which, as Peter pointed out, might bottle them up for hours—the children kept a tin box of crackers buried in the cave's clay floor. All in all the arrangements on the Island were so perfect that even Peter had begun to be a little bored by the place.

The Game and its secrecy had also begun to lose some of their original pleasure. Enid allowed Peter and Norman to linger longer over each kiss. Their faces grew flushed more easily. Their bickering about turns and time limits grew more tiresome to all of them. Lately almost every session had ended with Norman and Peter fighting and Enid going home angry at them. It had been just as unsatisfying today at the beach—even with the cool ocean nearby and the danger of being seen so real.

Peter asked himself how long he would go on playing the Game. If he could talk privately and clearly to Enid he would make her leave out Norman or he would quit it himself. But, meanwhile, he was unsure about her motives. She was the only one of them who had never missed an afternoon. Norman and Peter had each been absent once. The day Norman flew to Manila with his father in the sugar mill's pay-roll plane, Enid came as usual but had to go home early. And Peter was shy. He didn't say any of the things he had meant to say. When Norman asked him about it, he smiled and said he was pledged to secrecy. The day Peter had to mind his sister—when his mother went to the dentist and Anita, the maid, was sick—Norman also admitted to a wonderful afternoon, but he couldn't talk about it either.

Water fell on Peter's head in the sand. He looked up and Enid had emptied her bathing cap on him.

"You are sulking, Peter? Don't pay attention to what I said. I only meant that you are more serious than Norm, and sometimes I don't wish to kiss you because it's more difficult. There—" she knelt and kissed him—"come take me swimming. Norm is a bad swimmer. I don't dare go out far with him."

Peter got up sheepishly. She laughed and dashed down the beach. Peter tackled her in a breaking wave and they came up laughing and spluttering, with sand in their hair and ears.

8

"I want to swim to the island out there."

"It's probably farther than it looks," said Peter.

Norman swam a short way with them but turned back, shouting crossly when they started to outdistance him. He knew no stroke but an awkward crawl, and this was tiring in the waves. Enid breast-stroked prettily. Peter lay on his back and frog-kicked so that he would just stay abreast of her. Outside the little bay the well from the China Sea was long and steady and they could talk.

"Why am I difficult when I'm serious?" he asked.

"You act hungry," she said, "like a dog that sometimes bites."

"That's ridiculous." He swam silently, turning over in his mind all the good, friendly things in him and the wicked, lustful things in him that she might have meant.

"Enid, do you like me and Norm the same?"

"I don't know. I think I like you differently. Norm doesn't ask me questions."

"You mean you like him better?"

"Sometimes. But not to swim with."

Peter was filled with hope. After a struggle with himself he told her in a strange voice that he loved her.

"Fiddlesticks," she replied. *Fiddlesticks* was one of Peter's expressions. It amused her.

"Do you love Norm?" he asked.

"I like you both."

"I don't think we should kiss you the way we do."

"It's fun," she said. "I like it."

"But it's not like it used to be. It's more serious. Norm says he loves you too."

"When did he say that?"

"I don't know. A long time ago."

"He never said it to me except as a consequence."

"Are you glad we both love you?"

"I don't care. It's nice."

"I wish you would choose between us."

"Why should I?" she said, annoyed. "Are we halfway yet?"

"More, I should think."

"Good. I'm getting tired."

Peter's inquisition had come to a dead end. He concentrated malevolently on the little pile of rocks ahead of him. By the time they reached it, he was beginning to feel tired too. In the middle of the rocks they found a bed of sand and a tidal pool.

Enid flung herself down on the sand. "I could go to sleep."

"We should be getting back to the bus soon," said Peter. "But if we wait awhile the tide may change. We had it with us coming out."

"You mean it may be harder going back?"

"Unless we wait for the tide it will."

"Then we'll have to wait."

"Can I kiss you?" he asked finally.

"It's not your turn," she said without opening her eyes.

Peter got up and walked around the rocks. The bus was still hidden by the point. Norm lying on the beach was only a speck. The wind felt chilly and Peter's sunburned back broke out in goose pimples. It was lonely on the island, even scary. Mrs. Gibney would be furious with them for having disappeared such a long time. He picked his way back to Enid gingerly over the polyp-studded rocks. Her eyes were still closed and she seemed to be asleep. She lay on her back with her feet in the tidal pool. Her shoulders and legs were beautifully smooth and brown. Her damp bathing suit followed every crease and curve of her skin.

Peter looked at her with guilty fascination and repulsion. An unpleasant weightless feeling squirmed through his stomach. It would be easier if she were awake, so he knelt and touched the arch of her foot. She stirred. He smiled toward her face, but she didn't open her eyes. He stroked her shoulder where there was a mole. She didn't move. He kissed her. Even then she did not move. He kissed her several times on her neck and shoulders and then on her lips again. Her lips were slack and partway open. He stretched out beside her, put his mouth against hers and lay there quietly while excitement rose inside him. Suddenly he realized that his tongue was in her mouth. He drew it back and bit it.

Unclean! he thought violently. I'm unclean and wicked beyond all hope. But as he lay there another point of view recurred to him insistently. Her germs were now his germs. They lived in each other.

He extended his tongue again and touched her. It moved. It slipped into his mouth and out again quickly. He rolled on top of her, forgetting himself. She opened her eyes and looked at him curiously. He paid no attention. He was not embarrassed. He was not thinking. She closed her mouth and pushed him away, laughing.

"That's a good new way to kiss," she said. "But it's not your turn." She got up and looked toward the beach. "Norman is waving to us. It must be time to go back." She ran out on a rock and lowered herself into the water.

"The tide hasn't turned yet," called Peter.

"You can wait for it if you want," she answered, swimming.

He ran across the rocks, dived into the water and caught up with her. The wind was blowing from the shore. The water was cooler and more choppy than it had been. The tide was strong against them. It was going to be a hard swim and he threw himself into it gladly.

"You are not angry?" asked Enid.

"What for?"

"For making you come back?"

"No, I'm glad you did."

"Why?"

"I was forgetting about turns. I was losing self-control."

"Because of me?"

"Yes."

"There is nothing so wrong about that, is there?"

"Yes. No, I mean. I mean, I liked it but I mustn't take advantage of you."

She laughed and changed to a backstroke. "I'm cold," she said.

After a long silence he asked what he had wanted to ask for months. "Enid, do you . . . do you know about men and women?"

"What do you mean?"

"About how they have children?"

"It's none of your business," she said.

"Did your father tell you?" he persisted.

"I don't remember."

"How could you forget?"

"I haven't forgotten. But it was more than once. I learned gradually."

"Who told you gradually?"

"Oh, I don't know. The girls at school, I guess."

Peter was surprised. He hadn't realized girls would talk about it. Anyway, she knew and had always known, but she let him and Norm lie on her and think about her in the worst way. Of course it might be that Norman didn't. Per-

haps that was what she meant by calling Peter too serious—
because no question about it, his thoughts were the wickedness. *Whosoever looketh on a woman to lust after her hath
committed already* . . . But would Enid and Norman kiss
so long if it were only a harmless, friendly, thoughtless kiss
and nothing more?

"How much farther?" she asked.

"We're not even halfway yet."

"My leg hurts."

"Gosh, don't get a cramp."

"I can't help it. It hurts more each time I kick."

"Float a bit. Maybe you can relax it."

She floated and Peter tried to remember the lifesaving he
had learned in Scouts.

"It just gets colder and stiffer," she said.

"Try sidestroking and we'll go slowly."

They swam a few yards more.

"Oh!" she cried. "I can't straighten it."

She struggled and took a mouthful of water. Peter grabbed
her arm and held her up.

"Put your arm over my shoulder. I'll tread water while
you get the kink out of it."

She hung on, gasping. "I can't. It hurts too much."

"You have to."

She looked frightened, but instead of weeping—the way a
lot of girls would, he thought—she shouted at him angrily,
"I can't, you dope."

"All right, just stay there then." He ducked his face under
the water, reached down and sank his fingers into her
doubled-up leg. As he kneaded the muscles, she clutched at
his hair and thrashed about above him. The leg went straight.
He kicked hard and came up gulping for air, but he swallowed mostly water because she pushed him under again.
With a desperate effort he yanked his head from her grasp
and, remembering clearly what he had to do, caught her feet,
forced them together and turned her like a fence post or a
ladder. Then he came up the back of her, hand over hand to
the surface, and took a firm hold on her head from behind.
She grabbed at his fingers and tried to wrench them away
from her jaw.

"It's all right! Don't bend your legs again. I'll tow you."

"I was drowning!" She coughed water and let go of his
hands.

"That's right. Relax all over."

When she seemed completely past her terror, he shifted his carry, putting one arm across her chest and sidestroking with the other. It took him nearly half an hour to reach the beach. His legs were beginning to cramp too. And he was trying to accept and evaluate the impossible idea that they would drown. When he started to carry Enid out of the water, he couldn't, so he dragged her a little way up the smooth sand and flopped down beside her. Norman had only just noticed that they were in trouble. He had started to run for help in the direction of the bus, but now he turned and came back. He lifted Enid and carried her up to dry sand.

Peter started at the blood oozing from a place in his hand where she had scratched him. He wondered why her skin felt so neuter and lifeless in the water. The waves were washing his feet. He shivered and sat up. Norman was rubbing Enid's back with a towel. He was helping her into her terry-cloth shirt. When Peter staggered up to them, she was smiling and talking calmly again.

"It's awful having a cramp in the water. When you try to fix it, you sink. Peter had to swim me all the last part of the way."

Peter picked up his clothes. "We should probably go back to the others now," he said.

Norman helped Enid wrap her glasses and lotion and things in a towel and they set off. Enid limped a little and Peter felt stiff and stupid. To his relief he didn't have to make conversation on the way back because Enid and Norman talked nonstop about the Christmas dance a week from Saturday. In general, Peter hated dances because he had never been taught to dance formally and was in the process of learning by embarrassing experience. But now it didn't matter so much as usual. He was too tired and proud.

CHAPTER 2

From the lightness of the scolding Mrs. Gibney gave them when they reached the bus, Peter could see that she hadn't taken much notice of their absence. It was funny: where

Enid and Norm and he were concerned, Mrs. Gibney had a tendency not to notice things—or at least not to expect trouble. He guessed there was no denying it: they were all three of them teacher's pets. Mrs. Gibney liked *him* because he was a good student and took private piano lessons from her. Norm got in good with her by his nice manners and the care with which he washed and combed and dressed himself. Enid? Well, Enid was the biggest of her favorites and the hardest to explain. Peter thought it was because, being English, Mrs. Gibney believed in games and Enid was the only one of the pretty girls in eighth grade who ever went out and played Kick-the-Can and Prisoners' Base with the boys. Peter based his theory on a tongue-lashing he'd overheard Mrs. Gibney give the other girls one day for staying in class during recess and putting on nail polish.

"A more simpering, primping, silly lot of fillies I hope I never see," she hissed, her accent more British than usual. "You're trying to make my class into a jungle of competitive American adolescence and sex and I won't have it. The boys aren't ready for your nonsense yet, and neither are you."

At the thought of Mrs. Gibney's ignorance and innocence Peter smiled weakly to himself and shifted his weight uncomfortably from one foot to the other. Mrs. Gibney was in the process of taking roll call. Since Baldwin was the first name on her list and Peter had already answered to it, he was enjoying the special B-name luxury of letting his attention wander. Actually it was more than a luxury, he thought: it was one of the things that made him feel like him. He never would forget—or forgive—that teacher he'd had in Buffalo during his family's last furlough in the States. What a crazy, new-fangled idea of hers it was, calling the roll backward, starting with "Z"!

Mrs. Gibney had come to the last name on the list.

"Now let's see," she was saying. "Which four of you shall we put in the pickup truck for the ride home? Norman Diak, Peter Baldwin and Enid Larsen, you three seem to enjoy your own company."

Some of the kids giggled, but Peter hardly blushed.

"We need one more. What about you, Margaret Higgins? The fresh air will do you good."

"All right," said Maggie quietly. Maggie always said things quietly. She was a freshman in high school, a dark, pretty girl with a pale face and a lazy way of moving. Peter admired her for her self-composure, but he had hardly ever talked to her. Her grownupness prevented it. She was only one class ahead of him, but at dances she usually danced with one of the Gay brothers or with Charley French, and they were seniors.

Mrs. Gibney lined up her charges—there were twenty-nine of them, from eighteen-year-olds down to eight-year-olds—and marched them into the dilapidated bus. Meanwhile Maggie and Peter, Enid and Norman waited in the pickup truck for Antonio, the driver, to load in behind them the baskets and other debris from the picnic. Down the beach the rest of the teachers lazily gathered up their belongings and put them in the two cars, which belonged to Mr. Fincher, the science professor, and Father Gibney, the school principal and husband of Mrs. Gibney.

Antonio did not finish the packing until the bus already had a good head start on him. Then he shot off after it at breakneck speed, weaving back and forth wildly in a futile attempt to avoid jarring ruts in the dirt road and slashing leaves from the jungle of banana palms on either side.

Peter gave Maggie his beach blanket to help protect her from the outrageous shocks and lurchings. He himself half stood, half crouched, gripping the side of the truck firmly and watching for branches to duck. He was enjoying it as a game when he noticed that Enid had been jostled into a corner with Norman and was shamelessly cushioning herself on him while Maggie looked on. As long as the truck was in the jungle it was impossible to talk, but soon Antonio catapulted out onto the main road, a tortuous ribbon of concrete stretching from the port and airfield of Vispayan fifty miles through fields of sugar cane and then up the mountainsides to the resort city of Abanao. It was the only paved highway on the island of Panoc, but it was a good one, built by American engineers, and it allowed the children to relax a bit.

"Don't you think you should put your shirt on, Peter?" asked Maggie. "You'll catch cold in Antonio's prop wash." Maggie was untouchably rich. Her father owned a Piper Cub and was teaching her to fly.

"Antonio's crazy," said Peter, picking up his shirt.

"What were you all swimming in?" asked Maggie. "You're covered with scratches."

Enid pushed Norman, laughing, over to his own side of the truck.

15

"Those are my fingernails," she said in her blunt, sing-song way. "I had a cramp in my leg and he almost drowned me getting it out."

"You were frightened," said Peter.

"I certainly was. He had to swim carrying me for a long way."

"It sounds as if you were out too far," said Maggie. "Would you like me to rub some cream on your back, Peter?"

"No, I'm all right, thanks."

"It will make your scratches feel better and your sunburn, too," she persisted.

"Doesn't it smell or anything?"

"No, it's only cold cream. Come here and sit down." Peter did as he was told. Although it made him feel foolish, he liked having her rub his back—partly because her hands felt good but mostly because her attentions might impress Enid. After rescuing Enid, he had assumed she would be grateful, that she would, in effect, belong to him forever. He had been careful not to crow over Norman. He had taken pains to let Enid talk privately with Norman so that she could dismiss him gently without embarrassing him. But Enid had not even thanked Peter. He hoped she was somehow being discreet, but it was hard for him to appreciate it.

"Don't squirm so much," said Maggie. "Sit up straighter." He blushed and obeyed.

"Peter, why are you blushing?" asked Enid.

"I'm not," he retorted. Then, after waiting a moment, as if to prove his point, he said, "Thanks, Maggie. That feels fine," and got up to put his shirt on. His trunks were dry, so he pulled on his pants over them. As he buttoned up the fly it occurred to him that this last step in dressing looked the same whether you started from dry bathing trunks or naked skin. At the thought he blushed again.

"You're blushing again," said Enid.

"I don't know why," he asserted sullenly.

"Leave him alone," said Maggie. "Some people blush easily about nothing. I often do."

It was true: she did. But she was a girl and the kind of girl who always blushed about nice things, which she was ready to explain naturally and prettily with more blushes. Peter considered his own blushing an almost incapacitating weakness and he resented anyone excusing it.

"We're going to pass the bus," shouted Norman. They all

16

jumped up as the truck rocked toward the left.

"Get a water buffalo," screamed Norman.

"When's that thing going to grow up into a bus?" yelled back Fritz Laski.

"Blow me one of your extra kisses, Enid," shrieked Louise Newcombe. Louise was a raucous, overly plump girl who had played Truth and Consequences with them at the very beginning last summer. After the first few times they had left her out and she blamed Enid.

Apparently Louise knew more about the Game than Peter had thought. As the bus dropped behind, he was overcome with weariness and disgust. His feelings, the useless, wasteful feelings for Enid, were surrounded by a tangle of shame. What sort of person was he becoming? He lied to his mother habitually about where he had been. He went to church and took Communion without doing anything afterward about the promises of reform which he made in prayers. He was a prey to lascivious thoughts. Worst of all, he was constantly embarrassed. For some reason, when he had lost his straight-forwardness, he had also lost his calm and self-respect around people. It occurred to him that the words "state of grace" were more literal than he had ever imagined. Not being in a state of grace was the same thing as feeling constantly awkward.

"Peter, if you can't talk," said Enid, "let's sing songs or something."

He knew she didn't like to sing because she had no sense of pitch. And he knew she knew that he loved to sing. Her condescension made his temper worse.

"I'm tired and sunburned," he said. "Go ahead and sing if you want."

"I can't sing. You know it."

"Well, let's make a noise, anyway," said Norm. "We don't need him for that."

"Now I don't feel like it," said Enid. "He acts as if he had pushed me across the Pacific Ocean."

"Did he save your life?" asked Maggie curiously. She was knitting an athletic sweater for Charley French and gazing back toward the coast where the sun was setting.

"Probably," answered Enid. "But you wouldn't think so from the way he's acting, would you?"

"I don't know," said Maggie.

Peter felt he was being stripped naked and flayed but he

didn't dare say anything.

"Today he taught me a trick none of us thought of before," said Enid to Norman. "I will show you sometime."

She meant the kiss Peter had given her on the island of rocks.

She is a whore! he thought. It was the strongest word he knew except for "harlot," and that had the wrong sound.

"All right," he said quickly, "let's sing." And he embarked on "Billy Boy." Maggie, who sang with him in the choir, chimed in with her light, easygoing soprano. The others joined in unsurely.

They sang until it was dark and the road was winding among precipitous valleys in the Abanao Mountains. For a time they continued to suggest songs to one another, but these were the kind that none of them remembered beyond the first line. Finally, they sat back in the darkness and gave up even talking.

Peter planned how he would cut Enid out of his life: the excuses he would use to go home directly after school and the basketball practices he would take up during lunch hour to avoid talking to her. He could never explain his reasons to her. They involved religion, and religion—well, he was the son of a missionary doctor. He had always lived among missionaries, but his schoolmates had usually been ordinary children, the sons and daughters of businessmen working briefly abroad. He hated noisy piety, but he believed fervently in heaven and hell. He knew guiltily that he feared ridicule, but he *was* sorry for the unsaved.

Peter felt a hand on his: Enid's, he felt sure, although he could not see her. Norman was snoring in the corner at his left. He visualized Maggie still in the corner at his right, knitting. Now, without hearing a sound, he felt Enid move up beside him. She found his head with her hands and gently tweaked his nose. Then she stretched out and laid her head in his lap.

"It will probably rain tonight," she said. "Clouds are hiding all the stars."

"Yes," he said and tried to make his voice sound far away so that Maggie would not know how close together they were.

"Tomorrow's Monday," she said, "an ordinary school day again. Are you coming to the Christmas dance, Peter?"

"Yes."

"We will have fun," she said—and stopped talking. Soon, from the feel of her breathing, Peter guessed she was asleep. It was difficult having her head on his lap. And it dawned on him that the future, when he must carry out his freshly made resolutions, would be still more difficult. He felt dimly that she was blackmailing him. He could never quit the Game as long as she wanted him in it and was less afraid than he that people would find out about it. He had to see her every day at school. He had to dance with her at the Christmas dance. He visualized one listless, sensual, sun-soaked afternoon of indecision stretched out endlessly in front of him. It would be a sort of boredom, nervous boredom. They had conceived the Game out of wicked boredom last summer, and now by his own lies and her teasing he was trapped in boredom everlasting. If his family would only return to the States or go to some other mission field. If a war would only come as it had in Shanghai. But his father would not get a transfer or furlough for four years. And Panoc was part of the Philippines. The Japs would never dare to attack an American possession. Perhaps there would be an earthquake, a bad one. Or perhaps, perhaps . . . He caught himself praying foolishly—praying to God, who would certainly not listen to him when Enid's head was in his lap—for a cataclysm which he did not deserve anyway.

The moon came up behind the clouds. In its muffled glow he saw with relief that Maggie was probably asleep. Lights clustered off to the right. They would be Mananok Sugar Refinery. In a few minutes, then, the truck would round the cliff at the head of South Valley, and Abanao would lie below them, a jewel box of street lamps. He gently shook Enid awake. She stretched, looked around and puckered her lips at him. He shook his head.

"I was not nice to you, was I?" she whispered. "Maybe I didn't want anyone to know how wonderfully you saved my life."

She sat up and kissed him, using the new method. As he pushed her away he felt that the world had changed.

"You make me feel I am growing up," she whispered. "Norman doesn't. He's still a kid."

The truck descended into South Valley and the street lights awakened Maggie and Norman. They had hardly collected themselves when Antonio pulled up in front of the country club. Norman's house was just across the first green of the golf course, and Maggie, who lived all the way out at the end of North Valley, was staying the night at the club. Norman and Maggie said good night sleepily, then Enid and Peter held hands until they reached her home a little farther down the road.

"See you in English class," she said, and with a quick squeeze of his hand she jumped down into the darkness.

Peter lived on the hill below the Abanao Hotel. When Antonio let him off in the hotel driveway, he ran down the stone steps—a hundred and two of them there were—and burst into the house panting. His father was away again, but his mother was waiting up for him with a cup of cocoa. His father was often away. He led an ideal life roving the mountains and doctoring natives in out-of-the-way barrios. This time it was an outbreak of typhoid at Enao on the wild east coast. Drinking his cocoa and undressing, while he made up an untrue description of the picnic for his mother, Peter wondered how he could ever sleep with all the elation he felt. His good resolutions, his boredom and torment seemed far away now. He pondered his changeableness and fell asleep instantly.

# CHAPTER 3

Peter's mother had to wake him in the morning. When he came out of his room she was twisting the dials on the radio.

"I just heard something about the Japanese bombing, Oahu," she said. "I can't believe it."

"In Hawaii?"

"I don't know. I only caught the end of the broadcast."

"It can't be the island," he said. "Probably the gunboat, the one that used to come up the Yangtze to Nanking."

"I hope so."

"I'm late," he said. "Why didn't you wake me earlier?"

It was one of those mornings when he was imperious with his mother and found her accented English not musical but queer.

"Because you need your sleep, dear. It was nine o'clock when you came in last night and you had a tiring day."

20

Renée Baldwin was French. She had become a missionary and an Episcopalian by marriage, but she retained a solicitousness about the physical well-being of every male creature around her which Peter often found irksome. Before she could find another news report, he had wolfed down his breakfast and started for school. He took the short cut through the woods and arrived in chapel during the first hymn. By the time he had prayed and caught his breath Father Gibney was in the pulpit.

"Today we shall hold a service somewhat different from usual. As you all know—" Father Gibney paused "—early this morning—" he paused again—"without warning or provocation—" Peter held his breath—"Japan mounted a treacherous attack against our naval installations at Pearl Harbor in Hawaii. Our country is at war, so we must pray this morning for our leaders and our armed forces. We must all pray for ourselves that we may in our civilian capacities have Christian strength sufficient unto the troubled times ahead. Let us kneel."

As Father Gibney read the *Collect for Peace*, the prayers *For the President*, *For Congress* and *In Time of War and Tumults*, Peter concentrated on the words with growing excitement. Japan invading China was a small thing, but this, he realized, this was the whole world at war. His private prayer yesterday for a cataclysm that would distract him from boredom and wickedness had been answered on a vast scale. He hardly dared think about it. Not that it had happened all for him. The idea of asking for it had probably been planted in his mind so that he would be unforgettably appalled by the swift immensity of the reply. Thousands of sinners everywhere must have wished the same miserable wish. But he had been one of them, and God had answered. Enid was already growing remote and unimportant in the new excitement. How could he ever express or presume to express his gratitude?

School, announced Father Gibney, would go on as usual. As they came out of the chapel they heard the drone of airplanes. They broke ranks and shouted as they picked out first one and then another triplet of glistening specks high in the sky above them.

"Go get 'em, boys," shouted someone.

"Give 'em all you got, Yanks," yelled another.

Father Gibney restored discipline and marched them up

the hill to the buildings where the classrooms were. Peter had just sat down at his desk, had looked around for Enid and found she was not in her place, when a series of dull thuds rattled the windows. His classmates looked at one another, puzzled.

"It sounds like bombing," he said eagerly.

"Nonsense," answered Mrs. Gibney. "You saw all the American planes, didn't you?"

The building shook with another cluster of explosions.

"Well, that's the way the bombing used to sound in China," he persisted.

"It's coming from the direction of Camp Dewey," observed Jimmy Page. Camp Dewey was a U.S. Army post up on the west side of South Valley.

"Hey, we don't know those were American planes we saw," exclaimed Peter. "They were much too high to see the markings."

"You don't think we would let Japs simply fly over our heads like that without shooting at them, do you, Peter? There's a more sensible explanation, I'm sure," said Mrs. Gibney firmly. "We must remain calm and proceed as usual unless Father Gibney comes to inform us otherwise."

She called the roll, interrupted at intervals by more thuds. Half the children in the class were absent like Enid, kept home, Peter decided, by worried parents who didn't know what to do in case of war. Having seen bombings in China, he felt superior. The only thing to do was to behave normally and be lucky. He turned to Enid's enemy, Louise Newcombe, who had the desk on his left, and whispered, "It's more exciting when the planes come at night."

"I couldn't stand it!" exclaimed Louise loudly and nervously.

The building shuddered again. The explosions sounded closer.

"Peter Baldwin," said Mrs. Gibney, "if you have any thrilling war experiences to tell, perhaps you should regale all of us with them."

"I was only explaining," he said boldly, "that raids are prettier at night when you can see searchlights and tracer shells. I saw a Jap bomber in flames once over Nanking. It all fell to pieces in burning bits like a bonfire when you kick it."

"How delightful," said Mrs. Gibney. "I've seen night raids,

too: the Hun zeppelins over London in 1915. But what impressed my young mind were the beds hanging out of flats which had been cut neatly in half and the children weeping for parents who had been cut less neatly into smithereens. I don't want you to praise war in my class, Peter. Not ever again. Do you understand?"

"I'm sorry," he said.

The bombing continued, and Mrs. Gibney continued with the unreal English lesson. Peter wanted to get home and keep his mother company. She also hated war, and his father was away.

Finally Father Gibney came. Camp Dewey was indeed being bombed. Parents were telephoning about their children. Mr. Newcombe was outside waiting for his daughter. He had undertaken to deliver several other children to their homes at the same time. Mr. Fincher and Antonio were already busy running a taxi service for the first and second grades. Everyone must wait his turn. Transportation would be found for all of them. Peter slipped out during the excitement and ran home. On the way he noticed that the explosions had stopped. He found his mother making cookies. She had heard about the war on the radio but she had not heard the bombs. Anita, the maid, was making too much noise whacking the washing in the laundry.

## CHAPTER 4

After practicing the piano for a while and making sure his mother was not too worried about the war, Peter took a walk in the direction of Camp Dewey. Along the stretch of road in front of Enid's house he concentrated on a marble which he threw into the air and caught as he walked. There was no sign of Enid anywhere. The doors of the garage where Mr. Larsen kept the small truck he drove were left wide open. The truck was not inside, and the extra gasoline he kept in old Mazola oil cans along the back wall of the garage had gone too. It looked as if he had driven down to Vispayan and taken Enid with him. He didn't usually take her on his business trips.

As Peter wondered about it, he heard an approaching roar and jumped, startled, for the edge of the road. It was Mr. Higgins, Maggie's father, in his fancy little racing car. Not that it was a real racer with a number on it or anything, but it was low and open and bright blue, with room in it for only two people and a huge engine that hurled it along roads fast and straight like a giant wasp. Mr. Higgins was alone in it today and he forgot to honk a greeting at Peter as he usually did—as he usually did to any kid. Instead he rocketed past, intent behind dark glasses. He was going to the school, Peter guessed, to pick up Maggie. If he'd started from his lumber mill down on the coast or from his shipping office in Vispayan when the bombing began, he really must have made time up the mountain.

Peter felt twinges of dissatisfaction that anyone should be as excitingly wealthy as Maggie's family. As he battled to suppress them, he came to the golf course and decided to take the short cut across it. No one was playing golf or worrying about non-members trespassing this morning. It was such a radiant morning, such a strange morning for a war. The sun shone brilliantly, but the air still felt cool and clean, and last night's dew still sparkled on the grass. His sneakers began to get wet, so he ran. Left bare by the khaki shorts he wore, his legs warmed to the sun and the movement, and he lengthened his stride easily. He could run and run and run. Someday he would be a half-miler. Until then the world was at war and full of free, guiltless excitement.

Sprinting up to the fifth green, he was surprised to see bits of turf strewn about in the sand trap below it. He stopped short and climbed breathlessly to the top of the grassy plateau to investigate. The green was littered with red clods of clay. The flag and the cup had vanished. In their place was a hole five or six feet wide and almost as deep. In the silence, beauty and ordinariness of the morning, Peter could not believe what he thought he saw. He jumped into the hole and dug in the loose dirt at the bottom. His fingers struck on something hard. He pulled it out, a jagged piece of iron shaped like a Christmas tree. Bomb casing for sure; what he called shrapnel. And the little hole, the little mess out on the golf course in the sunny morning silence, was a bomb crater. A Jap pilot had missed Camp Dewey and shot a hole in one.

Feeling pleasantly scared and scornful, Peter dug up three more pieces of shrapnel, then walked on to the gates of

Camp Dewey. There the Filipino sentry said he could not enter; the camp had been bombed. But Peter wanted more souvenirs, and a short distance down the road where the sentry could not see him, he climbed over the low stone wall.

Camp Dewey was hardly more than an extension of the country club. A huge lawn, relieved here and there by arbored brakes of bougainvillea, groves of pine trees and walks of asphalt, swept up the hill from the stone wall to the top of the ridge. Up there were the soldiers' barracks and the houses for officers. But down below, Peter found, were many small bomb craters. He grubbed about in them until the sun was high and hot and nine jagged strips of bomb casing jangled satisfyingly in his pockets, tearing at the cloth and scratching the skin underneath.

He wondered whether the Japanese planes might not have damaged something more exciting than lawn and he began to work his way up the hill toward the buildings on top. He approached them through a covert of pines below Colonel Fleer's house. Colonel Fleer commanded the post, and his bungalow was a large one. Until the first war scare six months ago, when all Army and Navy dependents had been evacuated, he had had his wife and divorced daughter living with him. He was a thin, gray-haired man who always wore whites and attended all the cocktail parties. Peter had met him once at Norman's house and did not like him. He called Peter "Little Man" and told him he would be in for it at home because he had torn the sleeve of his shirt that day.

Peter skirted the colonel's house charily. It seemed to be empty and disappointingly undamaged, but he enjoyed stealing from bush to bush. The first of the officers' houses was equally dull . . . and the second . . . and the third. But the last had been hit. Its windows had been broken. Two sheets of iron had been blown from its roof. And there was a large hole in the wall of the kitchen. The ground outside the hole was wet, and Peter was about to look for the reason when he made out a man, an officer, kneeling by the sink inside. The little bomb must have broken some pipes which the officer was trying to fix. Peter scuttled onward to a large flowering plumbago. There before him spread the grassy parade ground. Beyond it stood the two barracks for Filipino enlisted men. A truck and a small tank were driving across the grass toward a crowd of soldiers at the end of the parade ground on Peter's left. Among the soldiers he could see other tanks and trucks parked here and there without any apparent order. Colonel Fleer was there too, in his usual white uniform. He and the soldiers were all intently watching something far away out to Peter's left. In that direction, he knew, the parade ground ended abruptly at a steep bank which dropped two hundred feet or more to a stream. Beyond the stream one could see a small barrio, a native village, and beyond the barrio—well, beyond the barrio there was nothing much to look at until the China Sea in the far distance. That must be what they were studying; otherwise Colonel Fleer wouldn't be using binoculars. Peter was puzzled. Why were they looking out to sea and why had they lined up their tanks and trucks in the open? Suppose the Jap planes should come back.

The Japanese planes did come back. Peter saw them, saw the red circles—"the fried eggs"—on their wings almost as soon as he heard them. They came buzzing along the ridge from the north, straight at him over the barracks. They were not shooting yet, and the soldiers on the parade ground had not seen them yet. Scrambling to his feet—and scrambling with fright internally—he shouted to warn the soldiers, but his voice came out weak and plaintive. He heard the machine guns and at the same instant he was knocked forward, flat into the plumbago bush. His ears rang with the whine of the planes and scolding of the machine guns. He looked at the soldiers to his left and saw them running and falling. The planes roared past and he started to get up but a big hand held him where he was.

"You damn fool kid!" It was the officer who had been fixing the pipes.

"They'll come back," said Peter.

"And you'd better get the hell out of here," said the officer.

"I'm not scared," he said.

"You ought to be. Quick! There's more coming."

The officer let go of him and ran to the pine trees down the hill. Peter scuttled after him and sprawled obediently on the ground as a second wave of planes passed low over the camp and strafed the parade ground.

"They're awfully small planes," he said bravely, when they had gone.

"Carrier planes," said the officer. "They're plenty big enough to kill you."

"Where are they flying from?"

'There's a Jap fleet off Vispayan. You can see it from the embankment."

"Gosh, are they going to land?"

"I don't know, kid. We lie smack on the invasion route to Borneo. If they do land we're not going to stop them. Colonel Fleer is going to drive our tanks down that mud bank and say he's destroyed them. Then we'll take to the hills. Go home and tell your father that. Tell him to get the hell off the island if he can. But tell him mostly to keep you indoors. Now beat it!"

The officer swatted him on the seat of the shorts, and Peter ran off down the hill. But he wanted to see the Jap ships. So he crossed the road leading up to the parade ground and stole back to the ridge through the woods on the other side of the barracks. At the top where the mountainside dropped away, there was a rock which jutted out over the brink. He had to climb the rock twice, because the first time, in his fear that the planes would come back and see him in his exposed position, he forgot to count the ships. Only a child would say there were swarms of ships without knowing exactly how many, so he climbed back and counted them: two aircraft carriers, twenty-five other large ships and ten smaller ones. He wished he could tell the difference between warships and transports but he didn't know enough except up close. He ran downhill through the trees, proud and still tense with what he had done. Rounding a turn in the path halfway down, he collided with someone. He rolled over and onto his feet and saw, with an audible sigh of relief, that it was only Rosario, Colonel Fleer's houseboy. Rosario had once worked for Norman's family. He recognized Peter as soon as he had picked himself up and dusted off the pine needles. He carried a brown cardboard suitcase and wore his Saturday-night suit of orange-pink silk.

"Mr. Peter! Boy! I dthought you were a bomb."

"What're you doing in the woods?" demanded Peter.

"I'm going to my barrio. You go home, too, ip you hope to lib long."

"Did Colonel Fleer say you could go?"

"Listen, Mr. Peter, don't tell him, please. He's awful darned scared. He's too scared to say what any man should do."

"Were any soldiers hurt in the raids?"

27

"Nine men killed bepore and more dthees las' time. Maybe ten more."

"Gosh, I better get home."

"Good-by, Mr. Peter."

Rosario headed north along the ridge, and Peter ran down toward the road. Still running, he kept to the woods and circled the golf course. He ran because he had to now: he was too excited to do anything else. He reached home gasping for breath. His mother wasn't there; she must be out shopping. Peter had to tell someone the news, so he started for the school to tell Father Gibney. Once more he ran. His chest hurt and he knew he would soon have to stop, but he wanted to tell people the news before anyone else and he didn't want time to think about it until he had talked to someone who would understand and explain what it meant to him. Japanese soldiers coming was nothing new. Twice in China—once in Shanghai and later in Nanking—his family had been in cities when the Japanese conquered them. Each time it had meant staying indoors for a few days and being searched and having things snitched and then going on with life in almost the ordinary way except that you felt sorry for the Chinese. But this time the Japs weren't fighting the Chinese. They were actually fighting the Americans. And Colonel Fleer, of the *American* Army, was running away. Peter's family had lived in Kobe for several years, and it was inconceivable to him that Americans should run away from Japs whom he knew only as servants around the house. If the Japs landed and the Army really did run away, he wasn't sure what would happen next. Would civilians be able to escape? If they couldn't, would they have to fight because they were Americans? Or would they simply go on living for a while like the Chinese: being ruled and pushed around by the Japs?

Peter slowed to a walk so that he could get back some breath before he reached the school and had to tell his story. As he entered the school driveway, Father Gibney drove down it in his old car, delivering the last load of children to their homes. Peter stood in the road and waved until the car stopped. Father Gibney got halfway out and spoke to him over the open door.

"Peter, you were not given permission to leave alone."

"No, sir," he panted. "But there are thirty-seven ships off Vispayan . . . Jap ones. Two of them are aircraft carriers. . . . And Colonel Fleer's going to smash up his tanks and things and run away to the hills. . . . A soldier . . . I mean, an officer . . . at Camp Dewey . . . told me nothing would stop the Japs if they land. He said everyone should get off the island."

"You went up to Dewey?"

"Yes. I wanted to collect some shrapnel. They machine-gunned while I was there. A lot of soldiers have been killed."

"Did you see the ships yourself?"

"Yes, sir. I counted them. If they land and we can't get off the island and they capture us, what will they do to us?"

"Probably intern us." Father Gibney pursed his lips as if he had just been asked an interesting question in Latin class. The children in the car all looked at Peter enviously. "Listen, Peter," continued Father Gibney. "I want you to tell your mother that she's welcome to come live with us until your father comes back from the coast. If there *is* a landing, the lawless element in Abanao may get out of hand. She'll be safer up here at the school with the rest of us."

"I'll tell her," said Peter, "but Dad'll come back quick when he hears about that fleet."

"Quickly," said Father Gibney, correcting him automatically. "Whom have you told about the fleet?"

"No one, sir."

"Then I'll have to see Mayor Ziegler. You go home and stay there. No more trips to Dewey. Understand? First thing we know you'll have the sentries shooting us on sight."

Father Gibney turned back into his seat and slammed the door. He didn't sound excited—he never would—but his car shot out of the gates as if Antonio were driving it. Peter didn't feel like going home immediately. He walked slowly up the driveway wondering what internment would be like if it really happened. It was hard to imagine Americans living together inside fences and being ordered about by Japs. Still, for the short time until reinforcements arrived and liberated them, it might be exciting. And it would probably keep him away from Enid—it would unless they interned her, too. He wondered. Could they? Or was she a neutral? In a lot of ways it would be fun having her along. If only she were American and more religious and less teasing and unscrupulous. Heck, what everyone should really do was go off in the hills and become guerrillas. That was the patriotic and exciting thing to do. Either that or Colonel Fleer should do his job and beat the Japs now.

Peter shuffled his feet and kicked disgustedly at the gravel of the driveway. He was entering the roundabout at the center of the clustered school buildings. Since the Army and Navy kids had left during the first war scare months before, there were few boarders in the dormitories, just the children whose parents lived on cane plantations in the lowlands.

Outside the boys' dorm, Johnny Partridge's parents were loading Johnny's clothes into their car. They had driven up from Vispayan for him as soon as they had heard the news on the radio. Peter told them about the fleet, and Mr. Partridge swore dirtily. He had a boat waiting to take them south, he said, and, swearing some more, he started hurling Johnny's things into the car any which way. He was scared probably that the Japs would block Vispayan Harbor before he and his family could get out of it. At least *they* still had a chance of escaping, thought Peter enviously. They jumped into their car and, as Johnny waved good-by, it kicked up gravel and leaped off down the driveway.

Peter turned glumly and went into the dorm to find the other boarders. The Gay brothers had just driven away with their parents too, so that left only Jimmy Page, Herb Campbell and Charley French. Usually he was afraid of Charley French because he was a senior and a lead-taker in hazing younger boys, but now he told Charley matter-of-factly about Camp Dewey and sold him two pieces of shrapnel for a peso fifty centavos. Herb and Jimmy bought pieces too, for a peso each. Then Peter went over to the girls' dorm and sold four more pieces. He had seven pesos fifty centavos and one more piece of shrapnel, the best, which he decided to keep. The windfall of money partly dispelled the sad, unsettled feeling he had had seeing everyone packing to run away. On the way home he chinked the coins in his pocket and tried to decide whether to go back to Enid's house after lunch and see if she had come home yet or to go downtown and spend the money.

When he reached home it was already after one o'clock and his mother was cross because he was late for lunch. He told her about the Japanese fleet, pretending that he had only talked to the guard at the gates of Camp Dewey. She tried not to seem too worried, but the fact that she didn't scold him for going near the place where the bombs were dropping showed that she *was* worried. He decided that there was no need to tell her about Colonel Fleer's running away yet.

"I wish there were some way we could get a message to your father," she said, pouring a bowl of soup for him. She used the expression *your father* not because of any stiffness. It was simply one of the French formalisms she had held on to through the years.

As Peter began to eat, one of the bellboys from the hotel came to the house with a note saying that Mr. Kahn, who owned the hotel, wanted to talk to Peter.

"What's this, *mon fils?*" asked his mother suspiciously when the bellhop had gone. "You haven't done something destructive, have you?"

"Of course not," he said resentfully. He'd thrown a ball through the big window in the hotel lounge two months before and it had been expensive to replace. She could have forgotten about it by now, he thought.

"*C'est bien,*" she said. "No need to anger yourself. When you finish talking to Mr. Kahn, come down to Yang's in the market. I'll need you to help Anita carry home the canned goods I've bought."

"Oh, gosh," he said, "all right."

"That's a good boy," she said, softening. "With your father away, you have to be especially helpful."

"Uhuh," he said. Being called a good boy and babied along didn't improve his mood.

"Did you tell Father Gibney about the Japanese fleet?"

"Yes."

"That's a good boy," she said again. She was ready to start for the market, but she paused absent-mindedly at the back door as if she weren't sure she had remembered to say everything she wanted. "Jeanette's spending the afternoon at the Barsinis," she murmured. "Perhaps after supper we'll all have a nice game of dominoes together."

He said nothing. He hated to play games with his mother. She always lost because she never tried.

"Be careful of cars on the way to the market, won't you," she said.

"Yes, Mother."

Finally she went out the door and left him alone.

Be careful of cars, he thought bitterly, sipping his hot soup, or bombs or machine-gun bullets. They're all the same to her. After the excitement of the morning and the grown-up importance of the news he had borne to Father Gibney he felt suddenly deflated. There hadn't been any more bombing for hours now. The excitement was all evaporating. And though he knew perfectly well he was being unreasonable, he blamed his mother for it. The prospect of hauling rice and kerosene and sugar up from market was a pall on the brightness of the afternoon. It had been the same way in China: war meant stocking the larder against all contingencies. But last time in Nanking most of the food had just ended up in the hands of the Japs. It would probably be the same this time, he thought. Of course, having the food would be a nice feeling: like living in a castle with a moat and a drawbridge. But hauling it was sure to be tiresome when there were so many other exciting things to do, like seeing Enid or checking on the whereabouts of the Jap fleet. Well, anyway, he'd be in the market, so at least he could spend his shrapnel money. He knew exactly what he wanted to buy: a hairbrush for his mother at Christmas and a bottle of silver Higgins ink for himself. He already had gold, brown, red, green, blue, yellow, orange, violet and black ink. Silver would complete his collection. Then, whatever happened to the little Chinese store which sold the ink, he could always finish drawing the huge ten-color map of the world with which he meant to cover one wall of his bedroom. Now that would really be a satisfying feeling!

Peter finished his soup and started up the hill to the hotel to see what Mr. Kahn wanted. On the way he ate his dessert: an apple and a piece of cheese.

## CHAPTER 5

The Kahns, who owned the hotel, were Jewish. It was a funny thing about Jewish people, thought Peter. A lot of the war in Europe and of what was worst about the Nazis had to do with their terrible treatment of Jews. And yet some good people like his father didn't like Jews, either. At home Dr. Baldwin sometimes called Jewish doctors "sharp practitioners" or "sheister cure-it-alls." When he was out, of course, he always spoke politely to everyone, even Japs. By speaking to

Mr. Kahn often enough, he had come to be good friends with him. Occasionally he still used to say that Mr. Kahn's thinking was "as crooked as a dog's hind leg," after they had been arguing about Dunkirk or the Russian campaign, but other times he called Mr. Kahn "a real gentleman," and that was the highest compliment he ever paid anyone. In the last few months the Khans had become such good friends that Peter's parents spent a lot of evenings on the hotel veranda talking. The two couples agreed on the important thing, which was that America ought to be in the war helping England. They also agreed on not drinking anything but a little wine, and that was important in Abanao, where Dr. Baldwin said most people were "treating their livers like darned fools and expecting everyone else to be a darned fool with them."

Peter went into the hotel by the back door of the Kahn's private apartment. It was a spacious suite of rooms on the ground floor with a fine view out over the park at the bottom of the valley. But it held an awful lot of annoying little knickknacks which he had to worry about knocking over and breaking. And where other people had plain mahogany floors which the maids polished by skating around barefoot on coconut husks, the Kahns had laid down thick rugs. The rugs got to smelling musty in the rainy season no matter how Mrs. Kahn kept airing and cleaning. They made Peter feel closed in and out of place. They reminded him that the Kahns certainly were a little queer and different. But as his mother said, you should never feel uncharitable about people simply because they were different. It was like that fat Mrs. Newcombe, who always suffocated you with perfume, calling Enid "the Nazi brat." Peter flushed with anger and protectiveness as he remembered overhearing her say it one afternoon at Norm's. He had wanted to hit her fat stomach—hit a woman in the stomach! Instead he had crept out the back door without even saying good-by to Norm or thank you to Mrs. Diak.

It was easier with kids. If they made fun of religion or talked about missionary baskets, you fought with them, and as long as they weren't smaller than you, you could tell by not feeling bad when you prayed for forgiveness afterward that you hadn't committed much of a sin.

Mrs. Kahn wasn't anywhere in the apartment, so Peter went out into the fresh air and down the back veranda toward the hotel kitchen. The apartment might be stuffy, but

33

he looked forward to finding Mrs. Kahn. She was a fat, jolly woman who cooked good fudge and sometimes acted sad about having no children of her own. Peter was fond of her and grateful that his mother had made friends with her and Mr. Kahn. Generally, he thought, where individual people were concerned, his mother was more right about prejudice than his father was. But she did carry it too far. To say you shouldn't ever be against a whole country or race was crazy. It would mean you couldn't fight the Japs. Not even after their dirty war in China, and not even now when they thought they could take on the Americans the same way. Boy, would they get a surprise! At least, most places they would. How could any American be such a coward as Colonel Fleer?

Mrs. Kahn was in the hotel kitchen arguing with Harry Gamoff, the White Russian chef.

"I don't care how you do it in Kiev, Harry. Who's in Kiev? Cream in the sauce means cream, not milk, so send a boy to the American Butcher Shop and get some."

"Hello, Mrs. Kahn," said Peter. "Did you want to see me?"

"Peter! I sure did. Nothing so good has happened to me all morning. You wouldn't believe how crazy and mixed up we are here. I have to go to the market before the other women buy up everything and start hoarding it, and I find Mr. Gamoff sabotaging the Newburg sauce for the shrimp. He should be back in Kiev where he could do some good with sabotage."

Harry Gamoff shrugged his shoulders and winked at Peter. Mrs. Kahn, without pausing for breath, took Peter's arm and drew him toward the entrance into the hotel dining room.

"There is an important magazine photographer from the States here and a beautiful tramp who is supposed to be his secretary or reporter or something. They are talking to Mr. Kahn in the dining room. They want to go to the east coast where your dad is, but they don't know the way and we can't find a guide for them. So, if I remember correctly, you do know the way because you went hiking with your dad last summer. Maybe you could tell them how to go. And maybe in return you could ask them to take a message to your dad and tell him to come back here at once and take care of his family and forget about the sick natives. What is important about sick natives when his poor wife is in such trouble?"

Having worked up a full head of friendly indignation, she propelled Peter across the dining-room floor and, continuing on a great circle route, turned herself back toward the kitchen.

"I have to do my shopping," she said. "But you send your father that message."

She disappeared through the swinging door marked "Out," and Peter found himself approaching a table at which Mr. Kahn sat with two strangers, a man and a woman. They were in sports clothes, and two knapsacks lay on the floor behind their chairs. Mr. Kahn jumped up and clasped Peter's hand warmly between his palms. He had a wonderful way of treating Peter formally and politely as if he were a grownup—not just any grownup either, but someone important.

"I'm so glad you could come over, Peter," he said. "Sit down and have some coffee with us. This is Miss Drayton from Singapore and Mr. Costeau from New York."

The strangers both said, "Hello, Peter." The man had a quiet voice that was slightly hoarse. The woman spoke clearly and straight-out, like an English schoolgirl. As for Mr. Kahn, he didn't have at all the same funny, loud accent as his wife but spoke very correctly. Each sentence was balanced and whole, and punctuated with a precise singsong emphasis that made Peter sometimes listen to the sound instead of the meaning.

"They came here yesterday," said Mr. Kahn, "to make photographs of Abanao for an American magazine. Today they have to leave because their editor-in-chief has cabled from New York that the war in Manila is a better war to photograph than the one here."

Having sat down, Peter was taking advantage of the talk to study the strangers, and so he was only half aware that Mr. Kahn had made one of his jokes. As he smiled politely, he saw that the photographer smiled too, but with real enthusiasm that brought out dimples in his cheeks and a river delta of crinkles around each eye. He looked like a nice sort of man. His face was small and weather-beaten and rather puckish. His hair was sandy-gray and thin and lay flat across the top of his head. He had a big barrel chest, and Peter guessed that he had short legs.

"The reason that they have to go from Banong instead of Vispayan," Mr. Kahn was saying, "is that the Japanese have been lucky in Vispayan. According to the information I received by phone, their air attack has closed both the airport and the harbor. What few planes are undamaged, and small enough to use the surviving stretches of runway, have already taken off. What few boats can still navigate the mouth of the harbor, past the hulks of sunken ships, are such cockleshells that no sane man would trust himself to them in the China Sea at this time of year."

"Gosh!" said Peter. He could hardly believe that Mr. Kahn wasn't exaggerating a bit and enjoying the fateful ring of his own sentences.

A nudge from the English woman drove the war from Peter's mind. She was offering him coffee, and that meant he had to look at her. He had been trying not to look because he knew her prettiness would make him blush. She was small and dark—compactly healthy and energetic—and she looked back at him with a live tomboy interest which didn't have in it any of the motherly kindness and condescension he was used to seeing in the faces of grown women. The look was so flattering that he didn't care whether he was blushing or not.

Peter was not allowed to drink coffee at home, but now, of course, he nodded and mumbled, "Thank you." As she leaned across to him with the coffeepot, he noticed that, though it was morning, she was wearing a trace of perfume and, though she was a woman, it was a man's shirt she had on. Involuntarily he glanced down the open neck of it and saw that there was nothing inside but naked skin. He blushed deeply. This time he minded blushing. He felt a hot, angry determination against her and he glared at her eyes unflinchingly. But her eyes were unconcerned, watching the coffee as she poured it. Evidently she was used to wearing no underwear and hardened to the guilty stares of people like Peter. Mrs. Kahn must be right about her being a tramp. Indignant and ashamed of himself, Peter looked away from her and fixed his eyes and mind on Mr. Kahn.

"I tried to get Dalag for them," Mr. Kahn was saying, "but he's been hired by Sam Bean for the same trip. Why Bean needs a guide to Banong, no one knows. Anyway, Peter, I told them that you could describe the trail down and that your father on the other end could help them rent a fishing boat for the voyage to Luzon."

"I guess so," said Peter. Like everyone else, it seemed—everyone but him, he thought bitterly—they were getting to escape. Then afterward, being newspaper people, they'd get to roam around and watch the war all over the world. Maybe they were immoral and sinful, but he envied them.

"I have a great many things to do," said Mr. Kahn, "so I'll just leave you with them, Peter."

As Mr. Kahn hurried away, the photographer said, "I guess the Kahns want you to give me a message to take to your father, Peter. Is that the way you figure it?"

"Yes," said Peter, smiling. "The trouble is Dad isn't in Banong. He's in Enao."

The photographer beetled his brows with annoyance and then looked resigned and slightly comic. "Where's that?" he asked.

"It's across the bay from Banong. Several miles if you go around on the land but only about half an hour in a boat."

"Well, that's no problem then," said the photographer. "Just tell me how to get to Banong."

"Dad only took me down there once," said Peter. "I expect I could follow the path if I saw it again, but I don't know if I can describe it."

"Why don't you start by telling me where it begins," suggested the photographer. He had such a funny, innocent look on his face that Peter couldn't resent the insultingly simple way he talked.

"You take a taxi to the lookout place at the end of North Valley," said Peter. "Then you get out and walk downhill."

He had given the simple question such a simple answer that both he and the photographer laughed. The woman sputtered a little but couldn't laugh because she had her mouth full of toast and egg. Peter hadn't noticed before that they were eating eggs.

"Are you having breakfast?" he asked incredulously. The rude question slipped out before he could stop it.

"Yes, Peter," said the photographer. "Breakfast in the afternoon. We're not such good people, you know. Last night we stayed up late and this morning we slept right through the bombing. That's why you have to help us. We're not prepared to face a war." He ran his hand ruefully through his hair, and the dimples showed on his cheeks.

"Don't mind if he speaks to you like a child, Peter," said

the woman through her mouthful. "He talks the same way to everyone. He thinks he's the only grownup in the whole world."

"Not a grownup, sweetie," said the photographer seriously. "Only a child wise enough to admit it."

Peter thought they were being silly, considering how things were, but he couldn't help laughing at the faces the photographer made. And both the photographer and the woman laughed with him.

"Now, tell me how to walk downhill," said the photographer.

They weren't really so silly. The photographer *was* treating Peter like a child, and the burden of proof lay on Peter after his foolish question about breakfast.

"I know!" said Peter. "Why don't I come to the lookout with you and point out the way. I'll remember better if I see the shape of the mountains."

"Fine," said the photographer, throwing down his napkin. "Let's go."

The woman abruptly leaned forward and pointed to the photographer's plate. "Jerry, you have to eat," she said. "I want you strong."

She said it not maternally nad not simperingly, the way some women would, but just straight out and athletically. The photographer made another of his faces, took a fried egg on his fork and gulped it down whole, like a huge pill. He had hardly eaten any of his breakfast. The woman, who was so much smaller, had eaten all of hers and several rackfuls of toast besides. The photographer took a mouthful of toast, chewed it twice and then looked foolish, as if he had run down and needed rewinding. Peter looked away, down the long drafty dining room, past the immobile fans on the ceiling to the hall where he could see Mr. Kahn at the desk with a pencil in his right hand and a ledger under his left index finger.

The photographer must have seen Peter was uncomfortable because he swallowed his mouthful and suddenly spoke in a serious tone of voice. "Pay no attention to my clowning, Peter," he said. "I only do it for this dumb brunette who thinks I'm funny. It really is important that I get to Manila. You see, for years I've only been allowed to tell the American public what it wanted to hear. Things like Corregidor is invulnerable. Or the Chinese guerrillas are brave fellows.

Or the Japs put their tanks together in silly little galvanized iron machine shops on the Yokohama waterfront. All these things were true, in their way, but the Japs have a lot of tanks now, and the Chinese guerrillas I took pictures of are mostly dead, and Corregidor can be sealed off and ignored the same way the Germans did with the Maginot Line. You see, they haven't published the other halves of my stories. And now that they'll listen to me, I have to get to Manila where I can cover the war properly and start telling them the truth. That's why you've got to show me how to get down off this mountain. You sure you can do it?"

"I think so," said Peter. He wondered if the photographer knew what he was talking about. Or was he simply angry at America and gloomy, the way Peter's father and Mr. Kahn sometimes were?

Luis, one of the hotel bellhops, came into the dining room carrying a shopping basket with two rifles sticking out of it. The photographer jumped up abruptly, took the rifles and started examining them. One was a light gun. The other was heavier, the kind with a telescopic sight that some of the people at the country club took with them when they went out to shoot wild pig or cimarron water buffalo.

"These are fine," said the photographer, squinting out the window down the telescopic sight. "Bang, you're dead, Jap," he said. "*Abu abunai*, Jap, you're dead."

Peter grinned, startled. He knew what *abu abunai* meant. It was what the Jap kids yelled at one another at their swimming holes when an *abu*, a kind of big horsefly with a bad sting, settled on someone's back. *Abu abunai* meant watch out for the stinging fly.

"*Abunai, banzai!*" said the photographer in a melodramatic whisper.

"I'm bery sorry to take such a long time," said Luis, shifting his feet uncomfortably. "Dthere are many people at Hinkel's hardware store. I hab to stand in line."

"It's all right," said the photographer. "How much were they?"

Peter realized with a rush of excitement that the photographer had bought the guns because he wasn't just running away like everyone else. He might be crazy but at least he would fight if it came to that. Peter longed to go with him into the hills, and all at once he wondered, *why not?*

"Hey," he blurted, "why don't I go all the way to Banong

39

with you? We can take Mother and Jeanette, my sister, and join Dad. Then, if he decides to stay in the hills, we can stay with him while you go off to Luzon in a boat."

The photographer put down the gun, cocked his head at Peter and looked at him quizzically. "And what makes you think your father and mother want to live in the hills like wild people?" he asked.

"Well, because if the Japs do land, it might be safer to live in the hills than be captured."

"Why do you think the Japs are going to land?" he asked, more seriously.

"Because of the big fleet off Vispayan."

"We don't know what you're talking about, Peter," said the photographer. His voice was suddenly hard and urgent and not especially friendly.

"Oh, I'm sorry," Peter said. "I forgot to tell you. There are thirty-seven ships, including two aircraft carriers. An officer at Camp Dewey told me there were Japanese. He had binoculars so he could see."

"Well, son of a bitch," said the photographer slowly. He dumped everything in Luis' basket out on a table and started shoving the contents piece by piece into the knapsacks on the floor. There was a bottle of whisky and some bars of Swiss chocolate and the rest was ammunition.

"Really, Jerry!" said the woman. "He's only a boy. They couldn't be Japanese ships. They haven't had time to get here yet."

"I saw them," said Peter indignantly.

"They started days ago, Margo," said the photographer. "This isn't an isolated attack on Pearl. It's a complete plan. I should have realized, but I thought the chip they've carried all these years might prevent them from taking the big view. Now it all depends on air power. We have to get to Clark Field." All the time he kept packing the knapsacks.

"You're in a flap, Jerry," said the woman. "How do you know the officer at the camp wasn't joking with him?"

"The planes came over and strafed while I was there," said Peter hotly. "They were the small kind they have on carriers, but they killed some of the soldiers, and Colonel Fleer is pulling out with the rest into the hills."

"You see how it is, sweetie," said the photographer with cold intensity. "No use being an outraged colonial. No use being a cool superior adult Caucasian. The world is for excited, murderous children now, so get that ammunition into your pack kwei-dee-kwei. I should hate to leave you behind."

The woman looked at him curiously and did as she was told.

"Why the hell you couldn't tell us this before, Peter," said the photographer, "I don't know."

"I forgot," said Peter. He resented the photographer's new mood of detached urgency. "I think you swear too much," he said.

The photographer put down his pack, looked at Peter with annoyance and then smiled.

"Perhaps I do," he said finally. "But as you grow older, there are times when you can't think of anything better to say."

Peter at once felt sorry.

"I suppose me and Mother and Jeanette going with you is a crazy idea," he said sadly.

"Pretty crazy," said the photographer. "But I'd like to have you as a guide. Where is your mother now?"

"Down in the market buying things," said Peter eagerly.

"Can you find her quickly?"

"Yes, she's at Yang's."

"All right, we'll see what she says. Don't get your hopes up because I don't think she'll agree. But there's no harm in asking, Luis, get us a cab and make it fast."

Luis hesitated. "I heard news on dthe radio at Hinkel's store," he said.

"Then spit it out," said the photographer roughly.

"Dthey say dthe Japs hab bombed many parts ob dthe Pilippines: Baguio and Clark Pield and Nichol's Pield near Manila. It is said dthey caught some op our planes on dthe ground. Also dthey are landing troops in Malaya. And in Siam dthey are adbancing on Bangkok. Hong Kong too—dthey bombed Hong Kong."

"God damn it," exclaimed the photographer. He sounded so angry that Peter inwardly blenched. He looked quickly at the woman and saw that she too seemed surprised. For a moment the photographer glared thoughtfully at each of them, then swung his pack off the floor and strode toward the hall where Mr. Kahn was still doing his accounts. The woman jumped for her pack, and Luis ran off to get a cab.

41

Very coldly, angrily and quickly the photographer paid his bill with Mr. Kahn, got Peter and the woman into the cab and ordered the driver to take them to the bank. The taxi driver sensed his mood and made the tires squeal as he turned out into the main road and headed downtown. A moment later at the curb outside the bank the photographer jumped out and hurried inside.

"He takes the news very seriously, almost personally," said the woman, getting out after him. "You wait here with the cab, Peter. I'll go inside with him."

"You dthink dthe Japs come, sir?" asked the driver as Peter waited.

"Not without a fight," said Peter. "And they won't stay long even then. MacArthur can hold Luzon against anything. As soon as he gets reinforcements he'll take Panoc back."

"Dthe Japs at dthe Jap stores downtown say dthey will be bosses," said the driver.

"Fiddlesticks," said Peter.

The more he thought about it, the more he knew that his mother wouldn't hear of taking Jeanette into the hills. Well then, perhaps she'd let *him* go so that he could bring back his father. After all, she'd said herself how much she wanted to send a note to his father. Peter imagined how it would be walking all night to Banong, finding his father, and walking back again without sleeping. The prospect was a little scary. Suppose he missed his father and had to walk home alone.

In a little while Mr. Costeau and Miss Drayton came out of the bank and the cab started again, down toward the business district. The photographer was still excited, but not so fierce as before.

"I wonder if that was fair, bribing the manager to cash such a huge draft," said the woman. "Other people with money in the bank may need it before communications get back to normal."

"They have plenty of sugar here they can use for currency," he said. "We have to have something we can carry."

"I should think carrying so much might be dangerous," she said. "How can you possibly need twenty thousand pesos?"

"Oh, I don't know," he said, brightening. "To buy champagne in prison, maybe? Or boots on the trail? Or information from friends? Or even consideration from enemies? There's no telling what you can spend money on in wartime, especially money like this that's backed by gold. You know it may be months before we see another bank. Suppose, for instance, we can't get to Manila. We may end up in the mountains somewhere, shooting a story on guerrilla activities. How would you like that?"

"I don't think I would," she said.

They lapsed into silence, and Peter hoped against hope that he could somehow go too. The possibilities for adventure and freedom seemed endless. The cab reached the bottom of the hill, passed the fancy clothing stores, the shops for tourists and the two new round-cornered modern buildings of professional offices, and then turned right onto the street beside the market. Several American women, well attended by servants, were buying up staples like rice and sweet potatoes at the open stalls.

"Stop," said the photographer abruptly to the driver. He leaned out the window, had the driver back up a few feet, and photographed one of the women shopping.

"We call sweet potatoes *camotes* here," said Peter, apropos of nothing.

"Thank you," said the photographer mischievously as he snapped shut his camera case. "All right, driver. Go ahead."

When the cab had edged its way around the crowded square, Peter had it stop in front of Yang's, a shop with a regular tin roof where his mother usually bought all her groceries except vegetables. With ebbing hope he got out and went inside. Anita, their maid, was standing guard over a heap of canned goods by the door. She said his mother had gone out with one of Mr. Yang's sons to buy kerosene in the open market, because Yang himself was already sold out of it. For a moment Peter was baffled. Then with rising spirits he saw that he had complied with the letter of the law. Going to the counter, he borrowed a piece of paper and a pencil from the cashier and wrote:

Dear Mother,

You said how much you wanted to get word to Dad about the fleet. Well, there are some friends of the Kahns here who are going to Banong and need a guide. They can't wait and I can't find you to ask permission. So, I'm going with them anyway, because it seems like a good chance. I'll be back tomorrow night with Dad. Please don't worry about me. I'll be fine.

Love,
PETER

He folded the note and handed it to Anita, telling her simply to give it to his mother when she returned. He was conscious that the note's air of well-meaning innocence constituted a sinful lie and he realized that his mother would probably see through it, but he suppressed his misgivings and started out of the store. As he passed the tobacco counter, a hand caught his shoulder and he felt himself jump and turn pale. It was Father Gibney, laying in a large supply of his favorite English cigarettes. He didn't seem to notice Peter's agitation.

"I'm glad I ran into you, Peter. I want you to give your mother a message. I've been to see Mayor Ziegler, and he and I have decided that in the event of a Japanese landing the whites in town will be better off if they gather at the school and hand themselves over to the Japanese in a body. Soldiers sacking a city are much more likely to rape and murder if they find isolated families here, there and everywhere. So we're organizing an Early Warning Committee of men with binoculars to stand watch over the coast from the various lookouts around Abanao. As soon as any Japanese set foot on the island we'll know and we'll notifiy people. If and when that happens, you're to make sure that your mother comes to the school with you and Jeanette at once. Understand?"

"Yes, sir," said Peter. "But I thought they were probably landing already."

"No, the fleet you saw—and by the way, you gave me a very good account of it—has steamed south past Vispayan. Unless it doubles back in the night or puts men ashore in the south—which I doubt because there are no roads—we are spared for the time being."

"Gosh," said Peter disgustedly. "Well, what about Colonel Fleer?"

"Oh, he's pulling out, all right. And it's probably just as well. If he fought here, he'd only make things more difficult for the rest of us."

"Not if he won," said Peter.

Father Gibney laughed approvingly. "Apparently he didn't think he could, Peter. And certainly if he's outnumbered, hit-

and-run is better for him than a pitched battle. Now, you tell your mother everything I've said and I'll expect you at Communion in the morning."

Peter nodded mutely.

"Good boy," said Father Gibney and turned to pick up his change.

Peter hurried outside to the cab, unsure of what he should do—or could do—or would do. First of all he had to say something to the photographer and the woman. They might not believe a really big lie without seeing his mother and talking to her, but if he told them a small lie now he could probably enlarge on the franchise it gave him later when he had decided what he was going to do.

"Mother doesn't want to take my sister into the hills," he said plausibly, "but I can go part of the way with you—far enough to get you started right."

"Good," said the photographer. "Jump in, then."

Peter did, and the cab moved up the hill through the crowded gambling district, past the Mark Price Saloon and the smaller gambling joints, over the ridge where the electrical plant was, and down into North Valley. The houses and shacks thinned out, and soon the road was bordered by truck gardens: beds of strawberries and melons, Chinese cabbage, asparagus and *camotes*.

Having the Jap fleet pass Panoc by was disappointing, thought Peter, but at least if he did go to Banong, he wouldn't have to worry about his mother and sister being captured by Japs while he was gone.

The photographer and the woman seemed content to stare out the cab windows and leave him in silence to think about what he was going to do. His mother would be worried sick, but she'd be worried sick just reading the note, and in the long run she'd worry more not having his father home for days than if she could stop worrying by tomorrow night. Peter chewed on the inside of his cheek. If he and his father walked fast they might even be home by noon. They would walk fast. That was what the natives called his father, wasn't it: *the doctor who walks fast?* The natives liked his father. One of them from Enao would be glad to accompany Peter home if his father had already left or gone somewhere else. His mother knew that. She probably wouldn't worry so much.

"It looks like much better soil here than in the rest of

Abanao," said the photographer.

"It's real black dirt," said Peter. "Everywhere else on the mountain is just red clay, but here they can even grow fancy vegetables like asparagus and artichokes."

The photographer was silent again. Out of the corner of his eye Peter noticed him squeeze the woman's hand. She smiled at him, shook her head, lifted his hand and put it down on his own knee. Peter wondered vaguely why they minded his presence when they were grown up and everything. What preoccupied him was the punishment he would get from his father for what he was doing. It would probably be a real licking with a belt. And, knowing that, his mother might not tell his father how hypocritical he had been. She hated to see him whipped, and it would be easy for her to pretend to herself and his father that he had really thought he was obeying the rules. What a disgusting liar and schemer he was! All the same, I may be doing the right thing, he thought stubbornly.

The cab started uphill again, leaving the truck gardens behind and passing between widely spaced bungalows with broad eaves and porches and brightly painted corrugated iron roofs. The luxuriant but carefully manicured gardens were ablaze with poinsettias. Between the flower beds grew lawns of thick close-cut grass, looking greener than most grass because it was set off by banks of red clay, the natural unimproved soil here on the hillside.

"Except for the pine trees it's like parts of Singapore," said the English woman.

"Up this end of the valley is where all the old Spanish families have their villas," explained Peter.

"They're beautiful," she said.

"I wonder what will happen to it all in the war ahead," mused the photographer.

"A man in Yang's told me that the Jap fleet has sailed by Vispayan," announced Peter.

"Thanks for telling us," said the photographer, shaking his head.

"You are a funny boy, Peter," said the woman. "I believe you're disappointed. Is that why you didn't tell us?"

"Well, it would have been kind of exciting to have an invasion," he said.

"It wouldn't either!" said the woman, and they all laughed.

"He didn't say fun, Margo; he said exciting," observed the

46

photographer. "All the same you're a dopey kid, Peter."

The cab abruptly came out at the top of the ridge on a circular picnic area where the road ended and the mountain dropped off steeply toward the shining ocean on the northeast. Jerry jumped out and paid the driver. While he and Margo put on their packs, Peter went and found the end of the trail which led down across the north face of the mountain through a forest of scrub pine. As he studied the contours of the ridges and valleys below, the photographer came up behind him and put a hand on his shoulder.

"Now you explain the way to me, Peter. I've paid the cabby to take you home."

"No, I told you," said Peter. "I'm coming part way with you. Once I get you past the waterfalls you only have to follow the stream, but before that it's easy to get lost on one of the side trails that lead off to little barrios here in the hills. You could waste hours that way."

"It's late," said the woman. "We don't want you walking home in the dark. It's a long way up the valley if you don't have a cab."

"Oh, I can call one," said Peter. "Our landlord, Mr. Espinosa, has a phone and he lives just down the hill. You can give me the cab fare if you want."

"It's nearly four o'clock," said the photographer. "You can come with us until five. Okay?"

"Sure. We can get round the falls by then," said Peter.

The photographer went back to the cabdriver, took some money away from him and told him not to wait. Peter led the way down the mountain—into the shadow left by the sun as it lowered on the other side. He went so fast that the man and the woman under their packs and rifles had trouble keeping up with him.

They reached the gorge about four-thirty. A while later the stream disappeared over the first of the waterfalls and the trail turned away from it up to the right. Trails to mountain villages began branching off farther to the right, and on the left trails down to pools between the falls where the natives went fishing and bathing. They were swell pools, Peter remembered, but he was having trouble remembering which of the many trails was the correct one. Each time he hesitated he was afraid that the photographer and woman might catch up enough so that they could easily and unignorably

47

shout to him above the roar of the stream and tell him it was time to turn back.

About half an hour before sunset Peter heard the photographer running behind him and realized that he had stretched his air of innocence as far as it would go. A feeling of stubbornness settled over him. He lay down on the carpet of pine needles and waited calmly for the photographer to come up to him.

"Where the hell do you think you're going?" said the photographer, panting.

"I thought I could show you around the falls," said Peter expressionlessly. "It isn't much farther."

"Then we'll find our own way. You just give me directions and get back up the mountain double quick."

"I think you take every left except one until you get back to the stream," said Peter. "Then you just follow the stream to the coast. Banong's up on the left side of the harbor."

"All right, skeedadle," said the photographer. "We'll manage."

"So long," said Peter sadly. "You will get a message to Dad about the war starting, won't you?"

"Yes, goddamn it, get going."

Peter turned and started slowly upward. When he came to the woman, he nodded gloomily. She laughed, took his hand and squeezed it.

"Good-by, Peter. You've been a real help. Hurry home now, won't you?"

"Okay."

She kissed him on the mouth and left him blushing. She had moist, full lips which conveyed a feeling of warm friendliness which he had never experienced either with Enid on the one hand or his real and self-styled grown-up "aunts" on the other. When she had gone, he sat down in the trail and absently matched triplets of pine needles in combat, interlocking their prongs and pulling them through one another to find a strong one which would win and keep a championship. He wondered what to do. He certainly didn't want to go home now after leaving that note, and he was scared to stay where he was in the woods with night coming on. Night was coming on fast.

He rose to his feet and started after the man and the woman. He ran softly, putting his sneakers down on the pine needles so that he could hardly hear them himself. At the second bend in the path he saw the man and the woman disappearing around the next bend. He slowed to a walk and followed them, keeping a distance which he gradually shortened as darkness fell.

## CHAPTER 6

The moon, almost a full one, was settling behind the mountain at Peter's back, and the sea in front of him, reaching out toward Luzon, darkened perceptibly. Now he could see that the sky was turning gray. In another hour or two it would be morning. He and the people in front had walked almost the whole night. He was very tired and a little scared. He had lost the people in front again. It was the second time. The first time they had taken a wrong left and gone down to one of the pools between the falls. He had had to wait patiently but frightened near the turning while they discovered their mistake, retraced their steps and got back on the right trail. But this time he wasn't sure where they were. He was moving slowly and cautiously because he thought they must have stopped to rest. With the moon gone, it was too dark to see anything against the trees.

Peter stopped short. He heard a murmur of voices. He inched forward and saw the glow of their cigarettes. They wasted an awful lot of time resting, he thought. He crawled up to them until he could make out what they were whispering about. Overhearing them might help keep him awake.

"I don't know. Your jauntiness," said the photographer. "The way you swing your hips. All that vitality packed into a pair of dungarees. It drives me like a motor, and I don't know how to turn the damn thing off."

"What do you want to tell me about it for?" asked the woman.

"Well, I've been seeing a very unpleasant caricature of myself tonight. I'm an old bearded moonshiner, see, with a keg on my shoulder. And I'm following a wild-haired mountain girl down into the glen. Only the girl hasn't got any clothes on. And as she strides along in front of me my eyes bulge and glitter in a way that's not at all attractive."

The woman laughed. "No, that's not very nice, is it? Somehow I don't picture myself that way."

"I know you don't. That's why I wanted to apologize for last night while I had a chance."

"You don't call that an apology, do you?" she said, laughing again.

"No, but it's a sort of explanation."

"Well, I don't need it, then. Last night was just as much my fault as it was yours."

"You're a sweetie," said the photographer.

"That's a dreadful American expression. I can't imagine why I like it," she said, rising to her feet.

"I'm so stiff I creak," said the photographer, getting up after her. They helped each other on with their packs and started moving again down the trail. Peter glided after them, blushing in the darkness and wishing that he hadn't eavesdropped. They were confusing people, the photographer and the woman. One moment they filled him with admiration and friendliness and the next with disapproval and hostility. They were like Enid: you couldn't help being fond of them, but they lived in a different world. They were careless and thoughtless about sin and they made it seem attractive.

A path branched off to the right.

That must be Father Mallard's turnoff already, he thought. He looked up at the mountainside above him and, sure enough, he could see a point of light about halfway up: the kerosene storm lantern in the tower of Father Mallard's church. Father Mallard was a fellow Episcopalian, and Peter had visited him with his father last summer. They'd found him in the study of his bungalow writing something. He had acted very queerly about it and covered it up with a lot of other papers as if he was afraid they might read it. Peter's father had said afterward that it was some sort of poetry that he'd been writing ever since he'd been sent out from the States.

"He's a queer duck," Peter's father had said. "He's much too young and impractical for a station out in the hills like this. It's having an unbalancing effect on him."

Peter started on down the path and then paused, remembering something else that his father had told him. Above Mallard's church, up on the ridge, was another trail which led down to the coast and came out on the Enao side of the bay, the side where his father was. It wasn't a good trail, his

50

father had said, but it was a pretty one. Suppose his father had decided to come home this morning and, instead of taking a boat across to Banong and using the main path, had chosen the route up the ridge. Then Peter would miss him.

There was no help for it. Feeling rather wild and light-headed from lack of sleep, Peter dashed after the photographer and the woman. Approaching the next bend in the path, he tripped over a root. The fall made him collect his scattered wits. The path had long since come out of the pine forest into the scrub jungle of the foothills. It was wider now and offered less cover than it had. He picked himself up and rounded the bend cautiously. He heard voices and dropped to his hands and knees. Hugging the edge of the trail, he crawled to where he could look down the next straight stretch. The photographer and the woman had a third person with them. At first he thought, overjoyed, that it might be his father. But as he studied the stranger in the dim light he was disappointed. It was Sam Bean, the man who had hired the guide Mr. Kahn had tried to get for the photographer. Peter couldn't see Bean's long triangular beard because he was facing away from Peter, but the sheer size of the man set him apart—close to two hundred and fifty pounds and none of it fat. He carried a rifle and had a pack on his back that was enormous.

As Peter watched, the big man half turned and handed a pair of binoculars to the photographer. "Pretty ominous, ain't they?" he said. "What do you make of 'em?"

It was Bean, all right. He talked with a funny accent that Peter's father said was from Vermont. He had a way of acting hearty and ignorant when he really wasn't—like a farmboy who had grown up pleased and pleasant because he knew he was stronger than anyone else. Actually he was an engineer—supposedly a good one—and so he must have plenty of education. But he'd married a Filipino woman, and that made him standoffish. The way he talked was like his long scraggly gray beard, a way of distracting people into thinking he was colorful. But he was really sort of frightening. The boys at the sugar mills said he was the strongest man in Abanao and could bend crowbars. Well, if someone was a frightening giant, it was probably only nice of him to let other people think he was colorful so they wouldn't have to take him too seriously.

After studying something down the trail toward the coast,

the photographer handed the glasses back to Bean. "They're not like any American ships I ever photographed," he said.

Now Peter saw what they were looking at: Banong harbor, which usually had only a few native fishing boats in it, was filled with the black shadows of ships. Big ships, too. Seven of them. They couldn't be Jap ones, he thought, or the grownups below him would be alarmed and doing something. Besides, the Jap fleet had sailed down the other side of the island. Peter lay on his stomach, watching fascinated and puzzled.

"Hev to wait for more light to be sure," said Bean, sitting down. "I sent Dalag, a native fella who's with me, down the trail a piece to watch for anyone coming up. No harm in us restin' so long as we don't take our packs off."

Peter remembered Mr. Kahn's wondering why Bean, who knew the mountains well himself, needed to hire Dalag, the thin, old frizzly-haired guide who took tourists pig hunting. Now, with a flash of excitement, Peter saw a possible reason. Dalag, he knew, had been a scout in the Constabulary, and Bean had once been in the Army Corps of Engineers. Maybe when the Jap fleet showed up and Colonel Fleer started running away, the two old-timers had simply decided to get together and do something about it on their own.

Bean leaned back against the trunk of a wild papaya tree and lighted a cigarette. The woman followed suit. The photographer meanwhile reached back over his shoulder and drew something out of his pack. Peter thought at first it was a sword or another gun, but it turned out to be a small metal tripod. He set it up in the middle of the trail and mounted a long-snouted camera on it which he aimed in the direction of the ships.

"I'll give you a bottle of Johnny Walker if you get anything," said the woman.

"We'll try five minutes," said the photographer, and squeezed a button on the end of a short black cord attached to the camera.

"Don't know as thet's wise," said Bean. "You might not have time to pack it up."

"I'm a fast packer," said the photographer.

"I guess you newspaper fellas get used to takin' chances," said Bean.

"I'm a magazine fella," said the photographer, watching

his watch and still pressing the button. "*Man* magazine. You ever hear of it?"

"Eyah," said Bean. "Don't see it too often, of course, and then I just look at the pretty girls mostly. You photograph many of them?"

"Only the ones with clothes on," said the photographer gravely. "But I do almost everything else."

Sam Bean chuckled: "Ever covered a war before?"

"I did a few stories on the war in China," said the photographer.

"You know what to look for, then," said Mr. Bean slowly. "That's good." He paused and eyed the photographer with boyish good humor. "Do much shootin'?" he asked.

The photographer looked surprised and then laughed. "You mean because my gun's brand new? Well, I just bought it. But I've done some hunting. I won't have an accident if you're worried about that."

"Good," said Bean again.

Peter heard a noise from the plain below that sounded like a salvo of muffled shots.

"Thet's closer than the village," said Bean. "You best pack up the camera."

"Only another minute," muttered the photographer.

"Oh, come on, Jerry," said the woman, getting up. "It isn't worth the candle."

The hillside was silent and beautiful. There was a gardenia bush near Bean. Its blossoms must be open because Peter could smell them. Maybe it was the perfume or maybe the effort of staring in the dim, eerie light, but he felt dizzy. He wondered if the tense people standing below him were real or dream people. In one of the gullies nearby a monkey chattered and a parrot squawked in reply. Then Peter heard running footsteps on the trail below. The photographer let go of the black cord, twirled the camera off the tripod and cased and packed all his things with a deftness that kept Peter staring.

Dalag came into sight, scrambling up the trail and grunting with exertion and excitement. "Japs coming," he breathed. "Soldiers cubbered weedth leabes. Not so par behind."

Peter turned and ran. They *were* Jap ships. After passing Vispayan they must have separated from the rest of the fleet and doubled back around the southern end of the island. Peter thought briefly of continuing on up the main trail

53

ahead of the Japs, but Enao and his father seemed a lot closer than Abanao. Besides, someone had to warn his father. If his father had only a few minutes' warning to get a small head start on the Japs he'd find some way of getting home up the mountain with Peter even if it meant cutting his own trail.

Turning into the path which led to the mission station, Peter could see the others following him at a run. No way of disguising how he had sneaked along after them now. No importance in doing it any more either. He gave up thinking and submerged himself in running and breathing.

It was a good half mile up to Father Mallard's village of parishioners—all steeply uphill. When Peter reached the top his chest ached as if it would cave in and his legs wouldn't carry him properly. He lurched up to the nearest of the native huts and confronted a woman who was winnowing rice on her doorstep, tossing it against the wind in a broad, shallow basket and letting the bits of husk blow away. Most of the natives were still in their hammocks. Peter could see them through the big window holes under the eaves of their shacks.

"Enao," he panted to the woman, and gestured helplessly with his hand. "Which way to Enao?"

The woman stared at him and pointed emphatically to the cliff up behind the church. She made a zigzag up the cliff with her finger and then pointed left toward the coast.

Peter grimaced and nodded his head in thanks. "Father Mallard?" he gasped.

The woman pointed to the church and gabbled at him in her dialect. He didn't understand any of it, so he nodded again and staggered away from her, straining to make his knotted muscles work.

By allowing himself to walk for a ways he smoothed out the muscles and reached the church on an even keel. The church was at the end of a hollow, a cul-de-sac, in the side of the ridge. Behind it the mountain rose almost perpendicularly, but he could see the opening to a path which zigzagged up the cliff, just the way the woman had indicated.

In the church Father Mallard was conducting Communion for two or three of the natives.

Peter half shouted and half sobbed at him from the door of the vestry: "The Japs are coming. I'm sorry to interrupt, but the Japs have landed at Banong and they're just down there."

He pointed, and Father Mallard got up off his knees. "You're mad," said Father Mallard. "They've sent you to tease me."

"Nobody sent me," panted Peter. "I'm going to Enao to warn Dad. I just thought I'd stop and warn you on the way."

Peter darted outside again through the vestry. Glancing back, he saw that Father Mallard had followed him and was smiling.

"Really!" shouted Peter. "I'm not kidding. The Japs will be here any minute."

"Then I'll give them Communion," said Father Mallard. "I'll meet them with a cross. Go back and tell the bishops that!"

He laughed, and Peter backed away from him. "I have to find my father," he said. "You better believe me."

Father Mallard laughed again, loudly, and Peter scrambled away from him to the foot of the trail up the cliff. He looked back and Father Mallard was still laughing. He turned his face up the trail and hurried as much as he could. His father had always said that Father Mallard was unbalanced. There wasn't any more Peter could do.

Several hundred feet higher, after a dozen or more traverses across the face of the cliff, Peter collapsed on a narrow ledge. He had to catch some breath. He could see down from this ledge and he was worried that he hadn't done enough to persuade Father Mallard. Maybe he *had* looked kind of unbelievable and crazy bursting into church that way. He wiped the sweat and tears out of his eyes and tried to see through the gray haze of exhaustion which hooded them.

The valley lay below him, as quiet and subdued as a Japanese print. A ribbon of morning mist marked the stream at the bottom. Above it in the growing light the mountains on the other side were beginning to show colors. He could distinguish black patches of rock face from the somber greens of vegetation. And here and there he could see bright splotches of orange, which he recognized as the flowers of a parasite that grew in the tops of the trees like mistletoe.

At first the little cluster of shacks below the church seemed deserted of life except for a few dogs and native children. Then he saw Miss Drayton in her white, immodest man's shirt. She was coming up the hill from the shacks toward the church. The photographer was behind her, Peter thought with tired pride that he had outrun them by a lot.

Father Mallard was still standing in his cassock outside the vestry door. As the photographer and the woman got closer to him he turned and ran back into the church. A moment later the natives who had been attending service came out of the church and walked down the hill. They paused and stared at the woman, but she went by them without stopping. So did the photographer. Neither one of them stopped at the church either. They kept coming until they were on the trail below Peter and he could no longer see them.

Now Bean and Dalag appeared. They took turns running up the path from the village and crouching in the bushes to cover each other with their guns. The sight of their professional soldiering excited Peter so that he felt less tired. To think he was out in the mountains involved in a rear-guard action against the Japs! It was almost like being a guerrilla. Then he thought of his mother alone and his father unwarned. He sobered quickly. He couldn't do anything more for Father Mallard, not when he still had to run all the way to Enao. He jumped to his feet, turned up the trail and stopped again immediately, staring with uncertain joy. Striding down toward him with long, stiff steps came a gaunt figure in denim shirt and dirty khaki trousers, with a simple bedding roll on his back and sneakers on his feet, the same as Peter himself.

"Dad!" shouted Peter, and threw himself toward him. They collided, and his father, gripping him by the shoulders, pushed him off to arm's length and stared at him anxiously.

"What in the merry heck are you doing here, big fellow?" he exclaimed.

"I came to warn you the war's started and a Jap fleet—" began Peter.

"Where's Renny?" demanded the doctor. Peter's mother's name was really Renée, but his father always called her Renny.

"She's home with Jeanette. I came down with some people going to Banong. They're just behind me. We bumped into Jap soldiers on the Banong trail so we had to turn up here."

"I know," said his father. "One of the Enao fishermen saw the transports and came and woke me up. Now listen, we're going to fly our boots home up that ridge there and we're going to arrive in Abanao before the Japs. But first I've got to go down to the village and warn Mallard."

"I already did warn him," said Peter. "He acted queer and wouldn't pay any attention."

"Goldarn it," said his father, hesitating, "the Presiding Bishop has no right to send us men like that! I've got to get him out of there, though, even if it means carrying him. Now you stay put until I come back, Peter. You understand?"

"Yes," said Peter.

Dr. Baldwin strode off down the trail, and Peter lay down to watch over the edge of the cliff. Bean and Dalag were already out of sight below him. There was no white person in the village now but Father Mallard. Any moment the Japs might come up from the valley, and his father might walk into their arms. Peter stared intently at the brink of the cul-de-sac where they would appear. Perhaps if they came and he shouted, his father might hear him.

He was still absorbed in keeping watch when the photographer and the woman lay down with their rifles beside him.

"You dopey kid," said the photographer. "What the hell happened? Did you get scared you'd have to walk home in the dark?"

"No, it wasn't that," said Peter. "I wanted to make sure someone warned Dad. And I guess I wanted to have an adventure, too."

"We just saw your dad."

"I know. Will you fire shots and warn him if we see the Japs coming?"

"That's what we're lying down for, silly," said the woman.

"Thank you," said Peter.

Bean and Dalag arrived and lay down on the ridge beside them. Dr. Baldwin emerged from the bottom of the cliff and ran into the vestry of the church. At the same instant Father Mallard dashed from the front door of the church, his vestments streaming behind him, and made for his bungalow. Peter's father followed him, and in a moment Peter could hear that his father was shouting.

"Lot of risk to take for a crazy man," said Bean.

"He isn't crazy," said Peter. "He's just unbalanced."

"He's crazy, boy," said Bean. "You can't make fine distinctions in wartime."

Mallard and Peter's father disappeared into the bungalow.

"Jap soldiers," said Dalag.

Peter looked at the head of the path leading from the valley and saw them coming up over the edge, running and fanning out to the shacks.

"Shoot your guns," he gasped. And as he said it, the photographer and Bean fired together. Only one Jap fell.

"Nice shootin', city fella," said Bean.

"Thanks," muttered the photographer. "I thought I was taking his picture."

They fired again. And so did Dalag and the woman. Two more Japs dropped on the ground, and Peter's ears ached with the noise.

"That time I missed," said the photographer.

"Don't waste your ammo, lady," said Bean to the woman. "Your gun's too small. It won't reach."

The three men fired again, and Peter realized that the Japs were firing back now. But it seemed as if their guns wouldn't reach either. Either that, or they were bad shots.

Suddenly Peter saw Father Mallard rushing up the path from the bungalow. He was carrying a suitcase. He got a few yards and then fell and didn't get up. The suitcase had broken open and a pile of papers had spilled out. They were skimming away in all directions over the packed red clay of the pathway.

His crazy poems, thought Peter. He clenched his fists and pressed them hard against his ringing ears. It couldn't be real. Peter prayed and insisted to God that it shouldn't be real. No one would do anything to his father because his father had never hurt anyone. He was a doctor. He had always helped people.

Peter continued to pray desperately, repeating any odds and ends of praise or pleading that came into his mind from the set rituals of Communion and Morning Prayer. He could see the Japanese soldiers running for cover behind the shacks. The sun was coming up. It was coming up fast out of the ocean on his right. It was so blinding that he closed his eyes. When he opened them the village seemed filled with tiny flashes of light. He blinked and heard a faint yell. The flashes of light were glittering metal. Bodies were leaping out from under the eaves of the shacks. The young men of the village were falling on the Japanese with knives. Peter shivered with excitement. It was like the Bible, he thought: the vengeance of a just and righteous God.

"Cease firing," barked Bean. Peter giggled. He suddenly found himself feeling relaxed and silly, and Bean's curt order struck him as surprising. It was the kind of thing you said when you were playing pirates. Yet Bean seemed to expect grownups to obey it and, sure enough, they did.

"Let's get on down there, Dalag," said Bean, more like himself again, but still rather stern. "Leave your pack lay."

He and Dalag bounded out of sight down the trail.

"I didn't realize you were such a marksman, Jerry," said the woman.

"I've never killed anyone before," said the photographer—said Jerry. "It leaves me with a nasty kind of excitement."

"I think Dad's all right still, don't you?" said Peter.

"I'm sure he is," said the woman—said Margo.

"It was nice of you both to stay and help," said Peter. "Thank you."

"Thank those native boys," said Jerry.

The last of the shooting had died out below. Peter saw that a lot of the villagers lay on the ground along with the Japs. As he tried to count the corpses, his father ran from the bungalow and knelt beside the crumpled body of Father Mallard. Bean and Dalag appeared from the woods and sprinted down the path to help him.

In the minutes that followed so much was happening that Peter in his daze could hardly keep track of it. His father had the natives make stretchers for Father Mallard and some of the other bodies out of nipa matting and cane poles. Jerry took pictures. Margo scribbled in a notebook, explaining by words and numbers what the pictures were about. Bean posted a guard of young natives at the head of the trail leading down into the valley and then went about from shack to shack routing out the villagers, forming them into columns and making them march off up the mountain. Dalag appeared back on the cliff with two young natives carrying spades. He had Margo and Jerry and Peter move out of the way while the young men dug a ditch from the middle of the ledge along into the woods on the uphill end.

"It is por dynamite," said Dalag when Peter asked him about it. "Mr. Bean will bring dthe dynamite dthat is kept in the store por pishing."

Peter looked down at the little *tienda* built of kerosene cans in the center of the village and saw that Bean had broken it open and was handing things out to the natives, who were carrying them away in gunny sacks.

"Think how it will sound in print," said Margo. " '*Man*

magazine photographer in thick of fighting on island of Panoc helps defeat Japanese in battle for strategic village.' "

"Nuts!" said Jerry, and went on taking pictures. Soon natives from the village began to file past on their way to the top of the ridge. The women carried baskets on their backs, supported by straps which ran across their foreheads. The bigger children walked in pairs, with bundles on poles between them. The old men in their G-strings, with old-fashioned spears in their hands, moved up and down the edges of the trail urging the others on.

To keep out of the way, Peter and Jerry and Margo found themselves a vantage point in a clump of bushes up the trail from the exposed part of the ledge. It was close enough to the brink of the cliff so that they could see down through leaves and branches into the village and not so far off the pathway that they couldn't also watch the activity back along the ledge.

Peter was beginning to worry again about his father. He was still down in the village extracting bullets and dressing wounds. He had dispatched four stretcher cases already, in addition to Mallard, and he still had two more that he was working on. Bean had left him to come up the hill with the dynamite. Only three men with guns remained to guard him. They and he and the four men who were going to carry the stretchers—and of course the two wounded men themselves —were the only live people left in the village.

Soon the last of the women and children and old men had disappeared up the trail. The young men with guns had taken up positions in the bushes around the end of the ledge. The ditch down the middle of the ledge was finished, and the men who had dug it were squatting beside the baskets of dirt they had taken out of it. A heap of dynamite stocks and some lengths of iron pipe had been unloaded beside the ditch, but no one was doing anything about putting them in. Then Bean arrived at a run and Peter saw why. That was his job.

"I'm going to find out what his plan is," said Jerry. He crawled out to the path and went and talked to Bean as he worked. Bean didn't even look up but went on tying the dynamite together in bundles and connecting the bundles with fuses threaded through lengths of pipe. As he moved along the ditch toward Peter and Margo, Dalag had his workers fill in the completed sections with dirt and cover the dirt with leaves and moss.

Jerry came back through the bushes and picked up his camera again.

"Well," he said, "Bean thinks there will be another patrol along any minute now to look for the last one. He says we've got to wipe it out. He says we may as well do it the same time we wipe out the trail behind us. After that, he thinks, the Japs will feel discouraged about pursuing us too hotly and we may be able to get all these women and children out of here safely."

"Where can we get away to?" said Peter.

"He plans to go down the ridge a ways and then cut north across the Banong trail. He says up that direction there's lots of swamp to hide out in."

"Nice swamp?" said Margo sarcastically. "We're not going to go with him, are we?"

"Sure. It's our best bet for a story. He's going to train these boys as guerrillas. He even promises, if we take good pictures of him, that he'll help us get a boat to escape in."

Peter started at the sound of a shot from below. He turned to look down over the cliff, and Jerry grabbed his leg as if afraid that he would slip over the edge.

"That must be what Bean calls his bear trap," Jerry said. "It's something he rigged up on the path below the village to warn us of anyone coming."

"Dad's finally started," breathed Peter. "He's got the stretchers almost up to the church."

The village seemed peaceful and deserted in the fresh morning sunlight. Then Peter saw tiny men in yellow-green combat dress running and stopping, running and stopping among the empty huts. They came fast—through the village and up through the bushes toward the church. Peter backed away from the edge feeling dizzy.

"Your father will make it," said Jerry. "Don't worry."

"There's an awful lot of them this time," said Peter. "Thirty at least."

"Do you think Bean knows what he's doing, Jerry?" said Margo. "Thirty professionals against one homemade land mine and a raggle-taggle of pig hunters and male and female journalists?"

"Sweetie, we can only hope," said Jerry.

Peter stared down the trail for his father. The ledge looked completely natural again. Bean was kneeling behind a clump of bushes at the end of it holding the fuse where it came out of the pipe in the ground and twisting his neck to see how the men were placed behind him. Peter closed his eyes and counted to twenty-five. He had to do something, and maybe when he opened them, his father would be in sight. He wasn't. Peter closed his eyes again and prayed that there wouldn't be any more shots.

The first stretcher came around the bend beyond the ledge. The bearers were trotting. Peter's father jogged along behind the second stretcher, followed by the three men with guns. Peter relaxed and let his eyes water quietly.

"Glad you made it, Doc," whispered Bean distinctly. "Your other patients are up the trail a piece. Best get back there and take care of 'em."

Peter's father looked as if he were going to say something, but from down the cliff only one or two zigzags away came the unmistakable grunt of a Japanese giving an order. The stretcher-bearers quickened their steps, and Peter's father strode past on the trail. Peter wanted to call to him but didn't dare.

"Go on, crawl back after him," whispered Jerry. "This is no place for a boy."

Peter obeyed, but his eyes were bleary, and as he neared the trail he put his hand on a dry stick, which broke with a crack.

"Sssst!" It was Bean looking around angrily. Peter gave up the attempt and stretched out in the bushes beside the pathway.

In a little while which seemed long, a Japanese officer came around the bend beyond the ledge. He was young and his uniform was dirty and he walked gracefully without the bowlegged swagger Peter expected. He paused at the end of the ledge and then walked gingerly across. He reached the edge of the bushes where Bean was hiding and called softly to his soldiers, who had grouped and waited on the far side. As he called, Peter thought he saw the flicker of Bean's match. The soldiers filed across the ledge after the officer, and the officer started coming toward Peter. He came and came. He passed Bean. He passed Dalag. He passed Jerry and Margo. The first of his soldiers were also over the cliff.

The fuse must have burned out in the pipe. It seemed to Peter that it was time for Bean to do something, no matter how foolish. As he thought it, Jerry rolled over onto his back, sat up and pointed his gun. The officer fell and lay still in the bushes at Peter's side. Peter hadn't heard Jerry's gun go off, because the dynamite had finally blown up. A brown mist of raining dirt hung over the ledge. The natives were all firing into it wildly. As the mist settled Peter distinctly saw a man standing on the other side of the ledge pulling the pin out of a grenade. For the first time he heard Jerry, right in front of him, firing his rifle. The man with the grenade dropped. Two more Japs ran out of the woods and tried to pick up the grenade. Jerry shot one. The grenade went off. and blew up the other.

Jerry was some shot! Peter looked toward him proudly and screamed with horror. A soldier with a bayonet had risen out of the bushes right in front of Jerry and was lunging at him. Margo's gun went off. The soldier paused in his lunge and came down on top of Jerry. Peter buried his head in his arms and looked at nothing more.

After a while the shooting lessened and finally stopped.

"I think we've killed the whole bloody lot!" It was the woman who said it, but she didn't sound much like Margo. Peter couldn't tell from the sound whether she was hoarse with rage or weeping. Farther ahead near the ledge a man was calling out plaintively in a high voice.

"I could use a hand," piped the voice. "How about some help. Goddamn it, I need help."

It sounded a little like Bean. Peter opened his eyes and looked up. Jerry was getting up in front of him. Jerry was alive.

Peter jumped incredulously to his feet and ran after Jerry to the edge of the crater left by the explosion. Bean was hanging from the branch of an upside-down tree which clung to the cliff by only two or three roots. A Jap soldier hung head down over a branch near him. Beyond the tree was all air. The dynamite had wiped out the ledge completely and almost swept Bean away with it. For a hundred feet over his head and as far straight down into the valley, the face of the mountain hung impassable. There was no sign of live soldiers anywhere, not even in the empty village below.

Peter left Jerry and Dalag hauling Bean up to safety and walked back across the battlefield. Jerry had a slash on his head from the bayonet of the Jap who'd tried to jump him. Bean had blood on his pants leg. Several of the natives were wounded too. Peter's father would be busy for quite a while, and Peter felt dizzy and sick and tired. He lay down in the bushes beside the trail and closed his eyes. He could hear thuds as the natives went around through the bushes with their bolos making sure that all the Japs were dead.

"You crybaby," he heard Margo say. "It's only a small gash. Head wounds always bleed a lot."

He heard deep-voiced sobs that were half sobs and half laughter and wondered if Jerry could be crying. It would be funny if he was. Peter would never have to worry again about holding back tears himself, if Jerry was crying. But Peter didn't open his eyes to find out. Either way it wouldn't be much to see.

Peter opened his eyes to find his father kissing him for the first time in years.

"Wake up, big fellow, you've got to go home."

"I wasn't asleep. I'm fine," he said.

"I couldn't believe it when I found they'd let you stay down here during the fight," said his father, shoving a thermometer into his mouth and holding his wrist. "I'm sorry I had to leave you like that, but I couldn't let Mallard go and do some fool thing that would get him killed."

"Is he all right?" mumbled Peter around the thermometer.

"I don't know yet," said his father. "He has a nice clean hole under his collarbone which shouldn't be serious at all. But he's got himself in shock and I'm afraid it may be something mental. I have to stay with him—I'd have to stay with these other cases for a few days anyway. So I'm sending you back home with a couple of native boys who know the trail up the ridge."

"Can't I stay with you?" pleaded Peter as his father removed the thermometer.

"Leave Renny all alone? Absolutely not. Did you get any sleep last night?"

"No," said Peter gloomily, hearing finality in his father's tone of voice.

"How about food?"

"I had lunch yesterday."

"I should have realized," said his father, smiling. "Finding you asleep like that, I was afraid you were sick."

"I wasn't asleep," said Peter. "At least I don't think I was."

"Well, we won't argue about it," said his father. "The boys are going to carry you on a stretcher. They have orders not to let you out until they reach the edge of town. Now, there's a good chance they'll get you there ahead of the Japs because the Japs have to look for trouble. But I don't want you taking any risks. Stay away from roads and sneak home through the woods. If Renny isn't there, try the school. The boys will follow you until they see you're all right."

"I'll be all right," said Peter.

"Here, take this. It'll give you a few hours' sleep and freshen you up."

"All the Americans are going to intern themselves at the school," said Peter when he had swallowed the pill. "It's a plan worked out by Father Gibney and Mayor Ziegler."

"Good," said his father. "I'll get news to you there, even if I can't come myself."

Peter got up. His father hugged him and gave him a big chunk of raw sugar and a loaf of dark bread from his bedding roll. Two of the men from the village were standing nearby with a hammock stretched on a cane frame. They grinned at Peter. Peter grinned back and got into the stretcher.

"Oh, one more thing," said his father. "Don't tell anyone except Renny what's happened. If it ever got back to the Japanese, I'd be a marked man."

"Gosh, that's right!" said Peter.

"Okay, off you go, then."

"Good-by, Dad."

"See you soon, big fellow."

The two natives started to jog up the trail. Peter looked back and saw his father help Bean to his feet and hand him a crutch made out of a forked stick. Behind them were a couple of men with rifles trained back over the chasm. But there were no Japs on the other side, and the exodus of the villagers had already begun. Laden down with bundles and babies, they streamed upward along the pathway. Even some of the old men had rifles now, Peter noticed—probably Jap ones. There were more bandages than there had been, too. His father must have been busy. Maybe Peter *had* slept for a while. His stretcher-bearers moved fast, and the other natives stood out of the way to let them pass.

Halfway up the column, a couple of zigzags higher on the mountain, Peter saw Jerry crouched beside the trail taking pictures. His head was bandaged with Margo's blue kerchief.

She was standing behind him holding one of his cameras.

"Good-by, scoop," she called as he passed.

"Good-by," he shouted.

"Thanks for putting us on the right trail," said the photographer, taking a picture of him.

At the top of the ridge Peter passed Dalag and a half dozen more men with rifles. His bearers exchanged greetings with them.

"My cousins will carry you home, boy," said Dalag.

"Thank you," said Peter.

Dalag and his men were standing in the left branch of the trail. Peter's bearers turned right and started up the ridge. Peter ate the sugar and the bread, lay back and waited for the sleeping pill to have its magic effect.

## CHAPTER 7

Peter awoke to the rhythmic jolting of his litter with a feeling of sensuous luxury. It was twilight and he looked at the fading blue sky euphorically, finding it difficult to come to with his usual suddenness.

When the stretcher stopped jolting, it was almost dark. Peter jumped out with a start. He had told himself that they wouldn't reach the top of the mountain until the middle of the night, but then he hadn't known really what time they had started. He was standing in an unfamiliar group of pines. He looked up the hill and saw a stone wall, and beyond it sky. The two men who had carried him were already untying the hammock from its frame.

Peter walked up the hill and looked over the stone wall. Gradually he realized where he was: not in North Valley where he had started but in South Valley, at the extreme tip of it, on the edge of the park which bordered the Vispayan Road. Beyond the wall was a lookout, a pavement of concrete where people could come in cars and admire the view. There was a car there now with its parking lights on. As Peter studied it warily, he realized that it looked a lot like the car of Mr. Fincher, the science teacher at the school. Then he saw Mr. Fincher himself, sitting on the running board beside his houseboy. They were pouring something into glasses out of a cocktail shaker. Around his neck, Mr. Fincher had a pair of binoculars. He must be a member of what Father Gibney had called the Early Warning Committee. The Japs mustn't have come yet.

Peter climbed over the wall and ran to him. "Mr. Fincher, the Japs have landed," he said.

It took a while to persuade Mr. Fincher that he was telling the truth. Peter didn't want to explain everything, so he just said he'd been out walking and seen some natives who told him about the Japs coming up the Banong trail. Fortunately, three of the Jap ships were still in Banong harbor, and there was still enough light to make them out with Mr. Fincher's binoculars.

"Just think," said Mr. Fincher, "a few more minutes and we couldn't have seen them. It makes you shiver, doesn't it!"

Peter waved to the two natives who had carried him up the mountain and wished he could thank them. They nodded and remained watching over the top of the wall.

"I may be considered something of a lightweight," said Mr. Fincher, motioning Peter into the front seat of his car, "but I'm not stupid. I don't need to be told twice about a Japanese invasion. What a cunning coup! To attack the *wrong* side of the island with part of the fleet that *didn't* pass in the night!"

"I wonder how come no one noticed the Jap ships earlier," said Peter.

"We only just started watching," said Mr. Fincher. "The committee didn't even meet until this afternoon. Everyone's been too busy swapping rumors, and pinch-hitting for run-away servants, and tuning the pops and squeals out of their short-wave sets. It's been perfect pandemonium all day."

Peter said nothing more. Mr. Fincher was driving down the valley so fast that Antonio in the school truck couldn't have kept up even if his whole pride had depended on it. By the time Peter recognized the golf course, Enid's house was already left behind, and he didn't see whether the lights were on in it or not.

"How soon do you think they'll be here?" asked Mr. Fincher, lurching to a halt in the hotel driveway.

"I don't know," said Peter. "It's only a nine-hour hike to Banong and they landed at three or four o'clock this morning."

"Any minute, then," said Mr. Fincher. "That calls for Emergency Plan A. I'll tell Mayor Ziegler."

He shot out back onto the main road, and Peter ran down the steps to his home. His mother heard him coming and met him at the door. She caught him by the shoulders and shook him angrily, but he saw that her face was drawn with worry and red with weeping. When he kissed her, she began to weep once more.

"I'm sorry, Mother," he pleaded. "I won't do it again."

She continued to weep and to shake him, calling him thoughtless and completely self-centered. When she would listen, he told her a little of what had happened. He didn't want to tell her all of it until he was sure she understood how secret it was. And he didn't need to, because the news of the Japs' coming was enough to make everything else seem unimportant.

She straightened up, very pale, and went at once into the kitchen, where she began to fill a suitcase with canned goods. Peter ate most of several meals which she had saved for him in the icebox and then, seeing that she was busy and no longer weeping, he went to his bedroom and stuffed some clothes and what few Christmas presents he had bought into his suitcase. He wished he had bought the hairbrush for his mother, but it was too late now. The shrapnel money, unused, still filled his pocket.

He heard a loud rap on the door and his stomach tightened. But it wasn't the Japs; it was Father Gibney.

"Renée," called Father Gibney, "you must go at once to the school." Father Gibney was the only person Peter knew who pronounced his mother's name correctly, the way it would be in France.

"The Japs will be here any moment," shouted Father Gibney.

"I know," called Peter's mother as she came to the door. "I'm already packing."

"I just wanted to make sure," shouted Father Gibney. "I still have to tell the Kahns and pick up the sisters at the convent."

Peter heard his mother opening the front door and Father Gibney running off up the flatstone steps outside.

"Thank you," called his mother. Apparently she hadn't told him about Peter's going to Enao. It was a good thing, too, Peter thought. It saved him from having to make up a bunch of lies about his trip.

When Peter had finished his own packing, he returned to the kitchen where his mother was.

"Don't pack too much, Mother. I'll call Anita."

Anita, the maid, shrieked when he awakened her. She always slept with nothing on and, like many Christianized natives, tried to be very proper. She didn't fully understand what he told her, but as soon as he had left the room, she got up obediently and dressed. He made sure by looking back through the keyhole. Seeing a native girl was not like seeing a white woman: a lot of the natives went about half naked anyway. He woke up Jeanette, his seven-year-old sister, and helped her put her clothes on. Then he got the other suitcases down from the attic. His mother had finished packing the food and was explaining to Anita that all white people might be imprisoned and that she should pack her most valuable possessions in case she had to return to her home in the lowlands. While his mother packed her own clothes and Jeanette's, Peter carried his wagon up to the street and loaded it with his own suitcase and the case of food. When he came back to the house, his mother had two more suitcases ready.

"I hope I've got all your father's important papers!" she exclaimed.

"Don't forget his medical chest," Peter said.

Peter went into the back yard and took down the clothesline. He carried his mother's and sister's suitcases, the medical chest and finally his father's suitcase to the wagon and roped the whole top-heavy load securely onto it. He felt cool and proud in his excitement. Back at the house his mother had filled a shopping basket with odds and ends and was checking through the rooms, snapping her fingers with dismay every time she found something new which was indispensable.

About eight-thirty they set off. Anita balanced her belongings in a hamper on her head. His mother led Jeanette and carried the bulging shopping basket. Peter pulled the swaying wagon. His mother worried that he would strain himself, but he distracted her with the problem of routes: they could go the long way around by road or take the short cut through the woods. She was all for the fastest way as long as Peter felt sure he could follow it in the dark. He said he was sure, so they crossed the main highway at the end of the hotel drive and proceeded up a side street past the big water tower. The side street came to a dead end at the edge of the woods. Here Peter realized that he couldn't pull the wagon up the path in the woods over all the rocks and roots. He would have to hide it in the underbrush and come back for the load piece by piece, after he had seen his mother and sister to the school.

He explained his change of plans to his mother as casually and reasonably as he could, but, as he feared, she was angry at him. She thought he had purposely tricked her so that he could go off adventuring. Packing and moving were the terrors of her life. She'd always counted on his father to make them easy for her and now she'd counted on Peter and he'd let her down.

"*Bien!*" she said sternly when she had finished scolding him. "You must take the case of canned goods first."

The short cut was genuinely short, but the cans of food were heavy and Peter found his self-possession leaving him as he stumbled along and felt the sharp edge of the case digging farther into his shoulder at every jolt. He spoke crossly to Jeanette because she held the flashlight carelessly and he couldn't see where he was putting his feet. His mother told him sharply that if he could not be gentle he should leave the food behind. Nothing was really important, he thought angrily, but getting safely where they could put Jeanette back to bed. He shifted the case to the top of his head and, finally, at odds with each other, they reached the school. At Father Gibney's house they found the servants laying mattresses for them on the floor of the screened porch. The nuns had taken the bedrooms, and two other Episcopalian families, the Marlowes and Barsinis, were bedding down in the living room and dining room. Father and Mrs. Gibney were at the boys' dormitory, trying to arrange accommodations for other families who had poured in from all over town.

Peter found that no one had seen anything of the Japanese yet, so he left his mother talking with Mrs. Barsini and went back to the wagon at the bottom of the short cut. Still aching in his shoulder from the case of canned goods, he decided that he must take the rest of the load around the long way by road. He tightened up the clothesline and pulled the wagon out past the water tower to the main highway. It was a fifteen-minute walk to the school this way, perhaps half an hour hauling the wagon. Except in front of the water tower and the entrance to the hotel, most of it was ill-lighted and lay through woods. Beyond the school there were houses again, all the way up past the golf course, but this one stretch was uninhabited, a land investment held by the school on one side and the Roman Catholic order of Dominicans on the other. Peter kept well over to the left-hand side of the highway and hurried across the lightless areas between street lamps.

He had gone about halfway when the street lamps went out. He looked for the glow in the sky above the business district and couldn't find it. The lights all over town must be out. He wished he had brought the flashlight. He knew the short cut in the dark—it was the way he went to early Communion when he served as acolyte in the chapel—but he didn't know the road. If he had planned ahead when he left Father Gibney's, he would have seen that he had to take the road and he would have brought the flashlight. After all, the electrical plant was one of the first places where a modern army struck. He had read how the Germans did it across Europe. Fifth columnists seized and disrupted the utilities to spread confusion before the Panzer divisions rolled in. Of course, the Japs weren't using Panzer divisions—they didn't need to—but it was a blitzkrieg all the same. He hugged the left side of the road, keeping one foot on the pavement and one on the gravel shoulder. From time to time the wagon ran too far left and stuck in the gravel. Then he would have to lift it out again.

How could a group of saboteurs keep the lights out for so long? The electrical plant was on the ridge between North and South valleys, so near the business district that Mayor Ziegler could easily send up a squad of policemen to recapture it. Probably the policemen had all run away. Scared-cat Filipinos! Peter had not heard a shot. It seemed cowardly that no one should be shooting. There were plenty of guns at the sugar refineries.

He wondered if his father would learn to shoot. Perhaps he would stay with Bean and become a guerrilla. No one knew the mountains better than he did. But first he should come back to Abanao and steal his family away with him. They could live in a hideout in the north while he went out and made raids. Of course, that didn't sound like him. Even if he decided that this was a time for killing as well as heal-

71

ing, he wouldn't think it was a good risk, involving his family. Well? Then he must come back quickly and be captured with them. He spent so much time away from home anyway. It wasn't fair to leave them now.

Stepping out with his left leg, Peter collided sharply with something hard that made him want to cry and dance and shake his bruised shin with fury. When it hurt less, he felt out in the darkness and found that he had walked into the concrete post marking the third kilometer from the center of town. He had gone farther than he thought. The school driveway turned off to the left only about twenty feet farther on. My, it was dark! He couldn't see either of the two stone columns which marked the entrance. In an outburst of happy relief he tugged the wagon out into the center of the road and ran with it the last few yards.

Slowing down and turning the corner into the drive, he noticed a cluster of jiggling lights coming up along the road behind him. Not sure what they were, he pulled his wagon over to the side of the driveway and watched them come. They were too small and close together to be car headlights. More like bike lamps. But there were so many of them. Five lights in each row, and rows stretching back as far as the bend. They looked like the ghosts of all the bicycle racers who had ever lived. He jumped into the ditch below the sign *Abanao American School* and crouched down, crawling with goose flesh. The first row flashed past him on the highway without turning in. He glimpsed a man in uniform huddled over the handlebars of the nearest bike, carrying a pack and a helmet on his back and a rifle slung over his shoulder. The next row was the same. The ghosts were only Japs.

He started to count rows. Six had gone by already. Seven . . . eight . . . nine . . . ten . . . eleven—there were five men in each row—twelve, that was sixty . . . sixty-five . . . seventy . . . seventy-five . . . eighty. . . . He counted for a long time. Occasionally there was a break in the rows and a lonely tandem went by with a small cannon on its baggage carrier. The tandems confused him, and when the last bike had passed he was uncertain whether he had counted 419 or 519.

Trembling, he pulled his wagon back onto the drive and up toward the boys' dormitory. He felt muddled and scared. How come the Japs were riding bikes? Where did they get them? He rounded the last turn on the wooded driveway.

From the windows of the dorm ahead he saw an eerie light flickering. For an instant he believed that the cyclists had been ghostly riders after all. The world must have been swept away and replaced by a spirit world while he was walking in the dark on the road. Then he realized, of course, that it was only candlelight—he must be dopey still from riding all day in that swaying stretcher.

The inside of the dormitory was completely changed. In the classrooms downstairs the desks were piled up on top of each other to make room for mattresses and sleepers. Each room had only one candle, and it was hard to see how to cross the floors without stepping on someone. Half the people were not really trying to sleep but were lying smoking or talking in groups or busy packing and unpacking suitcases. Some of the old men were snoring; some of the babies were crying. Peter recognized few familiar faces and even they looked somehow changed.

He had to find Father Gibney to tell him about the Japs and he half hoped that he might come across Enid, too. He hadn't seen her since the war began. Now that he was free of her he wanted to see what she looked like and to brag about his adventures—the ones that weren't secret. People swore at him as he threaded his way around the mattresses from room to room. They were so unreal, go ghostly, even here inside, that he didn't mind them. The snatches of conversation he heard seemed foolish and far away.

"One of our Jap laborers, just a press operator, had the nerve to laugh and refuse to help when we loaded the car," said a man in white flannels. "It couldn't have been more humiliating. Ordinarily I'd have slapped his face and paid him off on the spot. But the way things are going you can't tell whether they might not be put in charge of you someday."

Peter passed a young married couple. The woman was pregnant and the man looked worried.

"Don't worry, Martha," the man said. "God will provide powdered milk." Peter wondered fleetingly if God could allow Himself such little kindnesses, even for missionaries. God didn't give powdered milk to children with beriberi in China. On the other hand, maybe he had given Peter this war. And that was so much bigger for a need so much smaller that Peter obviously had no right to wonder.

Suddenly there was Enid. She was lying on a mattress in the corner with her head on her suitcase. She looked asleep and alone. Peter jumped over an empty mattress and stood at her feet looking down at her. He saw at once that she was not sleeping but eying the other people in the room with an angry, contemptuous curiosity that made her cheeks glow.

"Hello, Peter," she said. "You had better not talk to me. Nobody else does."

"Why not?" asked Peter.

"They don't like Papa," she said. "Who cares anyhow. I won't stay here long."

"Where are you going?"

"Papa's coming back for me as soon as he has found the Japs and told them we're Swedish."

"Where were you yesterday?" asked Peter. "I came by your house."

"We drove to Vispayan to meet the Japs, but they didn't land."

"They've landed now."

"But not in Vispayan. Somewhere else."

"Oh," said Peter. "Does your father know where to find them?"

"I don't think so," said Enid. "That's why he brought me here. He said it would be dangerous for me to meet them at night." Peter realized that he couldn't even tell her about seeing the Japs on bikes. It might be like giving information to the enemy. The thought hurt him. "I'm to stay here," Enid continued, "until Papa comes back for me. Then we'll go home and live there while they put the rest of you in prison. I bet you wish you were Swedish."

"They don't put civilians in prison," said Peter. "They intern them."

"What's the difference. You still can't do what you want."

"No," said Peter. "I'd like it better if you were there, too."

"I'm glad I won't be."

"I'll miss you."

"I think it will be exciting on the outside."

"It will only last a few months," said Peter.

"Don't be too sure," she replied.

"Anyway, we may see each other. They may not be too strict. I have to find Father Gibney now."

"Don't you want to kiss me good-by?"

Peter glanced around at the people in the room and saw they were all preoccupied. Quickly he bent and kissed her on the cheek. She laughed.

74

"Just like the first time we played the Game. You still don't know how to kiss."

"There are so many people," began Peter.

"And you think Papa's a Nazi," she said.

"No, that's not it."

He looked around again. Still no one was noticing, so he leaned over and kissed her on the mouth. She didn't open her mouth, so they kissed the old way.

"Thank you," she said—and Peter couldn't tell whether she sounded sarcastic or sad.

"Good-by," he said.

"You said that before. Go and see your Father Gibney." She smiled gaily and closed her eyes and turned her cheek down on the pillow of her suitcase. Peter stood over her a moment and then, remembering the people in the room enough not to look at them, he moved off unhappily. If only she were an American too!

He squeezed through the door into the fifth-graders room. A group of Seventh-Day Adventists he knew slightly were listening to a Bible reading in a circle by the door. "And the Lord said unto Satan, 'Behold he is in thine hand, only spare his life.' So Satan went forth from the presence of the Lord and smote Job with sore boils from the sole of his foot unto his crown." Yes, God moved inscrutably, but Peter didn't much like Seventh-Day Adventists: they were unpleasantly strict and pious. It was just like them to pretend that the war and its excitement made them into suffering Jobs.

All the same, he thought, those two women beyond the Adventists are being awful irreverent to talk so loudly.

"I didn't have any idea what to pack for," said one of them in slacks. "A weekend in the city or a month in the country? Heels or tennis shoes? Nighties or pajamas?"

"I know. And clothes are so important to morale," answered the other. "Jim said to bring good, solid, comfortable things, but, my dear, I haven't owned those sort of things since I last went on an Outing Club outing."

In the second grade, on a camp cot made up properly with sheets and blankets and a pillow, Maggie Higgins was fast asleep. Peter was surprised to see her. He'd thought surely the Higginses, with all their money, would find a way of escaping to Manila. He was surprised too that the rest of the family weren't with her. It must be they were in another room because there wasn't space for them around Maggie.

Peter smiled: it was just like her going to sleep, calm and beautiful, while everyone else fretted.

Not far away, Reverend Bax was dividing up a package of money among his fellow Lutherans. "You see," he was saying, "there was a run on the bank, so I couldn't get any money but what was in the church safe."

Peter thought of the twenty thousand pesos Jerry had withdrawn and wished he could tell Reverend Bax what a patriotic cause it was being used for.

"It's the privacy I shall miss," said an elderly lady in the next room. "Food doesn't matter really—not for a couple of months anyway, and it can't possibly last longer than that."

"Of course not," replied a white-haired gentleman. "When the Pacific Fleet gets here, I'll give them two weeks."

Peter saw the plump, pretty face of Mrs. Kahn and joyfully picked his way across the room to her. He asked her whether she had seen Father Gibney. She had not, but she wanted him to tell Mr. Kahn, who might be with Father Gibney, that she was lonely.

Peter entered the school dining room. On one side of it, sitting on the piled-up tables, was a drunken man in overalls telling a joke in a loud voice.

"So the wife yells out the window, 'You need more tail.' And the man with the kite hollers back, 'That's what I told you last night and you said to go fly a kite.'"

Peter didn't enjoy the joke, but he smiled at something else: on the other side of the room a group of elderly women—from their clothes, missionaries—were softly and draggingly singing the hymn "Shall We Gather at the River"—and warding off the evil spirit of the drunk.

Beyond the dining room, in the kitchen, Peter found Mrs. Gibney. She at least was acting real, overseeing the warming of babies' bottles and the preparation of breakfast. But she had no time for Peter; there simply wasn't enough oatmeal to go around. He escaped through the kitchen door, skirted the gymnasium and crossed to the other wing. There Father Gibney had his office, and it was obvious—Peter didn't know why he hadn't thought of it before—that with his house full, Father Gibney in his usual calm way would be getting a good night's sleep on the office floor. There was light in the office, but the curtains were drawn.

Peter knocked, and an unfamiliar voice told him to come

in. The room was full of men sitting around the long mahogany table where Father Gibney corrected papers. Father Gibney sat at one end and Mayor Ziegler at the other. Reverend Fisher, the Presbyterian minister, Mark Price, who owned the gambling casino downtown, and Mr. Kulhausen, the head of Mananok Sugar Refinery, were ranged along one side of the table. On the other side sat Mr. Kahn and two men whom Peter recognized only as bosses in sugar refineries.

"What is it?" asked Father Gibney. "We're having a meeting, Peter."

"I wanted to tell you something, sir. I thought I'd better tell you first."

"We're very busy, son," said Mr. Ziegler.

"I didn't know," said Peter. "I'm sorry. I'll wait outside for you, Father Gibney, if you don't mind." He turned to the door.

"Now wait a minute," said the principal. "Peter is the boy who brought me the news about the Japanese fleet yesterday. Have you been out scouting again, Peter?"

"Not exactly, sir."

"I told you to stay with your mother. One of these days I'll have to give you a good old-fashioned caning. What have you seen?"

"Japs, sir. Four hundred and nineteen or five hundred and nineteen. I lost track of the hundreds. They were riding bicycles in the direction of the golf course."

Mayor Ziegler and Reverend Fisher laughed unpleasantly.

"I really did," said Peter, blushing. "They had some tandem bikes, too, with small cannons on the backs."

"Laugh at him at your own risk," said Father Gibney. "Haven't you heard of the bicycle troops? Tokyo's very proud of them. They're lightly armed auxiliaries trained to operate on terrain where armor is impractical." Father Gibney explained Caesar's auxiliaries in the same tone of voice in Latin class. "Their cycles are lightweight collapsible affairs which they can pack on their backs cross-country between roads. Where did you see them, Peter?"

"I was bringing my wagon full of suitcases around by the road from our house. Just after I turned into the school drive I saw these lights coming after me from Abanao. I watched them go past from the ditch. They really were Japs because

77

they wore tight leggings. You know what I mean? And each of them had a rifle and a pack and a tin helmet. And the bikes were brown and yellow and green and didn't have mudguards. I thought I was seeing things."

"How long ago was this?" asked Mr. Kulhausen.

"Ten or fifteen minutes ago."

"After the lights went out?"

"Yes, sir. The lights went out just after I passed the water tower."

"They must have captured the downtown area without a shot," said one of the strange men bitterly. "I understand the police went home and buried their revolvers."

"On my orders," said Mayor Ziegler. "There's no point in antagonizing the Japs and risking civilian lives when the regular army has already pulled out. There'll be a time to fight later if Fleer gets reinforcements."

"Those bicycle riders are going to have one hell of a coast on the way down the mountain," chuckled Mark Price. "Can you imagine the hairpin turns at night? Jesus!" Mr. Price had an open pint of whisky in front of him. People said he drank too much and was disreputable, but Peter liked him.

"By tomorrow they'll occupy Vispayan," said the stranger. "Then where's Fleer going to get his reinforcements?"

"It's clear they've had good liaison with the local Japanese," said Father Gibney, "or they wouldn't dare push on so fast. It's my guess they won't try to take over the civil government until they've secured Vispayan and landed some armor and a general or two. In the meantime there's going to be looting. The Japanese civilians obviously hold a strong hand and we can expect them to play it highhandedly. My recommendation is that we undertake a foraging expedition to our own homes as soon as it's light. We must get as much food up here as possible before it's looted."

"According to the Geneva Convention the Japanese are obliged to feed us," said Reverend Fisher.

"According to Geneva conventions," remarked Mr. Price, "you probably aren't supposed to conquer island with men on bicycles. I go along with Gibney."

"It's obvious," said Mr. Kahn. "Otherwise we go hungry until they take us prisoners officially. And that may take days or weeks."

"I second Gibney's motion," said Mr. Kulhausen, "if it is a motion."

"I'll make it a motion," said Father Gibney.

"All in favor say 'Aye,'" said Mayor Ziegler.

Everyone raised his hand but the two strangers.

"Lindstrom, O'Connor? You're not in favor?" asked the mayor.

"I'm not going to be here in the morning," said the one called O'Connor. "I came in from Mananok with Mr. Kulhausen because he asked me to and becuse I wanted to know what was cooking. But I got my gear packed and I'm heading for the hills. Christ, someone's got to fight this war! Some of you men have wives—that's okay. But I'd like to move that this committee urge every bachelor in the place to come with us and fight. We can slip right out back here, work our way down the east ridge and cross the Vispayan Road before morning. By tomorrow night we'll be away in the northwest. That's rugged country. While the Japs mop up Fleer in the south, we can form a resistance movement that'll give 'em trouble for years, if necessary."

"Right," said Lindstrom, the other stranger. "I second."

"I'd like to point out," said Father Gibney, "that this community needs its able-bodied young men whether it's interned or free."

"This community can get along with its able-bodied young missionaries," said Kulhausen. "The single men with guts ought to be out fighting for their country. I wish to hell I could."

"Kulhausen," said Father Gibney, "you'd do well to remember that some of these missionaries have seen more danger and hard living in their lives than all your boys at the sugar refineries put together."

"I didn't mean anything personal, Gibney," said Mr. Kulhausen. "You served your stretch in the last war, same as I did. And I don't object to the old-fashioned missionaries who get the hell out into the back country and preach either. The ones that rile me are those pious young punks who sit around doing nothing at the United Denominations Rest Home or whatever it's called."

"You know as well as I do," said Reverend Fisher hotly, "that the people at the home have no work here because they're either refugees or new workers for the China missions who haven't been able to get to their posts yet."

"If I were your age and wanted to get into western China, I'd damn well find a way," said Kulhausen.

"There is a motion before us," said Mayor Ziegler. "All in favor raise their right hands."

Lindstrom, O'Connor and Kulhausen raised their hands. "All opposed?"

Father Gibney and Reverend Fisher raised their hands. Peter noticed that Mark Price and Mr. Kahn and Mr. Ziegler hadn't voted either way.

"Seems like a straight division between missionaries and sugar men," said the mayor. "But the motion does not have a majority, so the chair rules that Lindstrom and O'Connor can't use the authority of this committee for recruiting guerrillas. They'll have to do it on their own."

Lindstrom and O'Connor rose to leave.

"May I go, too?" asked Peter.

"By all means," said Father Gibney. "We'd forgotten you were eavesdropping. Mum's the word and no more adventures."

Peter wondered if he should tell Mr. Kahn that his wife was lonely, and decided not. Father Gibney still didn't know about his really big adventure, and it seemed best to leave well enough alone and escape while he could. He slipped out in front of the two men from the refineries and pulled his wagon down to the cottage where his mother and sister were. The fresh air felt good after the hot, smoky roomful of arguments. Things were confusing, he thought, and he was only a kid. He had to stay and be caught by the Japs and try to take care of his mother and sister the way his father wanted. Tonight, after the day's excitement, it seemed a pleasantly simple and restful prospect.

His mother was sitting on the front steps of Father Gibney's house waiting for him. She had been worrying about him again and was ready to be angry. He hastened to tell her about the Japs and their bikes. As he expected, the news blunted her grievance against him.

"It was senseless of you to go around on the road," she said distractedly. "Absolutely senseless and bad. Your life is much more important to us than a few pieces of luggage."

When they had stretched out on their mattresses on the porch floor, Peter told her the whole story of the battle on the cliff, and of Mallard and the other wounded, and of Sam Bean and his plans to organize a guerrilla group. When he had finished, his mother asked a few questions and they both lay quietly awake, staring up at the ceiling.

The battle and everything that had happened in his sleepless, hungry state seemed unreal now. But then, so did the Japs on bikes and so did the people in the dorm, talking by candlelight. The most real thing seemed to be the missionaries and sugar men arguing in his head. He was the son of a missionary, so he belonged on the missionaries' side, but most of what he had studied at school in American history —things like John Paul Jones and Sergeant York—argued for the sugar men. And so did his own body. The thought of Lindstrom and O'Connor escaping to the mountains and living free and defiant like Bean made his muscles tighten with restlessness.

If it weren't for Mother and Jeanette, he thought, and for responsibility and being obedient, I'd be out there now with Dad. Perhaps I couldn't fight but I could be a scout or a messenger or something. I can't understand why the young missionaries without families want to stay here. Why does Father Gibney say they ought to let themselves be captured? I should think everyone who isn't captured would give the Japs that much less chance to feel satisfied and contemptuous and invincible.

Mother's always said being a good Christian is the very opposite of being a sissy. If a kid blasphemes against God or missionaries you can fight him. If he just insults you personally you're supposed to turn the other cheek. I haven't always been so good about turning the other cheek and I haven't felt so good about it afterward either. But I never felt bad about fighting a kid who insulted religion. I thought it was the same way with your country. Fighting and even killing in a just war is allowed by every kind of Christian I ever heard of except the Quakers, and everyone knows how heroic the Quaker ambulance drivers were in the World War. Father Gibney fought in the last war himself. Maybe he thinks that the young missionary men are impractical people, like Dad says, and would only be a burden to the real fighters. But it seems to me it would still be better if they went into the hills and hid out. Father Gibney must have other reasons. After all, Dad has family responsibilities and *he* hasn't come back yet. He says he will and Mother's pretty sure he's trying, but I wonder.

Peter rolled over and licked his dry lips. The rights and wrongs were perplexing. Look at Enid. He could tell from what she had said that she was at least partly on the side of the Japs. And it was natural for her to be on the same side as her father. But it seemed so unnatural for any white family to be on the Jap side! He thought of sneaking up to the dorm and talking to her. What a hypocritical idea. He had pretended sometimes when he was playing the Game that he might teach her something about religion and he never had. It had always been an excuse.

I couldn't sneak out now, even if I let myself, he thought. Mother is still awake—and probably will be for hours, worrying about Dad. If I told her that wandering in the hills without proper food and shelter is fun, she would tell me not to speak of things I know nothing about. But I *do* know! Dad told me once: life in the hills is straightforward and beautiful.

He writhed again on the unbending mattress and listened to the cicadas. Try as he would, he couldn't make his mind stay quiet. It kept drifting back to war and loyalties, to families and religion, to Enid and the creases in her damp bathing suit at the beach. Finally, expecting punishment from his conscience the next day, he told his wicked self vengefully, Go on, think about her. And before his daydream had arrived at the first "consequence," the first kiss, he was asleep.

# CHAPTER 8

The Japs had come and they hadn't come. They had turned off the electricity, they had swept through the night on bicycles and then they had vanished. For two long days Peter had frittered away his excitement, cooped up in Father Gibney's house, angry at his mother, treated like a child who had never done anything, and strictly forbidden to go out, even as far as the dormitories. At least in the dormitories there were kids his own age. Of course the food wasn't as well cooked and there wouldn't have been as large a share of it for Peter. Having the convent sisters in Father Gibney's cottage cooking and cleaning to keep busy, but only picking at their rations, was nice that way. On the other hand, hearing them pray and seeing their solemn-cheerful faces around the house all day—when you didn't want to feel religious—

was dreary. Besides, Norm Diak was living in the boy's dorm along with Enid and it gave him an unfair advantage with her. Peter couldn't help imagining them together during the dull, confused hours while everyone waited for the Japs, and he felt jealous.

On the third day, Norm came down and paid Peter a visit. *His* mother allowed him to come and go, he said, as long as he didn't leave the part of the school grounds where there was regular mowed lawn. He said the food situation at the school was pretty grave. What the men had brought back from their foraging expedition on the first morning would last only three more days, and with the Jap civilians who had lived in Abanao before the war out looting the town and swaggering around drunk, with guns they didn't know how to use, it was too dangerous to go out for more.

"What's Enid doing?" asked Peter straightforwardly.

"I don't know," said Norm. "Nobody pays her much attention. She's there along with a lot of other riffraff. Dad says until the Japs brought them out from under their stones you never knew what a lot of mestizos and kikes and krauts there were in this town."

For a moment Peter was relieved as well as shocked. Then he was all shocked, and angry. "What do you mean?" he said. "Enid's Swedish."

"She's a Nazi bitch," said Norm. "I told Ma about the Game and she says so."

"The heck she is," said Peter, trembling. "If your mother says so, then your mother is a bitch."

They were talking out on the bench under the arbor in the front of Father Gibney's house, and they fought on the grass. Peter in his anger won quickly. He got Norm down and held him down by the neck. It was only when he noticed the color of Norman's face and the choking noises he was making that he let go and climbed off him. As Norman rolled around in the grass uttering cutoff, sobbing sounds, Peter was momentarily frightened, but when Norm started to breathe again, Peter found himself still angry. And when Norm didn't start to cry, he felt angrier still.

"Go home and apologize to Enid," he commanded.

"Stuff it," said Norm, jumping up. "Nazi bitch-kisser! Yellow-belly missionary!"

Peter didn't chase him far as he ran up the hill toward the dorm. *Yellow missionary* had struck home. Norman seldom said anything that he wasn't repeating from grownups, and Peter hated to hear the missionaries called cowards. He had been wondering about it himself for days now. He sat down on the bench and tried to calm himself by counting the buds on the passion flower vine up in the arbor over his head. Why should he worry about the missionaries? *His* father was a doctor—only partly a missionary. And *his* father was still out in the hills—no one could call him yellow. Anyway, there were as many missionaries as there were sugar men, so no one was bullying *them.* It was Enid who was being picked on. He saw her sitting wilted beside her mattress, a lone, friendless girl surrounded by hostile people, and his eyes smarted sympathetically. What was the matter with the grownups anyway that they acted impolite and different from usual because of excitement? Poor Enid! He imagined how she must feel, deserted and avoided even by Norm, who said he loved her only a few days ago. And when he was living in the same building, too! Then with a stab, Peter realized that she must think *he* had deserted her too. He couldn't leave it that way. He had to show her that at least somebody stood by her.

As soon as he had had lunch—while his mother read to Jeanette to put her to sleep for her nap—he very deliberately broke his promise to her and walked up to the boy's dorm. He found Enid in much the same position as he had left her in almost three days ago, only now she was reading a book. It was one of those books which must be good because everyone had it in their libraries: *Vanity Fair* by Makepeace Thackeray. He forgot the author's first name and he hadn't read the book, but the *Makepeace* had struck him on title pages and it seemed like a well-named author for her to be reading just at the moment.

She pretended not to see him when he sat down next to her mattress, and he pretended not to see any of the people sitting and napping roundabout.

"Hello, Enid. I've missed seeing you," he said straightforwardly.

"La, why if it isn't Peter!" she said queerly—and she giggled.

"What's the matter with you?" he asked. She blinked at him over the top of the book.

"Surely," she said, "if you haven't had occasion to pass my way in the last month, milord, you have no occasion

84

now. I find your presence altogether unsuitable to the seating arrangements I have made for the evening." Again she giggled, and Peter with horror wondered if loneliness had driven her mad.

"Enid, aren't you all right, or are you teasing?"

"You dare to talk of teasing, milord, after your caddish neglect." She broke out in ordinary laughter. "No, no," she said, "*caddish* is all wrong. I was practicing to talk like the lady in the book, and you swallowed it all, didn't you, even with my funny accent?"

Peter was relieved. He had never seen her smile more friendly nor her eyes more dream-filled—like doors left half open to the sun-soaked gardens of contentment which he sometimes imagined inside her head.

"You certainly had me worried," he said.

"I'm a lot like the lady in the book," she said. "Her name's Becky. She's a man-eater and everyone hates her and avoids her, except the men who are rich enough to afford her and not to care whether they're seen with her."

"Mother made me promise not to come up here," said Peter, "but I thought you might be lonely."

A flush darkened Enid's face and the doors in her eyes snapped shut. "If your mama is scared of me, she's right. I'll hurt you if I can," she said crisply.

"I don't mean she's worried by you," said Peter. "She's worried by my adventures. I was the first one to see the Japanese bicycle troops the other night, you know. And the day the war started I went up to Camp Dewey when the planes were still coming over and brought back the first news of the Jap fleet."

As soon as he had said it, he was ashamed of boasting, but to his surprise Enid didn't make fun of him.

"I didn't hear about that," she said. "Nobody talks to me much except for Mrs. Gibney."

"I know," said Peter. "They're not acting like Christians. I'm sorry."

"Who wants you to be sorry!" she declared fiercely. "I'm not a Christian either, and I don't need you being kind or pitying to me. When they lock you up, I won't feel kind about you, you can bet! Papa and I are going to live like kings. Papa says there will be German advisers with the Japs. I'm going to be a man-eater and get a handsome young one and make him take me to live in Berlin while you Christian

85

son-of-a-guns get old in a stinking prison."

"It won't happen like that," said Peter quietly. Hearing her so excited made him more than sorry for her. Perhaps the war really had broken the hold she had on him. As if any white person wasn't a Christian! You might not go to church, but it was crazy to say you weren't a Christian.

"I didn't mean it, Peter," she said in a moment, "not about you anyway. You and Mrs. Gibney have been okay. When you are put in prison I will smuggle in food to you."

"It's hard to talk," said Peter, "when you keep mentioning prison. What's happened to your father?"

"Oh, he comes in to see me sometimes. He says it will be safe for me to come home soon."

"Why do you want to be on the Jap's side?" asked Peter.

"It's better than the side of these people," she said. He looked around and saw that some of the grownups in the room were watching. He stood up.

"You're blushing," she said with a sudden smile.

"What do you expect when you talk so loudly and furiously?"

"I'll meet you on the Secret Island, if you like," she said.

"What for?"

"So as not to be so bored and so as not to talk with so many nosy people around."

"All right," he said. "Tomorrow morning?" What a hypocrite he was! He wouldn't really be able to change her ideas.

"Right after breakfast, about nine o'clock."

"Okay."

"Want me to give you a kiss?" she asked to embarrass him.

"Good-by," he said quickly, and hurried out of the room.

It was still dark the next morning when he woke up. Another night had gone and the Japs still hadn't come to take them prisoners. Perhaps the rumor was true that MacArthur had sent reinforcements to Vispayan and that the Japs were fighting for their lives. Mrs. Gibney—who lived at the dorms now, along with her husband—had paid them a visit the evening before and told them that she had it on good authority, but Peter sensed that no one really believed it, not even Mrs. Gibney herself.

What had awakened him was his mother getting up. She was humming tunes from *The Merry Widow* softly to herself as she dressed. He hadn't heard her so happy for days. It must be that she had been bored too. Having the Sisters doing all the work hadn't left much for her except to read Jeanette stories and worry about Peter. Now Mrs. Gibney had asked her to help with the breakfast at the dormitories, where they had been serving up the porridge, Mrs. Gibney said, "like cold-shapes. I mean it, Renny: just like blanc-mange." Peter's mother was proud of her cooking, even of porridge, and so naturally she had agreed to help. That was why she was getting up so early.

It was a good opportunity for Peter. She wouldn't be back until midmorning and he didn't think that any of the other grownups in the cottage—preoccupied as they were and eating in shifts because the table was so small—would notice if he went on an expedition and wasn't there for breakfast. Since the night of their packing and coming to the school, only one of the possessons he had left behind had really nagged at him. This was his collection of colored inks. The bottles were lined up on the inside ledge above the door of his closet at home. It was a good secret place, but even so he was afraid that the looters, who were supposedly breaking in everywhere, would find it and steal them. Now, before meeting Enid, he had plenty of time to go home and get them.

As soon as his mother had left for the dormitory, he jumped up, scrambled into his clothes and stole down the hall past the kitchen, where Sister Iona was lighting the fire, and into the servants' bunkroom. The room was empty because Anita and Father Gibney's maids had been sent home to their villages. He climbed out the servants' window and in a matter of minutes he was at the foot of the short cut, crouching in the bushes at the edge of the road by the water tower. In the half light the road looked awfully gloomy. He had never seen it so empty. Usually there were native women bringing *camotes* to market at this hour of the morning. Faintly in the distance, somewhere down in the town, he could hear men singing. They were out of key and out of unison, but the tune sounded Japanese.

Peter shivered and started across the highway. In the woods on the other side he made a detour, to avoid being seen from the windows of the hotel, and so arrived home from the rear. The house looked cheerless and unfamiliar, as if it had forgotten his family already. At the back door he was brought up short by a printed notice, a seal, pasted across the crack. *Property of Imperial Nipponese Army*, it read. *Trespassers will be punished with the best severity.*

Peter drew a quick breath and wondered if he shouldn't go straight back to the school. There was no question now that the Japs were in town. Why didn't they show themselves and stop acting spooky? He flexed his toes within his slimy, dew-soaked sneakers and shivered again. Having come all this way and taken so much risk already, surely he wasn't going to get scared and run off without the inks he had come for.

He jiggled open the loose catch on his bedroom window and hoisted himself in. The light was fainter inside. He found the inks and put them in the pillow slip from his bed. On his dresser was the piece of shrapnel from Camp Dewey. He pocketed it and went into the living room. What a mess! The looters must have broken in before the house was sealed. They had pulled down all the paper Christmas decorations he had wasted so much time on. They had gone through the desk and stolen the silver out of the sideboard. They had cut open the mattress in his parents' room and strewn the wadding all over the floor. Still, they had missed some things. His father's binoculars still lay wrapped in their yellow shammy in the bottom dresser drawer and a box of graham crackers, some cooking chocolate and a jar of peanut butter still stood on the shelves in the kitchen.

As he put the last of these things into his pillow slip he felt out of the corner of his eye that someone had looked in at him through the window. A second or two later, tumbling out of his bedroom window, with the tension of staying so long in the house turned to queasy terror inside him, he thought he saw a foot disappear around the corner of the house. He ran through the woods, up and around in complicated zigzags through the property of the Dominicans. Tears got in his eyes and blurred his vision, making him stumble. But he reached the road in spite of them, sprinted across it and hid in the bushes at the foot of the short cut. He couldn't run any farther without resting. Maybe he had left his pursuers behind long enough to catch his breath and make the uphill dash to the school. He fixed his eyes on the woods across the road, and then—boy!—what a reassuring sight: around the corner came Mr. Cumber, swinging his cane and walking his Scottie on a leash. Mr. Cumber was the American Negro who rented the cottage behind the water tower. He looked just as he always had when Peter was on his way to early Communion on prewar days. Didn't he know about the Japs? Perhaps Peter should warn him. But that was foolish. He must know. Maybe, being different, he thought the Japs would leave him alone. Or maybe, Peter realized, he didn't think the other Americans at the school would welcome him.

"You boy op doctor?" whispered a voice.

Peter whirled around, trapped and speechless, into the dark face of a native. The man was squatting and panting in the bushes behind him: a mountain man wearing only a G string. He put his hand lightly up to Peter's mouth, indicating that he shouldn't shout. Peter felt foolish and tried to compose himself. It was just one of the natives from Mallard's village. That was all it was that had been following him.

"Yes, I am the son of the doctor," he breathed.

"Gib dthees to woman ob doctor," said the man, and handed Peter a wad of tightly folded paper. "I shall go now. You are okay? And dthe woman? I shall tell the doctor you are okay?"

"Yes, we're fine," said Peter. "We're okay. Tell him we're okay at the school. We are living at the school." He pointed up the hill.

The man nodded and smiled. "I shall tell him."

The native disappeared into the bushes, and Peter, his hands still trembling, glanced at the wad of papers. They were folded many times and fastened with some of his father's adhesive tape. On the outside they were addressed: *to Renny and Peter Baldwin, personal and confidential.* Pleased and excited, Peter thrust them into his pocket and went up the hill.

Once in the safety of the school grounds he circled the buildings and climbed the wooded ridge beyond. From the ridge one could see out through the branches of the pine trees over a succession of steep mountain chains to the southwest coast, hazy in the distance. He paused for a moment, looking out and breathing the cleansed and cleansing air of the morning. Somewhere out there, beyond the thin column of blue smoke which rose from the charcoal maker's fire on the next mountain, was his father, still free. Peter wondered if he would see this view again soon, and thought of climbing his pine tree for one last look at it. His pine tree was a giant whose top stuck out above all its neighbors. Climbing it was almost spectacularly difficult, because there was one place where you had to let go of everything a full thirty feet above the ground and jump upward and sideways to grab a nubbin of a branch and swing yourself around the big trunk to a branch on the other side. It had taken Peter months to learn how—and to gather courage—to climb that tree. None of his friends had mastered it, so it was all his own. And from the top the view was very proud and peaceful. But this morning he had no time to climb it. He patted the bark at the bottom affectionately and plunged on down the far side of the ridge to the gully below. The passageway through the bushes to the clearing on the Island was soaking wet and he hoped it would dry before Enid came. He went across the clearing and crawled through the second tunnel to the Inner Keep. Under the vine-curtained ledge he dug up the tin box where he sometimes kept crackers, put the nine bottles of ink in it and reburied it. Then he returned to the clearing to read his father's letter and breakfast on graham crackers and peanut butter from the pillow slip.

The letter was in pencil—not as neat or clean as most things his father did, but easily legible. Since it was addressed to Peter and his mother, it began:

MY DEAR LITERATE ONES—AND YOU TOO, MY LITTLE JEANETTE:

Please forgive me for writing instead of coming. Peter will have told you about my troublesome patients. We got them safely put to bed across the road, but we couldn't find a place for them all under one roof so they are scattered up and down the water front, and I am going to be kept busy walking from one to another of them. Their accommodations are pretty shabby—with mangrove roots growing through the walls, cogon grass through the floor or rattans and orchids through the roof. The most serious case, of course, is the poet. He's regained consciousness but he's madder than even a poet ought to be. I don't dare let him out of my sight and may not be able to for some time to come. The big bearded fellow who runs things at the main inn on the north side of town where the poet and I are putting up says that for all he cares the poet can die of food poisoning unless I remain to look after him. In a way it's a form of blackmail. He wants me there to care for his other guests, present and future. I'd tell him to care for his own guests only I'm afraid that if I had the poet moved to the city his ravings would only antagonize people and get me in trouble.

To confuse matters further I'm indebted to the hotel-keeper and even fond of the scoundrel. Peter's probably told you how he stood by me the other day and backed me up with solid-steel credit when I was losing at gambling. He's a professional at this sort of thing and determined to make a success of it. I learned the other day that he was thrown out of the organized hotel-keepers' league because the brass in the organization didn't approve of his wife. As you can imagine, that makes him determined to be the best darn hotelkeeper on the face of the earth and show them all. Well, it's a foolhardy attempt, but if you could see the way he trains these boys of his to fetch and carry and light fires, you'd believe as I do that he may succeed in it despite all the big money against him.

Reading over what I have written, I can see that the things I wanted to say have become stilted and unclear just as they always do when I put them on paper. The best thing to do is to take my scribblings and throw them into the fire before posterity gets ahold of them and finds out what a darn fool I am. What I mean to say is that I miss you all very much. I feel I ought to be with you and then again I feel I ought to stay here. I wish, Renny, that you'd keep a diary and send it to me whenever you get a chance. I'll be communicating with you as regularly as I can by this same post. Later on, if you could ship off chapters of the diary by return mail, it would make my doctor's life seem a good deal more relaxed and natural. You write so much better about the little specific things that make life worth living. For my own specifics, which I'm incapable of putting on paper, you'll have to wait until I see you. It shouldn't be more than a few months. I think constantly of you with love.

TIM

Peter read the letter a second and third time, puzzling out his father's meanings. The other side of the road must be the north side of the Banong trail. The accommodations there must be mangrove swamps, forest clearings full of cogon grass, and cliffy places overgrown with rattans and orchids.

Peter paced up and down his own secret forest clearing in high excitement. The hideouts hinted at by his father sounded mysterious enough in themselves, but in addition, Peter knew, that whole area where they were, that whole northern part of the island, was marked *unexplored* on maps. In its swamps and forests Father Mallard, the poet, was mad and Sam Bean, the hotelkeeper, was teaching his men how to be good guerrillas—and light fires. Peter reread the confusing bit about the hotelkeepers' league. It seemed to mean the Army—that the Army had thrown Bean out when he'd been in it before. Anyway, it wasn't important. The main thing was that his father had decided to stay and be a guerrilla doctor. He called Bean's efforts foolhardy, but that was only for Peter's mother: he didn't really mean it.

In a way, Peter was proud. No sugar man could say anything against *his* family. But in a different way he felt his father had sent him home under false pretenses and left him all alone with the dull, dutiful, domestic end of things. He fell into a daydream of what might have been if he'd been a little older and could have stayed out in the hills. He was posted high in a tree watching the movements of the Japs on a jungle road and signaling with a mirror for Bean or the photographer to light the fuse which would blow them up. Then he was creeping up to a Jap campfire and overhearing their plans. Of course it wouldn't really be like that. That was kids' stuff out of storybooks. But it would have been something else equally exciting.

Coming back with a start to the letter, Peter realized that it gave orders for its own destruction. Don't let it fall into the hands of posterity. Posterity meant the Japs. He paced up and down wondering whether to burn the letter at once or show it to his mother. He had to show it to her. She would never forgive him if he didn't. He buried it deeply in his pocket.

The sun had come up over the ridge now and was shining into one corner of the clearing. He lay down on the steaming pine needles in the bright spot and thought he would relax a bit after all the excitement. The morning had been chilly and had started early. The sun soaking into his damp clothes and stiff joints felt wonderfully caressing and satisfying. After the noisy twittering of dawn, the woods were so quiet. It seemed hard to believe that Japs were conquering Panoc and guerrillas were fighting and marching in the mountains.

Peter was dreaming about trying to guard Father Mallard. With a mad, white-faced smile the minister kept disappearing like a jinni. Then Peter would have to hunt and hunt and hunt in tunnels of wet underbrush before he recaptured him. The dream had been going on so long that Peter had stood up automatically to start searching again before he realized that this time he was awake and the dream was over. Enid. Where was Enid? The sun was high in the sky. It was lunchtime. His mother would be back from the dormitories. He snatched up the pillowcase, ducked through the tunnel and hurried guiltily up the ridge.

"Darn Enid anyway. I should have known she was only teasing. How could I go to sleep at a time like this?"

As he breasted the top of the ridge he heard an ugly sound like a radio left on too loud. It seemed to be coming from the end of the driveway on the other side of the dorm. He circled through the woods and kept under cover until he was as close to Father Gibney's cottage as possible. All the while the radio kept blaring, unintelligibly loud. Before he walked out into the open, he put the cooking chocolate in his pocket, hung the binoculars around his neck and left the pillowcase stuffed in the crotch of a tree. If his mother saw the binoculars, he would simply tell her they'd been in his suitcase all along. Wow, what a noise that radio was making! He stepped out of the woods and, taking care to seem normally casual and absent-minded, he looked neither to left nor right, kept his hands deep in his pockets and sauntered across to the cottage. At the top of the front steps he saw with surprise that someone had taken up the mattresses from the porch. The suitcases were gone too. He ran inside and through the rooms. The breakfast dishes were unwashed in the kitchen, but there weren't any people there—nobody in the entire house.

# CHAPTER 9

Still stupefied from his morning in the sun, Peter stood gazing with disbelief at the unwashed breakfast dishes. Had everyone else been taken off to an internment camp and only he been left behind? Only he in all Abanao? No, the radio! Sure, what about the radio? It must be some important news which everyone had gone up to the dorm to listen to. But so loud? It seemed more likely that it would only be on so loud if no one was there to hear it. He imagined it with horror: an electric banshee howling in the emptiness of the classrooms like a dog deserted and locked in.

He dashed out of Father Gibney's cottage and across the garden toward the dorm. As he went under the passion flower arbor he came in view of the gravel turnabout in front of the school buildings and stopped short. The blaring radio was a yellow-and-brown sound truck pulled up on the driveway. On top of the truck stood a man in khaki uniform shouting into a microphone. Beyond him was a crowd of people lined up in ranks as stiff as corpses. Could this be the Japs? There were no tanks, no guns. Peter jerked his binoculars up to his eyes and focused on a pistol in a black leather case. It was at the belt of the man speaking. The crowd beyond were the Americans from the dorms, all right, but so different from usual, and rigid and remote. He swung the binoculars up to the face of the orator. He *was* a Jap, after all, but not a soldier in spite of his uniform, because Peter knew him. He ransacked his brain for the man's identity. Of course. It was the Jap civilian who ran the bicycle shop downtown. Who did he think he was anyway? Why, he wasn't even a proper Jap! He'd lived in Abanao for years. He was probably a Filipino citizen. Why was everyone bothering to listen to him?

Peter searched the crowd incredulously with his glasses and then he saw a real Jap, a mean monkey-face such as filled the whole screen in Chinese propaganda movies. He was leaning against the wall of the boys' dorm with a cigarette in his mouth and a kind of Tommy gun cradled in his arms. His uniform was yellow-colored khaki, mud spattered and ill fitting. He picked his teeth and as he did so his smile seemed especially cruel because three of his front teeth were gold or brass. Peter scanned the other edges of the crowd and found that all around it were more Jap soldiers with guns, stained uniforms and bits of wilted branches in their helmets.

So they really, finally, had come. Peter couldn't just walk up and join the other white people inconspicuously. The soldiers were only Japs but he did feel a little scared of them. And somehow he still thought he might fool his mother. Or maybe there was no way for him to be captured now. Maybe he had to back off, go around and over the ridge and join his father and the guerrillas. He realized with fading courage that he didn't even know where to look for his father.

A throaty yell at Peter's elbow turned him stiff and crackling. Minutes later, as it seemed, he spun about to escape and as he spun he saw a burly form in khaki hurl itself toward him. Even before the man's grip had closed on his shoulder he was writhing and twisting. He sprawled on the ground, rolled loose, got up and ran. *Matte!* He heard the order to stop shouted behind him and he changed course precipitantly amid the plumbago bushes. He dived up onto the porch and tumbled across the polished surface. *Smash* went a rifle behind him, and the wood above him on the wall splintered with a squashy sound. He jumped through the doorway into the house, ran down the hall and hid under the lower berth in the servants' room.

The trampling of feet on the front porch and up the back steps told him that there were two of them. *Sagashite.* "Look for it," shouted the one in back. As the shuffling footfalls banged through the house, Peter began to think. They had shot at him. They would kill him next time he ran. He had to give himself up but he couldn't remember anything to say in Japanese that made sense. In desperation he called out, "*Ohayo gozaimasu*"—"Good morning, sir"—and "*Wakari masu ka, kudasai*"—"Please, do you understand?"

They understood well enough and they came quickly. While one held a gun, the other kicked hard at him under the bed. Peter shouted hysterically and they dragged him out, bruised and weeping. They shook him and slapped him and felt him up and down to make sure he had nothing dangerous on him. They pulled the forgotten letter from his father out of his pocket, and Peter gasped in hopeless horror. Now he and all his family would be executed. He tried to struggle again, but the one who held his arms was strong and simply twisted one of his hands up his back until he had to stop. The other, who seemed to be in charge, dangled the letter in his hand and looked Peter over curiously.

*"Ikutsu desu ka?"* he asked brusquely.

Peter shook his head uncomprehending and the man repeated the question more slowly. Peter remembered it as meaning "How old are you?" and he thought he must be mistaken. But he counted off the Japanese numbers in his head anyway, found the right one and said, *"Jusan"*—"Thirteen." The Japanese both laughed, and the one behind let Peter go. Peter was about to lunge for the letter when the man in charge unaccountably dropped it on the floor and walked out of the room, leaving the other one lounging in the doorway, pointing his rifle at Peter and grinning. Peter picked up the letter stiffly and forced a smile in return. In a moment the noncommissioned officer came back looking pleased. Around his neck hung the binoculars. They must have fallen off Peter's own neck outside while he was running.

Talking and joking too fast for Peter to follow, the two soldiers took him by the arms and marched him up to the dormitories. He tried to shake off their arms so that he could walk alone, but they only held on tighter. The loud-speaker had stopped and all the Americans were staring at him. Peter looked down, chewed on his tongue, which was as dry as sandpaper, and devoted his whole attention to not crying again. When the soldiers let go of him and he looked up, there was his mother weeping and Jeanette looking frightened. Beside them was the Jap civilian from the bicycle shop.

"You see," said the Jap, "I torrud you they wurrud not harm him. Prease be quiet now, Mrs. Borrudwin." he went back to the sound truck, got on top of it and began speaking again. Peter's mother took Peter in her arms and shook him and kissed him and wept. Peter still struggled with his own desire to cry, but as his mother continued to make a scene, the desire left him. One of the Jap soldiers came up and prodded them with his gun, and his mother had to let go of him. He stood in line as stiffly as he could and looked straight ahead. He was sure people were still staring at him.

He had acted like a fool in front of them and, what was just as bad, he had acted like a coward in front of himself—almost begging for mercy from Japs! He had wept too and his eyes were probably red. He wondered bitterly if Enid had enjoyed seeing him humiliated. He hadn't noticed her in the crowd but he could imagine her smirk of mischief at the degradation she had brought him to with her man eating. Some guerrilla you would make, she could say; some guerrilla to be caught out in the open gawking through binoculars.

The harangue from the big, cheap Jap loud-speaker on top of the sound truck spattered and shuddered on. What little of it Peter could understand through the deafening hoarseness of the voice seemed like childish, repetitious stuff about what the Japs were going to do in Asia. They were going to establish some kind of government called a co-prosperity sphere and Asia was going to be for the Asiatics. From time to time the bicycle mechanic reached down into the cab for a bottle of Jap brandy, took a swig from it and began again more hoarsely than before. As the sun and the noise beat down on Peter, he gladly withdrew into his aching body and reviewed the causes for his shame. Sensuality, pride, restlessness, dishonesty, stupidity, cowardice: there was hardly a fault in him which the war he had prayed for hadn't made worse. Even now when he had caused his mother great fear and grief and jeopardized not only his family but a whole bunch of patriotic guerrillas, he found himself wallowing selfishly in his own misery. He shook his head to clear it. The letter! At least the letter was still in his pocket. He couldn't give it to his mother to read here or even destroy it here, but the responsibility of guarding it until he could do one or the other made him feel a little better. He reached out to his mother, smiled and squeezed her hand. She smiled back and nodded sympathetically. From now on, he told himself, he had to be dedicated to her and his sister, just the way his father wanted him to be. No more adventures. No more of Enid. After what she had done to him that much would be easy. He could stop standing up for her. She was on the side of the Japs, and the Japs—just as the taxi driver had said—were bosses now. He closed his eyes, briefly thanked God for saving his life and asked for help in carrying out his resolutions.

The bicycle mechanic reached down to take another

swig, and Father Gibney stepped forward out of the first row of prisoners, bowed to him and called him "Mr. Kono." Kono wiped his mouth with his sleeve and nodded curtly.

"Mr. Kono, this forcing of women and children to stand in the sun is arbitrary brutality in violation of all the international conventions regarding captured nationals—conventions to which Japan is a signatory. Unless you let these people go inside at once and start making provision for feeding them, I assure you as their spokesman we will file protest with the Swiss consul in Manila at our earliest opportunity."

Kono looked at Father Gibney with narrow, uncomprehending eyes and shook his head stubbornly. "You Americans," he announced into the microphone, "are a mercifurrul peoperul. We Japanese have no mercy. We are a proud peoperul. We are a fierce peoperul. We are not soft." Then he went on with his interrupted harangue and one of the soldiers pushed Father Gibney back into line with the butt of his gun. Peter wondered uncertainly how so many grownups could let another grownup, a principal of a school, be pushed around that way. With kids it was different. But adults got angry, they had self-respect, they had a breaking point. Father Gibney should get himself killed before letting them push him around that way. No, that was a crazy way to think. How Father Gibney acted was prudence and self-discipline. If the sun weren't so hot it would be easier to think sensibly. One of the soldiers who had captured Peter came to the end of his line, reached in to Jeanette, who was nearest him, and gave her a piece of candy. He held out another toward Peter, and Peter shook his head and glared in the direction of the sound truck. Kind to children! Only thirteen! Only *ju-san!* The Japs were always kind to children! Why didn't the soldiers have to pay attention to the speech? They ate rice cakes and sour balls, smoked cigarettes or walked down on the lawn to lounge and talk, or play dice. Only the Americans, the prisoners, had to stand still and pretend to listen. If one of them relaxed too much and got out of line he was prodded back into place. Some of the mothers, of course, had to be allowed to walk around a bit when their children cried, but the waves of sound from the truck blanketed everything. And most of the children simply sat overpowered in the sunshine, playing or sleeping in the gravel.

A white-haired English sugar planter from Vispayan stood

beside Peter on his right. As the afternoon wore on and more and more women and children had to go off into the building for a moment, accompanied by soldiers, the planter kept making explosive sounds under his breath. Finally he poked Peter and whispered, "The word for toilet is *benjo*. If you want to be polite to the little buggers, say *benjo, judasai*. Pass it on."

Peter told his mother that people wanted to know how to ask for the bathroom and she explained how to the woman behind her. A bit later Peter heard a woman in front, who had just come back, whisper to her husband, "He stood right over me and watched, so I waved him away angrily, and all he did was turn his back slightly. Believe me, I hated myself, but when you gotta go, you gotta go." Her husband snickered nervously and Peter felt disgusted. In some ways, he thought, it would be better simply to use the wall of the school, the way the Japanese soldiers did, than give them the satisfaction of thinking you were so dainty.

They had been standing about three hours in the sun and the bicycle mechanic's voice was hardly more than a thunderous hissing whisper in the loud-speaker. Father Gibney had been up to protest to him several times and even Mayor Ziegler had tried once, but all they had achieved each time was to make Kono repeat, like a set piece someone had made him memorize, "You Americans are a soft mercifurrul peoperul. We Japanese are strong. We have no mercy."

All of a sudden the English sugar planter beside Peter spoke out in a loud voice. "I say, Gibney, I think it's time we insisted on our rights instead of asking politely. These women are going to start fainting soon."

He stepped out of the ranks toward the sound truck, and as it stopped blaring the noncommissioned officer who had swiped Peter's binoculars shouted an order. Another soldier swung his gun at the English planter, hitting him in the head and knocking him down. Peter took a step forward and his mother grabbed his arm. No one else moved more than a step either. The planter got up by himself with blood oozing from a cut in his forehead and walked unsteadily back to his place in line. "The little buggers," he mumbled.

Father Gibney strode out to protest again and this time he interrupted Kono in the middle of a sentence. "Kono," he shouted, "this has gone far enough. Are you so drunk you don't realize what's in store for you after the war's over?"

"Excuse me," whispered Kono slowly. "You must orrul stay here in the courtyard to werrulcome the commanding Japanese officer. By no means must you reave this sunny courtyard untirrul he comes. I am drunk indeed, Father Gibney, but I do not think this war wirrul soon be over. Now, excuse me, I wirrul sreep and dream of the grory of Japan."

He put one leg and then the other into the window of the cab of the truck, slipped and twisted off the roof and miraculously came out of his contortion sitting right side up in the seat.

He nestled his head into the corner and closed his eyes. Father Gibney looked around hopelessly and one of the guards pointed a gun at him. Just then, somewhere behind Peter, Mark Price, the casino owner, spoke up jovially. "Looks like Gibney needs some support, boys."

Peter turned and saw the gambler lurch out of the lines of prisoners. Was he really drunk so early in the afternoon? A guard stepped up with a gun, but Mr. Price, with a broad drunken grin, swept the gun aside and reeled on across the gravel to the noncommissioned officer. He hauled a pint of whisky out of his back pocket and offered it to the sergeant with a big wink. The officer smiled foolishly and shook his head. Peter wondered how the bottle could be so full when Mr. Price was so drunk. The awful idea came into his mind that the gambler—feeling, like Peter, too proud to be taken out by Japs as a child might be taken out in kindergarten—had filled the bottle himself and then drunkenly decided it would be a good joke to make the soldiers taste it. If that was what he was doing, Peter was sure they would kill him. But Mr. Price made a broad, exaggerated shrug, pivoted teeteringly around on one foot offering the bottle to all the soldiers in the square and then took a big swig from it himself. Peter remembered what his father had said once: that the Japs had a peculiar sympathy and almost respect for people who are drunk. Was it possible that Mr. Price knew this and was putting it all on?

"Would one of you women who speak Japanese come out and help me?" shouted Mr. Price.

Peter's mother stepped forward tentatively, but Mrs. Gibney was before her. Mrs. Gibney walked out purposefully. Big in front, gymnastic and erect, Mrs. Gibney could look more purposeful than any woman Peter could think of. When she walked like that, she looked like a galleon with the wind behind her. Now as she sailed she spoke very fast and heartily in Japanese. Peter couldn't understand most of it, but he thought she was saying that many of the Americans there had worked all their lives to help Japan, that the good American gentleman was offering the soldiers a drink because they looked as if they had walked far and fought hard, and that they would be very rude to the good drunken gentleman if they refused to have a drink with him. Peter felt proud of the courage and cleverness of Mrs. Gibney and Mark Price and yet ashamed, too—ashamed that white people should have to act this way to save their lives.

The ruse worked surprisingly well. The Japs all had a swig out of the bottle, even the sergeant. And after that, while the bicycle mechanic slept in the cab of the sound truck, Mr. Price brought more whisky from his hoard in the dormitory and the rest of the Americans were allowed to sit down on the gravel and go back and forth to the bathrooms as they wanted. Occasionally a guard would shout at them if they seemed to be going anywhere else, but somehow bits of food were brought from the dorms—crackers and cheese and chocolate and peanut butter—and gradually the tension was replaced by tiredness.

Peter's mother wanted Peter to pray with her and thank God for his life and deliverance. But he interrupted her with embarrassment and impatience to give her the letter from his father.

"It's very important that no one knows what's in it," he said. "Take it to the bathroom or somewhere where it's private and then get rid of it afterward." She took the letter and went off with Jeanette, too excited and preoccupied to say anything more. While she was gone, he went to see if Enid was in the crowd. He couldn't find her but he found Norman instead.

"I'm sorry I beat you up yesterday," he said. "She *is* a Nazi, I guess. It was her fault I wasn't here when the Japs came."

"Forget it," said Norm. "Sure, she's a Nazi. That's how we first thought the Japs might be coming soon, because her old man came to get her and take her home."

"Oh," said Peter. "What time was that?"

"Right after breakfast. Say, what did the Japs do to you when they caught you?"

"Kicked me around a bit, but they're always pretty kind to

children, you know."

"Yes, I guess that's right. How did you like the way old Mark Price took over from Father Gibney? Wasn't that something? I guess you know now what I mean about the missionaries."

"Let's not fight again," said Peter. "They were both pretty brave in their ways, but I don't think anyone is acting especially well. We shouldn't have let ourselves be captured in the first place. We should have run off to the mountains."

"Are you crazy?" said Norm. "Dad says anyone who goes out there has holes in his head. The Army'll take care of the fighting. They'll be back as soon as the Pacific fleet gets here from Hawaii. What's the point in being heroes and getting killed just to avoid a few weeks of hard living?"

"I don't know," said Peter. "It just seems we ought to fight instead of acting so downtrodden and undignified."

"Good Christ in the foothills," said Norm. "You ought to talk to people instead of thinking. You get funny ideas."

Norm was always picking up colorful swearing expressions from the sugar men. Peter simply said, "Stuff it," and walked off. He wandered through the crowd looking at his fellow prisoners. Some of them were sharing chocolate bars and trying to talk and gossip normally. Some of them were praying in groups and trying to encourage one another. A few of them were asleep on the ground. None of them really had anything to say to anyone else. Peter felt lonely, unhappy and determined. His father was away doing what he had to do. His mother was only motherly—and, besides, he had to help her more than she helped him now. Enid had gone off to be an enemy. It wasn't much consolation to know that her going was the reason she hadn't met him on the Island. God was there, of course. He was there and everywhere always. But in spite of his fresh resolutions Peter felt he had lost personal touch with God. He had been afraid so for some time, but he was sure of it now because he needed God yet he still didn't feel like praying—not really praying with full truthfulness and repentance.

As he walked back to his place, he saw Maggie Higgins. She was sitting on the gravel with some of the grown-up country-club crowd, but he went up to her anyway and said hello.

"How's your sunburn?" she asked—and he felt how nice

it was of her not to say anything about how he had been captured.

"Oh, I haven't even noticed it," he said. "I guess your cold cream must have done some good."

"I told you it would. Say, where have you been all these days? I haven't seen you at the dorm."

"Mostly at Father Gibney's cottage. But I saw *you* the other night. You were in bed asleep." He blushed the moment he had said it, because it seemed as if he had been spying, but she paid no attention.

"It's been pretty tame around here," she said. "There hasn't been much to do besides sleep."

"I didn't see your parents."

"No," she said.

"I haven't seen them today either. Where are they?"

"They went to Manila."

"Why didn't you go with them?"

"I couldn't."

"Oh." She didn't seem to like being questioned about it, and he could see it would be embarrassing to be left like that for people to feel sorry for. "Well, I guess Manila is pretty old stuff to you," he said. "I've got to go back to my place."

"So long," she said.

"So long."

Not long after he got back to his place on the gravel, Jeanette and his mother returned from the bathroom. His mother looked very serious.

"Peter, I have to count on you now like a mature person," she said softly. "You won't ever make a mistake and talk about what your father was saying in that letter, will you?"

"No, Mother," he said. "I almost destroyed it and didn't give it to you. But I thought you had a right to see it."

She looked at him a little surprised and said, "I burned it and threw the ashes in the toilet. That's how secret it is."

"Yes," he said. She kissed him and asked him about what had happened in the morning. He told her quickly, coldly and truthfully, without embarrassment and without enthusiasm.

Not long after dark the Japanese commanding officer arrived. He came up the driveway fast, in an armored car which was followed by a tank that slowly turned a gun in its turret back and forth over the crowd. The Americans, the

103

prisoners, stood up even before they were told and formed lines and ranks. The armored car screeched to a halt and two men jumped out, both officers. The headlights of the Americans' cars and of the Japs' trucks surrounding the quadrangle were all switched on, and the prisoners stood blinking in the glare. When Peter got used to it, he saw that the two officers had climbed to the roof of the sound truck. One was an older man, in a neat green uniform with high brown boots, a riding crop and beautiful samurai sword which looked too long for him. The other was younger and his uniform fitted badly.

"On beharf offa Rieutenant Corruenrrul Miyanaku," shouted the younger one with difficulty—the older one clicked his heels and nodded curtly—"I procraim you prisoners of Japan. Iffa you co-operate and surrender your firearms immediatery to the Japanese Miritary Authorities, you wirrul not be harmed, but iffa you do not obey, one person wirrul be executed for every firearm which we discover." His voice rose to a shriek on the last words, and there was a silence afterward.

Then Mr. Price stepped forward, looking red-faced and barrel-chested and not so drunk any more. "We don't have any firearms, Colonel," he said. "Maybe we should have, but somebody said to leave that to the Army, so here we are, defenseless and dumb as the day we were born."

Mrs. Gibney translated only the first sentence, and Peter realized that now, not looking it, Mr. Price was a lot drunker than he had been before.

"Iffa you do not obey," said the Japanese interpreter, "we wirrul shoot by guns ten persons for every firearm which we discover."

"Listen, Colonel," said Mr. Price. "We don't have guns, and if anyone does I'll undertake to shoot him personally." As Mrs. Gibney translated, he stepped up to the sound truck, took off his rumpled brown linen jacket and shook it. All that fell out were a pipe, some matches and an empty pint bottle.

"Iffa you do not co-operate, you wirrul orrul be executed this instant," blared the sound truck. The colonel called Miyanaku spoke an order quietly to the soldiers and they all leaped to readiness and trained their guns on the prisoners. Everything was quiet, and then some scared-cat kid without any pride started sobbing. Peter turned to see who it was. Oh, well, Johnny Sharp. He was only a third grader. Besides, something was making him come forward and be scared. He was carrying something. Good gosh, a gun!

"I'm sorry," shrieked Johnny, "I'm sorry, I'm sorry, I'm sorry."

One of the Japs jumped forward, took the gun and passed it up to the colonel. The colonel looked at it and laughed. Then he fired it into the air. It made a small bang and Peter recognized it as the kind of bee-bee pistol for frightening vultures that a lot of the kids with money had been buying lately at the fancy new sports store downtown.

"What a nice toy," said the colonel, without help from the interpreter. "I wirrul send it to my son. Thank you, boy." He leaned down and showed the toy pistol to the soldiers, who all inspected it and laughed. Then the colonel barked something at them in Japanese and some of them went into the dormitories while others started going through the ranks, feeling the Americans up and down to search them.

"I hope no one has ried to us," said the colonel. "I do not want to shoot anyone. It is a great honor to take so many prisoners."

Peter knew that the Japanese were never supposed to surrender. He tried to feel scornful of such a primitive way of thinking, but once more he couldn't help feeling ashamed.

No one knew for sure whether somebody hadn't brought a gun, and the silence continued while the search went on. But no guns were found and the prisoners were herded into the girls' dorm, and Peter and his mother and Jeanette found a spot on the stairs with the Kahns. There they spent the night. Jeanette got some sleep, cradled from falling off the step by Peter's legs and kept warm by Mrs. Kahn's fur coat. The rest of them dozed, or moved for the people who kept having to go up and down the stairs, or picked at the cookies and chocolates Mrs. Kahn had in her knitting bag.

Sometime when it was still dark and Peter felt he had just fallen precariously asleep, his mother shook him awake. The Japanese outside were shouting and everyone was going down into the courtyard again. At the door, Peter, half asleep, was collared by Father Gibney.

"Your things from the cottage are over there in that heap," he said, pointing to a pile of suitcases and mattresses between two of the trucks. "Ask your mother which are the two most important pieces and then go find them. Carry the heaviest one yourself and give the other to her."

Father Gibney released him and grabbed the arm of Mr. Kahn. "They want the keys to our cars," he said. "The man at the card table over there. Not much else we can do. . . ." His voice faded in the hubbub. Peter knew which were the important cases: his mother's, his sister's and his own. He could carry two. While he was finding them, Mr. Marlowe and Mr. Barsini dug in the heap, too, getting in his way.

"You . . . have . . . fifteen minutes to prepare to reave," blared the sound truck. "You . . . aru . . . going to your permanent prace of internment. You . . . wirrul . . . be divided in four groups: men, women, chirudren ress than fifteen years, and aged peoperul over sixty years. You . . . wirrul . . . be on foot, so do not take more than hand baggages for your immediate personerrul use. The others . . . wirrul . . . be forwarded to you rater by truck."

Peter hurriedly opened his suitcase. It was topsy-turvy from being searched by the Japs. He dumped some of the clothes out of it and stuffed canned goods in their place from the food suitcase. Then he returned to his mother, gave her her case, took Jeanette and the other two suitcases and went to the place where the children were forming their separate ranks. His mother had been struggling not to cry, but other mothers were crying openly even in front of the Japs. It was especially hard on the ones with both babies and toddlers. They could take children they could carry with them but if they had several, the two- or three-year-olds had to come by themselves with the other children. Peter told Mrs. Barsini he'd take care of her little Ellen and he had Jeanette hold Ellen's hand while he took the suitcases.

Father Gibney was up by the sound truck talking into the microphone. Peter supposed Mr. Price was too drunk now to go on being the leader.

"I'm told we'll have to walk to wherever it is we're going," Father Gibney shouted. His voice was no longer precise, but tired and angry. "I advise everyone to stay in line and keep in well-lighted areas as much as possible." He'd forgotten the street lamps still weren't working. "Otherwise you may be encouraging the kind of incidents which certain people may want. We're a lot of mouths to feed. Let's keep it that way. God be with you."

After a while, as the children stood soporifically in their places, the men were made to march. In another while the women, weeping or calling back instructions and encouragements, followed them. The old people, Peter noticed, hadn't admitted to their ages and there wasn't anyone in the area reserved for them. When the women were out of hearing, some of the children began to cry. The soldiers offered candies around but they couldn't stop the crying that way, so in a short time they let the children start off down the road. At the bottom of the drive they turned left toward Enid's house and the golf course. Jeanette was very good and so was Ellen. Peter spoke to them from time to time, but the suitcases seemed unnaturally heavy and he had a hard time thinking of anything to say. As he walked, the cool morning air woke him up a bit and he remembered that at about the same time yesterday he had been getting up to go home for his inks. It was funny to think of the inks buried in the tin box. Nobody knew about them except him. Eventually they might become like treasure which belonged to anyone who dug it up.

Enid's house was full of candles and light and the radio was playing Japanese music. As the children slowly came up on it, stopping again and again for rests, Peter saw Enid's father and some Japanese in neat uniforms—probably officers —out on the porch. Mr. Larsen had a glass in his hand and the Japanese were leaving one by one, bowing and scraping their swords on the steps as they went down. There was a light also in the wing where Enid's bedroom was. The soldiers paused to watch the officers and to give the children another rest outside the house. Peter watched the window. As the children were prodded to their feet to start again, the blind went up and he thought for an instant, before the candle went out, that he saw Enid standing in her nightdress.

I'm going to be a man-eater and get a handsome young one, she said inside his mind. "You're going to come to no good," he retorted under his breath, vindictively. There she was living outside. Already her father was entertaining Japs and she wasn't going to bed until nearly morning. "You'll come to a bad end," he muttered. "You're only fifteen."

Jeanette said she and Ellen were cold, and Peter's eyes watered with sheer tired sentimentality because he couldn't do anything to make them warmer except walk faster.

The mile to the golf club took an hour. Then, as Peter had expected, they turned right up the road to Camp Dewey.

That was another mile and took more than an hour. Peter thought he could have run across the golf course with those two suitcases in about fifteen minutes, but after two hours they seemed as heavy as life itself—especially the one with the food in it. The column of children rested at the gates of Camp Dewey, and Peter took the bulky piece of shrapnel from his pocket and thought of hurling it back toward the hole from which it had come. But it was the only possession he had now except for clothes and food, and he put it back in his pocket. Feeling it scratching through his pocket was still a proud feeling.

They climbed the hill toward the parade ground. At the top, the two barracks for Filipino enlisted men looked desolately drab and deserted against the lightening gray sky. The two groups of grownups were standing separately, waiting on the grass in the distance. As the children started across the wet lawn, Peter almost stumbled over Mayor Ziegler. He was sitting on his suitcase at the edge of the parade ground and he was weeping. He was a fat, red-faced man, but he wasn't much older than Peter's father, and Peter couldn't imagine what was wrong with him.

"Can I do anything for you, Mr. Ziegler?" he asked.

The mayor looked up at him and started weeping more than ever. "Just go on, boy. That's more than I can do. Just go on if you can."

Peter turned away with an unpleasant hardness in his heart and gave Jeanette a nudge with one of the suitcases. What was the matter with grown men that they wept, and all those other people that they stood there like sheep on the wet grass? The Japanese outside the barracks were shouting back and forth to each other in confusion. It was obvious that they had no real plans for interning the Americans. They couldn't keep them in groups, at least not more than two groups, because there were only two barracks.

Peter was right. As the sun came up, the Japs separated the older boys like Peter from the other children and sent them to join the men in front of the barracks on the left, the one on the edge of the mountain. Meanwhile, the women and children filed into the barracks on the right. Until they had all gone, the soldiers kept the men waiting at attention in strict formation out on the grass. Then the interpreter announced that each of them could have three feet by seven feet of floor space and opened the doors to the barracks

108

which was to be theirs. The men marched toward the doors slowly at first. But someone pushed, and soon everyone was pushing and squeezing and running. It came back to Peter vividly that he had seen it before—on the Jap ship in China, when he and his family were being repatriated from Nanking. With a mixture of angry disgust and fear that he would lose out, he ducked under people and pushed and fought like everyone else. Being small and wiry, he squeezed through the crowd and into the doorway among the first. He didn't have to look around for the spot he wanted. He ran for the noncommissioned officers' room at the west end of the barracks and chose his floor space next to one of the three windows overlooking Vispayan and the China Sea. Out there he had seen the Japanese fleet, and out there he felt he would also see the American fleet when it came.

There were no *tatamis* to sleep on here as there had been on the ship in China and the double-decker bunks of the American Army had been looted. Peter dropped his case on the floor by the window, curled up next to it and waited in a jerky stupor—like a corpse nervous about the resurrection —for anyone to try edging in on his choice bunk space.

## CHAPTER 10

Is the Baldwin kid asleep yet?" whispered someone.

"What does it matter?" growled Harry Gamoff in the darkness. "He is a good boy. He knows how to keep his mouth shut."

"Horse shit! He's a missionary. That means he's always got to be nice and tell the truth nicely to the Japs."

Peter had been asleep, he thought, but he was awake now. It was amazing these days how quickly he jumped into full alertness—and how easily he went to sleep in the first place. It had something to do with the lack of real waking exercise on the one hand and the nagging dizziness of hunger on the other. That last whisper he had heard, ending up the way it did, nasal and sarcastic, came from Mr. Newcombe, Peter's enemy. It was funny about the Newcombes: there wasn't a single member of the family that Peter had ever been able to get along with. Before it hadn't mattered, but here in the concentration camp, Mr. Newcombe was an important, privileged person. He went out every day in a truck with the guards to buy the internees' food at the market in Abanao. A few weeks before, the Japs had caught him smuggling in liquor in a basket of *camotes*. They had slapped him around a bit and since then they had watched him so closely that he couldn't smuggle any more. He blamed it—as he did everything—on the missionaires. "One of those damn teetotalers must have informed on me," he said. That was the reason for his lying sarcasm now about Peter being nice to Japs and always telling them the truth.

"Knock that off, Newcombe," hissed a third voice authoritatively. That was Mark Price. After his handling of the Japs on the first day, the internees had elected him—disreputable as he was—to be chairman of their Governing Committee. "The point is that the kid's a kid," went on the gambler softly. "It has nothing to do with what you think of him or how you hate missionaires. We just can't take that kind of a chance. So shut up, all of you, and lie still and wait awhile."

Peter wondered what they were going to do tonight —something special, apparently. To do it they felt they had to wait for him to go to sleep. He wished they could trust him, and he couldn't see why they didn't. Of course, it might be that if the Japs ever took him out to Kempeitai headquarters for questioning, he wouldn't stand up under torture as well as a grownup, but then the Japs probably wouldn't torture a child either. Besides, the missionaires who *had* been taken out—three each day during the first numb, cowering weeks—and *had* been tortured at the secret police headquarters said they didn't see how anyone could stand up to it if he had anything to hide. They had nothing at all to hide. They were simply zealous young preachers who had caused the Japs trouble earlier in China and made the Japs think somehow that they were American intelligence agents. But they had to go through horrible things to prove their innocence. Dr. Bax, the Lutheran minister, whom Peter had talked to about it, had been given the water cure: filled full of water and jumped on until he thought his stomach would burst. He had also had his left shoulder dislocated so many times that he had never regained full use of it, but that didn't seem nearly so bad as the idea of being broken inside.

The awful part of it was that you might not stand up to

the torture even if you did have nothing to tell. Instead, you might invent lies against yourself so that they would stop hurting you and simply kill you outright. This, supposedly, was what had happened to the two young missionaries who'd been taken to Kempeitai headquarters and had *not* come back.

Peter shuddered in the darkness. The men around him were all busy breathing regularly and being quiet. Having them go to so much trouble on his account made him think that he might have to give in after all and move the way they wanted him to—move out of the private room he shared with them at the end of the barracks, out of the Staff Room, as it had come to be called, and into the cluttered open space, the Rest of the Barracks. He was sure the precautions they took because of him were unnecessary, but if they felt they had to take them, he would be a burden as long as he stayed there. It was bleak and sad to think of leaving his choice position by the window. He had only to look up and he could watch the stars. If he sat up, he could see the mountains in the moonlight, breathe the night air from beyond the fence, and sniff faint smells of chickens and pigs and free people in the valley below.

Peter had fought hard to stay where he was. The battle had begun about a month before, when Mark Price came to him and said that the men in the Staff Room needed more privacy. Most of them were on the Governing Committee and they had important matters to discuss which they couldn't do freely in front of a teen-age boy. That was the way Mark Price put it, but Peter knew that Father Gibney and Reverend Fisher were on the Governing Committee too, and they never came into the Staff Room at night to discuss things. The truth was that with Harry Gamoff running the kitchen, with Mr. Newcombe in charge of the marketing, and with Mr. Price in constant negotiation with the Jap officers at the guardhouse, there was more news, more tobacco, more whisky and more food to be had in the Staff Room than anywhere else in camp. Extra rations of all four were often served up after lights-out at night. The "extras" weren't large, but the unprivileged in the rest of camp whispered about them as unfair when everyone was starving. Naturally Mr. Price thought some of the whispers might originate with Peter. Mr. Newcombe had probably told him so.

Well, they didn't! It wasn't that Peter approved of the extras. For his own part, he had given up accepting handouts of food from Harry Gamoff long ago. But he excused them for the men in the Staff Room partly because they did more work to get hungry than anyone else in camp and partly because it had become a rule of life with him that people who let themselves be captured all behaved badly one way or another. This was the way of the men in the Staff Room, and he certainly would never have said anything about it outside. The only "extra" he might be tempted to gossip about was war news. If he had ever overheard anything hopeful, he would probably have passed it on to his mother through the fence between the barracks, the "commixing fence," as it was called. But the news Mark Price brought back from listening to the radio in the guardhouse was all bad. The Japs had taken Singapore and most of the Dutch East Indies; they had MacArthur bottled up in Bataan and were even landing on islands way down off the coast of New Guinea. So Peter never told his mother what he overheard but only the current crop of rosy rumors circulating in the men's barracks instead.

Having tried hard to mind his own business, Peter felt the efforts to move him out were bullying. The place by the window was his. He had found it and occupied it in the beginning and he didn't want to live outside with the sheep in the rest of the barracks. Well, not that he really thought all the people out there were sheep. The missionaries, especially the ones who had been tortured and survived, had the courage to keep turning the other cheek. But Peter had decided that he didn't have that kind of courage and that he was like his father: only half a missionary. He couldn't love and forgive the Japs in war. War was too complete, and he didn't understand—he still didn't understand—how people could want the Japs beaten and yet do nothing foolish and brave about it. The atmosphere around people like that, out there in the barracks, depressed him. They weren't themselves. If you knew them from before—as Peter did Mr. Kahn, for instance—they could sometimes talk like themselves, but most of the time they acted different: sort of suspended in air, clutching the end of a rope and trying to be absolutely still so that their hands wouldn't get tired and slip.

In the Staff Room you could see out over the mountains beyond imprisonment, and that was the way the men there seemed to be too. They might not be nice. They might be brusque and swaggering like Mark Price when he hadn't had a drink. They might be kind and hearty and dishonest like Harry Gamoff. They might be sentimental and fooling themselves like Mr. Kulhausen. They might be calculating and businesslike and cheat-the-Japs-but-win-the-war like Mr. Diak, Norm's father, who accounted for the food money the Japs printed for them. They might be gay and foul-mouthed and opportunistic like Donny Garver, the stranded California inventor who kept the marketing truck running and made *camote* peelings into a kind of hootch. Or they might be hateful coattail riders and apple polishers and butter-your-own breaders like Peter's enemy, Mr. Newcombe. But none of them were simply waiting for the war to end: they were living now and acting like themselves—if not their old prewar selves, then their new emergency selves.

Peter had not been able to tell Mr. Price his reasons for not wanting to move. The gambler was in too much of a hurry and Peter was too resentful.

"No, sir, I don't want to move," he said. "And you *won't* be able to get me as good a place in the barracks because there isn't one—not with the same view. And, anyway," he added foolishly, trying to find some sensible practical reason, "I don't think a bunch of bananas from the market is a fair trade."

"Make it two bunches."

"A zillion bunches wouldn't be a fair trade. If I wasn't in the Staff Room I wouldn't dare eat them anyway."

"Oh, for God's sake, you can come back to the Staff Room and eat them every afternoon. I'll keep them for you on a nail over my bed."

"Well, no," he said, cornered. "It doesn't matter how many bananas. I just don't want to move."

"All right, if that's the way you want it, boy, we'll simply have to put you out."

"But I've never told anyone anything outside," said Peter desperately. It didn't matter: Mr. Price had already turned and gone off angrily, leaving Peter to feel wronged and angry himself.

The funny thing was, Mr. Price didn't throw him out. Maybe it was because Maggie Higgins put in a good word for him. Mark Price was a friend of her family's and went and talked to her through the fence almost every day, asking if there was anything he could do for her. Maggie and Peter had been talking a lot lately, too. She was so obviously proud and lonely without her folks that he forgot to feel shy around her now—at least not with a fence between them, while he was waiting for his mother to come and Maggie was waiting for Mark Price.

Anyway, whatever the reason, Mark didn't put Peter out of the Staff Room. Instead, Father Gibney came to talk to Peter the next day, saying that it was no place for a boy among those profane men and that he would be better off among his own kind. With Father Gibney, Peter had a chance to explain a little how he felt about the window, but he didn't explain especially well. To Father Gibney, the minister who had confirmed him, it was hard enough these days to talk at all. And so after a lot of reasoning Father Gibney simply looked at him curiously and told him he was to come to Communion every day that week and pray for guidance.

Father Gibney had been holding his Communion services in the cubicle where he lived in the barracks. Peter hadn't been going regularly. A cubicle was the floor space for seven or eight men, marked off from other cubicles by piles of suitcases and hanging mats and blankets. It was hard to pray in the ugliness of Father Gibney's cubicle. Of course, it was hard for Peter to pray anywhere. Only when he was looking up at the stars at night from his place in the Staff Room could he still ask for help and understanding and feel that God was still listening and patient with him and able in His love to rain down on him a little answering peace along with the starlight. But drinking Donny Garver's hootch in place of sacramental wine and eating bits of rice crust from the bottom of the caldrons in the kitchen in place of wafers didn't have the same uplifting effect as Communion had back at the school chapel. Peter knew it was his fault. The change —the confused stubbornness—was in him, not in the inward power of the consecrated elements. But he fobbed off his guilt by telling himself that he was going through "a stage" —that's what his mother always called it—and that the make-believe and spiritual numbness he felt were moods which he would grow out of.

The next day as he took Communion in Father Gibney's cubicle and tried to concentrate on some way back to a state of grace, he found himself receiving a small measure of it by looking at the stars and the moonlit mountains inside his head.

114

It seemed as if God were clearly telling him to stay in the Staff Room—either that or the Devil was tempting him to think so. After receiving the sacrament, he went to the morning meal lightheaded and as full of inward argument as ever.

That afternoon, as he had his daily chat through the fence with his mother, she tried to persuade him to move out of the Staff Room, too. But she was easier to deal with than Father Gibney. So much feeling had built up among the missionaries against Mark Price and his bunk mates that Peter only had to state his rights legalistically. "It doesn't seem fair. I got the place in the beginning by my own good sense. Now they're trying to take it away from me because it's the best place in the barracks and I'm only a kid." His mother sided with him at once, and of course Peter felt at once that what he had said wasn't absolutely true. But it was nice to have her sympathy.

After the afternoon meal, when Peter had finished his work as a bus boy, he went back to his place in the Staff Room feeling dizzier and hungrier than usual. People hadn't left much rice on their plates that afternoon and the other bus boys, Norm and Charley, had been luckier about getting good plates to lick than he had. The water supply was still short from the time Colonel Fleer's guerrillas had dynamited the outlets of the reservoir, and the baskets the boys collected the plates in smelled nauseating from not being washed and from having food rotting in the cracks. Peter was all set to throw himself down on his mattress—the Japs had brought in mattresses along with the picked-over remnants of the baggage from the school during the second week—and have a self-indulgent, vainglorious dream about Enid. He didn't care: it would be a dream full of intrigue and spying in which Enid—wicked, beautiful and Nazi, with creases in her bathing suit—would get the worst of it. But when he reached the Staff Room, he found his mattress rolled up with a string around it outside the door.

Inside, there was no one except Mr. Newcombe asleep at the other end of the room. Beside the window the other mattresses had been spaced apart so that Peter's place had disappeared. Scalded with anger and the hot anxiety of an impending fight, he tugged the encroaching mattresses apart, dragged his own back to its place, and lay down with his eyes clenched shut to wait for someone to challenge him. He had hardly sprawled out when he heard Mr. Newcombe, not sleepy-sounding at all.

"Hey, kid, you don't live here any more."

"Go to hell," said Peter, his voice shaking. He had become hardened to hearing swearing in the Staff Room, but when he used it himself, he still meant it: a hell of real fire and anguish where people lay struggling, trapped under red-hot boulders and drowning forever in shallow pools of molten lava which lapped at their lips and stank of sweat and urine and sin.

"Why, you pious little phony!" shouted Mr. Newcombe. "I'll show you!"

He came across the room to throw Peter out bodily. Peter waited until he was close and then fought as unfairly as he knew how. He wasn't able to hurt Mr. Newcombe the way he really wanted to, because he had to put most of his strength into running and wriggling and wrenching free. And Mr. Newcombe sent him sprawling several times with some good hard slaps. But just the same, Mr. Newcombe saw he would have to kill Peter before he could win, so finally he gave up. When Harry Gamoff came in, he was sitting on the floor swearing and dabbing cotton on his bites and scratches while Peter sat on the edge of his mattress by the window, fearful but glaring, half sobbing and half catching his breath.

After hearing what was going on, Harry told Mr. Newcombe to keep hands off, sympathized with Peter and offered him a can of spiced ham to give in and move out into the barracks. Peter felt hurt more than ever, but he saw that he was winning.

"Go back and do sabotage in Kiev, Harry," he said.

Harry laughed. "Okay, kid. For myself, I'd as soon you stayed. I just don't want to see you make yourself miserable." He went to his mattress and started reading a murder mystery.

The next man to come in was Mr. Kulhausen. He was hot and tired from overseeing the garbage disposal crew. When Mr. Newcombe complained about Peter, Mr. Kulhausen said wearily, "Why don't you move, Peter? It would be easier for all of us."

"Because it's the only place I can see out to the hills where Dad is," said Peter.

Mr. Kulhausen had a son in the Army somewhere. He stretched out, closed his eyes and said no more. Peter knew he wasn't really asleep and he felt a little ashamed of having used the confidences Mr. Kulhausen had shared with him about his son.

Pretty soon Donny Garver came in, and Peter had already planned what he would say to Donny if he told Peter to move too.

"Hello, you little bugger," said Donny with surprise. "I thought they'd thrown you out."

"Go goose a moose, Donny," said Peter with a forced giggle. Donny was always telling people to do things to animals. "Go rape an ape," he would say, or "Go feel an eel."

Donny laughed. "Scientifically, that's the most interesting suggestion I've had in months," he said. "You know what you can do, Peter? Go get stuck by a bowlegged chuck." This was one Peter had not heard before and he laughed nervously.

When Mark Price came in, Peter and Donny Garver were sitting together singing "The Great Speckled Bird." Donny played the guitar and made up a new verse to sing every day. The great speckled bird was, of course, the American eagle. It stood for the Army and the Marines and all the things Donny would do Stateside after the war. When they had sung all the old verses that either of them could remember, Donny sang his new one:

*What a beautiful thought I am thinking*
*Concerning that great speckled bird.*
*Rita Hayworth will take me out drinking*
*And back to her home afterward.*
*She'll turn to me winking and say kind of slinking,*
*"The moon's started sinking and Donny I'm thinking*
*It's time that a girl should be felt and not heard."*

Here Peter chimed in with one of the many choruses.

*So keep the ice clinking*
*And keep the drink stirred,*
*And never stop thinking*
*Of the great speckled bird.*

"What the hell are you still doing here, Peter?" cut in Mr. Price. "I thought we'd got rid of you."

"I'm not going to go," said Peter. "I was here before any of you and I'm not going to go unless you put me out by force."

117

"But don't try *that*," said Donny. "He's maimed New-combe already."

Mark Price sat down on his mattress and took off his shoes. "Crazy kid," he muttered. "Why don't you want to go? Just give me one good reason."

"I want to see the American fleet when it comes, the same as I saw the Japs," said Peter.

Mr. Price shrugged helplessly and lay down. "They're going to advance lights-out to nine o'clock," he said wearily, a moment later. "They say we're using too much electricity. I'd have argued harder but I thought of you, Garver. It'll give you an extra half hour to abuse yourself."

"You can go to the zoo and visit the gnu," said Donny, striking chords on his guitar.

Peter had heard a lot of talk about sex in the Staff Room. Most of the specifics were things he had either heard or imagined before, but one fact stood out new and shocking: there were men—and, unless the men were complete liars, women too—who committed all the sins of the flesh, even adultery, and talked about them in private afterward as openly and shamelessly as if they felt no guilt about them. Donny Garver, in particular, seemed to see no harm in any possible use he could make of his body, and this was hard for Peter to accept. Sin he understood, but lack of guilt for it was incomprehensible. He vacillated between the idea that everything he heard was brave boasting or that these men were not ordinary sinners but confirmed servants of the devil who had deliberately exchanged their souls for peace of conscience in this life. The worst thing was that, except for being disgusted sometimes, Peter enjoyed their talk. Not only did it make him feel better about his own thoughts, but he preferred it to the more or less polite conversation in the rest of the barracks. There, the sheep spent most of their time discussing cookery. They lay on their mattresses during the heat of the early afternoon before the four o'clock shower cooled things off—as it usually did this time of year—and endlessly swapped recipes or bragged about meals they had once had in famous restaurants. A lot of them even spent hours down at the commixing fence getting new recipes to talk about from the women on the other side.

"Well, what are we going to do with the pigheaded kid?" asked Mark Price.

"Oh, for Christ's sake, Mark, pass an ordinance and throw

118

the little bastard out," said Mr. Newcombe. "See what he did to me?" Mr. Newcombe showed Mark a place on his arm where Peter had bitten him. Mark grunted uninterestedly and then gave the place a second look.

"Hey, Donny, what do you make of this?"

Donny walked over, examined the arm and whistled under his breath.

"What's the matter?" asked Newcombe.

"Come here, Peter," said Donny. "Open your mouth."

Peter opened his mouth and Donny nodded gravely. "What do you think, Mark?"

Mr. Price had a look down Peter's throat also and turned away with an expression of horror and disgust. "Good God!" he exclaimed.

"What's wrong?" asked Peter. He thought they were kidding but he wasn't sure.

"You've got no tonsils," said Donny.

"Bunch of clowns!" said Mr. Newcombe angrily. He threw himself down on his mattress and pretended to read a book.

"I submit that Peter isn't guilty of anything but biting the wrong sex in the wrong place," said Donny.

"I feel he brings us luck," said Harry Gamoff. "Without him—who knows?—I might burn the rice."

"Like you did this morning?" said Mr. Price.

"This? This was not burning," said Harry disgustedly. "This was only variety, to relieve the monotony of that insipid starchy flavor."

"Let's cut out the nonsense," said Mr. Kulhausen. "You've got the boy on tenterhooks and you ought to give him a decision. As far as I'm concerned he has good sense and discretion and I don't think we have any right to throw him out."

"Okay," said Mr. Price. "We all feel pretty much the same way, I guess, except for Newcombe. You'll probably burn in hell for it, Peter, but you can stay if you want to."

"Oh, thank you," said Peter.

"Christ only knows how you expect to exercise authority over men and women when you can't even tell a boy what to do," growled Mr. Newcombe.

"You better go see a doctor," said Mr. Price. And that was the end of it.

Mr. Newcombe had not said another word about Peter

until tonight. Whatever it was they were trying to hide from him tonight was important. He could see by the number of glows in the dark that every one of them was smoking, and he knew they would never waste cigarettes like that unless they were excited. In a way, he wished he could go to sleep so that he would not learn what they were going to do, but he supposed he never would be able to overcome his own excitement to that extent.

Apparently, though, he *had* gone to sleep—it was as if his thoughts had got sucked up and lost in the vast emptiness of his stomach—because when he next looked around the room the cigarettes had all gone out and the dark forms of the men had moved and were clustered together in the far corner. At first he couldn't understand what they were doing. They squatted in a circle around a faint light and a faraway voice rose and fell sputteringly. They were listening to a radio, of course. Somehow, Mr. Price had got a radio or Donny Garver had made one. Peter could hear some of the words: "Continues to deteriorate . . . MacArthur . . . Heroic defenders . . . Presumably by submarine." With a surge of excitement Peter realized they were listening to the news, not the Jap news, but the real news from Corregidor or Australia, or perhaps from KGEI all the way across the Pacific in San Francisco. He couldn't make sense out of the scraps he heard so he rolled over onto his stomach to keep watch. There was a knothole through the wall out which he could see a bit of the concrete walk beyond the fence—the walk which led across from the guardhouse to the barracks along the edge of the embankment overlooking the sea. As he watched he heard isolated words of the news broadcast and caught glimpses of his ten-color map of the world: of the fine blue line of the Irrawaddy River in Burma, of the black dots of Darwin in Australia and Novgorod in Russia, of the yellow boundaries of Yunnan Province in China, of the violet coastlines in front of Le Havre in France and Bengasi in Africa. The announcer spoke of news everywhere. It was such a big war and Panoc was such a small island. Peter wondered whether anyone would ever remember it and do something about it.

Suddenly, like the flicker of one picture in an old Charlie Chaplin movie, Peter saw Mr. Kono and Lieutenant Kanmori flash past in the knothole. They were headed for the barracks.

"Mr. Price!" he called softly. "Mr. Price!" The radio went off with a click. "Mr. Kono and Lieutenant Kanmori are coming along the embankment. Maybe they're drunk and want to talk to you again."

Mr. Price jumped to the window and looked out in time to see the two Japanese round the corner of the barracks.

"Put it away and get in bed," said Mr. Price urgently. As the others scurried about the room he tousled Peter's head and leaned down to whisper in his ear. "All right, smarty pants, thank you, but not a word to anyone about that radio, not even to your mother."

"No, sir," said Peter.

Just as it had been in China when Jeanette and Peter shared the same room and heard Dr. or Mrs. Baldwin sneaking up the stairs to catch them out of bed, so now everyone was quietly sleeping when the Japs came into the Staff Room.

"Attention, prisoners, prease," said Mr. Kono in a declamatory voice. "Mister Price, come forward. I wish to torruk to you. I have important communications from the commanding officer of Imperiarrul Nipponese Armies on the Iyurand of Panoc, Corrunerul Miyanaku, concerning eccresiaticurrul prisoners of war."

Mr. Kono shone a flashlight on each of the mattresses, and Lieutenant Kanmori trained his service revolver on the ones nearest the door.

Mark Price got up in the beam of the flashlight rubbing his eyes. "What is it, Mr. Kono?" he said.

"Before break of day," said Mr. Kono in his usual romantic way, "Corrunerul Miyanaku is prepared to set orrul those reverend missionaries with functions and parishes in Abanao at their riberty. You wirrul prepare a rist of those to be freed immediatery and they wirrul assemberrul at the fence at four o'clock this morning for transportation to their homes."

"I don't understand you, Kono. Do you mean you're going to release all the missionaries?" asked Mr. Price.

"Not orrul," said Mr. Kono. "The refugees and students of Chinese ranguage wirrul remain here. Onry those who have congregations to care for wirrul be set free. You wirrul prepare the rist immediatery whyurrul I wait."

There was no way Peter and his family could be considered as having congregations to care for in Abanao. On the other hand, they weren't Chinese-language students either.

121

He waited with little hope as Mark Price and Mr. Diak went through the list of internees checking the names. They passed the "B's" without mentioning Baldwin, and Peter's hope left him.

"There ought not to be more than twenty famuries," said Mr. Kono, halfway through the list. "That wirrul be enough for the morarul of the natives."

Peter dozed and woke up to hear Mark Price say: ". . . Baldwin. That brings it up to seventeen. Mrs. Baldwin isn't a minister, of course, but she helps Father Gibney with the native Sunday school."

What was he talking about? Almost no natives ever came to the chapel at the school and there wasn't any Sunday school. The white kids went to regular service. The native Anglican church in North Valley had a Sunday school, but Father Ambay, the Filipino minister, took care of that.

"Doctor Borrudwin has never surrendered," said Mr. Kono. "Untirrul he turns himserruf in, his wife must remain here."

"That's a funny way to look at things, Kono," said Mr. Price. "It seems to me Doc Baldwin is a lot more likely to leave his patients in the hills if he thinks his wife is free and fending for herself than if she's here in camp. He can't do anything for her here except look at her through a fence."

Peter felt a great admiration for Mr. Price. With one argument he was trying to do away with the commixing fence, remove suspicion of being a guerrilla from Peter's father and at the same time get rid of Peter from the Staff Room. Mr. Kono deliberated until the rest of the list was finished.

"I agree," he said finally. "Add the name Borrudwin. The ress mouths we have to feed the better."

A moment later he had taken the list and gone back to the guardhouse with it. Peter jumped up with a yell of excitement and started shaking Mr. Price's hand in thanks.

"Don't thank me for anything yet, Peter," said Mr. Price. "I knew you wanted to go and I wanted to get rid of you. But if things get tough out there, don't forget you can always send a message in to me by the marketing truck."

"Yes, sir," said Peter happily. The weeks of numbness and waiting like a dumb beast for the war to end couldn't fall away immediately, but Peter felt more healthy and excited and himself than he remembered being before, even on a full stomach. As he finished packing his suitcase the guardhouse turned the lights on. In the unnatural midnight brilliance he shouted good-by to everybody in the Staff Room except Mr. Newcombe, and ran outside with his case and down the front of the brightly lighted barracks to the commixing fence at the end. The guard there had no orders, but Peter talked to him until he called to the next guard and to the next and after a while the shouted word came back from the guardhouse that Peter might go through and help his mother.

She was in a state and not at all sure that she wanted to be released. Peter thought angrily for a moment that she was a sheep, too. Then he whispered to her that at home they would be able to get messages from his father.

"Besides," he said, "Mr. Price just told me that we can always come back here if we don't like it outside."

She kissed him anxiously. "*Bien, mon fils*," she said. "If you want to go so much, we will try it. It will certainly be nice to live in our own home for a while."

Peter had his mother and Jeanette out at the pickup point in front of the guardhouse—the house which had been Colonel Fleer's—before anyone else. For once the Japs were prompt. The pickup truck came for them before the sky had begun to show gray. It took them—the Fishers, the Baxes and Father and Mrs. Gibney—away from the barracks and the fence and the guardhouse, down the hill past the sentries and out onto the road along the edge of the golf course.

Rounding the corner of the country club, Peter looked ahead toward Enid's house. Now that he was out where she was, with the Nazis and the Japs, he felt a queer sort of disdain and wondered if she and her father were still entertaining Jap officers into the small hours of the morning. The lights of the truck swung onto the house and it was dark. Not a sign that anyone was even living in it. And then it was left behind, dark in the darkness, and Peter looked back with unexpected disappointment and nostalgia.

The truck did not stop at the school or at any of the other homes but took them downtown to the mayor's old offices. There they had to wait until all the missionaires to be released had been brought from the camp . . . and lectured by a Japanese Unitarian minister on brotherly love in the New Asia . . . and given arm bands identifying them as Americans . . . and made to sign papers saying that they would do nothing against the Greater East Asia Co-prosperity Sphere and would not go out of their houses except to

123

church or to market. At two in the afternoon, Peter, his mother and sister were released to walk home up the hill—up the hot, deserted main street—to their looted house.

## CHAPTER 11

Peter was on his way through the market. It was exceptionally early for him to be downtown. But he was always up at this hour; it was the hour he loved most, the time when freedom to come and go seemed most valuable and natural. The air was as clean as freshly laundered sheets, and in the infinite distance where it became sky it was faintly tinted as if with bleached bluing. Close at hand on earth, however, it was still full of damp darkness.

"Where's that baby, Rosa?" he said to a market girl who was taking off the canvas cover from her stall.

"You lazy boy, you have not helped me to make him yet," she shouted back raucously.

Rosa kept a banana tienda in the market. She was pregnant, but when he asked her where her husband was, she either denied her pregnancy or said Peter was the father. He had heard that the real father had run off to the hills with the guerrillas and so, though Peter could seldom afford Rosa's prices for bananas, he considered her a friend.

"Soon, Rosa, soon when I'm rich, I'll marry you," he called over his shoulder. The girls in the market gave Peter unusually good prices—prices as good as or better than they gave the poorest and shrewdest Filipinos. He sensed that they did this partly because he was a nice-looking boy, but mostly because he was the only one of the thirty-odd released Americans who came to the market often and joked and bargained with them.

Peter had heard that this morning Mrs. Fulgencia, the fat, rich, mean woman who owned a stall with a tin roof in the best corner of the market, was going to sell a few loaves of real wheat bread. According to the other girls, the flour for the bread came in some nefarious way from the bodegas in Vispayan, the storehouses where the Japanese kept the spoils they were gradually shipping back to Japan. Mrs. Fulgencia's stall hadn't opened yet and Peter was ninth in the queue waiting outside. He planned to give his mother a treat. She was always talking about wheat bread and this would be the first time she had had any since before internment over five months ago.

They were both the longest and shortest of Peter's life, those five months. It was hard to imagine a time when wheat bread was the lowliest food in the larder and yet, once he did imagine it, the five months, like a dream on awakening, seemed as if they had not really been. The freedom outside the concentration camp, after ten weeks inside, was not exactly what he had expected it would be, but it was good. It sure was! It heaped independence, responsibility and activity on him such as he had never known before. With Jap soldiers everywhere, his mother didn't like to go out of the house if she could help it, and so all the family business of choosing, bargaining, buying and bringing home had fallen on him.

The crux of living was money. By the standards of his mother's prewar budget she had only enough pesos to last two months. At first she had taken the sheeplike position that when this money was gone she and Jeanette and Peter would go back to the concentration camp and that would be the end of it—a nice holiday of health and normalcy in the war's craziness. But Peter, after the first happy week of gorging and feeling alive, had decided he would not be a sheep; he would not go back where his father and the guerrillas couldn't reach him; he had to help his mother make their money last longer. So he compiled endless lists of all the available things to eat in the market and by hard bargaining and hardhearted flirting with the shopgirls he found out what was the least you could expect to pay for each kind of food. Then he stubbornly set about persuading his mother that expensive vegetables like artichokes, asparagus, lettuce and spinach, which were grown on truck farms around Abanao exclusively for people who were white or rich, must be given up for cheap native greens like palm hearts, leeks, watercress and *camote* tops. Instead of apples and oranges and grapefruit they must eat passion fruits, guavas, pomelos, papayas and, of course, bananas. For the old imported white potatoes, there were *camotes* and strange lumpy local roots called *ubi* and *gabi*. As a substitute for canned milk there were coconuts whose meat could be grated on a serrated shoehorn nailed to a bench and then squeezed dry over the

125

milk pitcher in a piece of cheesecloth. In place of beef and veal there were chickens, pigs, peanuts and a dozen varieties of beans. There was crude sugar, too, molded in coconut shells into dark brown hemispherical lumps—and it was much cheaper than the granulated light-colored stuff which was left over from prewar days before the American sugar men had wrecked and dynamited most of the machinery in the mills.

Overhauling his mother's standard of living from top to bottom had not been easy. His mother was naturally frugal, he thought, but only with the ingredients she had been brought up with in France. Living from day to day, hoping for some word from his father or for a sudden American victory, she at first blocked his reforms with obstinate indifference. Coconut milk was allowed to go sour, *camote* greens were allowed to wilt and the family's tiny supply of canned goods—carried by Peter in his suitcase from home to school to camp and back home again—dwindled fast.

Feeling that all his efforts were of no grown-up use, Peter lost his domestic enthusiasm and became a listless nuisance around the house. Although he hadn't planned it like that, he saw now that he had struck on a better way of persuading his mother than the arguing he had used first. Like most grownups she probably thought children couldn't be logical but only happy or unhappy. And so when she sensed his unhappiness, she forgot her own and turned to the old remedy of keeping him busy. To do it she gave the new regime—which she called "going native" and he called "eating cheap" —a fair tryout. Jeanette turned up her nose at the new meals, and Peter's mother, in her pride as a cook, became absorbed in the challenge of making them taste better. Peter was chiefly interested in keeping his stomach filled, so the big thing for him was seeing the cost of living decrease by half. The experiment was so successful that he redoubled his efforts.

He pored over books of business arithmetic in the deserted school library and then went to see Mr. Espinosa, the Filipino landlord of the house where they lived. He persuaded Mr. Espinosa to accept promissory notes—at five per cent interest compounded annually and payable after the war in dollars—in place of rent. Then he got his mother to sign a paper asking the Protestant Episcopal Church at 281 Fourth Avenue, New York, to honor Mr. Espinosa's bill and pay it out of Dr. Baldwin's accumulated salary in case the Baldwins disappeared. Mr. Espinosa, a rich man whose many affairs had been slowed nearly to a standstill by the war, was so pleased with Peter's arrangements that he offered to lend the Baldwins fifty pesos a month on the same basis. It wasn't enough to feed the family but it was all Mr. Espinosa could lend and Peter thought it might be made to stretch.

He bought eight hens and a rooster and converted Anita's former bunk room into a coop. After a difficult week of chicken training and reading books on the subject, he persuaded the hens to lay all their eggs in the upper berth. His mother said the room smelled odious and made him clean it three times a week. He planted beans and peas in the back yard and taught Jeanette to weed and care for them. He bought a grinder for corn, rice, peanuts and cassava and successfully challenged his mother into perfecting breads and pastries from the flours he made. To replace his red wagon, which had been looted, he built a brown one out of wood, roller skates and the wheels of a derelict pram which he found in the gully back of the school. By using the wagon to run deliveries around town to rich Filipinos for the friendliest of the market girls, he started to get most of his *camotes* and bananas free. Trucks with gasoline to run on were becoming scarcer and the carting business promised to keep improving as long as the war lasted. He sold flour, too: mixtures of ground-up glutinous rice, cassava, millet and regular rice which his mother had worked out for making yeast bread. He gave out the recipe for the bread through Camelia, the girl who sold the flour for him at a percentage in the market. If only his mother had a larger oven, he thought, she could bake bread in quantity and he could sell the finished loaves instead of the raw materials.

Peter brushed the greedy thought aside. On the whole, his affairs were going far better than he could have hoped in the beginning. After three months of freedom half his mother's money—which she had thought would be gone at the end of two months—still remained unspent. He believed he could make it last at least four months more and he had a dozen plans to make it last even longer if he could only find the time.

Yes, time was the real problem. After tending the chickens and making the coconut milk and granulating the sugar and grinding the flour and spading the garden and chopping the wood for the stove, he didn't have enough time left for hauling with the wagon and earning money. (He also tried to keep up with schoolwork in bed at night. But it seemed unimportant. He did it only to please his mother and the Gibneys. And as often as not, he fell asleep in the middle of it.)

The answer to the problem of time, he felt sure, was mechanization. If he could get an electric motor somewhere to harness to the grinder he could make the coconut milk while the flour was making itself. That would give him a full two hours more a day with the wagon and in two more hours he thought he could probably add coconuts and sugar to the items he earned and didn't have to pay for. Then he might be able to keep his family out of camp almost indefinitely—perhaps even longer than the preaching missionaries like Father Gibney. The preaching missionaries—those who actually held services in church—had an easier time of it than the lay workers. Parishioners gave them handouts. Peter had once seen Reverend Fisher go through the market and fill a whole large shopping basket for thirty centavos and honestly seem to think that he had paid for everything he carried away. Naturally Reverend Fisher could not understand why Mr. Blackwell, the other Presbyterian who was free, ran through his share of the mission money so quickly. Some of the non-preaching missionaries had already had to go back to camp for lack of funds. Being grownups, they had had to obey the letter of the Jap regulations and go out only twice a week: once to church and once to market. So naturally they couldn't do any of the things Peter did to make money stretch. Why, simply going out to visit sick parishioners had got poor Reverend Bax slapped twice.

Where the Japs were concerned, Peter was an exception. He knew most of the sentries at the check points around town. And when he was making deliveries with his wagon and they stopped him, he could almost always get by without even having to give away a banana. Once, delivering some beer and canned oysters at Colonel Miyanaku's house, where Mayor Ziegler had lived, he had been seen by Miyanaku himself and nothing had come of it.

As Peter considered his advantages and his hopes, old lady Fulgencia opened her stall and began selling bread. By the time it was Peter's turn to buy he had found out that the bread was bringing a peso a loaf. For that amount he could buy six dozen bananas or eight kilos of *camotes*. It seemed prodigal and stupid, but he had stood in line for nearly an hour and he had set his heart on giving his mother a surprise, so he decided to afford it. As he put down the peso note, he felt as guilty as if he had lost money gambling.

The bread was wrapped in a plain brown paper and thrust toward him. He tucked it under his arm and hurried away. Before he escaped into the exhilaration of running up the hill he had to pause before the poster he was memorizing. The Japs were always putting up posters and Peter was keeping a collection of them written down. He didn't dare copy them out in public so he paused by one of them each time he was in the market and memorized a sentence or two, which he wrote out as soon as he reached home. This one, which was on the corner behind old lady Fulgencia's stand, was a particularly unbelievable one. It said:

To the people of Panoc!

Still certain of the Pananoca peoples living in and about Abanao continue to put the fire on some properties or to loot some things from the properties in and about Abanao. This is not good behavior anyway. When the Imperial Nipponese Army finds out those who intend to do so, it will shoot them by guns.

Affectionately yours,
Lieutenant Colonel Miyanaku

When the Imperial Nipponese Army finds out those who intend to do so, repeated Peter to himself, it will shoot them by guns. He turned away from the poster with the sentence firmly embedded in his mind and then suddenly it was gone. Not far in front of him stood Enid. He had seen her only three times since his release and then only at a distance in the market accompanied by her father. He was sure she had seen him those times, too, but she had never shown it by so much as a smile. Inwardly, again and again, he had damned her as a fickle, treacherous slut—it was a word he had learned in the Staff Room to serve for "whore" or "harlot" —and he had sworn an oath to himself that he would never bend his pride so far as to approach her and speak to her of his own initiative.

Now her father was not with her and she was smiling at him, so he approached tentatively. He meant to brush right past unless she said something pretty darned apologetic. He kept a stony face until he was only a few feet from her, but then she ran to meet him and caught him by the elbow and shook it and squeezed it.

"Peter," she said, "why don't you ever come to visit me? I can't talk to you here in the market. Papa says it's dangerous just to look at you, because you're American. But you could come and visit me privately."

"I thought you were busy entertaining Japs," he said sullenly.

"Don't be rude, Peter," she said. "Papa's away today. Come and have tea with me this afternoon. I must go and buy bread now. Good-by and see you soon."

She moved off abruptly and Peter saw that she had a servant with her carrying her marketing basket. No one else had servants. If she was that rich, her father was getting on with the Japs and didn't have to be scared of them. It was all a big excuse. This afternoon she just happened to have nothing to do so she thought it would be fun having Peter to tea. He wouldn't go. He couldn't go anyway because he had his hauling to do.

Putting Enid's invitation out of his mind occupied his thoughts all morning and robbed him of the pleasure his mother showed in the loaf of wheat bread. The game of getting the coconut milk made before breakfast and of finishing the sugar by nine and the flour by eleven and the wood and the garden by lunchtime had no pleasure in it either. By the time he reached Camelia's stall in the afternoon with a wagonload of flour to sell, the prospect of hauling seemed truly unpleasant.

But Camelia had a big job for him: three loads of fancy canned goods to take to the country club. The club was now used by the Jap officers on leave or convalescing from wounds. Delivering food for their private parties always seemed unpatriotic to Peter, but he did it anyway because he thought it might stop them from interfering with any of his other business activities. It was also a more pleasant run than most of his deliveries because it took him up along the road through the woods into the end of South Valley where Camp Dewey was. Except for Enid's house, that end of the valley—which had been entirely American—was now entirely Japanese. And since the Japs, except for private luxuries, handled their own food in trucks from the lowlands, it was seldom that they bought anything from the market or that Peter had an excuse to go up there.

Now, hauling a heavy load, he set his mind on getting the utmost in enjoyment out of the flat stretch through the woods, which followed on the long, hard climb up the main street. He had passed the check point at the top of the hill and there wasn't another until just before Enid's house. It had been several weeks since he had had the pine trees on both sides of him and smelled their resin. What with wondering if his father would ever send them another letter, it had been several weeks since he had enjoyed the thought of his father being a guerrilla out amid millions of such pine trees in the hills. Why, it had been several weeks since he had even thought of his colored inks buried among the pines in the Inner Keep. It might be time soon to get them out of hiding. With the rainy season coming on there would be days when he couldn't go out and he might have a few hours left after his indoor chores to work on the map of the world. Not that the map seemed important now, but he liked the expectation of making fine ink lines instead of hewing knots of wood and drawing lumbering wagons.

At the country club he was directed across the street to one of the big bungalows which had been owned by some friends of the Siaks. Two Jap soldiers, stripped to the waist, were scything the long grass in the back yard. Before the war the grass had been a neat lawn laid on good black topsoil from the lowlands and set off on the street side by a bank of the bright red clay which was the natural soil of the valley. Now it was mostly weeds and sword grass. Peter knocked on the back door of the bungalow and was let in by a woman in a kimono. She looked so poised that he wondered if she might not be a true Japanese geisha instead of an ordinary Formosan camp follower like most of the girls the Japs brought into town. Though the kitchen floor was only linoleum, she asked him politely but firmly to take off his shoes. He did and carried in the canned goods in their cartons and put them on the table. She stood by, paying no attention to the fact that he was white and treating him very correctly as a servant. He noticed with surprise, looking through the door into the rest of the house, that *tatamis* had been put on the floor and most of the furniture removed. The officer who lived there must be important.

As Peter brought in the last of the cases, a man appeared in the doorway from the dining room. He, too, was wearing

131

a kimono. He was over six feet tall, thin and slouched. He had a fish face and wore glasses, but he had a kindly, mild expression.

"You're an American boy, aren't you?" he asked.

Peter was surprised at how easily he spoke. He sounded more like an East Coast American than someone who had learned to speak English in Japan.

"Yes, sir. I'm the son of a missionary doctor."

"What's your name? I'm Colonel Kori."

"Peter Baldwin, sir."

"How do you happen to be in your present line of work, son?"

"We were released from the concentration camp and we didn't have much money," said Peter, as coolly as he could.

The man laughed. "Good practice for you," he said. "Someday you may have to work your way through college."

"What about you, sir?" asked Peter. "Did you go to college in Japan or the States?"

"You seem mighty sure I went to college," said the colonel, "so you ought to know which one. There's an old saying: You can always tell a Harvard man but you can't tell him much. Remember that."

"I will," said Peter.

"Good," said the colonel. "When you finish your job there may be a five-peso tip for you. Having you bring the fixings is a good omen for my first party here."

Peter went back to the market. He didn't know whether to be more impressed by the colonel's kindness or by his condescension and the fact that he was fighting against his former college classmates. When he returned to the colonel's house with the second load—liquor this time— only the polite geisha showed up to receive him, and Peter assumed that the five-peso tip would turn out to be boasting.

On the way back to market for the last load, as he was passing through the quiet woods, he noticed that a bare-footed native boy in a G string was walking along behind him. He wondered—as he often had in the last few months about natives who seemed to trail or watch him—whether the boy might not be following him shyly with a letter from his father. Pure wishful thinking. His father would long ago have sent word to them if he had known they were free. Probably he thought they were still in the concentration

132

camp where he had no way of reaching them. There was another possibility of course: his father might be dead. He had surprised his mother praying and weeping several times lately and he knew it was that possibility that made her do it. Sometimes when he felt sorry for himself in the role of breadwinner and imagined himself permanently lonely and responsible and fatherless, he almost wept too. Fiddlesticks. His father was too busy being a guerrilla to get in touch with them. That was all. He turned his mind—by choice—to the question of Enid. It must be boring for her without kids to play with and no time-consuming work to do such as he had. After all, she couldn't sit around entertaining Jap officers all day. She was still too much of a child and too energetic for that. He tugged at the wagon irritably and glanced over his shoulder at the boy.

As he approached the end of the woods, the boy was close behind him and Peter stopped to see if he would go by. But the boy stopped too.

"You want me?" asked Peter with hard, cold emphasis.

"You come?" asked the boy hesitantly. He was about Peter's own age.

"Where?"

"A priend op your pahder," said the boy. "He wants talk width you."

Icy and crackling with excitement, Peter had his wagon beside the road and folowed the boy into the woods. They went toward the school down into a marshy hollow.

"Hello, Peter," said a voice very quietly at his left. Peter whirled around and there was Costeau, the photographer. He was sitting, barrel-chested and bolt upright, on a mossy rock surrounded by ferns, looking like an out-of-place goblin. His puckish expression was the same as it had been at the hotel, but the rest of him was thinner and tighter and darker brown. On his knees he had the big rifle with the telescopic sight that he shot so well with.

"I didn't think it would be you!" whispered Peter excitedly. "I thought by now you'd escaped in a boat." He ran to the photographer and, not knowing what else to do when he got there, shook his hand enthusiastically. His enthusiasm was so great that in a moment it had turned to embarrassment.

"No, I stayed to take some pictures," said Mr. Costeau, flexing his fingers jokingly as if to make sure that Peter hadn't broken any of them. "Besides, boats are hard to come by. The one we're going to escape in, we're having to build ourselves."

"Where's Dad? Why didn't you bring him with you?"

"He's back at our base. He had too many patients to take care of."

"How's Father Mallard?" whispered Peter.

"Oh, he's with us—like God. But he *is* improving slowly. Your father expects him to reach the other end of his cycle in a few more months. Then he should be fairly reliable."

"Why hasn't Dad written to us?"

"General Sam didn't like it much when he heard about that first letter. He made your father promise not to send any more until we were better organized. By then you were in the concentration camp and we couldn't reach you."

"But we've been out almost three months," protested Peter.

"That long? Well, I'm sorry; we got our first inkling of it only a couple of weeks ago when one of our men came into town to buy a load of leather. He had it delivered to him out beyond the first two check points in North Valley."

"Hey, I delivered it!" exclaimed Peter—and the photographer had to raise his finger to his lips to remind Peter not to speak so loudly.

"Yeah, well that was it," said the photographer. "When he returned with this wild story about an American kid who hauled loads for the market women, we sent Enanak here to investigate—" he indicated the native boy—"and when Enanak reported back that it was you, I made a date with him for today and sent him to town to watch you. He's been following you around ever since so as to know where you'd be."

Peter took a quick look at the boy and realized, yes, he *had* seen him hanging around the market recently.

"He's a good boy. He gives me eyes and ears in places I can't go myself," said the photographer. "The only trouble is we don't communicate very well. Do we, Enanak?"

The boy started at being spoken to and, without appearing to understand, said, "Yes, Mr. Jerry."

"He did manage to convey to me that you're a very busy man, though, Peter. In fact, I get the feeling he's scared of you because he thinks you're a big operator."

"I'm trying to earn money so we can stay out of camp."

"That's what I figured." He paused and looked at Peter as if he wasn't sure what to say next. Peter had imagined so many active, exciting things about the guerrillas that it seemed funny seeing the photographer sitting quiet and polite on a rock. "Exactly why was it the Japs let you out of camp, Peter?" he asked.

"Because we were missionaries. They released all the missionaries who really belonged in Abanao and weren't just staying here waiting until they could go to China."

"You just happened to be on the right list, was that it?"

"Well, yes, sir, I guess so. I guess they decided it would look generous and impress the Filipinos."

"It's a big responsibility being man of the family at your age. Do the Japs give you much trouble?"

"No, sir. Sometimes they swipe things from my wagon when I go through the check points, but I've gotten pretty good at making them feel bad about it."

"How's your mother bearing up?"

"She's fine. She worries about Dad a lot and she gets bored staying home all the time, but she hasn't been sick or anything."

"Well, I've got just what her doctor ordered for her," said Mr. Costeau. He rummaged in his pack and took out a bundle of papers fastened with adhesive tape.

"Are those all letters from Dad?"

"Yep."

"Boy! Will Mother be pleased!"

"When I come again I expect you to bring me some answers from her."

"Oh, she's got a whole journal for Dad."

"Good." The photographer smiled and glanced at his watch.

"Could you tell me a little about what it's like being a guerrilla?" begged Peter. "I know Dad won't say much in his letters and I'd like to imagine what he's doing. I mean, is he good at it? I should think he would be, knowing as much about the mountains as he does."

"He's terrific, Peter."

"Does he do a lot of fighting?"

"Well, not too much. He's so busy doctoring he doesn't even have time to get sick."

"Does he do *any* fighting?"

"No, come to think of it, he doesn't."

Peter wondered why Mr. Costeau was babying him along this way.

"Are there a lot of wounded?" he asked.

"Not so many. Mostly malaria and dysentery cases."

"What kind of place is it where you live?"

"Oh, I don't know, sort of moist and woodsy."

"Yes, sir, but I mean exactly. You know, so I can see it when I think about it."

"That's just what I don't want you to be able to do. There are high trees and vines and monkeys and swamps. You don't need to know anything more specific than that."

"You don't trust me," whispered Peter.

"What? I'm putting my life in your hands just be being here."

"All the same, you think because the Japs let me out of camp and I bring groceries to them that I'm risky to talk to," insisted Peter. "I can tell you do."

"Well, you're wrong. Maybe I did ask you a few questions. After all, you've changed and grown since the last time I saw you. But I trust you completely. And working for the Japs is exactly what I *do* want you to do. If you're all through asking questions I'll tell you why."

"Yes, sir, I'm all through," whispered Peter unsurely.

"Why do you keep calling me sir?" asked the photographer irritably. "Do you have to call so many people sir nowadays, or what?"

"You see?" retorted Peter. "You think I'm kowtowing to the Japs when really the only reason I ever say sir to them is to make up for not bowing the way they expect."

Mr. Costeau smiled. "Peter, I don't care if you have to say sir to the Japs. But my name is Jerry. I'm not a Jap, I'm not in the Army and I'm not General Sam."

"Oh," said Peter. "Is that all you meant?"

"Yes."

"I'm sorry, then. Is General Sam Sam Bean?"

Jerry smiled again, and again he glanced at his watch. "That's one of the things you're not supposed to know. It began as a joke when Bean first started proving that that was what he ought to be. Now it's a code name full of awe and mystery. Thousands of Filipinos look up to it."

"I won't tell anyone," said Peter.

"Good. Are you ready now to hear my proposition?"

"Yes."

"How would you like to work for me?"

"As a spy?" breathed Peter incredulously.

"Not exactly. In a few months Margo and I have to start for Australia. Until then I need an assistant to help me round out this story I'm doing."

"Help you take pictures of the guerrillas?" asked Peter in astonishment.

"No, dopey. My story isn't all guerrillas—that's only what General Sam thinks. No, it's really the struggle of the whole island. I wish you could see some of the pictures I've taken: families crossing the mountain passes to get farther away from the Japs, cane fields burning, corpses hanging in reprisal, Jap truck convoys trapped by landslides and trying to shoot their way out, tribesmen dancing by their fires to declare war on Japan, children shooting rifles and old men wielding spears—and then Margo hanging out her panties on buttress roots in the rain forest. If I can get the pictures home, it will be the story of my career."

"Can I help you get them home?" asked Peter, more puzzled than ever.

"No, you can help me get Japs. That's what my story is short on. Enanak sees a few things when he's here in town but he hasn't the background to tell me. I'm hiring you to take his place. I need to know how the Japs have changed Abanao. In little ways. Little sensitive real ways. After you've told me, maybe we can figure out how to show it in pictures. Then maybe you can help me take the pictures. Some things we should be able to get with telescopic lenses from hiding places far off. Other things you may be able to take for me close up."

"I don't know how to use a fancy camera like that," said Peter, overwhelemed.

"I'll teach you. And I'll pay you too. From now on I don't want you accepting any odd jobs unless you think they may get you information as well as money."

"Wow!" said Peter.

"What do you think a fair wage would be?"

"Oh, you don't have to pay me. I'll do it for nothing."

"Look, you've got to live, don't you? How much do you need?"

"If I don't give up all my other work? Well, we can get along fine on another fifty pesos a month.

"What! Six dollars and twenty-five cents a week? You

137

want the Spies' Union to picket me? I'll give you two hundred pesos a month and a paper saying what it's for. Then after the war when your father wants to pay it back you can show him the papers and he won't have to. You see, he knows I'm giving it to you, but he thinks it's a loan to him, and I can't tell him it's not because he doesn't want you involved with me, much less acting the part of an agent. Understand?"

Peter saw that Jerry was watching him closely. "I understand," he said carefully. "Most any father has a tendency to protect his son too much and underestimate him, doesn't he?"

Jerry's eyes crinkled slightly and Peter expected to hear him say something sarcastic about sons who judged their parents, but the crinkles turned into a smile and Jerry let it pass.

"One of the things I'll want you to do," he said, "is take messages to Pete Wong who runs a gambling joint downtown called the Mark Price Casino. Do you know him?"

"I've seen him," said Peter, "and I've heard Mr. Price talk about him."

"Then you know more about him than I do."

"He used to be Mark Price's assistant," whispered Peter. "Now he runs the casino while Mr. Price is in camp. He's Chinese but he looks more like a Japanese wrestler because he's so big and fat and muscular."

"Good," said Jerry. "Maybe we can take pictures of him. I suppose it would be best if you knew why you'll be calling on him. It's because he's going to send us supplies: food and shoes and stuff. You see, General Sam has several hundred men now and they'll starve in the rainy season if Wong doesn't help us."

"Gosh, there are only a hundred and twenty people to feed even in camp."

"Well this is two to three times that many, and they'll all be depending on you. Now you understand why I didn't want you to know too many details. It's dangerous work and having too much information would make it even more dangerous, especially if the Japs ever picked you up for questioning. Do you know Rosa in the market?"

"Yes."

"All right, when you want to see Wong, you'll go to her and say Mr. Wong needs a load of Chinese cabbage or *camotes* or whatever seems sensible. That way you'll have an excuse for visiting the casino. And when Mr. Wong wants to see you he'll put in an order with Rosa. Rosa doesn't know what it's all about but she's on our side and you can trust her not to ask dopey questions. All right?"

"Yes," said Peter.

"Then here's your first message to Wong. See that he gets it this afternoon, and not a word about it to anyone, not even your mother. She's like your father and mustn't hear about it until after the war."

"And how! She'd have a fit!" said Peter, pocketing the note.

"Hmmph!" said Jerry. "You're pretty goddamn condescending about your parents."

"Don't swear," said Peter, grinning. He felt so happy and sure of himself now that he could talk back to anyone, even Jerry.

"You get sassy," said Jerry, "and I won't give you your pay." He held out two hundred-peso notes. Peter had never seen one before. He took them and stood gazing at them with disbelief.

"You'd better get Pete Wong to change them for you so as not to excite suspicion," said Jerry. He passed Peter a sheet of paper which said: "In payment to Peter Baldwin for services rendered to *Man* Magazine between May 20 and June 20, 1942: P200.00 (two hundred pesos). Payment and receipt of above amount are acknowledged hereinafter by Photographer Jerry Costeau and Temporary Employee Peter Baldwin"—then there were two lines for signatures.

"Is that the correct form?" asked Peter, trying to remember what he had seen in the business arithmetic books at the school.

"Well, Jesus Christ," said Jerry. "Listen, if it says what it means, that's all you have to worry about. So just sign it."

He produced a pen and signed the paper on top of his camera case. Peter followed suit. The position was awkward and his hand was so muscle-bound and unused to writing that his signature looked even more childish than usual.

"Where can we hide this document?" asked Jerry. "I don't want you to carry it around with you."

"I know a place," said Peter. "It would be a good spot for us to meet next time, too."

"All right, if it isn't far, show me," said Jerry when he had looked at his watch.

Peter led the way across the ridge to the gully, while Jerry, followed by Enanak, talked of the kinds of photographs he wanted Peter to be on the lookout for. Then Peter showed them the Secret Island and the two tunnels in through the underbrush to the Inner Keep. Jerry seemed pleased with the place, even though the vegetation was rather thin and scraggly after the dry season. Peter dug up the tin box from the clay under the ledge, took out the bottles of colored ink and stuffed them into his pockets. Then they reburied the box with the paper in it.

"I must be going," said Jerry. "Enanak and I have things to do on the Vispayan road. I'll see you again right here a week from today at two o'clock in the afternoon. All right?"

"Yes, sir. Don't worry about anything. I'll see Wong and I'll think about what pictures you should take in the meanwhile."

"Thank you, sir," said Jerry, making fun of him.

"I'm sorry," said Peter. "It's just that I'm excited."

"Don't be sorry," said Jerry. "You're going to be quite a spy."

Peter's career as a spy very nearly came to an end at the bottom of the main street where the road turned right toward the market. In his wild excitement he had ridden on his wagon, free-wheeling and belly down, all the way from the top of the hill by the water tower. Fortunately, it was still siesta time and there was no one in the street. He rounded most of the corner on two wheels, then hit the curb and rolled over and over across the dusty sidewalk. He jumped up shaken and hurried back to the curb to look at his wagon. It would still roll, but the rear axle was slightly bent. What a dope he was taking out his happiness in such an uncontrolled way. Still, he *was* happy. And he could buy a new rear axle, a better, more expensive one. He was a guerrilla agent now, and a news reporter, and he had a job and an income. He was practically a man. It surpassed all his most wishful dreams except for actually being in the hills and fighting. That might come next, after he had proved himself in town. He checked to see that the letters from his father were still safe in his toolbox and then he soberly trundled his wagon to Camelia's stall. As he picked up the load waiting for him, he arranged with Camelia to put a gift package on the camp marketing truck for Maggie Higgins.

140

It was something he had wanted to do for Maggie ever since his release. With her folks in Manila, she probably didn't have many people to do things for her. He had thought of it often, but now he could afford it.

On the way out of the market he stopped at Rosa's stall to say that Pete Wong wanted a case of Nestlé's cream. Rosa had to scurry up and down behind her counter and dig deep in the reserve hoards under it to get together that many cans. She called Peter a *bungao*, which meant, in her vulgar, joking way, that he was a well-grown boy—too well grown in certain parts—and caused her trouble in a way that she approved of.

He took the cream to the Mark Price Casino. Inside, beyond the beaded strings which served as a door, were several Jap soldiers playing card games with the Chinese dealer or talking to the girls. The number-one girl, Rainha, was at the cash register by the entrance. She was a Portuguese mestiza from Macao and so slim and long-legged and beautiful that it made Peter timid just to look at her.

"I have an order for Mr. Wong," he said softly.

"He's inside," she answered without looking up. "In the office."

"Thank you," said Peter.

The office was a bright, modern-looking room which came as a contrast after the dinginess of the casino. Pete Wong— big, smooth and rippling—lay on a wicker chaise longue smoking a cigarette and looking at the ceiling.

"I have some cream for you, sir," said Peter.

Wong looked up, recognized Peter, and got up quickly, his feet planted wide apart as if he were going to wrestle.

"So they've started" was all he said. He took the case of cream with the letter from Jerry, tucked in the flap on top, and shook Peter by the hand.

"Thanks. I'll get in touch with you if you don't get in touch with me first. But if you do get in touch with me, bring me cigarettes, not cream. Good-by, kid."

Peter hurried out into the daylight and hurried up the hill to get his load to Colonel Kori's house before the long delay became unexplainable. In the woods he was caught by the afternoon rain and, though he ran, he was quite wet when he reached the bungalow. The geisha met him as courteously as before and said nothing about his slowness. But as he was bringing in the final carton of liquor, Colonel

141

Kori emerged from another room wearing, not a kimono, but a dress uniform, and looking far less mild and kindly because of it.

"You were very slow this time, Peter."

He spoke affably enough, but Peter suddenly felt a dislike for him. He brushed the feeling back into the unswept closets of his mind—those closets held so much these days and hadn't been cleaned for so long that they felt as if they were bursting—and said matter-of-factly, "I had axle trouble. Guess I'm going to have to buy a new one."

"I've been wondering what kind of axles the boys used on those jalopies," said the colonel. "What are they?"

"Well, mine's just a piece of reinforcing iron padded out at the ends with sleeves cut from a pipe so that it fits into my pram wheels. The sleeves are held in place by pins the blacksmith put in for me. I keep the inside of the sleeves heavily greased so that they take the place of ball bearings."

"Whatever stops the wheel from working its way right off the end?"

"A couple of curtain rings welded to each sleeve."

"Isn't that something!" said the colonel. "Why don't you come in and have a drink with me until the rain stops and you dry off a bit. The first of my guests won't be arriving for almost an hour and I'm all dressed up with no place to go."

Peter had never had a drink except for Communion wine, which he liked, and Donny Garver's hootch, which he did not like. He was curious to try other liquors and this was a good excuse because it would be rude to refuse. Though why the colonel wanted to drink with a boy like him he couldn't understand. Maybe after going to college in the States he was simply lonely for the company of Americans.

"Just a short one for the road," said the colonel as Peter hesitated.

"All right," said Peter, "thank you." As he followed the colonel into the living room, he said, "Perhaps I can get a better rear axle this time. Some of the older Filipino boys have real steel bars and ball bearings that fit them. If I have the money, I expect I can find something like that myself."

"Maybe this will help," said the colonel, handing Peter the five pesos he had promised.

"Oh, thank you!" said Peter genuinely, with surprise.

The colonel sat down and the geisha brought out bottles

and glasses on a tray.

"Whisky, sake or brandy?" asked the Colonel.

"I like sake a lot," lied Peter, "but I haven't seen any whisky for a long time."

The colonel raised his eyebrows a little and said something quickly in Japanese. The geisha brought over a bottle of Johnny Walker to Peter and showed it to him.

"That would be very nice, thank you," he said.

"Long or short?" asked the colonel.

"Short, please," said Peter, thinking that a long one might be too much.

Again the colonel looked surprised. "*Whisky to kori*," he said to the girl, and she brought Peter a short, stubby glass of whisky poured over ice. Having heard jokes about children choking on liquor, he sipped at it gingerly. It burned and made his eyes water slightly, but nothing that would show. And though it didn't taste good like Communion wine, it did feel pleasantly warm inside his damp, chilled body.

"You're quite a man of the world, Peter," said Colonel Kori. "I suppose running deliveries around town the way you do is a fast way to get a liberal education."

"Maybe in some things," said Peter. "But I'm not keeping up with schoolwork very well."

"No, I can imagine," said the colonel. The geisha brought him his drink, a little brown liquid at the bottom of a huge round glass. "Your practical knowledge of day-to-day life makes me interested in hearing your opinions about certain things," continued the colonel. Peter said nothing. He felt that the colonel was being kind of slimy.

"Our big administrative problem on Panoc," continued the Jap, "is lawlessness. It prevents us from bringing in adequate supplies to feed the Americans in Camp Dewey and it raises the prices you yourself must pay for food in the market. The farmers around Vispayan are being terrorized and the trucks hauling produce up the mountain have to carry guards and move in convoys."

The colonel paused and looked at Peter intently.

"I guess the guerrillas are pretty active," said Peter impassively.

"I don't know. Are they guerrillas or bandits? General Wainwright ordered all American forces in the Philippines to lay down their arms three weeks ago."

"You can't blame some of them if they go on fighting,

143

though, can you?" asked Peter.

"Not if they're regular soldiers," said the colonel. "After all, surrender is never honorable, no matter what the conventions of war say. But most of these so-called guerrillas are hoodlums and jailbirds who try to pretend that stealing and raping and burning have suddenly become patriotic."

"I suppose people like that always take advantage of war," said Peter. "I know a lot of the looting of American homes was done by crooks and not—" he was going to say "by the Japs" but changed it to—"in any organized way."

"You're right," said the colonel. "The real soldiers who have become guerrillas may win or lose, but at least they're fighting for a valid military reason. Most of these irregulars, on the other hand, have no purpose except to grow rich on plunder. They don't want to win, any more than they want to lose. After all, the longer the war lasts, the longer they can continue to enjoy a parasitic life. To us Japanese, they are a nuisance, but they do no good to the American cause either, because they make law-abiding Filipinos think that all guerrillas are equally brutal and greedy."

"Maybe so," said Peter. He hadn't thought of it that way before, but he felt there must be something wrong with the colonel's reasoning. It sounded like advice for sheep.

"I'm glad you agree," said Colonel Kori. "It's such a joy to speak frankly and seriously about it to someone. Many of my own countrymen are extremists who say that all guerrillas, when caught, should be treated like common criminals. But here we are, neither of us wanting to do anything unpatriotic and both of us on opposite sides, and yet we can agree that one should make some distinction."

"Yes," said Peter, hoping that the subject would change. "This certainly is good whisky."

"I'm glad you like it. It's a pity Johnny Walker discontinued its White Label line, but for my money the Black is still as good as any Scotch you can buy." He swirled the drink in his glass.

"Going back to this problem of lawlessness," he continued. "I believe a lot of it seems straight from the open market down in town. I believe some of the hoodlums are in touch with the vendors. By making food scarce, driving up the prices and wholesaling stolen goods cheaply, the hoodlums help the market girls make fat profits. In return, the girls act as a clearing house for the spoils, channeling boots or food or ammunition from one gang to another according to what kind of article each group is poor or rich in at the moment."

"I guess that's possible," said Peter in an unusually soft voice. For a moment he had thought Colonel Kori knew about Costeau and Wong and was toying with him. Even to have had such a thought seemed dangerous. In the presence of a man like Kori, Peter thought, it would be best not only to look innocent but feel it, too.

"You're in a good position to judge," said the colonel in a conversational way. "Have you seen any sign of such activities?"

Peter thought for a split second of getting in good with him by telling him about old lady Fulgencia's peso-a-loaf bread, but he squelched the idea at once.

"I hadn't thought about it," he said. "I've been so busy trying to make ends meet that I haven't had time." The rain outside had almost stopped and soon he would be able to leave.

"No girls who suddenly have new things to sell? No big deliveries to unlikely buyers?"

"Nothing I can think of," said Peter, "but I'll be on the look-out." He stood up, hoping the colonel would let him go before he showed his fright and unsureness. His head and joints felt stiff, like wood, and he wondered if it could be the effect of the whisky.

"Nothing at all?" insisted the colonel. "I'm a little disappointed in you."

"Well, I did have one wagonload," he said. He paused and realized that he had been tricked, because of his stupid conceit, into saying something, which he hadn't meant to say, in defense of himself. Now he had to finish the sentence. He tightened the remaining fibers of self-control in him and set himself to lying his way out of it.

"It was canned cream," he went on quickly. "And I had to take it to a little shack built of kerosene oil cans—the last people you'd think would be buying cream. And the next week when I went by that way, up in North Valley, the shack wasn't there. They'd taken it apart and moved it somewhere else, I guess."

"I'll be darned!" exclaimed the colonel. "Which of the girls gave you the cream to deliver?"

"That was another funny thing about it," said Peter. "She

only had a stall in the market for two weeks. It seemed like it got emptier and emptier and then she closed up when nothing was left and disappeared. Her name was Anita."

"What was her last name?" asked the colonel.

Peter almost said "de la Cruz," which was the last name of Anita, their former maid, but for some reason he was thinking fast now and one of the rules he had just set himself for this game was to put together true things in a nonsense way, from places and contexts that didn't fit. So he said, "I don't know. I only know the girls in the market by their first names." Standing in front of his chair he felt ramrod straight and awkward."

"Won't you sit down and have another?" asked the colonel pleasantly.

"No, thank you," said Peter. "I'm afraid I have to go now. I'm having tea with Miss Enid Larsen." It sounded silly when he heard it, but he had hoped the "Miss" would make the engagement seem like one which could not be broken. He wasn't going to go to Enid's, of course, but it was the fastest excuse he could think of.

"Well, well!" said the colonel, looking surprised again. *Cherchez la femme.* And who, may I ask, is the lucky lady?"

"She's a Swedish girl who lives down the street," said Peter.

"I'll be darned! Just how old are you anyway, Peter?"

"Fourteen last February," he said. Seeing that he was going to be able to escape, he took the rest of his drink at a swig and followed it with a gulp of cooling air.

"You're quite advanced for your age," said the colonel.

"Thank you," said Peter.

The geisha stood beside the door, and Peter marched past her like a robot and so out through the kitchen.

"I hope you don't think I've been prying," said the colonel behind him, "but we want to fight a fair war and we don't think thieves add to the glory of either side."

"Of course not," said Peter. "Thank you for the drink, and I'm sorry I have to run." The words—imitated from ladies he had heard at the Diaks' house before the war—sounded forced in his mouth. He picked up the rope on the front of his wagon and started away abruptly.

"So long," called the colonel after him. "Come and see me again soon. I enjoyed the bull session." He sounded as over-hearty and over-American and slimy as he was. But he was

146

scary too, and someone to watch out for.

Peter waved acknowledgment and kept on going. He thought carefully over what he had said and it seemed better as he thought about it than it had when he'd said it. He certainly hadn't let on to anything except that the colonel made him nervous, and, what the heck, he'd have been nervous under those circumstances even yesterday when he wasn't an agent. The story about the shack of kerosene oil cans was a honey. The shack he was thinking of was actually one in the village below Camp Dewey. The girl was actually Rosa. The suspicious load was actually the water-buffalo leather that he'd delivered to the barefoot native out beyond the houses in North Valley. And the cans of cream, of course, were the ones he'd just delivered to Pete Wong. As for Colonel Kori, all his ideas and arguments were what Peter's father would call "crooked as a dog's hind leg." It didn't matter if there were bad guerrillas. Any guerrillas were better than none as long as they hurt the Japs. And even the most law-abiding sheep among the Filipinos would never go over to the Japs completely if there were guerrillas—or outright bandits— whom the Japs couldn't catch.

Peter felt good, rather peculiar and numb and full of self-pleasure and exhilaration. That must be the whisky. He ought to be careful, then, because people who drank didn't always know what they were doing.

His parents didn't approve of drinking, but it wasn't a sin like some of the lies he told or the thoughts he thought. And it certainly was an interesting feeling.

He was approaching Enid's house. It must be almost six o'clock and too late for tea, but if she happened to see him go by and ran out to ask him why he hadn't come, what would he say? That he had to make at least two more deliveries before curfew or he wouldn't have earned his quota of *camotes* for the day? He hated the thought of telling her how poor they were. But they weren't so poor now. He had a grownup's job and more money than they needed. It was a hard idea to get used to. He didn't have to haul any more loads today if he didn't feel like it. In fact, he was more likely to learn something about the Japs that would interest Jerry by talking to Enid than by carting vegetables for Camelia. Besides, he had told Colonel Kori that he was going to visit Enid and it was only prudent to make the lie come true. That way, no one could ever say it was a lie.

147

Peter hid his wagon under Enid's front steps, went up them and knocked on the door. She herself opened it. She had on a dress. Her hair was combed neatly. She was wearing lipstick. And naturally she looked angry.

"You're about two hours late, Peter. You don't expect to have tea now, do you?"

Peter felt much too happy to mind her scolding. "Sorry," he said. "I was delayed by a new colonel down the road. I have a feeling he's taking Miyanaku's place."

"Colonel Kori?" she asked, startled.

"Yes. Do you know him?" he said.

"You'd better watch out for him. Papa says he's a big shot who outranks Colonel Miyanaku. And he's not exactly taking Colonel Miyanaku's place either. He's here on some kind of special assignment."

"Well, so what?" said Peter casually. "I only had a drink with him."

"Tea?" she asked, breaking into a smile. "Or sake?" and she wrinkled her nose.

"Just whisky," he said.

"Oh, just Jumping Jehoshaphat!" she exclaimed. It was an expression she had learned from Peter and she knew he liked to hear the odd Swedish "y" sounds she put into the "j's." "You're probably drunk," she went on. "You'd better have something to eat and sober up before your mother sees you."

"Do you know what someone who's drunk looks like?"

"I sure do," she said.

"Well, do I look drunk?"

"You look like a mess," she said. "What did you get caught in, a rainstorm or something?"

"What do you think? Can I come in for a while or shall I go on home?" He looked at her steadfastly and felt no shyness at all. The months of war *had* changed things. She no longer appeared to him as a sinful, exciting game. Her aura of teasing bittersweet and the sickly excitement he had always taken in her girlhood were almost gone, and she seemed, as she stood there, hardly more than a tidy-looking young woman whom he didn't know very well. He wondered why he had stopped by in the first place. That was probably one of the peculiarities of whisky: it put things in proper perspective. With his new job he had more important things to do than stand around chatting with comparative strangers.

148

"All right, come in," she said. "But you *are* drunk. Maybe not very, but enough to be belligerent."

He followed her into the hall. She led him to a door and opened it and to his surprise it was a bathroom.

"You'd better get those wet clothes off and take a hot bath," she said, thrusting a towel into his hands. "If we are to eat anything I have to get it myself. Amelia has already gone home. She won't sleep here any more since the Japanese moved into all the houses roundabout. Usually Papa gets supper, but he's gone to Mananok and won't be back until morning."

She closed the door on Peter and he looked around. He had been in her house two or three times before, but he had somehow missed seeing this bathroom. It certainly was fancy. The washbasin and tub were green instead of white and there was a bench with a cover made of toweling to sit on while you undressed. He laid his clothes on the bench and got into the tub. It had a shower head over it but only one tap instead of four. The tap said *kalt* and *heisz* with an arrow pointing from one to the other. Probably it controlled both kinds of water for the tub and probably the tap for the shower had never been installed. He turned it on to find out and it rained freezing water down on him from above. Trying to get some hot out of it—or maybe *heisz*, he thought foolishly—he accidentally pushed it inward and the shower stopped and the spout for the tub started. By the time he had adjusted it for warm and found the soap in its curved, covered, built-in compartment and admired the fact that the soap was scented, he heard a knocking on the door and had to turn the whole contraption off again to hear what Enid wanted.

"Our meal is cooking. Would you like me to come in and rub you dry? That's what the Japanese girls do."

"Go away," said Peter. "I haven't even washed yet."

"I've put one of Papa's bathrobes on the doorknob outside," she called back. "You better wear it until your clothes are properly dry."

When he reached out for the dressing gown after finishing his bath, he was surprised to find that it almost fitted him. He had always thought of Mr. Larsen as much bigger than he was, but of course that was one of the reasons he was hungry so much of the time: he had been growing since the war started—four inches last time he had measured, and that was over a month ago.

149

He found Enid sitting before the drawn curtains in the *sala* smoking a cigarette.

"Want one?" she asked in greeting, and held out a pack of Jap ones.

"No, thanks," he said, taken aback. "I didn't know you smoked."

"I don't really. I just try them sometimes when Dad's not here."

Peter sat down awkwardly in the chair across from her. He felt silly in nothing but a dressing gown and the drink of whisky was no longer warm inside him. The shower had made him warm all over and rather tired.

"You're awfully thin," said Enid. "But you've grown a lot too. You're taller than I am now, quite a bit taller."

"You've changed some, too," said Peter.

"I've filled out a little more in front, that's all."

She was always so frank about physical things.

"Maybe I will have a cigarette," he said quickly. What the heck, he might as well try everything on a day like this. Perhaps the cigarette would give him something to do besides feel awkward.

"Good," she said. She jumped up, put one in his mouth and held out a fancy table-model lighter. "You're not supposed to inhale at the beginning," she said. "Close your throat and suck in your cheeks so that the smoke only goes into your mouth."

She flicked the flame into being and he did as he was told. To his surprise the smoke had a real taste—much better than the spills of paper or pine-needles-and-paper that he had ever puffed on before.

While she watched him in silence, he experimented with the feel of the smoke around his tongue and the shapes he could make with it as it came out of his mouth.

"Try blowing it through your nose," she said.

He tried and ended up coughing while she laughed at him.

"Let me see you do it," he said, annoyed.

"Oh, I've been practicing—" and sure enough she did it without any trouble. "Papa has to go off at night quite often these days," she said, "and without Amelia in the house, I try things so as not to get frightened. I know there's nothing really to be scared of. Papa leaves me a loaded shotgun just in case, and the Japanese soldiers are very well disciplined. It's the way they look mostly: so dirty and ugly. Not the officers, I mean. Some of them are quite intelligent and fun to talk to. We've had parties for them and I've stayed up until after midnight talking to them."

"I saw a light in your room the night they marched us to the concentration camp," said Peter. "It was almost sunrise."

"That was the latest night of all," she said. "I really expected something then. I was excited."

"What do you mean?" he asked.

"Well, Dad thought there would be Germans, too. But there weren't, and it's hard to talk to Japanese for very long. They're interested in different things and even the smartest of the ones who come here can't speak very much English."

"You must get pretty bored," said Peter. "There really isn't much to do without school and the other kids—not unless you work like I do."

"Papa has written to the Swedish consul in Manila asking if there is some way to send me home to my aunt in Lund in Sweden. At first I didn't much want to go, but now the war looks as if it may last forever."

"You mean because of Corregidor falling?"

"No, because the Japanese aren't going to take Australia."

"I don't know what you mean," he said impatiently.

"Well, Papa says they have to take Australia in order to make the United States want peace. If they would listen to the advice of the Germans, he says, they would risk their whole navy before giving up on it. But after those battles in the Coral Sea they don't think they can afford the price any more."

There was no question which side Mr. Larsen was on now. But Peter hadn't realized that the Coral Sea battle was important. Oh, he'd heard the name but he didn't believe in the news his mother and the Gibneys were always gossiping about. They no longer had short-wave sets to listen to America with and so most of their news was only guessing—like Father Gibney, who listened to the Jap radio from Manila and always reversed the figures, calling American losses Jap losses and vice versa.

"Do you want the Japs to win?" he asked Enid.

"I don't much care," she said. "Papa has always worked for German companies, so he wants the Japanese to win because they're allies of the Germans."

"What happened in the Coral Sea?" he asked.

"I don't really know. Everyone lost a lot of ships and that's supposed to be worse for the Japanese than it is for the Americans. I think the funny thing is fighting a battle in a coral sea to start with. It sounds more like a place to have a sailboat and drift around in the sun and maybe play the Game."

"It's really just part of the Pacific," he said, disregarding the last part of her sentence.

"Have you played the Game with anyone since that last time at the beach?" she asked.

"Of course not. Have you?" As soon as he had said it, he was angry with himself—not only for showing interest but also for feeling it. How could he be jealous about her if he didn't even know her well?

"Who could I play with?" she asked. "One of the Japanese officers wanted to kiss me one night. He recited poetry to me and tried to be romantic, but he said the words so badly that I had to make him talk about something else or I would have laughed at him."

"You better watch out," said Peter. "Japs do crazy things when they think they're in love. They're always killing one another and jumping into volcanoes and stuff like that."

"I know," she said. "Papa tells me never to say anything they might take as flirting. And I don't. That's why it's nice having you here. You used to say some fancy high-flown things yourself sometimes. Remember the stone heart you carved for me once, and wrote initials on with blood from your finger? I still have it, but you can't see the blood any more."

He blushed at the memory. She laughed but didn't say anything. Instead she got up and went to the sideboard.

"I feel like being bad as the devil," she said. "I'm going to have a drink, too. See!" She took a square bottle out of a drawer and held it up. "I know where I can buy another just like it, so Papa won't ever notice. We can hide this one and keep it for ourselves. Then when you come to tea in time for cocktails again, we can have some."

"We ought to have supper so I can go home before curfew," said Peter.

"There's plenty of time," she said. "Mostly I'm going to give you the cakes we didn't have at tea, anyway." She went to the kitchen, and Peter told himself to get up and put on his clothes and leave. It was so hot in the room with the curtains drawn that he didn't have any energy. That was the trouble, or maybe he had a fever. His face felt burning enough. Or maybe he really should stay to get more information about Colonel Miyanaku and the battle of the Coral Sea and the life the Jap officers led in Abanao. No, those were excuses. They were good excuses, but he knew he was going to stay whether they were good or bad. He could feel his heart growing as hard, angry and evil as any Pharaoh's. He had been good a lot lately. He had worked all the time and yet they were poor. Look at her! Everything was as soft and rich as the toweling cover on the bench in the bathroom. She had cigarettes and liquor like the Japs—and cakes for tea. Well, what was wrong about spending the money of your country's enemies? What harm was there in taking luxuries from the daughter of a Jap collaborator? If there was any sin in it, it could go back there in the bursting, unswept closets of his mind. He felt lazy and smooth-skinned under Mr. Larsen's bathrobe and he was going to stay and enjoy it until his clothes were dry.

Enid came back wheeling a tea cart. On top, on an ironed white cloth, were the bottle, a silver bucket of ice and a casserole warming over an alcohol lamp. Underneath were glasses, plates, utensils, jam tarts, water-cress sandwiches made with old lady Fulgencia's bread, and fancy little Jap cakes made with glutinous rice. Peter couldn't help sitting up straight and amazed as he looked at it, and Enid smiled with pleasure.

"You're supposed to keep the whole bottle cold," she said, pouring some of the liquor into a tumbler, "but we can't do that so we'll stir it up with ice."

"What is it?" he asked.

"Why don't you try some?" she answered, adding the ice.

"I will," he said. She looked at him and smiled. Then she filled two small glasses from the tumbler, keeping the ice behind by holding it back with a knife, and carried them over to the sofa. "You have to come and sit beside me if you want any," she said.

"All right." He felt aggressively calm, but his voice sounded slightly hoarse. When he sat down, one side of the dressing gown slipped off sideways and as he tucked it back between his knees, he had to blush again, of course. He looked at her quickly and she was watching him, but she still didn't make any remark about his blushing. When he felt so much older, why was it that the pumps for his blood didn't work in a more grown-up way, too?

"You certainly are thin now," she said. "Was it awful in the camp?"

"Mostly hungry," he said offhandedly.

"Your legs have grown hairier, haven't they?" She giggled.

"Don't act silly."

"I can't help teasing you; it's so easy. Taste your drink."

He did. It was strong and burning and tasted like some kind of candy or pastry he had had before. He made a face and found he could hardly whisper when he spoke. "What is it?"

"Swedish drink. Aquavit. Don't you like it?"

"Maybe I will," he said.

"Sure, you'll get used to it. I've had little glasses of it on special occasions ever since I was a small girl. We ought to drink a toast with it to King Gustav."

"Is he king of Sweden?"

"Yes."

"Okay, as long as he's not a German."

She showed him how to touch glasses, and then they drank. He sipped cautiously, but she tossed back her head and put down her glass empty. Laughing, she wiped the tears out of her eyes with the lapel of his dressing gown.

"That's the way they do it in Sweden," she said hoarsely. "Now I've caught up with you and I can have one to drink slowly." She went and poured herself another.

"Here's to that son-of-a-gun Norman, in camp," she said. "I hope they keep him there." She touched glasses with Peter again, but this time she only took a sip, the same as he did.

"The trouble is," she added, "we could never play the Game properly with only two of us."

"The Game was a silly thing," said Peter. "We're too old for it now."

"Fiddlesticks!" she said, laughing. "Too old for the rules maybe, but I don't think anyone ever gets too old for the Game itself. You remember how old Mrs. Regan was? The old lady who lived up back and died last year? Well, I saw her kissing her houseboy once."

"She was kind of nutty," said Peter. "But that's not what I meant."

"What did you mean, then?" She pouted slightly.

"Well, before, we used to pretend a lot of things: like loving you . . . or having rules . . . or that it was really only a game. Now I know more and I can't pretend as well."

"Don't you love me any more?"

"Not really."

For the first time since he had known her, she looked—for a moment—as if he had hurt her.

"I mean, not like grownups who can get married."

"Oh, well! But you're still my friend," she said, unclouding. "You don't hate me because of the war."

"Of course not. I simply mean that you could make all the rules you wanted and it still wouldn't be a game now."

"Would you fall in love with me like a grown man who wanted to get married?"

"No, that's one of the things I've learned. I could even hate you—I don't, but I could—and I would still want to kiss you. If a person isn't religious or ashamed and does just what he wants, he can be excited over almost anything. You should hear the men talk who *are* that way. Donny Garver —he's a man in camp—calls sex 'The Inglorious Itch.' He says, 'Any old back scratcher is good for it and the more curvy or twisted it is the better.'"

"Papa says talking dogs never bite," she said. He laughed and wished he could tell Donny. "Do you feel as if you are like this Garver fellow?" she asked.

"I don't know," said Peter. "You're the only person I've ever even kissed that way. But I have a lot of thoughts."

"Thoughts don't mean anything. If they did, we'd all be dead or son-of-a-guns. Why don't you kiss me and then say if it's silly or not?" Suddenly she looked vexed. "Damn it to the devil," she said. "I was going to make you ask me."

Peter faced around toward her and she pursed her lips. He reached out for her and his skin tingled. He touched her and his feeling of awkwardness decreased. Roughly pulling her down on him and swinging his feet up beside hers, he opened his mouth to her and watched the cigarette burn out in the ash tray beyond her ear. At first a part of his mind remained outside of the kiss, considering odd thoughts like the shapes two tongues and mouths together might make with the blue cigarette smoke. But then deep, hectic oblivion settled over

155

him and in the end she had to wriggle away from him and stand up.

"You certainly do get excited," she said.

Peter had his eyes closed and now he screwed them shut more tightly and lay still.

"You've broken a button on my dress," she said. "If you want to see how I've filled out, I'll show you. You don't need to break buttons." Peter made a choking noise and turned over on his face. "I'm going to sew it on," she said. "I won't be long."

After a while, when she was still out of the room, he opened his eyes and sat up and finished his drink. Hers was already empty. He closed his mind and waited for her to come back. When she did she said, "I feel funny. I'm going to have something to eat." She served two plates of meat balls out of the casserole. "Do you still not love me?" she asked.

"How do I know?" he said, cross at being questioned.

"You act so embarrassed about a kiss."

"No, I'm not embarrassed," he said. After another mouthful of the peppery meat balls he added, "I don't even think I'm ashamed exactly. It's something else. Something worse and more hardhearted. I expect it's one of the sins, though: lust or maybe pride."

"Fiddlesticks," she said. "How could it be pride? That's a cold feeling. It's not the way you were acting, or me either."

"Well, the thing is I didn't want to stop, and I didn't want you to be able to stop any more than I could. When you did, it made me angry."

"You think too much, that's the trouble. I didn't want to stop. I had to, that's all. If I hadn't, we'd have both been sorry, you bet."

"I guess so," he said. "Actually I think a lot less than before the war. I do things and try not to think."

"You talk better than you used to, even if you don't think," she said, smiling.

"Maybe I save it up while I'm doing all my jobs."

"What jobs do you do?"

"Chop wood, grind flour, haul loads in my wagon—stuff like that."

"That's why you're so strong. You almost scared me once. Did you know you hurt my arm?"

She showed him a small bruise near her shoulder.

"I'm sorry," he said.

"Well, maybe it wasn't nice of me, letting you kiss me when you were only wearing a bathrobe. I always have trouble being nice. When I was a small girl, I used to take boys to my room to show them my toys and Papa used to scold me about it and I could never really understand why."

"Now you know," said Peter. "I expect we're acting pretty funny, aren't we?" He grinned and she laughed. They had finished their meat balls.

"Your clothes must be dry now," she said. "If you go put them on, I won't feel so unfair. I'll pour us two half glasses of aquavit to have with our sandwiches and cakes."

Peter went to the bathroom, put on his shirt and khaki shorts and sang softly to himself the sentimental songs he could think of, like "South of the Border" and "Red Roses for a Blue Lady." Then he combed his hair and washed his face because it had lipstick on it. He felt so happy that he sang more and more loudly between the handfuls of water he threw on his face. His thoughts raced and his body, though it seemed lazy and detached, felt wonderfully healthy. When he looked as good as he could in his silly shorts, which had grown much too small for him, he hurried back to the *sala*.

At the door he stopped short. Enid was sitting eating a sandwich in a blue dressing gown.

"I thought it should be my turn," she said. "It's only fair I should see what it's like. You have your clothes on now so I can leave the stopping to you."

He laughed, but his flesh crawled with fear and excitement. "Suppose I can't stop?" he said, blushing.

"Then I'll learn to stop when it's hardest," she said. "That's something everyone should learn."

He sat down next to her and took a sandwich.

"Can't I really trust you?" she asked.

"I don't know," he said. "It seems foolish to me."

"But how can I learn to control myself if I can't practice with a friend?"

"You're making fun of me," he said in a low voice. "You're what they call a slut."

"Why, you get out of here then, you son-of-a-gun," she shouted, jumping up.

He remained sitting numbly and glared at her.

"You take everything too seriously and you don't know how to have fun without going crazy," she shouted. And she

157

crammed the rest of her water-cress sandwich into her mouth.

"You're crazier," he said. "You're stupid. You want to play games when we're too old for them."

"Go home, then. Go on home."

"I haven't finished eating," he said lamely.

"It's my food. Go on home."

"I won't," he said, taking a jam tart.

She stood absolutely still, her face moving as if she wanted to say something. Then she walked out of the room and into the kitchen. He tried eating a sandwich, but it seemed dry. He drank more of his fresh glass of aquavit, but it didn't taste strong any more. He went back to the bathroom and put on his still damp shoes and socks. Then he walked slowly out to the hall and called out, "Good night?"

No answer.

After waiting awhile, he stamped his way to the front door and slammed it behind him. It was dark. Under the front steps it was darker still. He stumbled in his crouching position and smashed his head against one of the beams which held up the floor. He wiped his forehead and felt the wetness of bleeding. He tried to drag his wagon out, but it got stuck on something. He struck one of the matches he kept in his pocket for such occasions, but being damp it fizzled. The others in the box were all the same way. He felt his wagon all over and found that a piece of rope had got twisted into the axle. He slashed at it with his knife, but when he pulled the wagon, the axle still wouldn't turn and he realized that a piece of the rope had jammed itself in under the sleeve of iron pipe.

He crawled out from beneath the house and wondered what to do. He hadn't been watching the clock and it might be almost curfew time. If he tried to go through the two check points on the road after curfew, the soldiers might shoot him. He could leave his wagon behind to be fetched in the morning, and go home through the woods. But without any moon, it would be hard to go through the woods unless he had matches to strike. He would get stuck in the tangles at the bottom of the hollows. The price of excitement was high. He put down his pride and turned to go up the steps again. As he turned he heard the door latch click. She had locked it. He ran up the steps and knocked.

"Who's there?" she called in a husky, trembling voice.

"It's Peter. I need some matches to go home with."

"You frightened me," she said, opening the door a little bit to look at him. "Why don't you go home?"

"Because I need some matches." She started to close the door again, but in the pushing which followed, he won and forced his way in.

"You're evil," he said angrily. "It's after curfew time. Do you want me to get shot stumbling around the check points in the dark? Last time I saw you, you sent me to the Island and they almost shot me then. Well, this time I'm not taking chances."

"I wish they had shot you," she shouted, slamming the door behind him. Her voice throbbed and was gruff and when he saw her in the light, he could see she had been weeping.

"You've been crying," he said.

"What if I have?" she shouted.

"I'm sorry," he said.

She slapped at him smartly. He ducked and her hand hit the bloody spot on his forehead. He automatically raised his hand to hit back, but she ran away into the living room and threw herself onto the sofa weeping.

"I'm sorry," he said again. "I wouldn't have hit you, not really."

"You're bleeding," she sobbed.

"You didn't do it."

"Of course I didn't, you damn son-of-a-gun. What did happen?"

He told her and she dried her eyes and fetched a washcloth and some Mercurochrome. While she dabbed his face she asked him coldly about the trouble he had had after waiting in vain for her last time on the Island—the time the Japs came. He told her the whole episode, and when his face had stopped bleeding they both apologized to each other.

"You're so excitable," she said. "I shouldn't tease you."

"No, I'm crazy and you're right: it can't be anything but a game when things outside are all so serious. Gosh only knows, I do like to kiss you."

"Do you really?"

"Of course. More than anything I can think of doing alone without you. More than getting up before sunrise or finishing a map or having a birthday."

So they kissed again and several times more while they ate the rest of the cakes. And each kiss was a game. Craziness and lust came back to him at intervals, but he didn't bruise her arm. He only did his best to feel lazy and tired and happy now that they were friends again. When she insisted on testing him, he met her challenges gently. Even when she showed him how she had filled out under her dressing gown and told him to reach out and touch her, he only stroked her skin lightly. All the same, it wasn't like a consequence in the Game. It was more like a caress. And finally, numb as he was, he had to pinch her and laugh. She laughed too and pulled her dressing gown closed and told him to go home. She gave him a flashlight and kissed him at the door.

"Be careful," she said. "I'll see you in the morning. By the way, if you have any good novels bring some and lend them to me, okay?"

"I'll see what we have," he said.

"Papa will be home by lunchtime. I'll bet your mother's fit to be tied."

He kissed her again and heard her lock the door behind him. Mention of his mother had reminded him of the letters in the toolbox of his wagon. He got them out to take with him. The way home was easy with the flashlight. He went down the road and cut off into the woods wondering if he was really happy or unhappy. By the time he reached home he was turning over the story he would tell his mother. She met him as soon as he had entered the door and her face looked carved and red, like a crudely painted statue of the Virgin Mary in Father Mallard's little church.

"What happened?" she demanded. "I've been worried sick about you."

"I had axle trouble with the last load," he said. "The Japs at the bottom of the hill helped me with it and gave me cakes to eat and sake. You mustn't worry about me, Mother. One of them even came up the hill and escorted me through the check point at the top. But I had to leave my wagon. It's still not right."

"You shouldn't accept sake even if it's hard to refuse, darling. Our family has a weakness that way. You're much too young to be drinking."

Her father had died of liver trouble. How could he help it, owning a winery in France and having to taste the wines as he did? She didn't disapprove of the vineyard, just of his drinking and dying. That was typical of women, Peter thought happily—like Enid approving of kisses but not of excitement.

Peter remembered the letters and gave them to her and that was the end of the talk, of course. As she read them he got ready for bed. Quite a while after he had turned the light out she came in and kissed him, her cheek clammy with tears.

"It's so marvelous," she said. "Your father is all right."

"I know. I'm sorry I kept you worrying."

"Did you talk to the man who brought the letters?"

"It was the photographer," he said. "May I tell you in the morning?"

"Of course, my son. *Mon petit fils!* You must get some sleep. It's so hard for you when you work like a man all day. Good night."

She went out quietly and closed the door. Peter damned himself casually for his hypocrisy and turned his thoughts to thoughtless pictures of Enid. What had happened seemed hard to believe now. The dreams of wickedness and intrigue were coming true. But what would Enid say and feel in the morning? And what would he feel? Had he really touched her curved white skin? The bittersweet sickness—it had returned more feverishly than before and he dared all the missionaries in the world to cure it. God could not help him now. Only the Japs, if they put him back in camp, could have any control over him. The Japs and Enid, of course. Toward her he was all weakness and sweetness, like a lazy-flowing stream of wild honey, pungent and poignant with the odd tastes of field flowers.

## CHAPTER 12

During the following months Peter felt that the flame of life, long smoldering in his green bones, had at last truly lighted in him. Everyone and everything in the wide, generous world seemed to feed it and pour into him volatile spirits—the unstupefying essence of what aquavit should be if it deserved its name. He drank the essence with every mouthful of the good food he ate and the good air he breathed. He wanted the blaze to mount higher and higher as long as he had fuel for it. In metaphysical moments he supposed that if it grew hot enough it might burn the blackness out of his sins and turn them to pure white ash. Then he might be ready to become a good man or even a saint, but that was a long dim time off and he gave as little thought to it as possible. For the moment he imagined the flame as a thing of self-sufficient beauty: a perfect cone like the ones in the solid-geometry book he looked at sometimes in the evenings. Only this cone was red at the steady core and gold at the dancing extremities and it rose from a perfect circle of black cinders. The black stood for God. The red stood for work and danger and Jerry. The gold, of course, stood for Enid.

When he had gone back to Enid's house for his wagon that next morning she was as sunny as the sky. As far as sin went for her, the touches of the night before had never happened. She asked him in for coffee and pastry. She kissed him without regard for the bright sunlight or the maid washing the dishes in the kitchen. And she promised him that next time her father was going away for an evening she would leave the blind halfway up on her bedroom window. If her father was to be gone both evening and afternoon she would leave it all the way up. Peter agreed to come by early every afternoon to look at it. Then, because her father might be back any minute, she made him take his wagon from under the house and go home to his work.

The blind was up at least once a week. Sometimes Peter wore Mr. Larsen's dressing gown and other times Enid wore hers. She worked out so many combinations of partial undress and dress for him or her or both of them that Peter became conscious of his clothes and particular about their state of cleanness and press. With furtive extravagance he had a pair of gray flannel trousers made for him by the Chinese tailor out back of Yang's grocery store. He kept these visiting trousers away from his mother, wrapped neat and flat and secret in an oilskin on the chassis of his wagon. When he was going for a visit he put them on in the woods along the way and combed his hair in a mirror which he had bought. When he was getting ready to go home, and the polite air of attending an adult tea party was no longer make-believable, and time and the curfew pressed, he generally

162

changed back into his shorts right in Enid's living room while they finished planning the rules for their next meeting. With practice, Peter became less shy and tempestuous, and Enid less critical of him. But the Game remained a game: looks and laughter, touches and, at most, caresses.

As the rainy season came to an end—along with the mildews and the smells and the exciting storms which bore down on the roofs and bore down the trees and blocked the mountain trails which Jerry had to come over when he brought Peter new assignments—the bittersweet was becoming almost routine. He was hardened to making himself numb and keeping fits of craziness and gentleness from taking possession of him. He was hardened most of the time to the pressure of guilt pushing at the closet walls in the back of his head. He kept his body lazy by constant activity. And his mind, which was less tractable, he kept as preoccupied as he could by making the intrigues and dangers of his life more complicated than they really were.

The one unmanageable time of the week was Sunday mornings, the hour of cinder-blackness when he knelt in cassock and surplice beside the altar serving for Father Gibney while his mother and Mrs. Gibney and a few others received Communion. He, too, put the bread and the wine in his mouth because, if he had not, his mother would have asked him why and would have been unhappy when he refused to tell her. But the bread turned his mouth as dry as dust—or as too many kisses—and he had to swallow each crumb as carefully as a pill to avoid choking on it. He knew that receiving the sacrament with unprepared mind and no intention of reforming was a grievous sacrilege and hypocrisy to add to his sins, but he knew too that he would do worse things for Enid if he had to. Occasionally, he hoped that he would not do worse, and he appealed to the God of Luck to make his hope come true. But Luck, he knew, was a pagan god and a weak one.

So far, at least, he didn't think that he had damned himself irrecoverably. After all, what he did with Enid couldn't be as bad as spilling his seed on the ground. At least she was there with him and he felt he loved her. Nor could it be as bad, surely, as lying with her completely. And he couldn't marry her. Even as grown up and independent as he felt, he knew he couldn't marry at fourteen. If she were an American and on the American side he might have pretended that he would marry her someday, but things being what they were, he couldn't use that excuse. And after the war, when sides and loyalties would no longer be important, was a time too vague and remote for him to fool himself with plans for it.

So each Sunday Peter faced his sins and totted up his accounts in black cinder-writing. The price of Enid and the golden flame was an accumulating thing which piled up back in the closets like promissory notes at compound interest which he would someday have to honor. Some Sundays the pile looked too big to pay back and he wondered hopelessly and rebelliously why it was that he damned himself for mental sins when perhaps he could insist on committing real ones and making damnation worthwhile. In such moods he deliberately imagined the real sins he might commit in order to violate the sanctity of the chapel more than he was already doing by his unrepentant presence. Other Sundays he wondered why the pile of his wickedness had ever seemed so high. After all, he had sinned in his thoughts as long as he could remember, so what was he adding now that was worse? But most Sundays, automatically genuflecting and carrying the missal and ringing the bell as the service progressed, he let the formal movements of the Mass evoke in him drifting memories of the old days, which he savored with a mixture of nostalgia and condescension. In those days before the war when he sinned pay-as-you-go with repentance afterward and no premeditation beforehand, the torture of guilt and remorse had been partly pleasurable. It had never stood still—cold and dead—before an unmoving background of fear and pessimism as his lust and hardheartedness did today. On the other hand, it had never had any redeeming framework of importance like his work for Jerry and the guerrillas, either. No, it had been easy. It had been childish.

Spying and running dangerous errands were the flame red of Peter's life, and in the light of flame red, hardness at the heart showed up as a practical necessity. It helped him to remain cool when he went through a check point with one of Jerry's cameras hidden among the canned goods in his wagon. It helped him not to feel so proud of his exploits that he ever bragged about them to Enid. Most important, it helped him to lie clearheadedly when he talked to Colonel Kori.

It also helped him—in a necessary but dishonorable way—when he had to sidetrack his mother's worry and curiosity about him. His simplest and most shameful tactic with her was to withhold his father's letters and dole them out as distractions whenever the situation demanded one. But during the rainy season there were long gaps of stormy weather between the letters, and whenever the last one was spent, he had to make do as well as he could with cajolery.

"Where were you tonight, Peter?"

"Colonel Kori asked me to help the geisha serve the guests after I brought up the stuff for his party."

"That Kempetai swine! You had a drink with him again, too, didn't you?"

"I had to, Mother. He mixed it for me himself and proposed a toast to Hirohito. You know perfectly well I can't refuse to drink to the Emperor. All I can do is think *Roosevelt* while I'm doing it."

She smiled in spite of herself.

Other times it was more difficult.

"Peter, I'm going to ask to be sent back to camp. Anything is better than having you out on the streets at night consorting with soldiers and drinking sake."

"Mother! We couldn't get letters from Dad then."

"That's my sacrifice, my son. I can make it."

"Well, what about Jeanette? We couldn't get goat's milk for her in camp."

"Jeanette can learn to like bean curd."

"Then think of me! I've grown another inch just this last month. How do you suppose I'd feel on two bowls of rice a day?"

Accusing his mother of selfishness made her stop to examine her motives and by the next morning she had persuaded herself that she *was* selfish and Peter was right. Actually, her concern about his drinking was a lucky thing. She knew so little about all liquors except wine that she accepted the smell of aquavit as the stink of sake and she never suspected what his real sin was. Still, she remained worried, and on several occasions Peter could see that she had asked Father Gibney to speak to him. With Father Gibney he was on dependable ground. He knew the minister would never ask him questions about sex—he wasn't shy, but his mind simply didn't run that way. And Peter's religious life was blameless on the surface. So Peter could always be sure that Father Gibney, too, would ask him only about liquor. And when he did— when he brought the conversation around to it—Peter was

165

always forearmed with words. It was easy to persuade Father Gibney that his mother, like Mrs. Gibney, worried too much. And then it was easy to distract him with some new bit of information—true or invented—about Colonel Kori.

It had turned out that Colonel Kori was head of the secret police on Panoc and was meant to mop up the guerrillas. As part of his job he had taken over control of propaganda and most law enforcement from Colonel Miyanaku. He confided in Peter—he confided in Peter in his slimy, purposeful way almost every time Peter delivered something to him— that Colonel Miyanaku was making him a lot of trouble by resisting his up-to-date liberal methods. For instance, the classes he held in public relations and detective work for the noncoms who ran the check points around town were criticized by Colonel Miyanaku as Western nonsense which might be good for an army of women but could only spoil Japanese noncoms. Father Gibney was delighted to hear of this friction between the colonels and he tended to agree with Miyanaku. Peter wasn't sure. It seemed to him that some of Colonel Kori's Harvard-man methods were effective —what he had done to the posters around town, for example. He had taken the nastiness out of them and also the awkwardness that made the Filipinos laugh. Now there was no more *shooting by guns* or *affectionately yours*, but only:

WANTED: The looter who calls himself *General Sam*.
REWARD: Five thousand pesos, dead or alive.
Filipino Citizens' Committee for Law and Order

After God, Colonel Kori was the fear in Peter's life. Peter had explained to him politely at their second meeting that he disagreed with him about lawlessness and that, as a patriotic American, he could never tell him about it even if he did ever happen to see something queer or irregular in the market. Jerry had advised him that this would be the best thing to say. But Colonel Kori kept inviting him in for drinks anyway, and Peter had come to fear and dislike him more, the more he saw of him. Colonel Kori had no self-control, that was the trouble with him. Or maybe he had too much self-control most of the time. In his daylight talk he was certainly calculating and slimy enough. But at the one party where Peter *had* helped serve the drinks late at night, Colonel Kori had gotten drunk and violent. He had made his geisha go and put on a Western-style bathing suit and do a disgusting dance for the other officers which he called "the American Bump and Grind." The other officers didn't like it any better than the geisha did—because she had been a real geisha once and didn't go in for that kind of thing. But all the polite disapproval Colonel Kori got about it only made him more violent and stubborn. He finally ended the evening by seeing something insubordinate in one of the guards at the door and beating the guard with the butt of his own rifle. He seemed so angry that Peter thought he would kill the man. No one stopped him either, but eventually he stopped himself, and they carried the poor soldier away somewhere. Peter learned later that the man had had a concussion and most of his ribs broken.

Peter's main concern with Colonel Kori, of course, wasn't his physical violence but his mental gentleness and the way he kept trying to trip Peter up. So far, the coldness in Peter's heart had stood him in good stead and he had not made any slips that he knew of. But he was still scared. He feared that the colonel—after Peter's stupid excuse for leaving at their first meeting—would find out about Enid and try to blackmail him. He prepared for this by getting used to the idea that patriotism was far more important than being considered good by his mother.

Then another possibility suggested itself which—though he feared it less—worried him more. Suppose Colonel Kori should speak to Enid and ask her to lead Peter on and listen carefully to everything he said. He could rely on his coldness when he faced the colonel, but not with Enid. She distracted him and made him do what she wanted so easily.

The idea that he might betray the guerrillas through Enid came to haunt him. Finally he saw that he would have to tell Jerry about her. He hated to expose himself to Jerry's worldly ridicule if he was being silly and shying at shadows, but if he was a poor risk and not worth the money he earned, when so much was at stake, Jerry had to know about it.

He had almost prepared himself for the shameful confession when one day he made it, not to Jerry, but to Miss Drayton, Jerry's girl friend, instead. He had been downtown with one of the photographer's Leicas, taking pictures for him of Pete Wong and Rainha. Jerry had said that Rainha and the

167

gambling den sounded too corny to miss and had given him very complete instructions. He had stood behind the hanging strings of beads in the door of Wong's office. The blinds had been drawn in the room behind him so that none of the soldiers in the casino would notice him if they looked toward the doorway. Then, being careful not to get the bright "contrasty" opening, which led out into the street, in the background of any of his "exposures," he had photographed Wong and Rainha going about their work. Jerry had given him a list of "stops" and "times" to use for those light conditions. The "times" were long, but the gamblers at the tables were not moving much and Jerry said that if their hands blurred, so much the better. Peter had spent all morning at it and had used up three rolls of film. He had enjoyed it, too, because Rainha was so beautiful. People said she was Wong's mistress, and whenever Peter looked at her, he felt that Enid and everything he ever did with Enid could never be so damningly wicked as he thought—not as long as there was a woman in the world so much more wickedly beautiful than Enid as Rainha was.

Returning to the Secret Island by a complicated walk in the woods that was sure to expose anyone who might be trailing him, Peter had been surprised to find Miss Drayton, or Margo as she liked to be called, waiting for him instead of Jerry. In some ways Margo was like Rainha or Enid because she too was beautiful and wicked. But in other ways she was the only one of these three special women he noticed whom he trusted as a friend. That was probably because she was forthright and uncovered in her wickedness and always talked to him straightforwardly without condescension. Then, too, she committed her sins for love of Jerry, whom Peter admired.

"Hello, scoop," she said. "Jerry's up your tree trying to photograph the Japs playing golf at the country club. How did it go?"

"I think I got some nice stuff," said Peter with breathless professionalism. "That Rainha is so pretty that composition hardly seems to matter."

"I hope it did matter."

"Oh, I watched out for it just the way Jerry said, but she *is* pretty."

"Sometimes you see altogether too much, even for a spy."

"Well, Jerry said he wanted a pretty girl in it."

"Did he!"

"Not any prettier than you. I didn't mean that. Just doing different things."

"Keep talking, scoop. You're in pretty deep."

"Please, Margo, don't tease me. You know how beautiful I think you are." He didn't mind at all if he blushed. He half hoped that the blush would coax her into a gentler mood. But she didn't respond as he had expected.

"Come off it, chum," she said. "That sort of conniving may work with your Rainhas and your Jap colonels but you're much too nice a boy to try it on me."

"I'm sorry," he said, flushing more deeply. "I do think you're pretty, though."

"Most men do. I'm not especially proud of it. I was born so." She said the last sentence out of the corner of her mouth, twisting up her face and switching into a cockney accent as she said it.

"Why did you do that?" he asked in surprise.

"It's something Mother used to say to me," she laughed. "Please, mum, I want a pound of butter." She contorted her face on one side. "What, mock me in me own shop?" She contorted it on the other. "Laws no, mum. I was born so." She spoke out of the first side. "Oh, indeed?" She spoke out of the second. "Yes, indeed!" She spoke out of the first. "Aaghow-oo."

Peter laughed.

"Margo, there's something I've been wanting to ask Jerry about, but I'd rather ask you because you're a woman and more my age."

"Your age!" She laughed. "That's even more conniving and oily than the last thing you said."

"I mean, you're more of a tomboy and you say things straight out, not squidgy and sentimental like other grown-up women."

"All right, I'll take it as a compliment. What's on your mind?"

"Well, I have a girl friend—" the words he had prepared began to slip away from him. "I . . . I have this girl I spend time with and her father's a Nazi and I'm scared of telling on you all because she might trick it out of me."

Margo looked surprised and thoughtful. "You're a little precocious, Peter. But I can see why you have a girl friend. What's her name?"

"Enid Larsen."

"Is she pretty?"

"Not like you. She's blond and she has freckles but she has a high forehead and a straight nose and wonderfully sunny eyes and, and—well, she looks nice," he ended lamely.

"How long have you known her?"

"Since before the war."

"Have you been kissing her?"

Peter blushed.

"Since before the war," he repeated more softly.

"That's a long time. Kisses are exciting."

"Yes!" he said intensely. It was a great relief to find that Margo, who was so pretty herself, understood and considered it natural.

"Have you done much more than just kiss her?"

"Some things more," he said, squirming.

"You haven't been going to bed with her or anything, have you?"

"Oh, no!" he exclaimed. "At least not the way I think you mean, not completely." He stared intently at the pine needles on the ground and wondered why he was being so truthful.

"That's an awfully stretchy word, 'completely.' You mean you haven't been in a bed with her or you haven't been in bed with her naked or you haven't actually done anything to her naked to have a baby or what the hell do you mean, Peter?"

"We've never both been naked at once," he said, resentful and almost inaudible. Why hadn't he asked Jerry? Jerry wouldn't have cared about all the details.

"I see. One of you gets undressed and the other doesn't and then you lie around petting, is that it?"

"Sort of like that."

"Well, if you want my opinion, that's one of the most ridiculous games for a boy your age that I ever heard of!"

"I know," said Peter. "But for me it's not really a game."

"Why don't you stop it, then?"

"I can't."

"Can't or won't?"

"Both. I guess I don't want to because of lust and I can't because I love her too much not to do what she asks."

"You know what's going to happen, don't you? One of these fine mornings you're going to wake up having gone whole hog. Then it will be ten times as hard to stop. And if this girl is as foolish as she sounds you may end up having a child and regretting it ever afterward."

"She isn't foolish," said Peter. "She keeps control of herself."

"That shows how much you know about it, chum! Petting is just as exciting for girls as it is for boys. Simply because she's shown more strength of character than you have so far doesn't mean she'll be able to hold off a great big self-indulgent hypocritical baby like you forever."

Peter couldn't help feeling a twinge of pride and pleasure in the midst of his shame. He hadn't thought of himself that way, nor of Enid's having a hard time resisting him.

"She's older than I am," he said dubiously. "It's her sixteenth birthday party the day after tomorrow."

"So much the worse. The older she is the more likely she is to want some real sex instead of just petting."

"No, she isn't like that!" he said, shocked. "She talks about how she's going to be a man-eater and I used to think sometimes that she *was* a Nazi bitch and only using me for practice. But she isn't really. I mean, if she's practicing, it's not for real life but only for another game. Everything for her is a game. It's because she reads novels and gets silly ideas from them."

"Well, I don't know your girl friend, Peter, and if you're bent on getting in trouble, come to Jerry first and he'll give you something to wear so at least you won't make her pregnant. But I warn you, if Enid's a normal, romantic girl who reads novels, a tumble in bed won't be a game: it will be a much harder thing for her to forget than for you. It isn't only that the physical results can be so dire; the emotional ones are equally bad. And if you're any sort of a man and you really love her and don't just think so because it seems like a good excuse, then you won't subject her to it."

Peter flushed with shame and anger. It didn't seem that Margo was being completely fair and straightforward any more.

"I do love her! I wouldn't ever forget afterward! I'd be going to hell for her!"

"Oh, Peter, you hypocrite. You and your precious soul. Hasn't she got one too?"

"She doesn't even believe in God. That's why it's a game to her."

"What a comforting thought for you! Did you ever stop

171

to think that if she doesn't believe in heaven, then she has to get everything she wants on earth? And if you spoil earth for her, what will she have left?"

"She'll have *me*," he whispered fiercely. "And it won't spoil anything for her." Why did Margo seem so excited and unfriendly and unlike herself?

"No, you're so wonderful. It won't spoil anything for her until you have what you want and remember that she's a Nazi bitch and go off sanctimoniously to forget her and find someone else who has your kind of a soul. That's all it will spoil for her!"

"I wouldn't do any of those things!" said Peter angrily. "Not any more than Jerry would!"

"What's Jerry got to do with it?" she said, puzzled.

"I saw the pictures in his wallet of him and his wife and children in the States," said Peter, blundering onward. "Does that mean he's sanctimonious and spoiling life for *you* because he can't marry you?"

"I don't know what you're talking about. Whatever it is, it's certainly no affair of yours."

"I know he's your boy friend," insisted Peter savagely. "So Jerry's committing adultery for you and that's a mortal sin, but you're *Miss* Drayton, so you're only committing fornication and that's not so mortal. But you think he's spoiling your life!"

"I think nothing of the kind!"

"Because you're in love. You're both breaking rules because you're in love!"

"That's none of your damn business!"

There was a silence while they tried to collect themselves. He hadn't meant to say what he had and he hadn't thought about it much beforehand. It simply seemed to him that if she and Jerry also did damning things for the bittersweet of lust or love or whatever it was, then she ought to be more helpful and sympathetic. But now already he was beginning to regret his outburst. He had hurt her more than he wanted. She sat tailor fashion in the pine needles with her head bowed and her fingers pressed against her forehead. If she cried he didn't know what he would do. But after a while she raised her face dry-eyed and discouraged-looking.

"All right, Peter," she said. "Perhaps I tried to be an adult and act superior and give stuffy advice the way Jerry says I shouldn't. But even if it didn't work, I want you to remember that Jerry and I are more than twenty years older than you and Enid. We have less of life left to gamble with. In fact, we have only this little bit of time on Panoc. Call it make-believe or wickedness if you want, but it can't spoil much. All it can do is make our past lives seem less unhappy when we come to look back on them."

"I'm sorry," said Peter miserably. "I wanted to say something that would hurt you, but I didn't really mean it."

"What if you did? I wouldn't blame you. I can remember the time when I resented grownups having all the pleasant things and doing them without worrying about getting in trouble. But I'm afraid in some ways you're more advanced than I was. That's the trouble with advising people: they're always slightly different and the better you like them the harder it is."

"Actually, I'm glad you said what you did. I hadn't meant to ask about sex, but you told me some things I'd never realized."

"What you really wanted to ask was whether you should go on working for us, wasn't it? I guess that was honest and self-sacrificing of you, but in a way it was a silly question, too. We *have* to depend on you. You're the only person in Abanao who can help us, and you already know more than enough to get us caught and beheaded if you start being indiscreet."

"I might not be so likely to talk about it if I weren't actually doing it," said Peter.

"Talk to your Enid, you mean? I think that's less of a risk than talking to Colonel Kori. And Jerry trusts your judgment in dealing with *him*."

"But I can feel hardhearted with Colonel Kori."

"Not like Enid, who wraps you around her finger?"

"She's a different world. Sometimes I forget about the war completely."

"Well, is she really a Nazi? Is she German?"

"No, she's Swedish, but her father is a Nazi."

"Does she think she loves you?"

"I don't know. She's sort of loving sometimes and other times she's just teasing."

"Well, I think you're clever enough and forewarned enough to handle her. I doubt that she would ever accept the job of collecting evidence to get you arrested anyway. But if she does seem to be prying someday, ask her why straight out. You'll be able to tell if she's been put up to it."

There was a rustling of leaves in the outer tunnel.

"That's Jerry," she said. "Next time we come I'll see that he gives you something to wear just in case. They're such nasty little things, maybe they'll shock some sense into you."

"You won't tell him all the details, will you?" begged Peter, ashamed.

"No, I won't need to."

"Thank you. I'm awfully sorry about the things I said."

Before she could answer, Jerry emerged from the mouth of the second tunnel. He was wearing clothes camouflaged with splotches of green and brown paint, and sprigs of leaves were pinned all over his cap. He was pleased about the pictures he had taken from the tree and pleased and businesslike about the ones Peter had taken in the casino.

"Great stuff," he said when Peter had made his report. "Couple more session like this one and we'll have Abanao pretty well wrapped up. Figured out any way we can photograph Kori and Miyanaku yet?"

"Well, two weeks from Tuesday is Emperor Meiji day. Camelia has to take down her stall because the Japs are going to put up a platform in the market and make speeches. I thought if you'd show me how to use one of your long lenses I might get Wong to build a shed or some sort of place where I could hide and still see up on the casino roof."

"That sounds pretty good, Peter. It sounds great if it's safe."

"Why don't I ask Wong what he thinks?"

"All right. Then if he thinks he can really hide you, pace off the distance from the casino to Camelia's stall so that I can give you the right lens."

"First I'll find out for sure if Colonel Kori is going to make a speech."

"Good. I'll be here two weeks from today, usual time. Don't worry if I'm late. Now that the rains have let up, Kori has so many patrols on the trails it's hard to get places on time."

"You going to stop at the charcoal burner's hut tonight?"

"Maybe, but it's better for you not to know. We'll give you fifteen minutes to clear the area before we start."

"All right. Good-by. I hope you come with him again next time, Margo."

"I'll try," she said. "Be good, won't you."

Peter ducked into the tunnel and scrambled out to the clearing. Here he paused. He was supposed to get going so that just in case Margo and Jerry were picked up he wouldn't be too close by. But he had to hear what Margo said to Jerry. Having told her his shame he felt both better and worse. The trouble was that no one could ever really help you if you couldn't help yourself. And he hated the thought of Jerry's knowing how weak and undignified he was.

He could hear Jerry describing how the Japs played golf. Then Margo said, "I had an awful time while you were gone. Peter confessed to me that he's practically sleeping with some Swedish wench and—"

"Peter?" exclaimed Jerry. "I don't believe it. He's pulling your leg."

"No, he was too ashamed of himself. That is, he was until I told him to give it up. Then he showed his stubborn streak, and I made the mistake of lecturing him and getting worked up over a lot of pious old saws. He saw what a fraud I was and finally he got angry and lashed out at me for making you an adulterer. God! I still feel dreadful. It was like being Hamlet's mother."

"Poor sweetie," he heard Jerry say. "You should have patted him on the tail and wished him well. That's all he deserved." There was a silence, and Peter waited until it was over before he crawled away.

"Aren't I committing adultery just as much as you are?" Margo asked as Peter crossed the clearing.

"Of course you are, sweetie, but it's such a big, meaningless word. We have a date to keep with General Sam."

Peter was away in the woods before the end of the next sentence. They didn't believe in sin. They didn't believe he was doing anything wrong except making himself unhappy. They just didn't know! But what a crybaby he was to have made Margo unhappy too! What a foolish crybaby to ask for help in something that was between him and God.

That night there was an uproar of shooting and shouting soldiers and squealing tires which lasted for almost two hours. The explosions sounded nearby, and Peter lay awake until morning wondering if Jerry and Margo had been involved in it. After breakfast when he went to the tailor's to try on a gray flannel jacket which he had ordered—secretly and extravagantly—for Enid's birthday party, he found out

175

that some guerrillas had ambushed a convoy of trucks near the top of the Vispayan road, practically under the noses of the Japs at the country club. The girls in the market were all afraid to talk about it except for Rosa, who, after spitting twice, said quietly, "Dthere was a big fight. Many Jap bastards killed." Then she spat again. "Pibe op our boys were taken also. Dthey say dthey will shoot dthem here in dthe market."

"When?" asked Peter.

"Who can tell?"

"Any of them Americans?"

"It is hard to pind out. Only twenty-pibe centabos a kilo, señora," she sang out loudly to a Spanish woman who was feeling the fancy white potatoes at the other end of her stall.

The execution took place the next morning. Peter went and watched it, though his mother forbade him and all the other released Americans had agreed to stay away. Peter had to make sure that Jerry wasn't one of the prisoners.

All five were Filipinos. They were brought into the market tied up like chickens. Behind them, soldiers carried in cheap pine coffins. The first was beheaded by the officer in charge of the killing. His sword was blunt or he didn't know how to use it. After the third stroke Peter hid his eyes. The second man was bayoneted by one of the common soldiers. The other three were machine-gunned. None of them acted especially patriotic but none of them cried out either, except the one who was bayoneted and that was only a strangled dying sound.

When Peter started home Colonel Kori was standing, watching the people, at the corner of the market place. He saw Peter and beckoned to him. Peter pretended not to notice and dropped his head, but as he started up the main street a soldier came up behind him and grabbed his arm and took him back to the colonel.

"Why didn't you come when I signaled to you, Peter?"

"I didn't see you," said Peter sullenly. "I didn't want to see you," he added, knowing that Colonel Kori valued him for his seeming truthfulness.

"You didn't like the execution, son?"

"It was filthy and cruel and uncivilized," he muttered.

"We have to be tough sometimes," said the colonel.

"Not that way!" burst out Peter. "It was like a servant we

176

had in China who poured kerosene on rats he caught and watched them run burning."

"I tried to stop it," said the colonel. "But they were Miyanaku's prisoners. Still, it may not do any harm."

"Maybe it will make some Filipinos scared of you but it will make them hate you more. An eye for an eye! A tooth for a tooth!"

"Nonsense. What did you do with your servant who burned rats?"

"Fired him."

"And I bet you never had another servant who burned rats."

"No, I don't think so."

"Because you fired the first one. Not being able to get another job as houseboy he probably took to stealing for a living and was killed by the police. After that the servant class was scared to burn rats near your house. But they didn't hate you or love you because of it. All right, that's your Scripture lesson for the day. Go home and think about it."

That afternoon Peter dressed in the woods. He put on his visiting trousers, a white shirt and tie, and the new flannel jacket that matched his trousers. As far as he could tell in his tiny pocket mirror he looked fairly neat and clean. He left his wagon with one of the soldiers at the check point just beyond the woods and gave him a whole peso to take care of it. After the execution he hadn't eaten any lunch and his stomach squirmed with emptiness and nervousness. Enid said she had told her father casually that she had seen Peter in the market and would like to invite him, so her father hadn't objected. But the birthday party was the first time Peter had gone to Enid's house when there was to be anyone else there, too. He didn't know who the other guests would be and he didn't want to look too childish to Enid if they were all men.

Enid's father opened the door when he knocked and Peter thought for a second that Mr. Larsen looked annoyed at the sight of him. Then he smiled broadly and said, "Oh, yes, you must be Enid's school chum. Go on inside and introduce yourself."

Mr. Larsen's smile was not a real smile, and Peter wondered how this man, with his fringe of hair, his shiny pate, his dark, gapped teeth, his jerky overprecise movements and his insincerity could be Enid's father. He went numbly into the living room. It was full of Jap officers: captains and lieu-tenants. And there in the middle was Enid. She had on a new dress: rusty brown with gold flecks on it that matched her hair. Her shoulders were naked and her hair fell down on them, gently curving on each side in a scroll over her collar-bones. When she saw Peter she came toward him and gave him one of her quick, sunny-shy smiles.

"You have a suit," she said when she was close. "You look nice."

Then she introduced him: Masaki, Hashimoto, Shinjuku, Anjiku, Ashi, Aki, Ito—the Japanese names blurred together in meaningless foreignness and discomfort. The soldiers clicked their boots and bowed and scraped their swords, and Peter nodded back at them more and more impatiently and curtly. He should never have come. Enid had already left him, and the lieutenant next to him was trying to talk to him.

"You are Gerruman?"

"No, I'm American," said Peter. "I'm a released mis-sionary."

"So?" said the lieutenant, and turned away.

A captain came up to Peter and said, "You are American boy?"

"Yes," said Peter.

"I am interested," said the captain. "You do not object to rivving under Japanese government?"

"I lived in Japan for years," said Peter.

"We have randed in Wisconsin," said the captain. "Soon orrul Americans wirrul rivv under Japanese government. Then you wirrul exprain to them it is not so bad."

"In Wisconsin?" asked Peter. He had heard this kind of nonsense from the soldiers at the check points. "That's a long way from the sea."

"So? From aeropranes we drop men everywhere. You think stirrul that America can gain the victory?"

"I'm an American," said Peter. "Of course I do."

"You are foowerish," said the Captain. "Your heart wirrul break for your native rand."

"Maybe. We'll see."

Before the captain could say anything more Mr. Larsen came to the entrance of the living room with another white man.

"Ladies and gentlemen, allow me to present Hauptman Kurt Hebel, military representative in Abanao of the Third

Reich. Heil Hitler!"

One Japanese captain returned the German's Nazi salute. The rest bowed politely while Peter stood unbending. A German, he realized numbly, had finally come. But it was too late, he told himself. Enid loved him now and wasn't interested in Nazi advisers. Besides, Captain Hebel wasn't young and handsome. He was plump and middle or late thirtyish. He had a white baby face and his hair was thinning. He presented himself to Enid and they talked German. She kept giggling because of the mistakes she made.

Amelia, the maid, served cakes and pastries and punch. There was aquavit on the tea trolley for anyone who wanted it. The Japanese officers, one after another, kept addressing polite but insulting questions at Peter.

*"Ich kann dich nicht verstehen,"* said Enid across the room. "If you wouldn't mind saying some things in English, I'm sure my German would soon come back to me."

"Is not goot, mine English," said the Nazi.

As soon as he'd eaten a little and been polite a lot to the Japanese around him, Peter got up and edged his way to the door.

Mr. Larsen was in the hall talking quite good Japanese, Peter thought.

"Thank you," said Peter. "It was a nice party."

"I'm sorry you can't stay longer," said Mr. Larsen. "It was nice of you to come."

Peter glanced over his shoulder and saw that Enid was still looking with all her attention at the Nazi.

"I have to be home," he said. Outside on the steps he waited a moment, thinking that Enid might still follow him out and say good-by. She didn't, so Peter returned to the check point, got his wagon, changed his clothes and went home.

"Was it a nice party?" asked his mother.

"So-so," he said. "Mostly foreigners."

## CHAPTER 13

The sheets were not as dry as Wong had said they'd be. Before light they had been damp and cold and numbing. Now, as the sun climbed, they were becoming steamy and tropical. Peter had been in the basket for at least two hours already, but that meant it was still only seven-thirty or eight. Another three hours probably before the speeches started. Peter wondered if he could stand it. It was a big oblong basket, the kind white people in the Orient called a *correy*. It was not the kind anyone usually kept laundry in, or fourteen-year-old boys either for that matter, but it did give him a little room to change the position of his legs when they fell asleep. And that was lucky because, doubled up as they had to be, they fell asleep often and seemed to be falling asleep oftener as time dragged on.

Cautiously he lifted the corner of the sheet which hung in front of his face and let in a little fresh air through the jagged hole Wong had torn open in the end of the correy. Through the hole he could see out over the brink of the flat concrete roof and across the market place to where the soldiers were still laying the floor on the speakers' platform. As long as no one was looking directly at him from in front, he was safe peering out. On the other three sides of the correy washlines of drying laundry curtained it off from anyone who might be up on the roofs of buildings roundabout.

The washerwoman was a cousin of Rosa's and the only person in the casino besides Wong himself who knew that Peter was there. The three of them—even though Wong ran the place—had crept up the stairs like thieves in the dark. The danger was that in nearly every room along the corridors was a girl with a Jap soldier. You could hear them grunting and giggling and you could smell the pleasant Japanese stench of sake and *shoyu* and pickles. Before the war, Wong said, the upstairs had been a real hotel, maybe not as good as Mr. Kahn's uptown, but good enough for respectable Chinese and Filipino businessmen. Now there weren't many businessmen, and Wong said this was the only way he could make the upstairs pay for itself. Girls were easy to find because so many were poor these days. From Mark Price's time only Rainha and a couple of others remained as proper casino entertainers. Peter wondered why Wong hadn't let Rainha know about his being on the roof in the basket. He wished she did know because then she might stop talking to him in the icy superior way she always did.

Boy, it was a lucky thing his mother didn't know where he was. Imagine trying to tell her that he'd spent the morning hiding in a laundry basket on a roof like this one! It sounded so funny that she probably wouldn't even believe him. What he had actually told her was that he was getting up early to deliver loads of freshly baked bread to the officers at the country club for their Meiji-day breakfast. And he didn't know whether she believed that either. He and she had had several arguments lately. She was bored from not going out much, he thought. Twice this week she had insisted on doing the marketing, but she could see as well as he could that she didn't get very good prices. Since Enid's birthday party she had asked him questions about *that Swedish girl*, too. But she was only guessing. And, what the heck, it was better to have her think he was visiting Enid than where he really was. Enid! She kept getting into his thoughts no matter how he tried to avoid her.

It was time to shift his position in the basket. He peered out through the hole and, seeing that the soldiers were not looking his way, he rolled himself carefully over the top of the camera onto his other side. The weight of the washing was considerable and the camera got in the way. The big lens on it made it so long, he had found, that he really had to scrunch himself up in order to get his eye down in front of the view finder. What a pity the long lens wasn't shortsighted enough to see the jagged basket work around the hole in the correy and photograph it as a frame for Colonel Kori when he started to rant and rave and boast and threaten and coax on that platform down there. When Panoc was liberated and the guerrillas could safely have names again, the pictures would appear in Jerry's magazine and Colonel Kori might see them.

A basket? he would say to himself. Of course! A laundry basket on one of the roof tops. I should have thought of that. But who could have taken pictures from a laundry basket? So? Yes. It must have been the American boy who brought me liquor and *canapés*. He really did know something after all. What a fool I was! What a fool he made of me!

Peter could see the colonel looking and cursing at the magazine in some air-raid shelter in Japan while Tokyo and Yokohama crumbled around him and a great American fleet stood offshore getting ready to land men for the final invasion. It was a glorious vision—and probably a silly one. Jerry himself said that the chances of getting the pictures to Australia were slim. It had to be in the next eight months or it would be too late. Another rainy season and the films—pack them with drying agents as carefully as he could—would be spoiled. And the boat Jerry was having built up there in the rain forest on the northeast coast still wasn't finished. The hull was complete but the fittings and calking and soaking up might take another month. Jerry had no idea how those strange, glass-hard, *lanau* woods would react to water. As for the voyage itself, even if the boat proved seaworthy, it might take three months or nine months; Jerry had no way of telling. But what a voyage! The idea of coasting down all the wild shore lines between Panoc and Australia—sailing by moonlight and hiding by day—seemed even better to Peter than being a guerrilla.

"Don't envy us yet," Jerry had said. "The eggs aren't hatched and the ridge isn't come to. We may not be able to stay alive for another month." Since the end of the rains and the attack at the top of the Vispayan Road, Colonel Kori had launched an all-out effort against the guerrillas. He had the hills crawling with men. He said he was planning expeditions into the northern rain forest itself. And worst of all, he had a half dozen or so planes flying for him now and they had begun to bomb barrios suspected of receiving the guerrillas during their marches back and forth from the north. For the first time, Peter was glad that his father was staying at the hideout with Mallard and the wounded instead of going out to do the actual walking and fighting.

If only Pete Wong could get more supplies to the guerrillas, they could fight back better. But that too was getting more difficult. Wong had sent Peter to Jerry twice lately with messages that had made Jerry swear with disappointment. Another time, just a week ago, Peter had disappointed the guerrillas himself. He had heard from Rosa that Wong wanted him and he had gone to the casino supposing that, as usual, he would take a case of liquor out to one of the rich Spanish families in North Valley and with it a small, mysterious package which he would give to a native who would stop him along the way. But when he got to the casino, Colonel Kori was there playing cards and drinking with Rainha. Wong was so suspicious of the colonel's dropping in that he gave Peter only the liquor and told him to scowl and shake his head at the native pickup man. As it turned out, the Japs at the North Valley check point didn't search Peter and so he had had to send the native away empty-handed for no good reason.

Although Peter wasn't supposed to know details of any of the deliveries, he felt fairly sure that the small ones he made himself were medicine. The big ones of canned goods or boots or ammunition were handled by Wong some other way. How, Peter didn't know, but he supposed that other Chinese businessmen in town helped him and that the goods were assembled at Wong's own home, which was up on the ridge in North Valley next to Mark Price's empty house. Here the guerrillas could approach through the woods from the other side of the ridge and carry away whatever Wong had for them without ever getting near a road or a street lamp. If that was the arrangement, it seemed to Peter that Wong should be able to supply the guerrillas with anything that was still available in the market, and except for ammunition there was still so much available in the market that Peter was puzzled by Jerry's recent disappointments. Of course, maybe it was simply a question of quantity. Peter didn't know how many groups Wong was supplying. Maybe some of Colonel Fleer's men—who were said to be fighting on in the south, though Fleer had surrendered—came to Wong too. So perhaps did Lindstrom and O'Connor, the two sugar men who had gone over the ridge that night Peter saw the bicycle troops. And maybe there were other groups. Maybe, too, Wong had some real reason to be scared, over and above Colonel Kori's coming to the casino to play cards with Rainha.

If Jerry went to Australia and there was no more photographing to do, and if Wong slowed down deliveries and there wasn't much to do for the guerrillas either, Peter would lose the excuses he made for his hardened heart and unswept mind. There would be nothing left to do but haul and hew and grind again to make ends meet, and nothing left to think but the long-postponed thoughts of religion and guilt and atonement. It would be the time of cinder blackness. The prospect was so full of gloom that there ought to be more he could do now to enjoy excitement while he still had it. But he could only peer out through the hole in the correy and watch the soldiers as they put up red and white bunting and draped the platform with ugly fried-egg flags. The market place was filling up with bustle and buying, with people who had come to get vegetables and go home patriotically early, and with people who had come unpatriotically to watch the show and listen to the lies and boasting. If only

Enid could be the same again—while he still had an excuse for sinning—the other parts of life would seem less bleak and uncertain, but since that awful day of the birthday party, she had gone as wrong as everything else. In the first miserable seventy-two hours he must have passed her house twenty-five times to look at the drawn blind on her window. It had often been drawn as long in the past and he knew that going by so often was something she would call "compromising and indiscreet," but he was forced to go by out of jealous fear and loneliness. Then on the fourth day when the blind was finally raised and he arrived as clean and dressed up and overjoyed as he could be for tea, she introduced him to the New Game.

"We can't play the way we have any longer," she announced at the door. "I've made up my mind it's silly and I'm too old for it. So if you want to come in and have tea and be my boy friend still, you must help me to practice conversation."

"Sure," said Peter hopefully. "We always talk a good deal anyhow."

"Not the way I mean. This has to be special polite conversation—not simply you and me talking but a man and a woman. You pretend you are a Frenchman with a vineyard like your grandfather. I'll pretend I'm in Paris for a year as part of my finishing. Papa says well-to-do Swedish girls always go to Paris or Berlin for a year when they are through school in Sweden."

"All right," said Peter, "I'll try."

When she had let him in and he had sat down in the living room and thought for a minute, he started off fairly well. "You are studying at the university, Mademoiselle?" he asked, mispronouncing the words slightly in the hope they would sound French.

"Oh, not seriously, Monsieur. A young woman comes to Paris mostly to learn the ways of love, you know."

"Is that so?" he said.

"You are probably here for the season," she said. "What do you think of it this year?"

"Well," he said dubiously, "I believe it's going to be a better year for red wine than for white."

"No, silly, not the growing season. I'm sure French lords have someone else to take care of the grapes. I meant the social season—the opera and the parties."

184

"Oh, well—I had a very nice time at the Costeaus' the other night." He felt pleased with himself for remembering a name that was French, but at once he realized that it was also Jerry's name and he wondered if the New Game was really finally that plan of Colonel Kori's that he had so often imagined and feared.

"Did you? I thought that dress Mrs. Costeau was wearing was impossible," she said, getting Jerry's name blessedly wrong. "I think those high necklines are ugly. I mean, don't you really prefer my dress?" she asked. She was wearing the new brown and gold one which she had got for her party.

"The gold is nice the way it matches your hair," said Peter.

She giggled. "Peter, I can't play unless you sound more French. You have to say it's ravishing or chic or something like that."

"*C'est formidable*," said Peter, remembering what his mother had always said when he'd told her something particularly fanciful as a small child. That pleased Enid, and soon, remembering phrases and turns of accent used by his mother, he had become quite good at pretending to be French. But Enid still didn't think he was social enough. She wanted him to admire her and flirt with her and he found it difficult to say things roundaboutly instead of blurting them out. Finally tea was over and she didn't offer him any aquavit, even though, having just bought the last bottle himself for ten pesos, he knew she had some hidden away.

"I suppose I better be going," he said, hoping that she might relax the new rules to make him stay longer.

"So soon?" she said, getting up. "What a pity. It's been charming."

She saw him to the door in relentless silence.

"Can't I kiss you once?" he begged in desperation.

"Only if you say such clever things that I can't help it. That's part of the New Game."

"Oh, go to the zoo and visit the gnu," said Peter, not very hopefully.

"What's the gnu?" she asked, puzzled.

"An animal with horns," he said.

Then for some reason her face lighted up and she giggled.

"A sort of antelope or goat, I think," he added proudly.

"Or man perhaps?" she asked archly. "Really, Monsieur, you must learn to trust me."

She pouted slightly and Peter, not knowing what she was
185

talking about, remained silent.

"All right, just once," she said.

He kissed her as long and well as he knew how, and though she still seemed to enjoy it, she stuck to her new rules and made him leave immediately afterward.

"Next time," she said, "you must be a Spanish man from Rio and you must try to be clever all the time."

Peter was about to ask whether people from Brazil didn't speak Portuguese, but he thought better of it and left—left the heartbreaking boredom of the New Game, knowing that he had failed at it miserably.

At home he asked his mother what a man with horns meant and she asked him in return where he had heard the expression.

"From Colonel Kori," he lied.

"That barbarious swine," she said, as she always did nowadays of Kori. "It means a man with a wicked, unfaithful wife."

And that was the way Peter felt it was. The cold stupidness of talking went on, and Enid no longer cared for him except as a fool she could practice with—not a man with horns but a boy and fool with horns.

Peter unclenched his fists in the correy and carefully changed his position under the damp, steamy sheets. People in the market below had begun to wait for the speeches to start, and the Jap soldiers were standing guard at the completed platform.

Yesterday, when the blind was up again, a new element had entered the New Game. While Peter was pretending to be a young English lord meeting Enid at a gambling place on the Riviera, someone knocked at the front door and when Enid went to see who it was, it was the German adviser. She had invited him to tea, too, and he had brought her a potted gardenia bush. Gardenias grew in every garden in Abanao, but Peter might have thought the Nazi had brought her a diamond necklace the way she carried on. After all—after everything—she was a Nazi bitch and Peter didn't have to feel sanctimonious about thinking it. During tea the conversation was even stupider than when Peter and Enid were pretending alone. Not that Peter entered into it. The German kept saying how nice it was to see an Aryan girl, *a true edelweiss of an Aryan girl*, and Peter said nothing at all except to answer questions when they were asked of him.

186

"How do you learn your education?" inquired the German.

"I study nights," said Peter, "but I'm falling way behind."

"Dhis is not goot for bote of you," said the German. "If Rommel vins dhis new battle at El Alamein as ve know he must und if Paulus takes Stalingrad before dhe end of dhe mont as he cannot fail to do, it vill be a long war. Our positions in Egypt und on Volga vill be impregnable. Dhe Fuehrer vill have achieved what he meaned to do. Naturlich only a stalemate can come of such a situation, howaber it vill be called war still. It vill endure. Dhat is vhy in my opinion, you must return to Sveden, Enid."

"I'd like to, but Papa can't save enough money right now."

"Vell, you must bote find some means to attend school or you vill become dummkopfs of no culture or standing."

"I'm not so pessimistic about the war situation as you are," said Peter.

"Ach, vhat do you know? All dhat you hear from bote sides is propaganda. You must be able to see intelligence reports to know vhat is happening. Und I tell you it vill be a long war, ten years at dhe least."

"Fiddlesticks!" said Peter.

"You must not talk about it, either of you," said Enid. "You are on different sides and I find it tiresome to hear you both being so patriotic. I'm sure Kurt is right, but that makes no difference."

"You are absolutely correct, edelweiss. I apologize."

Not long afterward the German stood up to go.

"Won't you stay for a glass of aquavit?" she asked.

"No, dhank you, it is to a drinking that I must go. Howaber, I vill see you soon, I hope."

He clicked his heels and handed her an envelope. She tore it open and looked pleased.

"You vill do me dhe honor?" he asked.

"I don't think I have anything else that evening," she said, and paused a second as if thoughtful. "No, I definitely do not."

"Vonderful," he said. "I vill say *auf Wiedersehen*, then." He added a *good-by* to Peter, clicking his heels, and went out.

"Are you going to a party with him?" asked Peter jealously.

187

"Maybe," she said. "You better leave now before Papa comes."

"Aren't you even going to kiss me?" he asked.

"Oh, Peter, can't you see how silly it is now?"

"Only once," he said, writhing inwardly at his own stubborn humility.

"All right." She kissed him quite nicely and pushed him out the door. The shame of his awkwardness and pridelessness, even now in the privacy of the correy, made him blush and twitch like a beggar. If he had any self-respect he wouldn't go near her. She would soon get tired of that Nazi, with his cocksure correctness and his silly heel-clicking compliments. Then she would want Peter to come back and play the Old Game, and if he had any pride he would wait until she did.

A sudden increase in the market noises and a tramping of soldiers' boots made Peter cautiously lift the corner of the sheet and look out again. At almost the same moment he heard Wong's voice behind him.

*"Goran nasai, dare mo nai,"* said Wong awkwardly. "See, there's no one." Peter heard the sheets on the lines thwacked as if with a gun butt. Then he heard the dragging of boots. It must be a soldier walking about on the roof making sure no one was there to shoot or look down on the speakers below. When the boots came close to the correy Peter held his breath. A blow struck him in the side and, suppressing a gasp, he realized that the soldier had prodded his gun butt into the correy of laundry. But there was nothing more.

*"Ikei sh'ta!"*—"Go below," commanded the soldier, and Peter could hear the two of them tramping their way downstairs to the street.

There had hardly been time to feel frightened and there was no time now to enjoy the feeling of having squeaked through. By the time Peter had focused the long lens and adjusted the stop and time dials according to Jerry's instructions, Colonel Kori had begun speaking. Peter was so busy watching for the right gestures and expressions that the speech was over without his knowing what Colonel Kori had said. But he thought he had taken some pictures which showed Kori looking as cruel and cold and hypocritical as he was. Colonel Miyanaku spoke longer and wasn't as interesting to photograph. He made no guestures and his long, earnest, severe face had no expressions. Peter took only three

188

pictures of him and heard every word that he said. Mostly he just said that Japan had conquered the Philippines for keeps and the Filipinos better behave better.

As soon as the two colonels had marched away from the podium and Peter had put the cap on the snout of the long lens, the correy was dragged across the floor to the top of the stairs and Rosa's cousin pulled the damp sheets off him. He scrambled into the stairway, hid the camera in the old graham-cracker box in which he carried it, thanked the washerwoman and went downstairs to Wong's bedroom on the second floor to give his report and check out. The corridors upstairs were deserted and smelled stale. Probably the girls who were supposed to clean them had had to be outside that morning listening to the speeches.

Peter was about to knock on Wong's door when he heard Rainha's quiet, icy voice inside.

"I don't care about your damn American friends, sweetypie. Did they invite me to the country club in the old days? Did they ever ask you to join, you poor Chinaman? All right, no! So any Jap *binnibai* who invites me now is fine. I go with him."

"*No, leche da cabron!* You don't go"—"no, by the milk of the whore," swore Wong in corrupt local Spanish. "Not if you want to stay my girl and work here. You go with that policeman, I don't know you. I don't even rent you a room to defile yourself in."

"All right, Peão," she said, snapping her icy voice at him with special precision. "I *am* going. Get a new woman to run your second-class house and stick to the white bosses like a yellow peão, but *I* am going."

Peter was standing on the hinged side of the door, and when Rainha stormed out through it, it banged against him without her seeing he was there. He waited several full minutes and then knocked.

"Come!" Wong was watering a small indoor tree of ornamental oranges and his hand was steady—just as if he were as calm and lazy as always.

"You get good pictures?" he asked with no more than a glance at Peter.

"I think so. Jerry asked me to thank you and tell you these will be the last."

"Good, and I want you to tell Jerry to tell Sam that I'm through for a while too. They can have the big order tomor-

189

row night but that's all. Maybe I'll get in touch with you again sometime, but for now I've had it."

"But . . ." started Peter.

"Don't argue, kid. We have to lie low, both of us. You ought to understand, so tell it to Jerry. You don't come here. You don't ask Rosa to come here. And if I ever think it's safe again, I'll let you know."

"I can't tell him just that," said Peter.

"Sure you can. Good-by, kid, that's all."

Peter went down the stairs knowing that the bottom had fallen out of his life and trying to keep his thoughts straight. Rainha was going to the country club with a Jap and Wong was not going to make any more deliveries except the big one tomorrow night. Those were the two things he had to tell Jerry, but there were other things he had to reason out to himself. Why was Rainha going to the country club? Because there must be a big Meiji-day party there tonight. Why had Enid received an invitation from Hauptmann Kurt Hebel, the Nazi? It wasn't to go with him to one of the old movies which had started playing again at the cinema. Nor to meet a few of his friends at a small party. No, this was a Jap Meiji-day ball, a big drunken dress occasion and Enid would be the only Aryan edelweiss—the only white geisha—in the entire hall.

With concentration Peter remembered where in the woods he had planned to leave his wagon and what mixed-up route he had decided to take to the Secret Island with the case of camera. Putting all else out of his mind, he executed his plan as carefully and precisely as he knew how. If this was to be his last assignment, he *ought* to carry it out extra well. If there was danger, as Wong said, he *had* to carry it out extra well.

When Peter had crawled into the Inner Keep on the island, he stood up into the muzzle of Jerry's rifle.

"You forgot to whistle," said Jerry.

There was a bird—Jerry called it a whippoorwill, but neither of them had ever seen it—which had a call you could imitate perfectly if you could whistle high enough. Beginning on the fourth line above the top of the treble clef—more than two octaves above middle C—you whistled a G-sharp, then a short F and a long-drawn-out G-natural. It was a good way of identifying yourself, but they had been careless about using it lately.

"Wong says no more deliveries for a while," announced Peter. "Partly he's just upset because Rainha is going to the Jap celebration at the club tonight and he and she had a big fight about it, but I think he really means it too."

Jerry looked at Peter and shook his head. "Everybody's jumpy and nervous," he said. "Everybody but Peter. Make you a general and we'd have won this war months ago." He put an arm over Peter's shoulder and jostled him gently.

"Hey, quit it, Jerry. You know I'm just as scared as anybody, and it's awful gloomy to think of everything coming to an end like this."

"I know. Well, maybe if you lie low for a while, the pressure will ease up and you can get back into business. What's the story on Rainha? Just because she goes to a Jap party, does that mean she's turning informer?"

"Oh, no!" said Peter. "She's mad right now, but she's really very cool and sensible and grown up. Besides, I'm not sure she knows much. She didn't know about me being on the roof this morning."

"Thank God for that," said Jerry. "You think it's safe for you to stay in town? Or shall I take you to your father?"

Peter's heart leaped. Before he could say anything he remembered his mother and sister and Enid—Enid alone and trying to flirt her way through, surrounded by hundreds of Jap soldiers.

"Would you take Mother and Jeanette, too?" he asked.

"No, they're innocent and safe, and I could never get them past Kori's patrols. I'm just asking you. If you believe there's real danger of your being arrested, I'll take you with me."

"Oh, I don't think there's that kind of danger yet. And I couldn't leave Mother and Jeanette anyway."

"Good. I didn't think there was, but I had to hear you say so yourself, General."

"I got some terrific pictures of Colonel Kori, I think," said Peter, quickly changing the subject. "Miyanaku wasn't so interesting so I only took three shots of him. The last ones are still in the camera. This is the exposed roll and here's the one I didn't use."

"Thank you. You know, when I get back to the States, Peter, I'm going to spread your name around. So keep notes on what you see and hear during the rest of this war, understand? When it's over, I can turn them into money for you."

"Aren't I going to see you again?"

"I don't know. I may be here at the usual time two weeks from today, but don't worry if I'm not. Our boat's almost ready and if it's moderately watertight I'm going to get started. I've put your Christmas bonus in a separate tin box underneath the one with the receipts. I thought you'd be better off not carrying it around with you. Besides, you shouldn't open presents before Christmas."

"Thank you," said Peter in a tight, quiet voice.

"Here's this month's salary and our paper of agreement."

Peter took the money and they both signed the paper. While they were digging up the tin box to put it inside, Jerry said, "Oh, Margo sent you a present, too. She wouldn't tell me what was in it, but she said you knew and you didn't have to wait until Christmas if you needed it before then."

The moist feeling of saying good-by to Jerry grew dry in Peter and turned to mud and dust. Margo's present must be those things he would never need for not making Enid pregnant. He stuffed it quickly into his pocket.

"Don't you want to open it now?" asked Jerry. "I'm curious to see what it is."

"No, it's really something for my girl friend," he said coldly.

"Margo told me about her," said Jerry. "I was surprised. I thought with all your other excitements, you wouldn't need a girl too. In fact, I thought, making you an agent and all, we'd solved the prehistoric problem of adolescence once and for all."

"I guess not," said Peter impenetrably.

"Have I said something wrong?" asked Jerry. "After all, I have a son your age. I'm interested in these things."

"It's private," said Peter.

"Okay, okay. But remember: real love is never slavery. Otherwise it wouldn't last. It would end up in civil war and an emancipation proclamation."

"I'll remember."

"You don't want my full five-dollar lecture?"

"Not when everything is breaking up, Jerry. Margo already gave me a lot of advice about girls. Besides, Enid's taken up with a German Army captain and I'm going to be too busy working, now that you've gone, to see her even if she wants me to."

"Okay. Then take good care of your mother and sister, huh?"

"I will. And you give my love to Dad, please."

"I always do, even when you don't mention it," said Jerry with his old look of wry amusement.

"How's Mallard?"

"The same."

"And Margo and General Sam?"

"They're fine. Stop hanging around asking questions."

"Sorry," said Peter.

As they shook hands Jerry said, "You remember how to act if they do pick you up and grill you?"

"I think so."

"Be a child. Don't admit to anything, don't understand anything and above all don't try to argue or be reasonable. Be as spoiled and picked-on as you can ever remember being with your mother. Throw tantrums if you like. Don't overdo it, of course, but don't forget either that they think you're a child and you can go pretty far. Being a child is a tremendous weapon to have."

"I won't forget."

"Good. I'll give you five minutes' start. And I'll see you in New York if I don't see you in two weeks. Right?"

"Right," said Peter. Feeling like a crab at the bottom of a very black ocean, he scuttled off through the tunnel.

After doing the chores and eating supper and reading to Jeanette while his mother caught up on her journal—the journal for his father, which, though he hadn't the heart to tell her, would be read by no one but her now—Peter went to bed and tossed and turned. He saw the Japanese dancing Western dances. He saw them watching with hungry, drunken eyes while Enid waltzed with the Nazi. He saw the Nazi asleep with his head on the table and Enid invited to dance by a polite Japanese lieutenant. Then he saw the other Japs cutting in more and more frequently until Enid looked scared.

Peter got up, slipped into his clothes and out the window. He knew he could do nothing: it was the first really pointless, childish adventure he had indulged in for a long time.

There were guards all along the road around the golf course and he circled through the woods almost up to Camp Dewey before he found a place where three of them had clustered together to have a drink of sake. Quickly he crossed the road and headed out into the wide-open moonlight on the greens. He crawled a lot and made pretty good use of the hillocks and rough between the fairways, but he didn't feel that it mattered much if he was seen and shot at. That was silly! The idea that getting killed would make Enid love him forever was pure wishful nonsense. He approached the club house more cautiously. There was more planting here, but also some paths to cross and some officers out smoking from the party. Finally he established himself in a group of plumbago bushes near the club house veranda and lay down to wait. It was chilly and he felt as numb and sleepy as he had that morning in the correy of damp sheets. The music inside certainly sounded civilized enough. It was all pleasant Viennese waltzes and American hits from the old days.

Peter awoke from stupor because he thought he had heard a familiar voice. The moon was setting and he must have slept for hours.

"You can't beat the Americans," said the voice. "They're too well meaning and sure of their own goodness, too damn careful and hard-working and cool-headed. But I think it's nice of you to try. While you're ahead of the game it's nice to think you'll continue to win. And it's nice to enjoy yourself."

Peter looked away from the sinking moon and up to the veranda to identify the funny-sounding, familiar, dream-confused voice. But in the low, mottled moonlight he could see only that it was a woman—a rather white woman.

"Don't you feel the same way, college boy?" went on the voice. "You're so almost American like me you ought to feel the same way."

"Sometimes like now I do and sometimes I feel so Japanese I know we will win. I'm a son-of-a-bitch when I feel really Japanese, you know." Peter couldn't see the man speaking because of the shadows, but the voice had the same slurred and familiar dreamlike quality as the woman's.

"Everyone I like is a son-of-a-bitch. They have white tongues and yellow tails. You know what?"

"No, what?"

"You'll have me shot for the way I talk. First I gotta dance another one of those funny stiff dances."

The woman's face withdrew into the shadows and Peter saw their backs silhouetted against the light at the door leading into the ballroom. The music inside was Japanese now and Peter could tell from the occasional guttural screams and stamps that the officers were taking turns doing old Japanese story dances. Had he seen the woman and the Jap or was it a dream? If it was real the Jap would be Colonel Kori. But Colonel Kori spoke more clearly and he would never take a moon-white, funny-talking girl like that to a dance when he had his own correct, attractive geisha from Japan. Peter shook his head repeatedly, trying to get the sleep and the moon out of it.

After a while as he squatted tailor-fashion in the plumbago bushes and took healthy deep breaths to wake himself up, he was attracted by the sudden flare of a cigarette lighter near the door to the ballroom. Again it was a man and a woman. They lighted their cigarettes with faces close together so that he couldn't see them and brought the two glowing ends over to the railing where the sparks got tapped off into the bushes below. The woman was the first to speak.

"I don't want to go back in there, Kurt."

Peter had no need to shake any more moon out of him. It was Enid: wakefully, definitely and at last.

"Is not polite," said the German, "but if you vant to go home, I take you."

"Take me to where you live, Kurt."

"In dhe mittel night, edelweiss? You should not even dhink of it. Vhat are you? *Sechzehn?*"

"It doesn't matter. I'll be your mistress. I want to go back to Germany with you next year when you are circulated."

The German laughed. "Not circulated, edelweiss, r-r-rotated."

"You think I'm just a little girl?"

"Vell, I don't know. But I dhink I could find more experience in some of dhese girls at dhis dance."

"Kiss me."

"*Schlecterdings!*" exclaimed the German, laughing. "Sure, I vill kiss you."

Peter dug a small hole in the soil among the plumbago roots.

When they had finished kissing, the German said, "You are a bad girl. Have you also slept vidh men?"

"Not yet," said Enid. "But I'm sure I'd be good at it. I have a passionate nature."

"*Sogleich* I take you back to your papa! In two yahrs come to see me vhen I have become less honorable. You kiss

195

like vun of Hitler's *Jugend*."

He led her down from the porch.

"I am a man, edelweiss, und you vill find if you kiss men like dhat, you vill make dhem crazy soon enough."

"Won't you take me back to Germany?"

"I have no money. It vould be easier to treat you wrong and dhen run avay."

They passed out of hearing down the path to the gate of the country club. By the time Peter had worked his way to the edge of the road . . . and found an opportunity to cross to the other side . . . and run through the woods to Enid's house . . . and stolen out to the roadside again by her front door, the Nazi was walking off down the street whistling a hymn tune, "A Mighty Fortress Is Our God." Peter waited until the light went off behind the blind in Enid's room and then went home himself. Nothing had happened. All bad things were a dream. Enid was a child like he was. Enid was his child no matter what she did, and as soon as he learned to talk better he would be as much of a man as she was a woman—maybe more. He picked up a handful of pine needles and threw them into his face in drowsy ecstasy. They and the aging night smelled good. When he reached home, he quieted himself, crawled in at the window and got in bed in his clothes. Not much time could be left for sleeping before morning came. There was a sudden noise in the darkness and he heard his mother's voice.

"I have been praying for you here by your bed, Peter. Where have you been?"

## CHAPTER 14

Peter's mother would not be put off. She turned on the light and kept him from his sleep with questions and worrying.

"I've been doing an errand for the guerrillas" was what he blurted out in his first fright. But when he realized that the lie was worse than the truth, he gave way to numb resentment and stopped caring what he said as long as it was false.

"All right, I've been out seeing a girl," he said.

"That Swedish trollop?" said his mother.

"No, one of the girls downtown. She entertains the Japs at Pete Wong's gambling den. Boy, you ought to smell the *shoyu* and pickles in the corridors down there. You know how I love *shoyu*."

"What *are* you talking about?" she asked, trying to be calm and sarcastic. "Have you been drinking sake again or are you trying to be rude?"

"I guess I'm drunk."

"I can't smell anything."

"That's because I got it all through the nose. I was really up at Camp Dewey sneaking aquavit under the fence to Mr. Newcombe. As I passed it in to him I took a sniff of each bottle to make him mad."

"Peter, stop it!" she said, shaking him. But he had opened the closets of his mind to a coal chute and it felt good to rattle the contents out into the street in a cloud of dust and confusion.

"Actually, I stole some strawberries and canned cream from Camelia in the market," he said. "I thought it would be safest if I ate them at night in the woods."

"Is that what you really did?"

"No, if you really want to know, I was just delivering a load of those things men wear so as not to make women pregnant."

"Peter!" she said, shocked and angry. "How dare you talk that way? As if you didn't disgust me enough without trying to do it on purpose."

"Well, you know that Nazi German who came here a couple of weeks ago to teach Colonel Miyanaku how to waltz? He said he had to have them at once, tonight, and I had a hard time getting them for him."

Taunting his mother with cold preposterous notions that crept onto his tongue, he felt more drowsy and detached all the time. Finally his mother saw she could not make him unhappy and gave up.

"Your head is full of wickedness," she said, turning off the light. "You're lying to God as well as to me. I only hope you don't have to marry some native girl."

"Maybe I already have."

"Oh, Peter, try to pray before you sleep. Then in the morning perhaps you will be able to talk more honestly."

He must have slept better than his mother because when he awoke the sun was no longer shining in his window—but already gone past up into the radiant center of the day—and his mother was on her knees again beside the bed.

"Have you been here all night?" he asked groggily.

"No, *mon fils*. I have one or two better things to do. You have a sister, you know."

"I'm hungry," he said.

"Are you ready to tell me the truth yet?"

"I didn't do anything bad."

"Then you can tell me about it."

"No, I can't. I've promised to keep it secret. That's why I had to tell you so many crazy things last night."

"Those crazy things as you call them were awful lies. They worried me as much as anything you could have done. Merely to think them shows how wild you're growing. If it were normal times I could send you to boarding school, but since I can't, I've made up my mind to go down to the police office today and ask for us to be put back in the concentration camp."

"You won't really do it. You'll back down again."

"You have a lot to learn, *mon fils*. I should have done it months ago. It would be better to have you thin and sick than the way you are."

"I'll go to Colonel Kori, then," said Peter. "I'll tell him you're crazy worrying about Dad. He doesn't want me sent back to camp because he thinks I may be useful to him outside, so he'll see to it that your application gets lost."

"Have you become a traitor too, along with everything else?"

"Of course not," he said coldly.

"What do you call it when you go to the Japanese and tell them your mother is crazy?"

"Well, if you do such crazy things . . ." he began.

"No, *mon fils*, it is you who are crazy. You who are endangering your soul. And only for bread. For bread alone!"

She began to weep silently.

"It's silly doing that," he said.

"How can I make you listen to me? If your father were here you'd act differently."

"Stop crying," he said.

"How can I help it? I can't control you."

"Don't cry," he pleaded. But she continued to sob in silence.

198

"All right, go to the police station," he shouted. "I'll go see Colonel Kori."

He put on his clothes and she remained by the bed weeping.

"Mother," he finally said softly. "I promise I did nothing bad. I have to meet the guerrillas sometimes and I have to see Colonel Kori sometimes. Sometimes I do see Enid, too, but will you stop crying. Please, Mother. Please stop."

"Where were you last night?"

"I was at the country club—outside the country club listening to the people talk on the porch. I had to find out something and I finally did, but I went to sleep in the plumbago bushes for a while first. That's why it took me so long and I was home so late."

"Did the guards know you were there?"

"Of course not," he said indignantly.

"So they might have found you asleep and shot you. I don't know that this isn't another lie, Peter, but if it's the harmless thing you really did last night, it's all the more reason why we must go back to camp at once."

"You don't believe the truth," he said bitterly. "And if you did, you'd still want to do the same dumb, sheepish thing and go back to camp. I ought to know better than to tell you the truth."

She didn't answer, so he went to the kitchen and choked down some rice and coconut milk. When he had finished eating he went back and found she had gotten up off her knees and gone to her own room and was putting street clothes on Jeanette.

"Looks like I really do have to go see Colonel Kori," he said.

"Stop talking about it, then, and do it," she replied. "Jeanette and I are going out too."

"Maybe I can get him to have you put back in and me left out. Then I won't have to worry so much about money," he said.

She looked at him angrily and scornfully and said nothing.

Peter waited outside near the woodpile until he saw his mother actually come from the house with Jeanette and go up the stone steps and turn in the direction of town. She looked back once, by the corner of the hotel, and Peter seized the opportunity to start out purposefully across the wooded hill toward Colonel Kori's house. This was much

199

farther than she had ever carried a threat before and he waited in the outskirts of the pines to make sure that she didn't turn back. But she didn't, and as he continued on his way, he became less and less sure that she was bluffing. He was bluffing and he knew it. He would go back into camp before admitting to Colonel Kori that there were chinks of weakness and disagreement in any American family, much less his own. If he still had important work to do, it might be different. But even then, to explain why his mother wanted to go back to camp, he would have to have a likely story, and he couldn't think of a likely story which didn't contain some element of truth in it that might implicate someone in the knowing eyes of Colonel Kori. His mother had to be bluffing! It would be so silly to get put back in camp by a mother when he had worked so hard and succeeded so well in having the money to stay out. Oh, sure, she was bluffing. She was too scared of the Japs to go near the police station anyway.

As Peter turned over the chances and thought of all the hundreds of excuses she could use to back down, he came to Enid's house. The blind was already up. Well, why not? It was already afternoon. He had breakfasted in the afternoon like Jerry in the hotel. And if he had no important work to do and wasn't really going to see Colonel Kori, he might as well visit Enid and have his last taste of the bitter in the bittersweet. At this very moment his mother might be asking to go back to hunger and imprisonment. He might not see Enid again for years. He might never see her again on earth. He went to the door and knocked and Enid opened it. She was still in pajamas.

"Oh, Peter! Papa just this moment left. Go and wait in the bathroom while I give Amelia the afternoon off. I'll have to be subtle about it so don't get too impatient. It may take a while."

Waiting in the bath behind the shower curtain he heard the murmur of voices and felt foolish. Was this any way to spend his last hours of freedom? He could be out in the woods or up his own giant pine tree or saying good-by to Camelia and Rosa or burying his colored inks again in the Inner Keep or maybe down at Wong's wasting money gambling so that he would deserve what his mother might be doing. But he felt that his thoughts were foolish and angry and he didn't know *what* his mother was doing.

"Come on out," said Enid finally, opening the bathroom

door. She was still in pajamas but—even before getting dressed—she had combed her hair. She had a nice smell of perfume, too, probably left over from the night before.

"*Comme tu es belle* this morning, Mademoiselle," said Peter, jumping out of the bath and plunging into the role—his most successful one—which had been decided for him at their last meeting.

"Oh, let's not talk politely today," said Enid. "I'm so tired and disgusted this morning. I went to a dance last night with Herr Hebel and I don't think he can get me back to Sweden any better than Papa can. I'm not even sure that his intentions to me are honorable."

Peter had to remember that Enid didn't know he'd been watching them the night before.

"Do you love him?" he asked.

"I try to," she said. "But only in some ways. You are more of a friend to me, I know."

"Why do you want to go to Sweden?"

"Because I want to do something and not stay home all day. I should be in school and growing older. But Papa wants to show people what a good father he is and what a good house he keeps for me. So we don't even save up passage money in case there ever *is* a ship."

"Maybe we could have our own school," suggested Peter eagerly. "I have all the high-school books. I'll bet if we read them together and talked about them, we could learn them fine."

"Maybe, and maybe we'd just end up kissing. Besides, it's not only the books. They're easy to read when you have nothing else to do. I read a lot of novels. And most of the things in them are things to do, not read. I want to grow up: ride horses and go to real dances and drink in restaurants and smoke with a long holder and have lots of friends like you, Peter."

"I don't," he said unhappily. "If I were in a school or anywhere, I would only be in love with one person. I'd like to run on the track team and swim and play tennis and basketball and maybe it would be nice to have all the other guys for friends, but I would only love you. If you weren't there I suppose I might love some other girl. I don't know. It would take a long time to change over, I know that."

It was so remote and philosophical that he wasn't embarrassed to say it and she looked quite pleased to hear it.

"You're very nice," she said, "much nicer than I am. I don't think I'm good enough to fall in love and get married to anyone. I don't have the right feelings. But I know you're my best friend. Maybe you'll always be. So I promise if I ever get sad and tired of being worldly and man-eating, I'll ask you or write you a letter to find out if you still want to marry me."

"It's hard to think so far ahead, isn't it?" said Peter.

They sat down together in thoughtful silence on the sofa, and in a while he said, "I'd like to kiss you before I go."

"Sure, you can kiss me, but don't go yet," she said.

"I didn't mean go from here."

He was about to explain the possibility of being put back in the concentration camp, but when he looked at her, he saw she had turned toward him on the sofa and was waiting to be kissed. Under his hands the silk of her pajamas slid over her skin and he felt almost as if it were one of those old difficult times again when she was the one wearing a dressing gown and it loosened up around her and he had to think about Colonel Kori and his father and Rosa in order to keep a storm of craziness from blowing up in him.

After a while she jumped up. "Let's have some aquavit," she said. "I still have that whole bottle you brought me."

He remembered people at Norm Diak's house saying they never drank before five o'clock or they never drank before noon. It was afternoon now, but it was before five o'clock and even before lunch on this particular funny day. Still it might be his last day out of camp and it was certainly the first day in a long time that Enid had been nice to him.

"Sure," he said.

When she had poured it, they both said *Skol* and emptied the tiny glasses Swedish fashion and laughed and kissed again. They had another and in a while Enid said, between kisses, "It's not really the Game, Peter, but I would like it if we could both of us take off our clothes."

He said nothing.

"I don't mean so that we would have a baby. That would be awful. But couldn't we just try it a little bit without you going crazy? Couldn't we just see how it worked and then stop?"

"We don't have to," he whispered, enunciating clearly and desperately, like a snake. She doesn't know what she's doing, he thought. The sin will be all on me. "I have some things

202

which will stop you from being pregnant."

"Where did you get them?" She seemed surprised and even shocked.

"From a guerrilla woman I meet in the woods sometimes," he breathed. For himself, what he said didn't matter now and for Margo it didn't matter either because she would be sailing to Australia any day now.

"I didn't know you had done it before with native girls," she exclaimed, looking somewhat frightened.

"My gosh, I haven't. This woman is English and grown up and she's already in love with someone, someone important. I just told her a little about you and she said I would need some of these things."

He jumped up and found the Christmas present still in the back pocket of his khaki shorts.

"I'm scared," she said.

"You have to now," he hissed. "I've given myself to the devil already just by asking."

Her mouth twisted in a smile as if she were going to giggle, but she didn't. Instead she got up quickly while he stood over her.

"Go and put on Papa's bathrobe," she ordered. "I'll pour us both a glass more of aquavit."

When he came back—after washing his face, as well as un-dressing—his hands were trembling. Enid was not in the living room and he called out for her anxiously.

"I'm here," she said, and came in from the kitchen. She was so much quicker than he that she had already gone to her bedroom and put on her dressing gown. Now she was bring-ing out two brimming glasses of aquavit, which she carried poised high in each hand—just the way Peter had to carry the candles in church sometimes, but far more gracefully.

"This is the way we Swedish girls carry the candles on Christmas Eve when we sing 'Santa Lucia,'" she said.

How could they think the same thoughts unless they were in love? thought Peter.

"We will go to Papa's room," she continued. "He has a big bed. He has girls in some nights so I know it's the right sort."

She led the way through the hall into a large bedroom which faced out across the overgrown back garden toward the quiet woods. While he pulled the blinds she placed the candles of aquavit on the bedside table and sat down. Turning, he found her watching him with flushed cheeks.

"I'm still scared," she said. "Are you sure it's all right? The things you have are good?"

"The woman who gave them to me is very worldly," he said. "She's been a man's mistress for a long time and she hasn't had any children."

"Aren't you scared, though?" Enid asked.

"I don't care if I'm scared or not," he said.

"Why don't we just play the Game and see what happens."

He laughed hoarsely. "All right, as long as you never push me away and say I'm getting crazy."

"Okay, sure," she said.

Though he hid it, he felt as unsure as she did. They kissed and then they stopped to drink. They kissed again and their dressing gowns loosened and finally slipped off. They laughed at each other and kissed again and laughed again and stopped to drink again.

After many kisses she said, "Are you sure you want to?"

"Yes," he said intensely. "But I'm not sure exactly how to start."

"Haven't you ever looked at the grownups' books?" she asked.

"They seem simpler than you."

She giggled, but only with nervousness. "I think it's like this," she said. "Go ahead and try it."

"That's right," she said encouragingly. "Go ahead now and don't worry about me."

"It's nice," she said a bit later. "It doesn't hurt now at all."

He covered her mouth quickly with a kiss. Now that it was started he didn't want her to talk any more, especially not about her body.

"Is that the end, do you think?" she asked later.

"I don't know," he said hoarsely, with half his mouth against her shoulder.

Between kisses and talk of *after-the-war* they finished their drinks and Enid went back to the kitchen to fill the glasses. While she was gone, Peter stared fixedly at the ceiling and clutched the blanket tight around his neck, trying to keep out the heavy cold of damnation which drifted in on him from the edges of things. Then Enid came back. She was white and straight and unembarrassed and he wondered how she could be so beautiful and so brave too. He pulled her quickly to him and threw himself on the warm mercy of her flesh.

The dark edges dissolved, the cold weights lifted and his dismal soul vanished into a burning star, the only star in edgeless nowhere.

"It's getting chilly when we're resting," she said.

It was already dark and Peter felt the end of the day closing on him like a vise.

"You don't say much any more," she said.

"I'm a little tired and stupid."

"It was a lot for a first time," she said. "I'm quite sore but I'm getting better at it."

"The aquavit after it cools off in me always makes me stupid," he said, hoping to change the subject.

"Maybe we're just hungry. It must be long after teatime."

They ate meat balls and bread and peanut butter, sitting in the kitchen in their dressing gowns. Until they had finished they said nothing at all except "There's no moon tonight," "Would you like some salt?" and things like that.

"It's funny," said Enid, wiping her fingers on her napkin after sucking a gob of peanut butter off one of them, "it doesn't seem so clever or man-eating, does it?"

"Did you really think it would?" he asked sadly.

"Oh, I don't mean it wasn't good. But I don't feel wicked. I just feel lonely. I wish you could stay and spend the whole night here."

"Isn't your father coming home?"

"Not until tomorrow afternoon. He's at Mananok again."

"I'm scared of being alone now too," said Peter. "But I can't spend the night. I could stay until you're asleep, though."

"Could you? Oh, Peter, you really are the best friend I shall ever have, I bet."

When they had gone back to the bedroom, turned off the lights, opened the window to the fresh dark air behind the blinds and taken each other in their comforting arms, Peter said, "You still don't love me, though, do you? You were only practicing for Captain Hebel."

"I guess I was, but it seems a long time ago. Maybe now I love you; I don't know. I need a few days to see what I really feel."

"Mother went to the police station today," he said. "She was going to apply to have us put back in camp. I don't know how long it will take or whether she even did it, but I may not see you again."

"I thought you were earning enough money to stay out!" she exclaimed—and she sounded truly alarmed and disappointed.

"It wasn't that. She thinks I am going to hell."

"Oh, Peter, is that why you were so determined? Did you really want to go to hell?"

"I decided to go to hell for you months ago."

"I'm sorry," she said. "But it was worth it, wasn't it? We did it nicely. We were never very embarrassed. Even you never seemed especially embarrassed."

"I've thought about it a long time. There wasn't much left to be embarrassed about as long as you really wanted it and didn't giggle or say anything."

"I didn't either! I'm proud of the way we acted. You never thought I was cheap or disgusting, did you?"

"I felt a little disgusted a couple of times but only afterward with myself."

"Men in books often feel that way too. Especially if they're not married."

"It wasn't a strong feeling. Mostly I didn't think much of anything. I guess it was because you were so nice. You've never been so nice before."

"Neither have you, and it's a good thing too, I bet."

They laughed and hugged each other.

"I'm going to miss you terribly if you go back to camp," she said. "Maybe I do love you. How do you tell about love when you aren't ready to marry the person?"

"Just by the feeling, I suppose. It's such a queer mixture of things that don't go together, like sweet with sour, and strong with weak, and reckless with safe and cozy. At least that's how it seems."

"Yes, I had some of those feelings. The awful thing is that if you go back to camp I'll be lonelier with feelings like that than I would have been without them. I'll have to go to Sweden even worse than before."

"Yes," he said bitterly, thinking of the Nazi.

"Why are we so happy being sad?" she said suddenly after a silence. "Let's not be sad. Let's have a good time while we can." She tried to tickle him, but he wasn't ticklish, so she bit his arm and when he said *ouch* she kissed him.

"Soon I am sure to go to sleep," she whispered after a while. "But you must promise to try to come and have tea with me again if they are going to put you back in camp."

"I don't need to promise that," he said.

"Even if Papa's here, I'll send him away somewhere."

Peter awoke with a start and sprang from the bed. The blinds showed light outside. He ran across the room and peered out. The ragged weeds in the back garden were trying to look beautiful—moist and flushed, as the girls at Wong's also tried to look in the glow of the morning. Judgment morning, and the sky was already teasing him. It was as pink and fleecy as the crib of a newborn girl. It was as soft and rosy as the cheeks of an unwanted Chinese baby which would have to die in the next famine. This time there would be nothing he could tell his mother. There was nothing he could even tell himself. He was drained of all will power and certainty. He was tired and dry-mouthed and his bare feet grew cold against the floor. Should he wake Enid? Her face was gray and peaked and her mouth seemed twisted as if she were wincing from turning an ankle or barking a shin during play. No, he didn't want to see her trying to make herself look pretty, and she probably didn't want to see him this morning either. He leaned over and touched her forehead as lightly as he could with his lips. She stirred and rolled away from him, turning her face to the wall. Perhaps she felt a little of the disgust, too. It was funny how disgust could be mixed the way it was with tenderness. Such a sad longing and love for his sin. Such a tender forgiving knowledge of all her weakness and such a weariness with his own.

He forced himself to hurry from the room. By the time he had put on his clothes, piece by tired piece on the bench in the bathroom, dawn was already past and the light was growing colder, hardening into the full light of justice.

He had everything that was his. Was there anything else? Oh, yes, the aquavit. He took the half-filled bottle from the kitchen into Enid's own empty little bedroom in the front of the house, where he hid it in a drawerful of underclothes and stockings. Then, sentimentally, he lowered the blind as a signal to himself not to come to tea that afternoon. As he turned from the window and the bureau full of her clothes, he noticed a book lying open on her bed. He glanced at it to find out what she was reading and saw a cold, hard-edged drawing of a naked woman in the position to lie with a man. It was one of those books by doctors. He had read two of them carefully and he knew they had been helpful, but now their heartiness seemed false and their frankness dirty. Enid must have looked up the drawing while she was changing into her dressing gown. It was like her. It endeared her to him and at the same time it was frightening and repulsive. He ran from the room and the house. In the hard, brightening light on the street outside he tried to look ahead toward the first darkness within him: the fear and anger of his mother; but he couldn't. The street was gray before him and he was coming to the gray stone hut of the Jap check point. He could circle around it through the woods, but he didn't; maybe they would shoot him for being out so early and he wouldn't have to face anything. He walked toward the sentry on guard outside and, sure enough—he had almost expected it—the Jap uttered a guttural cry of excitement and began running heavily toward him, pointing the blade of his bayonet as he came.

## CHAPTER 15

The soldier with the bayonet was only twenty or thirty yards off now, and Peter recognized him as the man he had paid to take care of his wagon the afternoon of Enid's birthday party. He must recognize Peter too and that meant he wouldn't shoot. It meant that before getting settled in hell, Peter still had to live out his life of disgrace. Of course, it also meant that he was in trouble with the Japs for being out so early.

Funny how the soldier kept running forward, flashing his bayonet in the sun, when he could see it was only Peter. He must be trying to scare him. After all, going toward home, intead of away from it, at this hour of morning, sure made it look as if he had broken curfew. But what a fuss they were making. Now the other soldiers had piled out of the stone hut and they were training their rifles on him too. Maybe if he cut loose and ran they would still shoot him. But now he was scared to be shot, wasn't he! His fine, foolish despair had crumbled in the face of a little fear. It might be wrong to want to die, but dying took courage—and he was weak. He put out his empty hands and walked slowly toward the Jap soldier as he came panting the last few yards up to him.

"Aaagh!" screamed the Jap and lunged at him with the flashing bayonet. He was only feinting—just trying to have some fun with him. Peter stood as still as he could and when the Jap saw that he didn't flinch much, he put the bayonet against Peter's chest and held it with one hand while he used the other hand to pat Peter's clothes and make sure he had no weapons. Then he escorted Peter back to the check point. The other soldiers, lowering their guns, looked on curiously. The noncommissioned officer in charge of them waved his pistol at Peter, pointing down the road with it toward town.

"Sa! Ike! Hayaku!" he ordered brusquely. "Come on, let's go, on the double."

One of the soldiers gave Peter a push in the back to start him in the direction the noncom wanted, and as Peter staggered forward the noncom fell into step a few paces behind him.

"Nan desuka?" "What's the big idea?" asked Peter, trying to sound superior.

"Shiranai," muttered the noncom. "I don't know." And "shiranai" was all he would say to every queston Peter asked him. It certainly was a lot of fuss to make about being out too early.

They went single file through the woods to the edge of town. As they passed the entrance of the hotel driveway, Peter prayed to Luck that his mother would not be looking out one of the windows at home and see him. Not that it made much difference. If they took him to the jail for a few hours the whole town would know about it anyway. Father or Mrs. Gibney would hear about it and tell his mother. After staying up all night worrying and weeping and probably thinking that her threats had made him run away to the guerrillas, she would hear he was at the police station, she would find out that he had been arrested practically in front of Enid's house, and she would realize that he had spent the night of her own prayers and vigil in Enid's comfortable bed of sin. After that she would not forgive him. She would have less cause to forgive him even than God.

They reached the bottom of the hill and turned left past the Roman Catholic cathedral toward the police station. Feeling on him the eyes of passing Filipinos, Peter stared straight ahead. Maybe they would think he had done something patriotic if he looked proud enough. After all, he *had* worked for the guerrillas. That wasn't why he was being taken to the police station, but if they thought it was—he being only a child—it might be an inspiration to them and make them resist the Japs more stiffly. The vainglorious notion shriveled inside him, and out of its dried pod rolled hard, round little peas of jeering and sneering. If he had any courage he would call out and tell the Filipinos to spit on him—or, better, to stab him before he turned informer. Didn't he know the names of other guerrillas besides Margo and Jerry? Ones who weren't sailing off safely to Australia? Then what right had he to give the Japs an excuse to arrest him and prod his mind, bursting and unclean as it was, and maybe open up leaks in it? He had insisted like a baby on having his own way. For a sickly game of girl-loving and skin-loving, he had endangered hundreds of brave men.

Why did it all have to happen today when he was so tired? he wondered. Sure! So tired and self-pitying and guilty! he replied. But scorn and self-reproach didn't help. As the Jap noncom shoved him in at the door of the police station, he felt fear. The flesh of his brain seemed to be swelling up stiff and stupid with it. Being out too early was probably only a pretext to have him picked up and questioned. That was what he had better be prepared for anyway—if he could be prepared for anything.

At the police desk, two quick, unintelligible sentences were spoken, and Peter was taken immediately by a Jap guard out back across the courtyard to the cell block. He had never seen the cell block before. On two sides it had no proper walls, just bars running from the concrete floor up to the wide-eaved roof. Behind the bars stood a closely packed crowd of Filipinos. Most likely the profiteers and the patriots, the wife killers and the owners of short-wave sets, were all there mixed up together, he thought. They watched him come like creatures in a cage. Then he was shoved in with them and the iron gate was slammed behind him.

"*Et tu*, Peter?" said a familiar voice. Peter jumped and whirled around to see, of all people, Father Gibney. Not only Father Gibney but beside him in the crowd Reverend Fisher and Reverend Bax too. Peter's mind lighted up with hope: it was all dreaming. The night hadn't really slipped away from him. He was still in bed with Enid and it was time to get up and go home. She would be warm and smooth beside him and he could touch her once more before he left her. Oh, why did he torture himself? This was the wishful yearning of someone unrepentant and damned. He had to face the truth. For the guerrillas he had to.

"What did *you* do?" asked his voice, probing the reality of Father Gibney.

"They've cleared us all off the streets," said Reverend Bax. "It's nothing we did."

"I thought it was because I was out too early," said Peter dully.

"Oh, no, I'm sure it was the shooting," said Father Gibney with a mysterious smile. When Peter looked blank, he added, "You did hear the shooting, didn't you, Peter?"

"No."

"Ah, the sleep of innocence!" said Father Gibney. He was only trying to be normal and jovial, but his choice of words seemed dreamlike and God-sent, and it made Peter wince. "There was quite a battle last night," he went on. "Somewhere in North Valley, to judge from the sound of it."

"We think this General Sam they're so afraid of staged a major attack," said Reverend Bax.

"My gosh!" gasped Peter. The night before had been the night for the big supply pickup, Wong's last delivery—and Peter had forgotten about it. Had they been watching Wong? Or had they simply bumped into the guerrillas marching off with cases of provisions? If they'd been watching Wong they must know about Peter too. He was in for it. He was really in for it. And he had to keep things straight as never before.

"That's only speculation, of course," said Father Gibney. "But it's pretty clear that whatever the noise was they think we may be implicated."

"A boy his age!" exclaimed Reverend Fisher. "What could he possibly have to do with it?"

"Well, frankly, Fisher, he's had a good deal more opportunity to do something than we have," said Father Gibney. "At least he's been able to move freely around town without getting his face slapped. What I don't understand is why they're bringing him in so late. What time did they arrest you, Peter?"

"About half an hour ago, I guess."

"Isn't that funny," said Reverend Fisher. "They came for the rest of us at two this morning."

"Not only that," said Father Gibney indignantly. "They packed our wives into a truck saying that they were going to take them back to camp immediately! Have those poor women been sitting out in the chilly air ever since?"

Peter saw that Father Gibney was looking at him for an answer.

"I don't know," he said, bewildered.

"Well, when they came to arrest you and pick up your mother, were our wives sitting outside waiting in a truck?"

"Oh, I see what you mean," said Peter. The Japs must have come for him in the middle of the night and found only Jeanette and his poor mother at home. No wonder he'd almost been shot by the men at the check point. There must have been an order out for his arrest. And his mother! The panic she must have been in, there by his bed. First the shooting and then the soldiers getting her up off her knees, ordering her to pack to go back to camp at once and demanding to know where Peter was. *Oh, my gosh, my gosh.* He felt like dancing about and shaking his hands as if he had burned them. Or as if he were a small child again and had broken his father's microscope after repeated warnings never to touch it.

"It's a simple question, Peter," said Father Gibney sharply. "Were they or weren't they?"

"I don't know," he said faintly. "I wasn't there."

"You weren't there!" exclaimed Reverend Fisher.

"Where were you?" asked Father Gibney.

"Well, you see, I got up early and went down toward the end of South Valley. They arrested me on the way home when I tried to come back through the check point at the edge of the woods."

"How early did you get up?" asked Reverend Bax with amazement. Before Peter had to answer there was a commotion in the jail and he saw that the Jap guard had brought in a pail of boiled rice. The Filipinos had gathered round him and were taking their shares in old tin cans.

"I don't know exactly," he said, "but it was awfully early. Maybe right after the shooting. Maybe it was the shooting that woke me up, even though I didn't hear it."

"You mean to say," said Father Gibney, "that you may have got up at one-thirty this morning and been traipsing around the streets with your cart ever since?"

One of the Filipinos handed Father Gibney the bucket of rice, and he was distracted while he put it down between them. Since the Americans didn't have tin cans to eat out of yet, the Filipinos had left their shares at the bottom. Peter noticed that they were more than fair shares and he gratefully picked up a mouthful between his fingers. Father Gibney gamely followed suit. So did Reverend Bax. But Reverend Fisher merely looked into the bucket and then away.

"Well?" demanded Father Gibney.

"No, I didn't have my wagon with me," mumbled Peter. "I just went down to the pass at the end of South Valley to watch the sunrise. I've been meaning to do it for a long time but I've never waked up early enough before." He was lying, but it *was* something he'd always wanted to do. "Then when I got there," he continued, "it was so early I fell asleep on the bench at the edge of the lookout."

"What an extraordinary thing to do," said Reverend Fisher, looking at him with an unsure, fishy expression.

"What a night to do it on!" said Father Gibney. "You realize how bad it looks, Peter? The only thing in your favor is that you were found in South Valley instead of North Valley, where the shooting was."

"*Baka! Sugu ni ano otoko-no-ko o tsure-te koi.*" "You idiot! Bring that boy to me at once!" It was Colonel Kori. He was standing just outside the door of the cage. As always, he was slouched from the shoulders up—as if his back couldn't support the whole long length of him. But now his head, hanging from his shoulders, seemed to bounce a little on his rubbery neck and his eyes seemed to study the ground more contemptuously than usual. The guard had opened the cell door and was pulling Peter out roughly after him.

"What are you doing to that boy?" shouted Reverend Bax.

"Keep your head, Peter," called Father Gibney.

"Your greatest weapon is being a child," Jerry had said. "Be one!"

"What's the big idea?" Peter shouted at Colonel Kori. "Leave me alone. I haven't done anything."

"I thought you'd rather be in a special jail," said Colonel Kori mildly. "I had to arrest you after the unpleasantness last night but I don't have to keep you in with the natives."

"What about Father Gibney and the others? Can't you put them in the special jail with me?"

"They're not friends of mine," said Colonel Kori coldly. He turned himself round by a swing of his big hips and led the way across the courtyard to a ragged hole which had been cut in the concrete wall around the prison. On the other

213

side Peter realized that he was in the courtyard of the American Butcher Shop where Australian beef had once been kept under cold storage and the best local pigs and goats had been brought and slaughtered under hygienic State-side conditions. Now, he had heard, it was the headquarters of the Kempeitai. On the left of the courtyard coming from this direction was the old store. On the right were the slaughterhouse and the storage rooms. Colonel Kori turned and entered a door on the right. The inside of the slaughterhouse —a big plain concrete room that you could wash down with a hose—had a bunch of chairs and floodlights and things in it now. At one end was a table with a bowl of Korean apples, a loaf of wheat bread and a bottle of wine on it. Peter tripped over a coil of rope on the floor and almost crashed into a *hibachi*, a kind of small Japanese charcoal stove made of pottery. With the guard's rifle jabbed into his back, he scrambled to his feet and ran after Colonel Kori, who was waiting with a look of annoyance at the door of the corridor which led to the cold-storage lockers.

"Sorry I had to bring you through our torture chamber," he said, "but we haven't built a separate entrance to the cells yet."

Peter shuddered and tried to look blank.

"I didn't believe torture was really necessary when I first came here," went on Colonel Kori conversationally. "But you'd be amazed how these natives value their bodies. No respect for their God-given minds at all."

He stopped in front of one of the cold-storage vaults and unlocked the door.

"There you are: the most luxurious private prison on the island." Peter saw nothing inside but three windowless walls, a mattress with a blanket on it covering the floor, a toilet bucket in the corner and two big iron eyes on the ceiling for hanging meat hooks on. Colonel Kori swept Peter into the room with the hand he wasn't using on the door, and Peter stumbled and fell on the mattress.

"I'll be back to ask you a few questions later."

"I'll freeze to death," screamed Peter. He jumped toward the closing door, but it was too late. He pounded on it with his hands, but he knew it must be almost soundproof with all the insulation in it and it was far too tight to rattle.

He sat down on the mattress to freeze and die. He looked at the blanket, picked it up and threw it away from him over to the door. Then in a little while he realized that he wasn't getting cold. The freezing mechanism wasn't turned on. Oh, he was such a baby. Always imagining things. Now was the time to think. To find out what they knew and didn't know. How could Colonel Kori have gotten on to the supply pickup? The Chinese in town wouldn't ever have told. Nor the Filipinos either, the ones who knew anything, because if it wasn't their neck it was the neck of a close relative in the guerrillas. No, but there was another possibility, an awful, absurd, insistent one. Perhaps Enid had sneaked out during the night, when Peter didn't even hear loud gunfire, and told Colonel Kori that Peter knew a guerrilla woman. Perhaps Colonel Kori, remembering that Peter often visited the casino, had put two and two together in the middle of the night and sent soldiers at once to start watching Wong's house. Then perhaps the soldiers had arrived during the supply pickup and started the battle at once or perhaps they had gone to get help first.

He wondered if he could be just supposing. It had seemed as if Enid really meant it when she said she loved him. But she fooled him so easily, and Colonel Kori was probably the one person who could find a way of getting her back to Sweden if he felt like it. Besides, unless she'd been expecting it, she ought to have acted more surprised and curious about this English woman who was a guerrilla and met Peter in the woods. That was what he'd told her, wasn't it? But she hadn't asked a single question except whether the woman was worldly and really knew about love. Yes, it all seemed logical and possible and the other explanations he could imagine seemed vague and hard to grasp. Enid herself, coming from her sweetness and softness and sin, must have betrayed him. And that meant that he was a traitor, because he had given her the information to do it with. Traitors were shot. Fornicators were damned. He had committed awful sins against God and country and he ought to be condemned and cast out by both of them.

A means of escape flashed into his mind, wild and lurid. He had been born in Japan. He had a claim to Japanese citizenship. Perhaps if he told Colonel Kori everything, he would be allowed to go back to Japan and live out his damned life unknown and unscorned. Kotosan, his ammah—the nursemaid who had taken care of him until he was seven—would probably find a place for him in her family. Her house was small but it was clean. The filth was all underneath between the foundations. But her father was polite and full of deference—even to a tiny child, if it was a white child. Yes, her father was humble beyond belief. He was what Peter would have to be if he tried to become a Japanese.

Oh, what dreams. What dopey dreams, as Jerry would say. He might as well die now as try to become a Jap. What about Jerry? Had Jerry been at the supply pickup or had he already left for Australia? No, all the guerrillas weren't caught or Colonel Kori wouldn't want to question him. There was a shred of string by which he could pull himself back to humanity. There was also more treachery he could still perform—and that was more like him. If they tortured him, he would probably let the half-redeeming shred of string slip through his fingers and betray everything that was left. Couldn't he die? It must be better to die than give in to sin and treachery completely. Sure! If he had the courage and could think of a way.

Remembering Norm Diak's purple face when Peter had nearly choked him once, he tried to throttle himself. But it didn't work. You really didn't need your hands at all, if you had the courage to die. All you needed was to hold your breath long enough. But each time he tried it, at the last minute when his whole being began to throb and his chest ached, he gave in and said to himself, Next time. Next time I'll be better at it.

He was only playing another game. He couldn't kill himself. And if he couldn't he had to think and work out a way of doing no more harm than he had already done. His mind chattered and flashed with disconnected words and pictures. He had to make a firm, simple beginning.

I don't know how much Colonel Kori knows, he thought, and if I lie he'll soon see I'm lying and he'll torture me until he can be sure from my screaming and fear and cowardice that I'm finally telling the truth.

*Be a child. Throw tantrums. Be as unreasonable as you've ever been with your mother. Don't admit to anything. Anything at all.* Jerry's advice was the only advice he had to follow, but it was hard to apply when you were scared and in pain and had lost your hardheartedness—and when you faced a subtle, torturing policeman instead of an unhappy, distracted mother who loved you.

The thought of his mother, fearing he was dead and trying to reach him with love and prayers across the salt sea of sadness, overwhelmed him and he began to weep. He felt such a confused mixture of homesickness and affection, humility, guilt, desire, pity and self-pity, what did it matter which one he was crying for? He struggled a bit to stanch the tears and preserve the silence, but they got the upper hand, and soon he was sobbing and gasping with childish abandon. After a while he found himself listening with pleasure to the sounds of his tears' subsidence. In that grave of a room where there was no other sound but the distant whir of air-conditioning machinery through the vent in the ceiling, it was good to hear his voice. The sorrow in him gasped and sighed against the silence like surf against a shore when you weren't too close. He began to feel better.

Suppose Colonel Kori has a microphone hidden here, he thought. I will have to be careful not to talk aloud to myself when I don't mean to. But what if I do mean to? Maybe then I can say things which will help me. He tried to imagine what would be most likely for him to say aloud. Prayers, of course. In the old days he had been quite proud of his ability to make up extemporary graces and prayers at table or in Sunday school. Being an acolyte, he could remember lots of phrases from the prayer book and throw them in for their fine sound and weight. This time, however, he would have to compose the prayer carefully in his mind beforehand. He had to persuade Colonel Kori in it that he knew nothing about guerrilla activities and that he had been out at two o'clock in the morning for a harmless reason. He would have to do the first by barefaced lying. But he didn't have to lie about the second. If he could bring himself to overcome his shame and be desperate and betray Enid as she had betrayed him, Colonel Kori might be convinced by his own sensuality and cynical pagan wickedness. In fact, a story of fornication might distract him and interest him as well as persuade him. Suppose, though, that Enid hadn't betrayed Peter. Well, then he didn't need to use her name in the prayer. If she *had* told on him, Kori would guess the right name and begin to suspect Enid's motives and distrust her story. And if she hadn't betrayed him, then Peter could appeal to Colonel Kori's romantic Japanese honor and beg not to have to betray her. Even if Kori insisted on knowing her name, it would be a separate investigation. It would at least give Peter time to find out how things stood.

He fell on his knees and went over the prayer several times before he said it aloud.

"Almighty and everliving God," he intoned finally—his voice was hoarse from weeping and his hands were hypocritically folded before him. "I would not presume to call out to you if it were not for your manifold and great mercy. I know there is no health in me at all and I acknowledge and bewail a most grievous sin of the flesh which I committed last night with a girl. I don't expect pardon, O Lord, but I beseech you, in spite of the blackness of my soul, to grant that I may not drag down others in my own punishment, nor add to the burden of my sins by telling Colonel Kori foolish lies when he tortures me and when I give in to my miserable body and try to save it. Don't let me make up malicious things about the girls in the market or even about the Japanese soldiers at the check points. I do not know what I have done or what they want to find out from me. But I'm weak and frightened of being hurt and if they torture me I might invent stories about innocent people. So I humbly beg you, O Lord God, if it's not your will for me to be released unhurt, then let me die without hurting others. Somewhere in the New Testament you said that when lust is conceived it brings forth sin, and sin when it's finished brings forth death. I had great lust and it led to great sin and now if you can't grant me a lifetime to make atonement, please grant me a quick death. Also please don't let the girl have a baby. For ever and ever, Amen."

The blasphemy of using a prayer this way had begun to frighten him and he hadn't ended as eloquently as he had begun. But on the whole he felt better about himself. He couldn't do any more until Colonel Kori came back to question him. He lay down on the mattress and spun a dozing trance out of the patterns he could see in the meat-hook eyes overhead.

Peter had been gazing comatose into the incandescent vortex of the wire-caged light bulb on the ceiling for hours and hours. He felt as if it must be night or the next morning, but he didn't want to be as foolish as the man in the story in one of the high-school English books Father Gibney had given him who let his hair turn white because he had been shut up in a tomb for ten minutes and thought he had been there for days. Instead, Peter played games with the patterns of the meat-hook eyes and the shadows cast by the wires around the light bulb and listened to his stomach. It had rumbled and growled when he had first awakened. Later it had twisted and knotted in cramps. Now it was quiet. If they were going to starve him to death he could probably make it faster by doing exercises and using up his energy, but he felt so precariously suspended in numbness that he didn't want to move and excite himself.

Lying still, he heard a creaking and a rattling afar off and then a voice.

"Well, I'm glad to see you're resting well, Peter." It was finally Colonel Kori. "Sorry I took so long getting around to you, but I had to question the other prisoners first."

"What time is it?" asked Peter in a flat voice.

"A lot later than I intended. I've had a long, trying day, so I hope you're ready to co-operate."

Peter looked past the policeman's legs and up through the open doorway to the windows on the other side of the corridor. It was dark out. And silent, too, he realized. No sounds from the street at all.

"Why should I?" he asked hopelessly.

"Because you're hungry and you don't want me to hurt you."

"I don't know anything," said Peter dully.

"You know the names of guerrillas. You've met some of them and run errands for them."

"If that's what you think, go ahead and beat me up. I'm unhappy anyway. I don't care if you hurt me. I hope you kill me."

"Poor Peter, so pathetic and childish! But being a child works both ways, you know. I may be sorry for you but I can also be dead sure that you don't want to die. There's too much life ahead of you, too many things you've never tried. And as for your unhappiness, you know from experience that it won't last. You can dry your eyes and you'll be laughing and playing games again in five minutes."

"Not me," said Peter with conviction. "I wish you'd shut up and get it over with."

Colonel Kori knelt down Japanese fashion on the mattress and looked at him earnestly. "Rudeness won't help you, Peter. Childishness won't help you. Lies and red herrings won't help you. If I can't get co-operation out of you by twisting your arm, I can pull off your fingernails or yank out

219

your teeth. If you don't respond to your own pain, I can use someone else's. Would you like to see Pete Wong being tortured? Would you like to see your girl friend raped by ten soldiers one after another? One way or another, no matter how unpleasant it is for me, I can always get what I want out of you, so be sensible and tell me now before you're hurt."

"You don't dare do anything to Enid," said Peter. "She's a neutral."

"O-ho! That little Swedish number. I'd take a whack at *her* myself. And if you think Sweden's going to make a fuss because a Japanese does the same thing to a naughty Swedish girl that an American boy does, you'd better think again. Neutrals are used to getting screwed by both sides."

Colonel Kori laughed at his dirty joke, and Peter turned his face to the wall, flushing with helpless anger. He had been tricked into revealing Enid's name when he hadn't meant to. Colonel Kori wouldn't really do anything to a Swedish girl. That was all bluff and provocation. But Peter would never be able to tell now whether Colonel Kori had eavesdropped on his fake prayer or had been in cahoots with Enid from the beginning. It all depended on whether or not he had known her name before Peter had told him. Hate flooded into Peter and with it energy and a little alertness.

"All right, now you know where I was last night," he said bitterly. "But you trapped me into telling her name. It was dishonorable of you to make me tell on a girl."

"More than it was of you to tell?" jeered the colonel. "Don't kid me, Peter. I know what the honor of an American boy is worth when it comes to girls. The only person he doesn't want to know about his exploits is his mother. So I'll make a deal with you: you tell me the names of your guerrilla friends and I won't tell Mom the name of your girl friend."

"I don't know any guerrillas, and Mother already knows about Enid. That's one of the reasons I'm unhappy." It was a cold, hopeless game, but from playing it Peter felt that he was regaining a little of the old hardheartedness.

"I happen to know you've been bringing messages from the guerrillas to Pete Wong."

"You're crazy," said Peter. "I don't even know who Pete Wong is."

"Come on, don't be stupid. Everyone in town knows Pete Wong."

"Oh, you mean the guy who runs the casino. Sure, I'm just dopey from looking at that light bulb."

"Who gave you the messages for him?"

"Nobody. The only stuff I ever took to him were cigarettes and things he ordered from the market."

"Don't forget I've seen you come to the casino, Peter. And the time I saw you, your cart was empty. I went out and checked on it while you were in the office giving your message to Wong."

"I didn't give him anything. He gave me a load of liquor to deliver to the Cerillos up in North Valley."

"Then who are those people you meet in the woods? Don't tell me they're all girls you play pokey-pokey with because I happen to know different. I've had men following you."

"You have not!"

"How do you know?"

Peter had fallen into another trap. What Colonel Kori was going to say next lay in wait for him just the way he himself had often lain in wait to see if anyone was following him in the woods.

"Because I do go into the woods sometimes just to sit and think," he said plausibly. "I have a secret place where I hide and I don't believe even a red Indian could creep up on me there without me hearing him."

"Very charming and childish, but what you really mean is that you take elaborate precautions to make sure that you're not being followed when you go to meet your guerrilla friends."

"I would if I had any," said Peter scornfully. He had caught Colonel Kori bluffing. Perhaps all the other things Kori pretended to know were bluffs and guesses too.

"You're making things bad for yourself, Peter," said the colonel severely. "Shall I tell you how I really know what you've been doing?"

"You just did. You've had people sneaking around watching me."

"No, I trusted you, Peter. I thought we were friends. But one of the natives we captured last night broke down and talked."

"I don't believe it. If he told lies about me, why don't you go ahead and behead me or bayonet me the way you did

221

those poor guys in the market?"

"Because I've grown fond of you. I don't want to hurt you. I want to give you a chance to confess so that I'll have an excuse to let you go."

"You're a liar. You don't care for me. You hate me just like you hate all Americans. I'll bet when you were in the States they flunked you out of college or something." Peter stood up and stretched rudely. Colonel Kori, kneeling in front of him, seemed to be looking at Peter's shoes. Peter glanced at them himself to see if there was anything wrong with them. There wasn't. They were nearly new sneakers and they didn't have a single hole in the sides yet.

"I have a terrible temper, Peter," said Colonel Kori softly. "Don't provoke me into doing things I'll feel badly about later. Can't you see how utterly hopeless it is for you? I'll get the names out of you one way or another, but I don't want to see that fine manly young body broken and that promising young mind half crazed in the process."

"It doesn't matter how cruel you get, I won't be able to tell you any true names. They'll be made-up ones, just the same as if you were a bully twisting my arm; I'd cross my fingers and say anything to get you to stop."

"And then run off hooting derisively?" asked Colonel Kori sadly. "I've watched kids. I used to be one, believe it or not. But where are you going to run to? I'm trained to recognize lies and I know from experience that they only make the tortures last longer. There's always another hair or tooth or fingernail or eyeball for the next lie—and the next—and the next. Eventually you tell the truth just so you can die."

Looking into the watery mildness of Colonel Kori's eyes, Peter suddenly felt sure that he was facing the devil. He must try to be more hardhearted. Torture couldn't last forever unless the devil could get him to hell and make God abandon him completely. But God hadn't abandoned him completely or He wouldn't have let him see through the devil's disguise. If Peter could hold out until his body was crushed and mutilated and his mother pitied him and forgave him and started praying for him again, then God might relent and curb the devil's power over him.

"I've thought about your stupid, uncivilized cruelty quite a lot," he said. "Eventually even if a person's innocent he finds a lie that the Kempeitai believe and then they let him die. That's what happened to two of the missionaires who

222

were taken out of camp for questioning at the very beginning. The main thing is to save the best lies until later when you're sure they'll be believed. That's what I'm going to do."

"No, Peter. I'll never let you die until you give me the truth. Lies don't work with me."

Colonel Kori rose from his knees and stood close in front of Peter, towering over him and stinking of sweat that seemed sweet and not musky like a proper grown-up man's.

"Fiddlesticks," said Peter. "You're just a Jap."

Colonel Kori grabbed him by the ears, tilted his face up to the light and looked down on him eye to eye.

"Who's General Sam?" he shouted.

"I don't know."

"Who's Fernando Moro?"

"I don't know."

"General Sam's real name is Sam Bean, right?"

"I don't know."

"Who's Henry Cheng?"

"I don't know."

"Who's Tim Baldwin."

"I don't know . . . oh, that's Dad. But he wouldn't be a guerrilla. He wouldn't fight or kill anyone. He's a doctor."

"Are you hungry?"

"I don't know. I mean, yes, of course I'm hungry."

"All right, let's go have something to eat. I've got a surprise for you."

Colonel Kori turned away abruptly and stepped out into the corridor. "Come on," he said gruffly.

Was it all over? Had Peter won already? Or had his eyes told Colonel Kori what he wanted to know. One of the natives Kori had asked him about was a guerrilla captain, but the other was no one Peter had ever heard of. Probably it was a made-up name thrown in to see if Peter's eyes looked any different when he didn't know something from when he did. He followed Colonel Kori down the passageway in a daze of uncertain expectancy.

Colonel Kori stood at the end of the corridor pointing toward the table of apples and bread and wine. "There you are," he said.

Peter ducked past him, ran to the table, snatched up an apple and bit a big mouthful out of it. He mustn't stop being unreasonable now. It might still be all a trap.

"Now you can't starve me to death until tomorrow night at least," he shouted, with his mouth full of apple.

"I have no intention of starving you to death. I've brought you here to eat and see a friend of yours." Colonel Kori waved his hand limply toward the other end of the room. Peter let his eyes follow the hand and he choked with terror and disgust. There up on the wall was Wong, his thumbs fastened to the ceiling by cords behind him and all his weight supported by them and by the arch of his back and by a tiny ledge on the wall, maybe only an inch wide, which he gripped with his bare toes. If his feet slipped, his shoulder muscles would collapse and there he'd be all hanging broken from his thumbs, with his arms turned back-to-front.

"Have another apple," said Colonel Kori. "Then we'll ask Wong some questions."

There was a strangled noise from Wong, and Peter saw that he had a tight gag across his mouth which was dripping with spit. His eyes bulged and there was blood trickling down from his shoulders. Peter imagined him, strong and gentle as he had been, watering his ornamental oranges or fondly slapping Rainha on the seat of her black velvet slacks, and Peter turned cold with sweat and shuddered uncontrollably. He clenched his teeth on the apple and bit the core out of it.

That's what they'll do to me, he thought. And if Wong didn't tell anything I can't spoil it. He spat the core of the apple into his hand.

"Dirty Jap!" he screamed. "Dirty Jap! Dirty, filthy, rat-burning Jap!" He hurled the pieces of the core at Colonel Kori and jumped closer to the table, took a bite of the loaf of bread and flung it after the spitty fragments of the apple. All the apples in the bowl remained, and as Colonel Kori advanced across the room Peter spat on them one by one and pelted him with them. He saw that he was making Colonel Kori as white-faced and angry as he had been that time he beat up the guard at his party. It would all be over soon and Peter felt swept away by a wave of fearful joy. He grabbed the wine bottle and struck at Colonel Kori's head, but the bottle slipped from his hand and struck only a glancing blow. Peter lunged forward and forced Colonel Kori backward. He seized Colonel Kori's raised hand and bent it the way he wanted. He was stronger than Colonel Kori!

"You're weak," he sobbed. "You even smell weak."

Colonel Kori was crying out for help from the guards outside. Peter pushed him up against the wall, kicked him with his knees, butted him with his head and pommeled him with his fists. Colonel Kori couldn't do anything. Colonel Kori was soft and squidgy. Colonel Kori—the whole huge height of him—had to go down like Goliath. He had to go down like a palace of Philistines before Peter's killing, pillar-toppling, God-given, last-minute strength. A blow from behind knocked Peter aside, and before he could gather the dazed pieces of himself together and get up, Colonel Kori had risen above him, whitefaced and swinging a rifle. Thud, pain, thud, pain, and finally, after repeated thuds, darkness and death.

Dirty Jap, dirty Jap, dirty rat-on-fire Jap. The chant went on and on and the brightness was as stupefying as the core of a light bulb.

The last expensive bottle of aquavit flew aimlessly across the fiery radiance, slipped through the stinking clouds, the yellow, billowing sin-scented mists, and sank inadequate and untouched out of reach.

Hell was blinding, painful, boring and long, as it ought to be. But Peter spat at the devils who came to taunt him. He wasn't theirs forever. That feeling of triumph at the bottom of things meant that God would let him out in the end.

All patterns, patterns, pain and patterns.

And then one day Peter awoke from torment. He was in paradise or back in the cold-storage locker. The ceiling was white and bright, but the patterns were different. There weren't any meat-hook eyes. There weren't any sulphurous clouds. There weren't any electric-light bulbs. The light was like sunlight.

"Arru you awake?" asked a voice. It was a nurse. A chinese or Jap nurse all in white. He was still on earth.

"Yes," he said sadly. "How's Pete?"

"You arru recovering, Pete," she said.

"I mean Pete Wong."

"I do notta know Pete Wong. You arru Pete Borrudwin. I come back soon." She moved away from his line of vision, and Peter subsided into disinterest.

Knowing he was alive, he knew not long afterward that live people were shaking him awake, but he didn't hurry to open his eyes. When he finally responded, he saw Colonel Kori. Funny.

"Hello, Peter, how do you feel?"

Peter looked around for the nice Jap nurse who had been sorry for him, but she wasn't there.

"What's the matter with me?" asked Peter after a while.

"Slight concussion, a broken leg and some ribs fractured," said Colonel Kori. "You had a nasty fall off the top of that table when you tried to fight us."

"I thought I was stabbed by a bayonet."

"No, just a fall," said Colonel Kori. "You're rather brittle."

"I am not! I'm not brittle. It takes a lot to break my bones because I've broken some and I know."

"You haven't changed much. Too bad you couldn't have told us what we wanted to know. Wong had to die and several others before we got the names we needed."

"I didn't know any names," said Peter.

"Who is the man who takes pictures?" asked Colonel Kori.

"I told you I don't know."

"Who's General Sam?"

"I still don't know."

"And there's a woman, too, isn't there?"

"Ditto," said Peter, trying to speak rudely.

"Fernando Moro, Olympio Smith, Henry Cheng?"

"Ditto."

"Well, I suppose I should bring you back to headquarters and start all over again with you, but you've been pretty well punished already and it doesn't make any difference to me how their graves are marked."

"Go away, then," said Peter.

"I'm going. I do hate to leave all these loose ends, though."

Peter looked at the ceiling.

"By the way, that girl friend of yours is great. Looks like a million dollars."

"Who do you mean?" said Peter.

Colonel Kori snorted. "All right, if that's the way you feel. But listen: you say anything about what happened to you at headquarters and I'll see that your mother and everyone else in camp hears how you play pokey-pokey on dark nights with little Swedish girls. Understand?"

"I won't say anything," said Peter.

"Good. I hope you recover quickly." And Colonel Kori walked out of the room.

## CHAPTER 16

It was a private room that the Kempeitai had given Peter in the Abanao Hospital and his special nurse, Ringosan, made it more private. She wouldn't tell him what patients were in the rooms adjoining. She wouldn't tell him what was going on outside in town. She wouldn't even tell him what date it was or how long he had been there. Instead, she chatted about food and clothing and life in prewar Japan—or about Peter's father, whom she had heard of in the hospital in Tokyo where she had got her training. She was a nice girl in her homely, provincial way and she was always cheerful and friendly. What kept her from talking about anything close at hand on Panoc was fear of Colonel Kori. If Peter grew tired of her chatter and wanted to get rid of her for a while he had only to tell her that he had not fallen from a table but had been beaten up by Colonel Kori in a temper tantrum. Then she would run from the room with her hands over her ears and not come back for an hour or more. Peter didn't much mind her uncommunicativeness. Most of the time he didn't want to talk about anything nearby either, and sometimes he felt he would be satisfied to remain in the quiet white room chatting about distant things with Ringosan for the rest of his life.

Peter couldn't believe that Colonel Kori was really through with him. Lying still in bed, he tried to prepare lies, confusions and rebellions against the time when he would have to return to the torture chamber. It was difficult to plan coherently, because Ringosan and the other nurse who woke him up at night were always giving him sleeping pills, which sapped his ability to concentrate. As well as he could reason it out, Jerry, Margo and General Sam were still free and that business about marking their graves was all bluff. Otherwise Colonel Kori wouldn't be asking questions about them. Well, if they were free, there were only two possible reasons why Colonel Kori would let Peter go. Either he was ashamed of

227

what he had done and afraid of doing it again or he was convinced that Peter didn't know anything. Since Peter didn't believe either possibility was real, he waited fatalistically for Colonel Kori's next visit.

But the visit didn't come and as the days gathered into weeks Peter found himself forgetting sometimes that it had to come. Ringosan brought him stacks of old novels to choose from out of the hospital library and when he wasn't asleep he read them or gazed out with longing and fear on the green world beyond the window of his room. The hospital was up on the west end of the ridge separating North from South Valley. It was on the same road as the police station and the American Butcher Shop but all the way out at the end of it. Peter's window looked south, through the branches of tall pines and across the park at the bottom of the valley toward the Abanao Hotel and home on the other side. Some days one look out the window—even if it was only a glimpse of the bandstand in the center of the park where he had gone occasionally with his father to hear the Saturday-evening band concerts—was enough to send his mind scurrying back to the world of the book he was reading or to ring for Ringosan to close the curtains. Other days he would lie looking out for hours, oblivious to all thoughts and feelings but those of a remote boy back in the before-the-war.

One evening during the fifth or sixth week a Filipino doctor came into Peter's room and cut the cast off his leg. The next morning Ringosan announced that he must get out of bed and start learning to walk again. He protested that she was only trying to repair him for Colonel Kori to break, but she seemed hurt that he didn't appreciate her nursing and in the end he gave in. A few days later as she was helping him toddle around the bed she told him that a white girl had come to the nurse's dormitory in back of the hospital the night before and had asked to speak to "the nurse of Peter Borrudwin." It was, of course, Enid. She had asked all about Peter and whether she could come to see him. Ringosan said she could not but bravely offered to deliver a note if Enid would like to write one. The note lay unopened for two days on Peter's bedside table. He knew that it would be painful to read it and would distract him and confuse the narrow purposes for which he lived, but he couldn't bring himself to tear it up. Perhaps Enid had betrayed him and the guerrillas to Colonel Kori and perhaps not, but either way it was his reckless talk which had given her the opportunity and put the temptation in her way. Blaming her for his own fault, he had then betrayed her to Colonel Kori and exposed her to his jeers and foulness. Perhaps she didn't care about that, but even if she didn't, Peter owed her something and she had a right to force herself in on him if she wanted. He wished that she could have been satisfied to remain in her own happy world and leave him alone, but the letter was there and finally he had to read it:

DEAR PETER,

That was a dirty trick you played on me, telling about how we had dinner together. But I forgive you. Colonel Kori says you were under great stress because you thought you knew some important secrets which he might try to get out of you. I'm glad it all turned out okay and I'm sorry you had a bad fall. Captain Hebel has been transferred to Manila, but Colonel Kori thinks he can help Papa get me back to Sweden. Please write me a note if they will let you.

Love,
Yes, really a kind of love,
ENID

Peter tore up the letter in tiny pieces and threw them away one by one in the never used ash tray on his bedside table. He had never smoked cigarettes except with her. He had never drunk except with her. He had never felt grown up at all except with her. And he had never loved anyone but her. It was a nice letter she had sent him, too. But he still didn't know whether or not she had betrayed him. And he was sure that all the confused feelings her letter called up in him would never be solved and made straight. He had stood up to Colonel Kori and gained a chance either to die well or to live and expiate his sins. One or the other he still had to do and whichever it was Enid had no place in it.

All the same he owed Enid an answer, especially when she had taken the risk of coming to the hospital to send him a note and forgiven him for the way he had betrayed her. So two days later he asked Ringosan if she would deliver a letter for him to the white girl, Ringosan blushed and said she would as long as Peter would let her read it—only her and not Colonel Kori, she promised. Peter let her. It wasn't as if he had written anything mushy.

DEAR ENID,

I appreciated your letter very much and I'm glad that you forgive me. I hope you like Sweden fine. I'll never forget you.

Love,
PETER

"It is very short," said Ringosan.

She delivered the letter the very next morning before coming on duty. Enid was still in bed so she left it with Amelia, the maid.

One evening about a week later, Peter was walking up and down in front of the window of his room getting some exercise before he went to bed. It was his eighth or ninth week in the hospital, the nurses had stopped giving him sedatives and he was finding it increasingly difficult to sleep at night and keep his thoughts from roving beyond the novels he had read in the daytime. The dark trees of the park below sighed and creaked restlessly in the wind and Peter was planning a scene full of temporizing lies and infuriating insults for Colonel Kori. He was well now, though he wouldn't admit it to Ringosan. He had recovered both from his beating and from any hope that it was all over, and he was ready to face the next encounter.

While he was pacing, he was surprised to find that Ringosan had come in in her street clothes, as she often did now in the evenings after going off duty and changing and eating, and was watching him from the doorway.

"You are orrul werrul now," she said. "Tomorrow, Corrunerrul Kori says, you wirrul be taken back to camp. The truck wirrul come for you at six o'crock. That is before I am on duty, so I came now to bid you good-by."

"To camp?" said Peter. "Oh, no, that's just what Colonel Kori says, but he doesn't mean it. In a day or two, if I'm smart, maybe I'll end up back here in the hospital."

"I have a retter for you," said Ringosan nervously.

Peter took the letter and read it at once.

DEAR PETER,

Your note was awfully brief. I am not going to

Sweden right away and you can bet I am bored without you. Pretty soon I'll find a way to visit you.

Love,
ENID

"Good-by," said Ringosan, and before Peter had thanked her for her weeks of kindness, she was gone. Peter tore up Enid's letter, rang for the night nurse and waited impatiently for her. As usual, it was nearly half an hour before she came. He told her coldly that it was his last night and that he had to have a sleeping pill. She protested, but he was so insistent and irritable that she finally gave in and brought him one. Confident of its magic, he settled down in bed to go to sleep quickly and gather strength for the ultimate test, which he expected on the next day.

When the night nurse awakened him she had a soldier with her. It was even earlier than six o'clock because the sky out the window was almost completely black still. The nurse brought him his shorts and shirt all neatly pressed and clean. He put them on hurriedly, along with the socks and sneakers under his bed, and followed the soldier out down the dark, antiseptic corridor, past the lighted island of the nurses' station, down the wooden stairs and out a side door into the street. There an automobile was waiting for him with a second soldier in it behind the wheel. The wind of the night before had stopped and a cloud had settled on the ridge top, burying the hospital and the pine trees in soft white mist and cutting off the view across the valley toward home. The damp chill of it made Peter wish that he had on his gray flannel visiting trousers. But he had left them back beyond the mist in his wagon, hidden among the stacks of firewood under the house. He climbed in between the two soldiers. The one who was the driver released the brake and, saving fuel-alcohol like a Chinese cabby, let the car glide off down the hill without switching on the engine. Peter turned and watched the hospital slip away into the mist. It looked cold and white. Still, it had been a home of sorts, perhaps the last he would have, and he wished again that he had said a proper good-by to Ringosan.

From its ghostly start, the automobile quickly picked up momentum, and Peter found himself thinking not of the ordeal ahead or of the hospital behind but only of the next hairpin curve in the descent from the ridge. There were four of them. The first, to the right, was easy. The second, to the left, made the tires squeal. The third forced the car over into the left-hand lane and Peter waited for the driver to put on the brakes. But he didn't. At the end of the next straightaway he began to turn left even before the corner. The tires squealed. He aimed at the pine trees on the inside of the curve. The back wheels lost their grip on the road. The car shuddered along sideways through the mist, plunged for the pines on the inside, wagged toward the embankment on the outside, hurtled right, left, right and left again and finally shot out of the mist, going straight and whistling along between the rows of huts which edged the road at this end of town. The driver nudged Peter with his elbow and roared with laughter. The other soldier grinned foolishly and Peter took a deep breath to vent his excitement. The idea crossed his mind that the whole mad incident had been arranged by Colonel Kori to rob him of composure and drive the carefully laid battle plans out of his head. When Peter had calmed himself and suppressed the intoxication which had risen in him, he looked out the window again and saw the Roman Catholic cathedral. The driver let in the clutch, starting the engine and slowing the car down so that he could turn the market corner and head up the main street with some semblance of good sense and dignity. Only then did Peter realize that the butcher shop and the police station were already far behind. He was being taken toward Camp Dewey. It was a trick to put him off his guard. Perhaps it was simply a mistake. But suppose it was genuine. Suppose Colonel Kori had given up and was going to let him live.

Peter suddenly felt nervous, embarrassed and confused. Somewhere in the back of his mind he knew that he feared the scorn and disgust of his mother and the condemnation of the rest of the community. But for the moment he couldn't remember exactly why it was that his mother knew of his shame and fornication, nor even why she should be too unforgiving if she did know. After all, he had life instead of death ahead of him and in time he could expiate his sin. It wasn't an altogether mortal one. In some cases—between natives, for instance—it was considered fairly venial. He relaxed back into his seat feeling weak, tired and deflated.

The car flashed through the check point where Peter had been arrested. He realized that he had already passed his home and hadn't even noticed it. Now they were approaching Enid's house. There it was on the left. He looked automatically to see if the blind was up. Naturally it wasn't. She would not be awake yet. But he found that the sight of her window still moved him. The inclination to sin had not left him. Living had not become simple.

The country club came into sight ahead on the right. Across the road from it was Colonel Kori's house. Maybe that's where they were taking him. The thought was a flash of energy, almost like hope. And almost like disappointment, the car passed Kori's house without slackening speed. Peter closed his eyes and counted up the sensations of being alive: in his stomach, hunger; in his nose, the stench of fuel alcohol; under his arms, the cold wetness of spent excitement; in his feet, the vibrations of machinery.

He opened his eyes in time to see the green of the golf course where he had first dug for shrapnel. Then the driver shifted into second for the climb up the hill, and the sentries at the entrance of the concentration camp carelessly saluted. The car heaved up onto the edge of the parade ground and the soldiers jumped out. They escorted Peter to Colonel Fleer's old house, where the officers of the camp guards slept and did their paper work, and left him sitting on the porch in full view of the barracks while they went inside to report. In a few minutes Mr. Kono came out yawning and combing his hair.

"Werrulcome back to Camp Dewey," he said. "Prease sign this."

"What is it?" asked Peter.

"Onry your paper of identification," he said. "You wirrul put your fingerprints here beside your name." Kono produced a small ink box, and Peter did as he was told.

"Go to the guard at the fence and he wirrul ret you through I expect you wirrul find your mother and Mrs. Gibney and the others of your sect horrulding service in the big hut."

Kono turned away, and Peter walked out alone across the parade ground. He felt a little hurt and foolish that they didn't bother to guard him better. It was as much as to say that he wasn't brave enough and his broken leg wasn't well enough for him to try running away. Still, it was nice being alone. There was no mist at this end of the valley. What few small clouds there were in the sky were strewn about and the pink of dawn was only just fading out of them. From the stoves in the cook shed behind the barracks the smoke rose in a still, vertical column. Camp had changed. The chicken-wire fence around and between the barracks had been replaced by a single massive stockade which encompassed both barracks and a good part of the parade ground as well. Outside, the grass was high. Inside, it was neatly cropped and dotted with shacks and lean-tos which had not been there before. As Peter approached the big gate in the center of the stockade, the guard shouted, "*Hayaku*"—"Hurry up"—and Peter quickened his steps. He was let in through a small door to the right of the gate. The parade ground inside was deserted and he set out across it slowly and unsurely. Before meeting his mother he would have liked to go to the Staff Room and fortify himself with a little of the easy pagan tolerance which clung to Donny Garver and Mark Price. But he couldn't do that, so he limped toward the big shed in front of the barracks which Mr. Kono had pointed out to him. It was roofed with tin from kerosene cans, laid on like shingles, and its walls were made of nipa palm matting. It was held up off the ground by untrimmed pine logs. Through the flimsy nipa partitions Peter heard the murmur of devotions from inside. Coming closer, he recognized the voice of Father Gibney and picked up the thread of a Communion service.

". . . to all bishops and other ministers, that they may, both by their life and doctrine, set forth Thy true and lively word and rightly and duly administer Thy holy sacraments . . ." A long-forgotten piety and excitement stirred in Peter at the sound of the beautiful formal words. ". . . give Thy heavenly grace; and especially to this congregation here present, and to Thy brave young servant Peter Baldwin, now absent and in the hands of Thine enemies; that, with meek heart and due reverence, they may hear and receive Thy holy . . ."

Peter Baldwin?

". . . And we most humbly beseech Thee . . ."

Peter Baldwin?

". . . to comfort and succor all those like Thy child Peter, who, in this transitory life, are in trouble, sorrow, need, sickness or any other . . ."

What awful blasphemy. Couldn't Father Gibney have guessed how it really was? Peter limped quickly around the nipa-matting church with a thought to correcting the horrible mistake inside.

When he reached the door at the other end Father Gibney was saying, "For as the benefit is great, if with a true penitent heart and lively faith we receive that holy sacrament; so is the danger great, if we receive the same unworthily. Judge therefore yourselves, brethren, that ye be not judged . . ."

Peter had judged himself and he knew he was not fit to receive Communion. But was he fit to enter the church? Even worse, if he went in now, wouldn't it seem like a kind of miracle—a fake one—after they had been praying for him and he didn't deserve it and he couldn't tell them why?

All the same, he had to begin somewhere. He had made promises and he could feel a real yearning pulling him in toward the altar. He waited until the General Confession had started, when he knew Father Gibney would be turned toward the cross and away from the door, and then he limped in and knelt low in the back of the shed where no one would see him until the service was over. His entrance had made some noise, but no one turned to look.

As the service progressed, Peter began to see what expiation would mean for him. He had expected he would have to suffer scorn and rejection for what he had done. In his first horror at hearing Father Gibney call him "brave servant" in the middle of the beautiful prayer for the Whole State of Christ's Church, he had wanted to tell the congregation that scorn and rejection were all he deserved. But he couldn't ask them to make him suffer without itemizing reasons. And he couldn't confess without involving Enid on the one hand and Jerry on the other. And as long as there was any doubt that Enid had betrayed him or any chance that some of the guerrillas were still free in the hills, he couldn't name either one of them. He was back in his old trap of telling lies by saying nothing and of damning himself simply by being alive and breathing. But it wasn't altogether the same as before, was it? He no longer wanted to do it. He *had* repented. He *had* been ready to face the consequences. He had wanted to change. And now he didn't know. Was it possible to atone simply by remembering his sins himself and blaming himself for them? Was it possible when he was still being a hypocrite outwardly and receiving praise which he didn't deserve?

"Please God," he prayed, "can't you make it easier? I'm ready to try to be a just and righteous man or a minister or even a missionary if that's what you want, but it's going to be difficult to make myself better if everyone thinks I'm already good."

He felt happier after praying. It was the first honest prayer he had made in a church for more than a year. But he had not received any absolute answer, and no assurance that he would be saved if he could keep himself inwardly honest and self-accusing and not let himself be corrupted by his outward hypocrisy. It was as if God stood very far away and said severely: "Let's see how you do."

When Father Gibney had spoken the benediction, Peter stood up by the door. The candles were put out by Father Gibney himself, because he had no acolyte. As he turned from the altar, he saw Peter, started with surprise, and then, giving a hearty laugh, he forgot to put down the candle snuffer or make the final genuflection but strode down the aisle toward Peter.

"Good boy," he shouted.

"We heard about you through the grapevine," he said, shaking Peter's hand. "We heard indirectly from the Filipino doctor who treated you in the hospital. You stood up to them until there was nothing they could do but beat you up. I'm proud of you."

"How about you?" asked Peter dazedly. "When did they let *you* out?"

"Oh, we were in only for a week. They hardly bothered to question us."

Peter's mother wept and kissed him, and hugged and pinched him.

Mrs. Gibney shook his hand, like Father Gibney, and said, standing even straighter than usual, "It's wonderfully good to see you, Peter. Perhaps we can get you back to your studies now, eh?"

Sister Iona, speaking for the nuns who stood by watching with the Marlowes and Barsinis, said, "We will thank God for your deliverance, Peter, just as we prayed for it."

Overcome, but with shame rather than the joy of reunion, Peter stood woodenly and let their praise and jubilation wash over him. When they had all gone and left him alone with his mother, he said, "What's the date, Mother?"

"January the third. Oh, *mon pauvre*, didn't they even give you a calendar?"

"Gee whiz," he said. "I missed Christmas and New Year's both and I never even noticed them."

"Have you had breakfast yet?" she asked when she had finished crying.

"No," he said, so they left the church and went to stand in the serving line outside the cook shed in back of the barracks. The line had just started to move, and as the news that Peter was there spread through it, people turned to stare at him. He tried not to notice but he couldn't help wondering how many of them believed—as some had believed of the missionaries who came back from being tortured in the first few weeks—that he had sold his conscience to the Japs to stay alive. Well, what difference? He had sold it to Enid.

Suddenly the people in the line began to clap their hands. Peter didn't know if they were applauding him or making fun of him. Either way was equally bad. He blushed and wanted to run away. Then he saw that the clapping was for Harry Gamoff, who was coming down the line in one of his prewar white chef's hats, with a broad smile on his face and carrying three dishes of rice on a tray.

"Compliments of the house," he announced in a loud voice. "Today I bring you your breakfast personally. Tomorrow you have to stand in line for it yourself. Come round to the Staff Room later and maybe we'll have a surprise for you."

"Thank you, Mr. Gamoff," said Peter's mother.

"Come around about ten o'clock, Peter," he said.

"Okay, Harry. Thank you," said Peter falteringly. He took the tray, and his mother led the way to the place where she lived. It was a nipa shack about twelve feet square out near the stockade on the downhill end of the women's barracks. She shared it, she said, with Mrs. Gibney and five of the other missionary women who had been out of camp. Peter could see through the raised iron flap over the window that the bunks were hung up high by two-by-fours from the roof beams, and that shelves and crude pieces of furniture were compactly arranged to make living and working spaces underneath. On one side of the shack—and almost as big as it—was an open porch thatched with palm leaves and floored with split climbing palms. To some extent, the porch made up for the crowding inside.

There was a rough table on the porch, and here Mrs. Baldwin told Peter to set down their portions of rice.

"I'll get the sirup," she said, and went inside the shack. Peter sat down on a bench. If only everyone would stop being so kind, and just give him a bunk and a book to read, maybe he could collect himself and face life without feeling so dejected and tired.

Two hands covered his eyes from the rear. "Guess who?" asked Jeanette.

"I don't know. Father Gibney maybe or Mr. Kono?"

"No, dopey, it's me. See!"

"Wow, you've grown."

"I have not. You just never noticed me when we were out of camp. D'you know I'm going to school now?"

"That's terrific."

"You don't look specially beaten up."

"Why should I?"

"'Cause I heard they beat you up. What did they really do?"

"One of them got mad at me and hit me with a gun and broke some of my bones."

"I bet that hurt."

"Not so much. I went to sleep in the middle of it."

"What a dopey thing to do. They might have broken something right off while you weren't paying attention."

"I couldn't help it. I was knocked out."

"Did you see stars?"

"I guess so. How come you're not dressed yet?"

"Because Mother always gets the breakfast and I don't have to put on my clothes until I've eaten it."

"Jeanette, start eating or you'll be late for school," called their mother out the window.

"Mine's mixed with goat's milk," said Jeanette. "I get to have goat's milk until I'm ten. Then I have to have just sirup like you and Mother."

Mrs. Baldwin came out of the shack with a glass jar of boiled crude sugar sirup and a plateful of grated coconut.

"The sirup is part of our ration," she said. "They hand it out once a week. The coconut is an extra which Mrs. Gibney bought at the store."

"Store?" asked Peter.

"Over there next to the gate," said his mother, pointing, and Peter saw what looked like a vegetable stand protruding from the inside of the stockade.

"It's run by Mrs. Kono," said his mother. "People with money live off it almost entirely. There are stoves out back now where we can do private cooking if we have anything to cook."

"Do we still have any money?" asked Peter.

"Yes, it's all here, just as you left it. I simply snatched up the cardboard box that night and brought it in with me. Two hundred and forty-three pesos. I counted it for the first time only the other day. And I saw that you had added some since the last time I looked. I don't see how you did it. The last few months outside you never used any of my money at all."

"I had some more too," said Peter sadly. "It was in my wallet." He reached automatically for the back pocket of his freshly laundered shorts, and to his astonishment the wallet was still there. He jerked it out and looked inside. Every single note of his seventy-three pesos was still in it. The bills were fastened together by a paper clip and with them was a piece of paper stamped with an official seal and scribbled with the words *Approved, Colonel Kori.* Perhaps Kori really had been ashamed about Peter—or even sorry for him.

"Isn't that surprising?" he said, laying the wallet on the table. "They washed my pants and then put it all back without taking any of it. You better keep it with the rest."

"Did you really earn all that running errands?" asked his mother.

"Sort of. Anyway I earned it all."

His mother picked it up with a worried look and rose to take it inside. "Jeanette," she said, "hurry up or you'll be late for school."

Jeanette bolted her last few mouthfuls of rice and goat's milk and, kissing Peter, followed his mother into the shack. What did his mother think? That he had accepted money from the Japs? He had done enough bad things for her to worry about without letting her be unhappy over imaginary ones.

When she came back out to finish her breakfast, he said, "You don't have to worry about that money, Mother. I earned it honestly. The pay was high because I did some dangerous things."

"For the guerrillas?"

"Sort of," he said.

"Funny. I knew you had to meet them to get the letters from your father, but I never realized they would ask you to do things for them. Father Gibney says you were the obvious choice as a messenger boy and we should have guessed it. I suppose I should have told him about the letters from your

239

father and he *would* have guessed it, but Tim said not to tell anyone."

"Yes," said Peter flatly. "Anyway, it's all over now. Let's talk about something else."

"How do you like my porch?"

"It's nice. When did they start letting men and women eat together?"

"A few months ago, I think. There have been a lot of changes in camp since we were here before. Things are much better organized than they used to be."

As they finished their rice and sirup in the pleasant morning sunshine, she enumerated the improvements and tried hard to be entertaining and matter-of-fact—almost as if she were talking socially to a grownup she didn't know very well. An honest, energetic young Presbyterian minister called Mr. Catlow, she said, was chairman of the Governing Committee now and the Staff Room had lost its power and privileges. A young Baptist and a young sugar man with advanced degrees in mathematics and engineering respectively had been appointed to assist Harry Gamoff on the serving line. They divided up the rations with such scientific justice that there was hardly a rice grain's difference between any two portions.

Poor Harry, thought Peter. In the old days, if a friend like Peter had been brought back into camp, Harry would have chiseled a fatted calf out of everyone else's rations so as to spread the friend a feast. Now the authorities watched him so closely that the biggest show he could put on was to wear his old chef's hat and save his friend from having to wait in the chow line.

The only one of Peter's old bunk mates who was still in power, said his mother, was Mr. Newcombe. He had moved out of the Staff Room long ago and had somehow weathered every political storm since. But it looked now as if his cushy job of buying all the food for the camp might soon be abolished. According to Mrs. Gibney, who had become an interpreter again, the new commandant of the guards, Captain Hira, didn't like the marketing truck going downtown every day and was thinking of having the camp supplied with Jap Army rations trucked in direct from the lowlands. If the rations were really regulation, they would have less variety, perhaps, but they would mean far bigger servings. The only people who preferred to go on with the old system were Mr.

Newcombe and some of the big sugar refinery families who still had lots of money. They had become so used to living on delicacies from Mrs. Kono's store that they wanted to decrease the quantity and increase the quality even of what little food the common mess already supplied.

On the whole, though, no one in camp was starving now and no one was getting fat—except, of course, a few unfortunate women who could get fat on rice no matter how little they ate of it. No one was getting out of doing a fair share of work now either. Except for the worst invalids, every internee had to put in five hours a day at hard manual labor or slightly more at softer jobs. The five-hour details were the wood gang, the garbage crew, the *camote*-patch tenders, the pot washers and the D-GOOD FECITS which reportedly stood for "Donny Garver's Organization of Diligent Fixers, Experts, Carpenters, Inventors, Tinkers and Smiths. The six-hour details consisted of more sedentary chores like caring for the camp's herd of goats or picking stones and weevils out of the rice before it was cooked.

There was also one nine-hour detail, and whether or not it should be nine hours was the subject of the latest camp controversy. The enlightened new commandant, Captain Hira, had brought in books and had a school shed built for the children. Young ones like Jeanette, who was in second grade, attended the school from seven to twelve in the mornings. Teen-agers Peter's age had to go on a regular work detail in the mornings, so they attended from one to four in the afternoons and then again after the second meal, from five to six. The controversy was about the teachers. In a work force of a hundred-odd—not counting those sick with dysentery, and considering the fact that someone was always thinking up new jobs which had to be done—four adults seemed plenty to devote to the education of the camp's thirty-two children. The camp committee had ruled in the beginning that each teacher could handle two grades during the morning and either English, history, foreign languages or math and science for the various high-school groups in the afternoon. Since the teachers would be working only with their brains and wouldn't be burning many calories, the long hours would be no hardship.

The trouble was that the teachers didn't find it so. They found that they had no time left for private affairs like washing their sheets, and the two men teachers had just quit in protest and gone back to their short, energy-consuming jobs on the wood gang. People without families said, "Fine: let the parents teach their own kids in the afternoons when they've finished the important work of the day." At the other extreme, some of the parents said that not only should the teaching staff be doubled but the teen-agers should be relieved of work so that they could devote all their energy to studying. Peter's mother backed a compromise plan whereby the ten high-school kids should have to work only four hours a day and there would be thirty-six teachers who taught an hour a day each and had it count as half an hour of manual labor. This way the children would get the benefit of all the specialist knowledge in camp and the teaching load would be spread so thin that it would hardly be noticed. For instance, under such a system, Peter's mother would be delighted, she said, to teach French conversation.

As she rattled on over the empty plates of rice, Peter watched the wood gang file out through the gate in the stockade with saws, axes, wheelbarrows and guards. They would go down the ridge a ways, fell some pines, saw them into logs and haul them back to stoke the cook stoves. He could see from the pile of logs under the nipa-thatched lean-to opposite his mother's hut that they were several months ahead of themselves and could probably weather a whole rainy season without cutting more. Camp had certainly changed all right. In the beginning, people had been so sure of speedy liberation that they had considered doing things in advance pessimistic and unpatriotic. Now *patriotism* and *liberation* seemed to be fuzzy, far-off words which meant no more to most people in terms of day-to-day camp life than *philosophy* or *The Second Coming* had meant in day-to-day prewar life. It was almost as if camp had swallowed up the world and taken its place. Things outside were happening on Mars or some other planet. They were sick things to think about here because here everyone was lean and healthy and energetic. Everyone had jobs to do and interests to pursue. Everyone had a place except Peter. Camp had changed and left him behind. He was still dreaming of wars and gods and devils which only existed on Mars.

Shaking his head clear of such dopey thoughts, Peter looked at his mother and saw that she had changed too. Her hair was almost completely white now—which looked rather nice, he thought—but there were lines around her mouth and a twitch in her eyebrow which did not look nice. When she had finished describing the squabble about the school, he said, "I'm sorry I caused you so much worry, Mother."

"You only did what you had to do, *mon fils*. I was the foolish one to worry so."

"Your hair's turned white," he said.

"Well? I've been wanting it to finish turning for years. Now it has and it looks much better."

He shook his head doubtfully, and after a short silence she said, "It was mostly that one dreadful night. I know now that you were out helping the guerrillas, but at the time I thought you had run away or gone to live with some native girl or—oh, I don't know, I don't know what foolish things I thought."

So she really does believe I was a hero, he thought bitterly.

"You gave me so many silly excuses," she went on, "the night before when you stayed out too late watching the officers at the Meiji Day Ball."

"What makes you think I was helping the guerrillas?" he asked unsurely.

"Well, weren't you? Father Gibney said you must have been. He said it was very clever of you to circle around through the woods after the attack and present yourself in South Valley instead of North Valley. He said it was the one thing which might save you."

"I told him what I did," said Peter. "I went down to the lookout at the end of South Valley to watch the sunrise."

"That may be what you told him, but I know that you were out all night because I waited up for you."

"I didn't want him to know we'd had a fight, so I said I'd gotten up about one or two o'clock. But actually I spent the whole night on the bench at the lookout."

"All right, my son," said his mother with a sad smile. "If that's all the Japs could get out of you in two months, then it's good enough for me."

Peter realized dully that he could never break this chain of lies. Accepting pity and praise from his mother was a worm-like thing to do, but even if Enid really had delivered him into the hands of Colonel Kori, he still wouldn't tell his mother about her now. His mother was happy. She thought all her worry had been for a good cause.

243

"Did you really ask the police to put us back in camp that day?" he asked.

"Yes, I really did. And when they first came that night I thought that was why. I thought it would be all my fault if you got into trouble about not being home."

"I'm sorry," said Peter. "I could probably have stayed home that night."

"Perhaps if I hadn't been such a foolish woman and gone to the police, you would have stayed home. I'm sure the guerrillas could have gotten someone else to do your job just that once."

"Maybe, maybe not," said Peter. He was trying to remember whether his mother's threats had really been important or not in making him go to Enid's that afternoon. So much had happened since that he could no longer be sure. "In some ways I wish I could tell you about it," he said.

"Well, don't if you've promised not to. The main thing is you're back with me now and all I'm interested in is having you strong again and forgetting the whole terrible business as soon as possible."

"Okay," said Peter.

"I don't suppose you heard from your father, did you?"

"No, but he was all right. He was back at the hideout in the north. Colonel Kori mentioned him to me once as a possible guerrilla, but I could tell that he thought it was only a trick or a wild guess and I didn't say anything different. I just said Dad was out in the hills somewhere being a doctor and wouldn't ever be a guerrilla because he liked to cure people, not hurt them."

"Thank God you had the good sense," she said. Perhaps he'll still be able to turn himself in if Father Mallard recovers. It's a terrible burden for you at your age, Peter. You have done very well and you don't know what it means to me having you back."

The numb hypocrisy and loneliness of Peter's position increased as the day went by. When he paid his visit to the men in the Staff Room, he found none of them there—they were all out working—but they had squeezed their mattresses together, found a mattress somewhere for him, put it by the window overlooking the China Sea and hung a sign over it which said PETER'S PLACE. He lay down and dozed on it for a while and then returned to his mother's shack. She

was just back from doing three hours in the vegetable cleaning room where she had met Mrs. Kahn. Mrs. Kahn had invited them to have *extras*, the lunchtime snack, with her
and Mr. Kahn on the porch of the women's barracks. It
turned out that Mayor and Mrs. Ziegler and Father and Mrs.
Gibney and a Mr. and Mrs. Steinmann were there too. The
snack was fried rice with an egg on it for each person, a loaf
of rice bread flavored with mashed banana and a bottle of
rice wine.

All the guests said they hadn't eaten such a lunch since the
war started and Mrs. Kahn said over and over again that she
wouldn't allow anyone to ask Peter questions because he had
had a terrible experience and probably didn't want to talk
about it. So they talked about it for him and toasted him in
rice wine and talked on and on about the mess the Japs were
making of things in Abanao. Peter hardly said two words
during the whole party, but toward the end of it he found
himself nodding his head to stories of Jap stupidity which he
knew nothing about, and when Mr. Kahn insinuated that
maybe the Kempeitai had given Peter the water cure and
that maybe it was internal injuries as well as a broken leg
which had kept him in the hospital so long, he didn't even
have the energy or strength of character to deny it.

After lunch, when he had fed to the full on self-disgust, he
excused himself from his mother and went on a tour of the
stockade to try to digest his meal. His leg ached and he felt
very tired, but he didn't want to go to the Staff Room and
rest because the men would be back from their work details
now and he couldn't face them. Instead, he started around
the side of the women's barracks from his mother's shack to
see what was out back. The stockade enclosed even more
ground to the rear of the barracks than it did in front. The
trees had been cut down along the ridge almost as far as the
lookout rock from which he had long ago counted the Jap
fleet. Up that way, he could see, was the *camote* patch. It
sounded from the way people talked as if the patch was almost ready to deliver its first crop. Closer to the barracks,
along with the laundry shed, bathrooms and cook house
which had always been there, were several new buildings.
The big one way over on the embankment must be the infirmary. The shed next to it was probably the school. Then
the smaller shacks must be for people to live in. Peter followed the stockade away from the dwellings. It bent down

the hill for a ways to include a small enclave of pines before climbing back to the ridge top and to the *camote* patch in the far corner.

Peter limped gratefully into the pines and lay down on the carpet of needles. Below him, where the woods ended and the swath cut for the stockade began, there was another shack, but he didn't bother to wonder what it was for. He felt weak and feverish. Too much excitement probably. Too many lies and people after the quiet of the hospital and the undemanding company of Ringosan. The murmur of life in the camp lapped at his outer ear and he wished it wasn't there. Or maybe that he wasn't there but back in the hospital behind the white mist.

"Hello, you dreamy little bugger," said a familiar, faraway voice. "What are you doing out here? Escaping the plaudits of the crowd?"

Peter opened his eyes and saw Donny Garver.

"Come on, on your feet. I'm going to give you the privilege of being the first to see the greatest invention of our century."

He dragged Peter up and led him by the elbow toward the shack below. "What would you think distinguishes a weevil or a small hunk of rock from a civilized, properly husked grain of rice?"

"I don't know."

"Naturally you don't or it wouldn't be the great discovery it is. But you might have hazarded a guess. You might have suggested something complicated like buoyancy or specific gravity. And you'd have been wrong, of course. It's far simpler than that. Like all insights of true genius, it seems almost self-evident now that it's been discovered."

They entered the shed, and Peter saw that it was a workshop full of benches and caldrons and handmade tools.

"The headquarters of the D-GOOD FECITS," said Donny. "Wooden clogs, shelves, tables, stools, cook pots, kitchen knives, jewelry, coconut graters, ax handles, soap, lipstick, pot-washer's hand lotion—you name it and we either make it or fake it. But here's the ultimate achievement." He pointed to a large funnel-shaped hopper which was poised above a slanted hardwood board and a tray made of roofing iron. The tray was divided into several sections. "Behold," said Donny. He pulled a stopper out of the bottom of the hopper and rice came pouring out. It struck the slanted

246

board, bounced toward the tin tray and mostly fell into the largest and deepest division of the tray. The dust was stifling. Peter rubbed his forehead and found it slimy with sweat. When even Donny was so enthusiastic about domestic details, it must be Peter and not the others who was the sheep in camp. A sick sheep too, he thought. A sick shep from Mars.

Donny stemmed the stream of rice and turned to him with pride. "All right now, what is it that distinguishes a weevil from a polished grain of rice?"

"Your machine?" asked Peter, groping dizzily for a workbench to lean against.

"Oh, go feel an eel, you miserable little bugger. It's bounce. Pure and simple bounce. Look here." He pointed to the smaller sections of the tray.

Peter tottered over to him and saw that one of the sections had mostly weevils in it, one mostly unhusked grains of rice and one mostly pebbles and chunks of grit.

"You see what I've done for you?" said Donny. "I've given you schoolteachers. I've released all those poor women from the servitude of the rice-sifting detail. Now they'll have no more excuse to sit on their thin asses all day gossiping and fingering the food I eat. Why, after what I've done, I expect the camp committee to set up a harem for me out of the plumpest and assign the unlucky skinny ones to doing my laundry. Then I'm going to sit back and grow rich selling byproducts: whole-rice flour made from the unhusked grains in this division, tooth powder from these high-quality pieces of grit here, and from the weevils a delicious *pâté* for people who want more protein in their diets."

Peter lurched out through the dust, reached the doorway and threw up in a pile of sawdust.

"Well, for Christ sakes," said Donny. "You *are* an unappreciative audience."

"I'm sorry," gasped Peter. "I don't feel well."

When he had finished, Donny helped him to his feet and led him back toward the barracks.

"Come on, I expect all you need is a look out that old window of yours. Then, as soon as you feel better, I want a run-down on Jap torture methods. And I don't want you being coy and modestly heroic either. I want the details, especially about the machines. It doesn't seem to me anyone's given much thought to the branch of engineering since the days of the rack and the boot. I once dreamed up some simple little

247

contrivances to use on a girl in Frisco which would have made Peter the Cruel drool. But I never built any of them because there wasn't any market for that sort of thing. Now the market's better, I imagine."

They reached the Staff Room and Donny left Peter on his mattress while he went to fetch a doctor. The other men in the Staff Room, he said, were probably out behind the barracks playing poker.

Peter must have dozed off before Donny came back because the next thing he knew he had been moved and was in a cubicle in the camp infirmary surrounded by walls of nipa matting. A woman he didn't know was nursing him. She said that he had a fever of 105° and that the doctor thought it was some kind of dengue. After that, whenever he was awake he knew that he was hectic and slightly drunk and delirious, so to be on the safe side, he shut his mouth and said nothing to anyone; not to his mother or Mrs. Kahn or Mrs. Gibney or any of the other people who came to visit him. It was a new form of interrogation, a new kind of hidden microphone, and he spent all his clearheaded hours impressing harmless things to say on his mind so that he would pour them out the next time he became delirious. His mother was always there watching him, like the devil in a new mask, but when he had told her several times in his drunkenness that that was what she really was, she began to leave him alone with the nipa matting.

# CHAPTER 17

Alone in a cube of whitewashed matting, unhappy on his own remote planet, Peter convalesced from dengue and made stern resolves about his future. To gain redemption without the help of any outward punishment he saw that he would have to be not just good but almost perfect. And the only way he could come close to being perfect was to avoid all temptation and keep himself from being sucked into the activity and easy solace of camp life. In moments of weakness and self-pity, he thought that it was a hard penance to impose on a boy. Even if he succeeded in it, he wasn't sure that he would be forgiven. God still seemed to stand a long way off and to say, "We'll see." But Peter had controlled his mind in fear and in fever and he thought perhaps now he could control it in life too. For help he counted heavily on two hospital habits, silence and loneliness, and he continued to cultivate them carefully after his temperature had gone down and his jaundiced skin had begun to grow white again.

When Dr. Dyson, the head of the camp infirmary, finally discharged him to return to the men's barracks, the first thing he did was to go to the Presbyterian chairman of the Governing Committee, Mr. Catlow, and ask to move his mattress out of the Staff Room. Donny Garver's talk and humor were a temptation which he had to escape. And when he told Mr. Catlow that he wanted to move because he didn't want to get into bad company, Mr. Catlow was quick to agree. The sleeping diagram of the men's barracks showed that only two cubicles had less than their full quota of occupants. One was the cubicle of the old men, the other the cubicle of the Seventh-Day Adventists. Mr. Catlow recommended the second, but Peter chose the first. He knew that the old men were all sugar refiners and as foul-mouthed as anyone in the Staff Room but he felt that they would make sin seem less desirable to him than the pious talk of the Seventh-Day Adventists.

Peter moved his mattress in the afternoon while the men in the Staff Room were all out back playing poker. It wasn't until the next day that Mark Price stopped by, wet with sweat from a morning on the wood gang, to ask him why.

"What the devil is this, Peter? You given up waiting to see the American fleet come sailing in window of yours, or what is it?"

Peter had been reading the Bible. Since he wasn't well enough to work on a regular detail yet, reading the Bible was his main occupation. He put the book down, embarrassed.

"I've just got some things to think about," he said, "and I wanted a place with some peace and quiet to do it in."

Mr. Price snorted and seemed about to go on his way; then he hesitated and said, "I don't suppose you saw or heard anything of Peter Wong down there at the butcher shop, did you?"

"They showed him to me," said Peter. "He was pretty nearly dead."

"You think they killed him?"

"I don't know. I didn't see him die."

"Poor bastard," said Mr. Price. "If I ever see that bitch again I'll strangle her."

Peter snatched up the Bible and rudely pretended to read it again in a vain effort to keep out the words. If Mr. Price meant Enid and if he knew that she had betrayed the guerrillas, he ought to blame Peter. But he didn't because he was sinful and tolerant himself. His easygoing point of view was the worst kind of temptation.

"Okay, boy, if that's how you want it," said Mr. Price. "But don't forget we've got a place for you if you ever feel better."

It didn't matter what Mr. Price thought or even what Enid had done. Peter was still at fault before God. By careful mental manipulation he forced the conversation out of his consciousness.

Later the same day, Donny Garver paid him a call. "Now what the hell kind of a wild hair is this, Peter? You going to stay here?"

"Yes."

"Well, what are you doing? Studying to be a saint or something?"

"No, far from it," said Peter quickly, frightened by the danger of spiritual pride. "I just want to be alone so I can think for a while."

"Yes, but why? Did they make you say the Lord's Prayer backward or wet your pants or turn Buddhist or what?"

"Please go away, Donny."

"Now listen, if they finally broke you down and got you to squeal on Wong, don't worry about it. He was cooked anyway."

"I didn't do that. I just want to be left alone."

"All right, be stubborn. Make yourself miserable. But when you're fed up with this pious crap, come around to the shop and I'll teach you some real theology at the workbench."

"Okay."

For the next week or so, Mark and Donny and Harry Gamoff stopped by at Peter's new bunk place occasionally and chatted just as they had when he'd been in the infirmary. But as they came to see how little he enjoyed talking to them, they gradually gave it up.

One night a few weeks later as Peter was falling asleep, he heard old Mr. Illingdon say to old Mr. Kraskowitz, "Well, another day another dollar. If the damn Yanks don't come for us pretty soon, Kraskowitz, we're going to go as crazy as the poor stooly kid. What the devil do you suppose is keeping them?"

Little by little Peter had gained for himself the kind of reputation or at least suspicion that made him suffer and gave him a penance outside his own mind. Of course his mother treated him the same as always and Mrs. Kahn still forced extras on him, but Peter felt sure that even they had begun to suspect he was guilty of something.

As Peter grew stronger on the food his mother bought for him at the store, he started school and took on a work detail. He began by helping the old men clean the grounds. Then he washed pots for a few weeks and finally, after helping to harvest the first *camote* crop, he graduated to the wood gang. He worked hard and silently and kept himself well tired.

Soon even Ray Henry, the strongest man in camp, couldn't fault him on the other end of a two-man saw. In school he didn't do so well. Except for geometry and algebra, he found that his studies tempted his mind to stray beyond the increasingly strict boundaries he set for righteousness. When he found temptation in his books, he directed his mind to other things. The return of his strength and energy made it harder every day to find things which were not in some way tempting. Even the brief prayer he said at night for Enid—in which he tried to lighten the burden of guilt he had put on her and remind God that she was lonely and motherless and uninstructed—often left him with a sadness and nostalgia which weren't fully repentant.

His schoolmates—even Norm Diak, who worked with him on the wood gang—soon gave up their efforts to find out about his adventures and began not to notice that he was there in class with them. Of course the girls, especially Maggie Higgins, to whom he had sent food parcels from the outside, tried to be kind to him from time to time, but they were all pretty well taken up with their own lives. As well as schoolwork and regular work, they had dates and boy friends now. The Japs had opened the school to recreational activities in the evenings and when the last class let out at six there was always a line of couples waiting outside to go in and play cards or cribbage at the study tables.

This was the time of day when Peter found it most difficult to remain out on the planet of shyness and silence to which he had banished himself. He was the only one of the boys who did not stay after school doing homework and reserving a table for his date. The girls went to their barracks and took showers and put on a little of Donny Garver's lipstick. Then they came back and played bridge or did their homework with the boys. Later, if the night was fine, most of them spent the last hour before lights-out walking on the parade ground or necking in the clump of pines out by Donny's workshop.

Peter sometimes took walks, too, but not often, because he didn't like to have his loneliness noticed and it was difficult not to be seen. Either he had to stay in the open where the searchlights on top of the stockade could suddenly pick him out of the night and expose him to everyone else, or he had to skulk among the trees of the pine grove or in the shadows of the shacks where he was always in danger of stumbling over commixers. It was bad enough if the commixers were unmarried, but if they were married it seemed more embarrassing still. Not that there was much danger they'd be more than kissing. The Jap guards were always poking about in the woodshed and other dark corners and if they found couples doing anything which was likely to increase the population, they took them to the guardhouse and made them sit all night under bright lights on the porch where everyone could see them and laugh at them. One or two of the couples who had been married for only a short time before the war were apparently thick-skinned enough to chance the consequences —anyway, they were careless enough to get caught repeatedly. But most of the married people were either more discreet or more abstinent. After all, babies to feed were a serious danger, and fear of them wasn't restricted to the guardhouse. There were a number of older internees who didn't just laugh and gossip about people who carried commixing too far, but criticized them, cut them socially, and even tried to get the Governing Committee to pass laws for reducing their rations and punishing them.

Peter had no opinion about the commixing question because he did his best never to think about such subjects. He only wished there were some way he could go out walking nights when he grew restless, and still avoid pity, embarrassment and the difficult thoughts which were dredged up in him by the sight of lovers. His best alternative was to go out back of the cook shed, where the eaves had been extended to cover the poker table, and listen to the old men gossip and reminisce about food and drink and women. But it wasn't long before Peter had heard all their stories many times and extracted from them as much disgust with the vanities of the flesh as he ever would. So most evenings he lay on his bunk doing the last and hardest problems at the bottom of the chapters in his geometry book. More and more, this was his one pleasure in life.

While he was studying, he usually had for company old Mr. Kraskowitz, lying in bed on the opposite side of the cubicle. Kraskowitz was a sick, unhappy old man who seldom moved out of bed except to fetch his chow, and seldom spoke to anyone but Mr. Illingdon. Some nights it would have been hard to know he was still alive except that when he was smoking he periodically tugged at his sheets to flick live coals off them, and when he was making pleasure for himself he grunted a bit. To know that he was simply there —either dead or alive—was easier: he could be smelled. The other old men had never managed to get him to take more than two showers in any one month. This was bad enough, but worse still were his stiff gray sheets. They had been washed only once since the beginning of internment and the moment he disturbed them to get into bed they polluted the air of the entire cubicle.

Disgusting as old Mr. Kraskowitz was, Peter had developed an odd affection for him, a combination of pity and of gratitude because he held up a mirror to Peter's sins and showed him what was in store for him if he failed in his efforts to reform and atone. It was a sin for Peter to judge Kraskowitz's soul by the condition of his body—and Peter knew it and tried to cleanse himself of it—but everything Peter could learn about the old man's life confirmed him in thinking that it hadn't been a good one. Kraskowitz had come to the Philippines as a young man, fought for a month in the Spanish-American War and been wounded. For nearly half a century since then he had lived off his pension, growing fat, drinking as much as he could afford and being waited on by a succession of native mistresses. Internment was a long night for him—with few cigarettes, less whisky and no girls—to be slept through if possible.

In the presence of Mr. Illingdon—a waspish old Scot who made tomato pickles for himself and kept them, on a shelf beside Peter's bunk, until they had gone rotten or sometimes until Peter had knocked them off—Mr. Kraskowitz referred to Peter as "the pious punk." But in the evenings, when Peter was doing geometry problems and no one else was in the cubicle, Mr. Kraskowitz sometimes made an effort to be sociable.

"D'ya get it yet?"

"Yes, but the next one's harder."

"I used to do the same crap when I was a kid."

That was all there ever was, but it seemed to show that Mr. Kraskowitz sensed Peter's odd affection for him and appreciated it.

One evening when Peter had been back in camp about four months, he was working on a particularly tough problem: given the radii of a right triangle's inscribed and circumscribed circles, to construct the right triangle. He had been working on it for two evenings now and Mr. Kraskowitz had twice asked him whether he had got it yet, and he had just had a fresh idea and *was* getting it when Mr. Kraskowitz said, between puffs on the cigarette which dangled from his mouth and dropped ashes on his sheets, "New man in camp today, I'm told. . . . Japs beat him up pretty bad. . . . Illingdon says they got what they wanted out of him and then put him here in camp as an informer. Bad business that."

"Where did they put him?" asked Peter, describing an arc with his compass.

"Staff Room with the rest of the goddamn crooks," said Kraskowitz.

"What's his name?" said Peter, sure now that he had the solution and eager to get on with it.

"French name. Sounded like *cookstove* or something like that."

Peter put down his compass. "It wasn't Costeau, was it?" he breathed.

"Yeah, I think that's it. You know him?"

"Sort of," said Peter. He put away the half-finished geometric construction on the shelf beside his bed and unscrewed his light bulb until it went out. For the first time in months there was a blaze of firelight in his mind, and for one short moment the guerrillas and Enid and life danced before it, and the problem of sin drifted off into the shadows

254

where it could scarcely be noticed.

But Jerry was supposed to be in Australia. If anything happened to Peter, Jerry and Margo were the only two people alive who could say that he had ever done anything more than be a child. It was a proud, pagan idea, but Peter knew that he had had it at the back of his mind every since the day he had gone to Kempeitai headquarters.

It couldn't be Jerry! The Japs couldn't have captured Jerry any more than they could have captured Peter's father. Even less, perhaps, because Jerry had that boat to take the pictures back to the States in. Besides, Jerry tortured? Jerry an informer? Worldly Jerry, who loved everything that he laughed at—not like Donny Garver, who only laughed and never knew whether he loved or hated? Jerry who loved Margo and felt no shame about her? It couldn't be Jerry! It couldn't be Jerry! If it were Jerry, Margo would be with him.

When Mr. Illingdon and the other old men had come in from the stoves and gotten in bed, cracking old jokes, and the lights had gone out, and they had all started to snore or joined Kraskowitz in lonely efforts to recapture the pleasure of old lusts, Peter climbed out softly from his berth and stole along the aisle between the two rows of cubicles. At the end of the aisle there was a kerosene lamp burning, with wick trimmed low, so that men could find their way down the outside stairs to the bathrooms. By the light of the lamp, Peter found the Staff Room door at the top of the stairs and opened it gently. He skirted the boards that creaked and without making a sound arrived at the bunk space which had once been his. The moon, sinking into the China Sea, poured light in through his window and there under the window, his head on the outside and his feet against the wall, was Jerry.

His face was white and drawn and full of pain. A white sling, to hold his arm in, lay empty on his chest. His hands lay as quiet as fallen sparrows beside it. In the moonlight Peter saw that one of them, the left one, had dark bloody scabs instead of fingernails and on the other the last joint of each finger had been removed completely and replaced only by a cap of dirty bandage. Peter winced and looked back at the mobile, crinkly face which had always seemed so wise and amusing. Its eyes were wide open looking at the moon. Now they rolled upward and stared at Peter. Peter looked back at them and wanted to say something, if there were any words to say what he felt, but the head shook slightly and the eyes turned away and Jerry rolled over onto his side, sighing. Peter crept around him and saw that the eyes were closed and Jerry to all intents and purposes was asleep.

Hurt and horrified, Peter made his way back to the cubicle of the old men. Jerry couldn't have any practical reason to pretend that he didn't know him, not when the other men in the Staff Room were asleep and it would have been easy to smile and whisper a hello. No, the reason was obvious: Jerry's eyes were condemning Peter for the ruin of those hands and the ending of Jerry's career as a photographer.

Peter prayed for help and found that all the hopeful, dignified words which had flowed from him these last months had dried up. Perhaps he had passed the test of internal atonement, perhaps not. Anyway, the amends he had to make now and the punishment he had to suffer now were all outside him. He had to give Jerry every possible chance to scorn and accuse him. That was the only way Jerry might vent his anger and come to forgive him. At the same time he couldn't let people know that Jerry was a guerrilla or had been a photographer. It might be that Colonel Kori hadn't killed him only because he couldn't connect *the man who takes pictures* that he'd asked Peter about in the hospital with the Jerry Costeau he'd captured. Somehow Peter had to follow Jerry around and stay near his accusing eyes without people suspecting anything.

## CHAPTER 18

After a sleepless night, Peter got up at five o'clock and served for Father Gibney at Communion. But the familiar ritual and beautiful words of the service failed to have their usual calming effect on him. Later in the morning, after breakfast, he found that his work on the wood gang failed to have its usual numbing effect either. When he had finished wheelbarrowing logs and came to his hour with Ray Henry on the two-man saw, he worked jerkily and Ray swore at him. He made up for it with conscious effort and sawed correctly until Ray himself declared a take-five. But Peter still felt jerky and not smoothly tired and when he stretched out on the pine needles in his G string—the work clothes he wore to spare his one patched pair of khaki shorts—the dazzling morning sunlight failed to stupefy him as it usually did and only made his brain seem to boil more furiously.

Until now, Peter realized, he had never fully believed in Enid's betraying him. The thought had been only a metaphysical possibility which he could use, when he needed it, as a whip to punish his wicked mind. But now Jerry's unfriendly, pain-filled eyes seemed to confirm the hints of Mark Price—hints which Peter had never dared to ask to have clarified—about the bitch Mark would like to strangle. And now Peter saw in Jerry the results of what the bitch and he had done—nothing metaphysical but all real and irreparable —and it was more than he could face. The wrecked body seemed too real to be only thought about. No amount of guilty anguish and vicarious suffering could ever make up for it. It demanded action, and what action was there? It was a broken microscope which could not be fixed and paid for no matter how many odd jobs Peter did nor how much allowance he saved. It was a path that led back to its own beginning. There was no place to start on it and no place to end. After spending the night going around and around on it, Peter couldn't concentrate on circling any farther. Instead, he found himself blaming and hating Enid. He found himself twisting and turning on the pine needles just as he had twisted all night on his bunk. He found himself listening to the other resting members of the wood gang as they talked about Jerry and spread the vicious rumor that Jerry had bought his life by agreeing to become a spy in camp. Peter even found himself daring to blame them for stupidity.

Heck, he thought, if the Japs want to find out about whisky or news smuggling they don't need a spy. All they have to do is keep their eyes open. It's not hard to see how some of the guys on the wood gang leave notes and empty bottles in the woods and pick up different notes and full bottles later from the same hiding places.

Peter knew he couldn't defend Jerry against the charge of being a spy without showing a suspicious amount of feeling, but during work breaks later in the morning, he took refuge from the tired hopelessness of his guilt by thinking of other practical ways he could help Jerry. The first thing he must do was speak to the Kahns. They were the only people in camp besides Peter who knew Jerry and could spill the beans about his being a photographer. So at noon, as soon as Peter had eaten the extras his mother had ready for him, he went to the porch of the women's barracks and found the Kahns having lunch together. There were dozens of other couples all doing the same thing at their tables nearby and Peter wondered how he could say anything without being overheard.

"So look who's paying us a visit, Fritz," said Mrs. Kahn. "Seems like we should know him but it's been so long."

"Hello, Peter," said Mr. Kahn warmly. "Sit down and have some extras with us."

"Thank you," said Peter, "but I've already had mine."

"You'd think he was a Hindu or something, the way he fills up so easy," said Mrs. Kahn. "Here, here's a spoonful of peanut butter. If I'd known you were coming I'd have baked banana bread to put with it."

"Thank you," said Peter.

"You don't look so good," said Mrs. Kahn. "Kind of pale and thin. You should remember you have friends and stop trying to starve yourself to death."

"I came to ask you both a favor," said Peter.

"You know we'll always do you a favor, Peter," said Mr. Kahn.

"I guess it's not really a favor," said Peter, getting an idea. "Mostly I just came around to tell you that that new man in camp is a dentist and maybe he can fix your teeth better than Doc Sharp. You remember you were complaining a while back."

"You mean the man they suspect of being a spy?" asked Mr. Kahn.

"Oh, that's just a rumor," said Peter. "I don't think there's any truth in it."

"We thought maybe he was that newspaper man—" began Mrs. Kahn.

"No, he's a dentist," interrupted Peter. "He's that same dentist you introduced me to at the hotel the day the war started. You remember? Jerry Costeau? He went out pig hunting and never came back?"

"Dentist, I don't remember," said Mrs. Kahn. "But Costeau, I do remember and that tramp of a—"

"Of course you remember, Ellen," cut in Mr. Kahn. "Doctor Costeau. He had the suite. I'm trying to recall if he was traveling alone or did he have someone with him?"

"He was traveling alone," said Peter firmly. "And you said, Mrs. Kahn, how it was such a pity a nice-looking young fellow like that didn't have a wife or a girl friend to go pig-hunting with."

"All right, so that's what I said," said Mrs. Kahn. "But I wish you people would keep it in mind that I'm a simple woman and I can't be expected to remember everything."

"I guess the favor I was going to ask," said Peter, "was the same one you did for me when I came to camp. The dentist doesn't have any baggage by his bed."

"So he'll need clothes," said Mrs. Kahn. "Naturally we can't have him out back at the laundry tables doing his wash in the nude. I'll take up a collection. What size, please?"

"He's built about the same as Mark Price or Father Gibney," said Peter. "I'll try and get you exact measurements for making alterations later."

"That would be a help all right," said Mrs. Kahn.

"Good," said Peter. "Thank you for the peanut butter." He was still holding it untouched on the end of his spoon. "Guess now I can eat it and go to school."

"Well, it was nice of you to drop by," said Mr. Kahn. "You've saved me a trip to the Staff Room to find out if it was the same Costeau who was the dentist."

"Yes, it is," said Peter. "Actually I don't know that he'll be able to help you much with your teeth. His hands are . . ." Peter's voice had become untrustworthy, so he shrugged, put the peanut butter in his mouth and didn't finish the sentence.

"Yes, I heard he was in bad shape," said Mr. Kahn.

Peter nodded and chewed on the peanut butter.

"Good of you to visit us," said Mrs. Kahn, shaking her head with bafflement. "Nice to see you so talkative again."

Peter waved his good-bys and went to the school shed still holding the peanut butter in his mouth and trying to find saliva enough to swallow it.

As soon as the irrelevancy of school was over, Peter went to look for Jerry. He found him out back of the cook shed playing in Mark Price's afternoon poker game. Mark ran the game according to strict democratic rules. There was no limit on bets, but if a person didn't have cigarettes or bananas or Mickey Mouse pesos to bet with, he could use I.O.U.s. No matter who signed them the I.O.U.s had to be accepted and were all valued in the same way. They were written in terms of pesos and were payable after the war if anyone lived so long. Naturally an I.O.U. peso which represented what everyone expected would be a good solid after-the-war peso had to be worth more than an inflated Mickey Mouse peso. So the rule was that it was worth half of what Mark figured a prewar peso would be worth if anyone was still fool enough to put one into the game.

Peter settled himself inconspicuously in the chimney corner to watch. He saw that Jerry, like almost everyone in the game except for Mr. Kulhausen and Mark Price, was playing for I.O.U.s That meant Colonel Kori hadn't left him any money the way he had Peter. It meant that Jerry wouldn't be able to buy extras at the store. And Peter caught himself being glad of it because it also meant that Peter could take back the money that was his from the cardboard box in his mother's shack and use it to buy extras which he would leave anonymously on the shelf at the end of Jerry's bunk. As if bits of food can make up for what you've done! he thought bitterly. He wished he could go and stand directly behind Jerry so that he could see the bandaged stumps of the right hand holding the cards inside the sling and watch the painfully slow dealing of the nailless fingers on the left hand. But he couldn't without being obvious, and, besides, Jerry could see him fine where he was if Jerry wanted to look. But Jerry never raised his eyes to cast him a single scornful glance. Jerry kept his head slumped over his cards and over his crippled hands and said nothing except "I'm in," or "I'll see you," or "I raise," or "I fold," or, when he was dealing, "Five card draw." His position looked so dead and his voice sounded so flat and his face was so completely lacking in the old whimsical crinkles that Peter began to wonder—and caught himself feeling relieved at the thought—if Jerry wasn't still partly unconscious from the tortures and perhaps didn't recognize Peter. But no, Jerry was paying a good game of poker and winning more pots than anyone except Mark Price. If he didn't know Peter, it was the only thing he didn't know. If he didn't know Peter, he was being awfully careful not to look in Peter's direction.

When light failed and the poker game broke up and the other players went off to commix with their wives and sweethearts or read at their bunks, Jerry remained at the empty poker table, listening lackluster to the old men who had begun their evening gossip around the chimney. Peter stayed, too, lurking in the shadows and multiplying his misery. Neither of them entered into the old men's conversation. In fact, Peter realized after a while that Jerry wasn't even listening to it but was sitting there in the dim light, only thinking despondent thoughts and dreaming sad dreams. When it was finally time for lights-out and Jerry got up to follow the old men into the barracks, Peter was still sitting unseen on the edge of the laundry table about twenty feet off in the black shadows. He saw Jerry lift his limp right arm with his left hand and place it in its sling as if it were an inanimate object. Then he shambled away toward the barracks and Peter remained behind, envisioning how he must have been hung up by that arm and imagining how the muscles in it must have felt before they finally gave up and stopped working forever.

That night Peter stole into the Staff Room again, removed Jerry's clothes from the window ledge where they had been left to air and took them out to the kerosene lamp at the head of the stairs. When he had measured them and written the measurements down, he returned them to the window ledge without anyone being the wiser.

During the next three weeks Peter grew more silent than he had been. He grew sullen. He gave up his homework, and his geometry book lay unopened on the shelf beside his bed. When Father Gibney asked him what the trouble was he said shortly that he was sick of studying. When his mother asked him for an explanation he said he was just sick, not feeling well, a touch of the trots. The truth was, of course, that he was spending all his after-school hours in the unhappy vicinity of Jerry: kibitzing at the poker table or hovering about the chimney corner or pretending to visit old friends in the Staff Room. Donny and Mark and the others didn't understand the visits. They saw that he didn't say anything except to answer questions, but just the same they seemed to hope that he was becoming less religious and they kidded him about falling from heaven.

The funny thing was he *was* falling. Suffering Jerry's scorn and lack of recognition didn't seem to be doing any good. Peter was beginning to feel that in spite of his months of training in self-discipline and abnegation, it didn't much matter what way he directed his thoughts. All ways proved equally sinful and damning when he analyzed them. Sin was everywhere and wordly thoughts were inescapable. During

261

daylight hours, when the sun was still shining, he hungered for worldly news. He wanted to know why Jerry was in camp and what had happened to his father and Margo and the other guerrillas. He found himself wanting to know what punishment had been meted out to Enid—Enid for whom he still tried to pray.

But the bad hours came after the sun and the electric lights had gone out and the logic of possible events could no longer hold his interest. Then his thoughts became disconnected and uncontrolled. They had no light to see by but the shining white specter of Jerry's hands and no center to focus on but the slump-shouldered expression in Jerry's open eyes. The first few hours when there was something to do were relatively easy. He lay awake until Jerry's eyes ought to be closed and then he went to the Staff Room and put a pack of native cigarettes or a hand of bananas or a new article of clothing from Mrs. Kahn on the shelf by Jerry's bed. If the night was warm and dry he would take the clothes Jerry had been wearing out back to the laundry tables, scrub away at them in the dark and hang them deep in the forest of laundry lines until the next night when they would be dry and he could smuggle them back to their place by Jerry's mattress.

When everything had been done that could be done and there was nothing left until morning, Peter faced the real horror of each day: insomnia and fantasy. He lay awake fitfully thinking peculiar, bitter thoughts: wondering, for instance, if his father had been forced to use a gun yet and turn Jap-killer, or day-dreaming of revenges on Colonel Kori. In the graveyard silence of restless, sighing souls which filled the barracks after lights-out, there was a solution to Peter's life. It was to have died a violent, honorable death. And almost every night he relived the one great chance he had had. He might have snatched up the wine bottle from the floor and smashed Colonel Kori to death with it. Or he might have pushed Colonel Kori in the way of the guard who came running up with the swinging rifle butt. Or, having found Colonel Kori was weak, he might sensibly have strangled him instead of wasting his moment of triumph in ineffective pommeling.

When dreams of violence that might have been and of death that should have been were rehearsed and played out, queer theological notions ate their way into his conscious-

ness and squirmed about there like worms. In spite of tiredness and Jerry's scorn and all the mortification he could bring
to bear on himself, he saw that the careful reconstruction
work he had done on his soul was crumbling and the devil
was raging at will through his strong, sleepless body. His
months of trying to atone seemed now to have been months
of selfishness and spiritual pride. Perhaps some people could
expiate any sin, even the irreparable damage done to Jerry's
body, even the damage to Jerry's soul which seemed to show
in his bitter, despairing eyes. But Peter wasn't sure. How
could anyone atone for hurt to another person's soul, hurt
which might lead to the person's damnation? Anyway, if
some saints could, Peter couldn't. When he tried to think
good theology the thoughts twisted themselves into blas-
phemies and curses. Who was Peter Baldwin, he wondered,
that he should be worth so much worry and unhappiness to
himself? At most he was a scrap of lost or mildewed film or
a memory in the mind of Jerry, who despised him. Why
couldn't God relieve him of a soul so that he could just die
whenever he wanted and not have to be immortal? If you
took away the trivialities that made him Peter and got down
to pure soul, it wasn't Peter any more anyway, was it? It was
just soul, no different from anything else that was eternal,
no different from all the rest of the heavenly white sugar and
hellish black pepper. With a soul Peter was no better than old
man Kraskowitz, another drop to be added to the bucket
of damnation. Whether the drop shone for another sixty
years in the sun or stood dully for only a couple more years
on sheets made waterproof by gray dirt was unimportant
compared to eternity. But take the soul away and Peter was
at least better *off* than old man Kraskowitz. He was younger
and healthier and he hadn't used up a fraction of the sinful
energy in him yet.

"Go out and play," his mother had always been saying to
him as a child. "It isn't good for boys to mope about indoors."
And it wasn't. It led to thinking. But what she should have
said, he thought, was "Go out and get killed while you're
still innocent. Go and fall off a high tree before you begin
thinking too much. Go to the hills and find a good death as a
guerrilla before you damn yourself." His bitterness convinced him that he was no longer redeemable. It was, he
thought, the final most mortal sin of all, spiritual despair.

One day Peter cut school entirely and spent the dragging afternoon hours watching the poker game instead. When the gong rang for the second meal, Mark Price leaned toward poor, crippled Jerry and said, "You don't need to get up, Costeau. You can barely carry the goddamn slops anyway. Stay here and I'll bring it to you. Talk to Peter while I'm gone. He's been through some of the same things you have and he's been hanging around for weeks as if he wanted to compare notes. I'll be back with your chow in a half hour or so."

Mark and the others left and Peter stood still in the chimney corner, shifty and apprehensive. Jerry rubbed each of his eyes in turn and then slowly dealt a game of solitaire with his good left hand.

"All right," he said at length, "if you've got to know all about it, I guess I'm the only one who can tell you." He looked around to make sure they were alone and then jerked his head at Peter. "Come here. I'm not going to shout. I guess we can trust Price but I don't want to take a chance on anyone else."

Peter moved over from the chimney corner and stood beside him.

"After the Japs picked up Wong and the others at that supply drop," murmured Jerry, continuing to play solitaire, "some of our boys escaped and got back to our base in the north. The Japs must have tracked them because one evening about a week later, while we were still waiting around for Bean, who was supposed to have escaped too, the Japs suddenly closed in. How they'd moved so many men into the area without our scouts and patrols seeing them, I just don't know, but by the time we realized they were there, they had us sealed off with our backs to the sea. We tried to break out a couple of times during the night without any luck. Mallard got killed. So did Enanak. Remember him?"

"Yes," whispered Peter.

"Well, they kept coming in and by morning they had pushed us into the mangrove swamps along the shore and chopped us up into a dozen little groups. Before light Margo and your father and I waded out through the mud and the trees to our boat and rowed off in it while we still had a chance. We moored again a couple of miles to the east and hid all day in a tangle of mangrove roots listening to the butchery of the mopping up. That night your dad left us. He said, now that Mallard was dead, he was going to walk back to Enao and turn himself in as if he'd been hiding in the hills nearby, treating the natives since the war started. I thought he might be here in camp by now. You haven't heard anything from him?"

"No," said Peter.

Jerry lifted a stack of red and black cards in his game and went on playing silently as if he'd forgotten Peter was there.

"What happened to you and Margo?" asked Peter timidly.

"We kept on rowing," said Jerry in a monotone. "We came to the northeast tip of the island and the biggest, most god-forsaken mangrove swamp of them all. We found a hummock in it above high tide, built a hut on it and lived there for three months on fish, palm hearts and love, while my film turned to moldy glue and we wove a sort of sail for the boat out of palm tassel. When it was ready we shoved off again and headed south, sailing nights and hiding days. We got about halfway down the coast when one night I was having a bout with malaria and in my fever I let Margo keep on sailing under a bright moon. I guess some fishermen saw us and reported us. About dawn the pilot of a Jap patrol plane caught us heading for shore and gave us one burst of his machine gun. He riddled Margo and left me unscratched. The boat filled with water, Margo drifted off and I hung on to the hulk, dopey and delirious, until a Jap motor launch picked me up and took me to Banong. Since then, as you can see, your old pal Kori has been questioning me and trying to tie me in with the guerrillas. He's put me in camp now for a few months to see if I won't grow fond of life again and tell him something. From the way he talks I guess Bean got away and organized a new outfit. Kori thinks I helped him with it. But the only people I can still hurt are you and your dad. That's why I don't want to talk to you."

Jerry stopped talking and Peter didn't know how to start.

"What's the matter? Cat got your tongue? I'm not going to speak to you again so if there's anything else you want to know, let's have it." Jerry's face twitched irritably, like old Mr. Illingdon's.

"You think Dad's dead?" breathed Peter.

"I don't know. He's a pretty rugged man and the Japs can't have too much on him. Maybe turning himself in to some small-town mayor, he got hung up in red tape. He could be sitting in the Enao jail just waiting for the Japs to come and pick him up." Jerry took a bottle from his pocket and had a swig. "Courtesy of Donny Garver's still," he said. "He gives me a ration to keep me from radiating too much gloom."

"Does your arm hurt a lot?" asked Peter.

"Only when I can feel it," said Jerry, looking around as if he wanted more company. "What did Kori do to you? Tell me about it. Entertain me."

"He didn't do much," muttered Peter. "I knew he had a bad temper and was sensitive about some things so I made him mad and he beat me up. After my leg was better and I got out of hospital, I don't know whether he was sorry for me or could see I was no danger or wanted to let me have time to be ashamed of myself or what. Anyway, he told me to keep quiet about how he'd lost his temper and said if I didn't he'd tell Mother about Enid. Then he let me go."

"Who was Enid?"

"The Nazi girl I used to see."

"Oh, yes, your girl friend. See, I forget things all the time. I don't see why you want to talk to me." He had another small swig from the bottle.

Peter felt tears forming in his eyes.

"I know you ought to be sarcastic," said Peter, "and I'll go away if you say so, but I'd do anything to make up for your hands. Saying sorry about them seems so childish."

"Yes, my hands are a mess," said Jerry. He held up the bottle to see how much was left in it, and seeing it wasn't much, he returned it to his pocket with a sad shake of his head. "Kori had heard from somewhere," he continued, "that there was a man who took pictures, so he made a shrewd guess and tackled my hands first. After he got this far he decided to save some for later."

"You never admitted it was you, though," said Peter, doing his best to sound proud and enthusiastic.

"No."

"Just like Wong. They even hung you up by the arms like Wong."

"I wish they'd killed me like Wong," said Jerry. "But they will. I'm not through yet."

Peter turned his head away. The tears were beginning to get too big and to dribble down his cheeks.

"Come on, I've got enough troubles of my own," said Jerry coldly.

"Why don't you blame me?" burst out Peter. "You talk and

talk but you don't blame me. Your hands keep me from sleeping nights, but *you* don't say a thing, you just talk."

"What do you mean?" asked Jerry dully.

"I mean blame me. Scorn me for what I did."

"I don't know what you did. All I know is you get clothes for me and have them washed and put food by my bed. Thanks a lot."

"You *do* know," sobbed Peter. He felt that he should let Jerry continue to make fun of him and get some kind of small revenge, but it seemed so unlike him. Jerry should shoot him, perhaps, but not go on rubbing in salt in such a petty way.

"All right, what? Did you lose one of the shirts you got for me or something?"

"Stop it," shouted Peter. "I told Enid."

"Your girl friend? The Nazi girl? Well, what did you tell her?"

Peter's mind went blank. He had to explain now what had happened and he couldn't remember.

"Those things Margo gave me to wear," he said, groping. "I told Enid about them and she told Kori and he went to Wong's house and stopped the supply pickup and that was the end of everything."

"You slept with the Swedish girl," said Jerry slowly, as if he was beginning to understand. "That was something Margo wanted me to find out about. Did you? Did you sleep with her?"

"Yes," said Peter, "but that's not so important. The real thing is you and the way I betrayed you through her."

"Oh, I see," said Jerry. "Oh, how I wish Margo were here!" The derelict of a whimsical smile twisted his mouth. "You're such a dopey kid," he went on. "You told me yourself who was going to betray us, as you put it. Rainha. Our Judas was Rainha. She runs the casino now. I saw her myself at Kempeitai headquarters. She came by to ask Kori a favor, poor slut, but he had already discarded her. He wants a different girl every week if he can find one white enough. The whiter they are the better bragging they make when he's describing them to poor captive wrecks who'll never make love again."

"Rainha?" repeated Peter stupidly.

"Yes, Rainha. Don't you remember telling me about her blowup with Wong that day?"

"I saw her that night, too," said Peter, seeing it again through a mist. "I saw her making up to Kori at the Meiji Day Ball on the porch of the country club."

"Well, what's your trouble, then?"

"I wasn't sure it was her. I fell asleep in the bushes waiting to see Enid and Captain Hebel and I was still groggy and couldn't be sure it was her. But it must have been. Nobody but Rainha and Colonel Kori could have talked like that."

"So you forgot it?"

"I guess I must have wanted to think it was Enid who betrayed me," said Peter.

"That's the Swedish girl again," said Jerry, rubbing his eyes with his good left hand. "The one you slept with. Yes, naturally you thought that was why you were picked up and questioned by Kori. I can remember the same kind of stupidity when I was your age. Maybe you had more serious and plausible reasons. I don't know. I was a Catholic and that made it pretty bad, I remember."

"Here comes Mark Price with your dinner," said Peter.

"Good. I guess we'll have to talk again so we can finish this. Maybe tomorrow or some other day, same time and place. At least I don't have to hike sixty miles between meetings any more."

Jerry waved at Mr. Price almost cheerfully, and Peter hurried away to stand in the fast-dwindling chow line. He was at the counter before he began to realize what had happened. His entire life for months seemed to have become invalid. He had forgotten how to think except in terms of his own sin and now the thoughts which came to him, out of habit, were all inappropriate and meaningless.

He got his food and started for the door, to go out and eat it on his mother's porch and talk for a change. No, he couldn't do that. He didn't know how to talk yet. He might say all sorts of stupid things. He didn't even know what to tell her about his father yet. He sat down at one of the mess tables in the cook shed to sort out the tumbled mass of his thoughts. It was a good place for it. Now that commixing meals were allowed on the porches of the barracks, the tables in the cook shed were used only by the loneliest people in camp. He had used them a lot lately.

But today will be the last time, he thought. It's not that I'm suddenly happy. Logically, I should still be guilty of the same sins I was punishing myself for before Jerry came into camp. Only now, compared to the responsibility for Jerry's hands, they don't seem so heavy. Maybe, since I made up part of my guilt, I exaggerated the rest too. Or maybe I've already done my penance. Anyway, I feel different.

He finished eating and returned to his bunk, giving the poker game a wide berth. As he pursued his thoughts, he found that he could look back on Enid with simple regret instead of fear. He found, too, that he couldn't concentrate on the logic of morality and salvation, and even that he resented it for the way he had become tangled up in it. The one thing that still seemed important to think about was Jerry. Jerry had changed. He thought he had to die. But maybe Colonel Kori wasn't going to drag him back and torture him again any more than he was Peter. Besides, it was possible to escape. Peter could plan it and once Jerry was in the mountains he could find Bean. Bean had always been expecting to make contact with American submarines. Now that the war was turning tide, he might. And for a case like Jerry's, the sub captain would take a passenger. Maybe in Australia or San Francisco or New York some surgeon could repair Jerry's hands and arms. The main thing was to keep Jerry talking so that he would begin to enjoy living again and would want to escape.

Peter had a thousand thoughts to think—more thoughts that seemed urgent than he had had for months. Trying to get to them all before he forgot any, he fell asleep in his clothes long before lights-out and slept through until morning.

## CHAPTER 19

The moon was brilliant and the shadows it made on the ground from the pine boughs overhead were spidery and beautiful. Everything about the night was beautiful. The earth, giving up moisture to the air, repaid it for the rain which had fallen the previous afternoon and added the scent of resin and needles by way of interest. A dog howling miles away in some barrio on the other side of the ridge seemed to open the darkness of the camp to the darkness of the world, tearing down the stockade and setting Peter free.

Creeping through the shadows of the pine grove, Peter felt as if he were inhaling the moonlit beauty and extracting happiness from it. It was a simple thing to feel—like morning sunshine or the sweat of sawing or the taste of boiled rice. But it was the kind of pleasure to be noticed and made the most of because it showed him that he was beginning to be alive again. The only thing that detracted from it, he thought, smiling, was the goat manure he carried in a cloth pouch on his belt. Even that proved something perhaps. He didn't really believe the stuff was helping much in what he was doing. He continued to bring it along because it amused him.

He had paused, but now he moved on through the pines, careful not to make any sound. There was no danger of stumbling over commixers now because it was four o'clock in the morning, but he had to be careful not to arouse the sentry on top of the stockade. At the edge of the pine grove he paused again. The sentry, as usual, looked half asleep, slumped on the rim of the crow's-nest from which he watched. Soon his relief would come around on the outside of the stockade and call to him, and he would call back, and stretch, and deliberately climb out of the crow's-nest and down the ladder or whatever there was on the other side. Then the crow's-nest would be empty for a few seconds until the new guard climbed up to replace him.

Enjoying the fine night, Peter waited for the new guard patiently. The pleasures of life which weren't simple pleasures of nature were still difficult for him to grasp. In his months of guilt, deepening gradually as they had into the despair of Jerry's hands, Peter had raised around himself a heavy stockade of silence and shyness through which he found it was difficult to escape. Sometimes he wondered whether, if he ever did escape from it, he would still find the people he cared for waiting unchanged outside. His mother was still separated from him by her own worried unhappiness. Telling her what he'd done and thought he'd done might explain to her why he'd been acting strangely, but it would also make her worry more. He could only wear away at her unhappiness by being cheerful now himself and chattering about inconsequential details of camp life. But it wouldn't be gone completely, he knew, until she heard something definite and hopeful about his father.

The Gibneys were equally unreachable, but that wasn't

their fault. It was his own. He had developed a peculiar shyness around them, particularly around Father Gibney. The reason for the shyness puzzled him, but he thought it probably had something to do with his shyness and uncertainty toward God. Jerry had said once in his cynical way that what Peter needed, after being so proud and overscrupulous as to judge himself and reason with God, was a go-between to apologize for him and put relations back on a polite, formal basis. Peter didn't trust the Catholic theology, half forgotten and half invented, which Jerry expounded to him some nights. Most of the time, Peter thought, it was only bitterness and bunkum inspired by Donny Garver's *camote* brandy. But in this one matter Jerry was probably right. Father Gibney was God's formal representative and Peter ought to confess to him and ask his help in regaining a healthy religious perspective. The trouble was: every time Peter began to talk to Father Gibney he seemed so informal and so much of an old family friend that Peter found himself asking a few abstract theological questions and letting the conversation die.

The same feeling of constraint and awkwardness—as if he were talking to everyone over a bathhouse partition—pervaded all his relationships. The other kids at school were especially hard to approach. They were so used to his shyness that they took it for granted and left all the work of overcoming it to him. They seemed hardly to notice how much more he said in class now or how he tried to talk with them. Maggie Higgins was the only one who ever listened and ever said anything sensible in reply. And she had grown so beautiful—so pale and blushing, so thin and paper-skinned, so top-heavy and intense, with her long black hair and blazing blue eyes—that it would have been difficult to talk to her without feeling shy even before Peter had begun to cultivate shyness. All the other kids were taken up with love affairs and isolated from friendship two by two. Norman Diak couldn't pay attention to anything now but Candy Kulhausen, with whom he necked for hours every night in the woodshed. Jimmy Page was preoccupied with Nancy Barsini and the poetry he was always writing to her. Fritz Laski was stuck on Louise Newcombe—stuck with Louise Newcombe—and Peter didn't want to talk to either of them. Herb Campbell was dating Ruth Page, Jimmy's younger sister, and the two of them played together in the bridge tournaments which were held evenings in the history room. Even Maggie Higgins had a lot of dates—with Charley French, who graduated from high school and was now topper on the wood gang. But Charley spent most of his evenings with Mr. Illingdon's grown-up mestiza daughter, Bonny, who was, as Peter had heard her say herself, "a hot chick and all for laughs."

The new guard grunted on the other side of the stockade and Peter tensed. The sentry on top stretched as usual and clambered from the cockpit and out of sight. Peter moved from the pine grove and out across the open space, which bordered the fence. The open space, or Bufferland, as it was called, was lighted by a string of electric-light bulbs festooned along the top of the fence all the way around camp. It was out of bounds to the internees and as a result the grass in it was uncut and reached almost to Peter's waist. Walking through it made a pleasantly soft swishing sound.

In front of the barracks the Japs were more neat about Bufferland and kept it scythed down so that it would look good when a visiting general or admiral came to pay the camp a cursory inspection. It was out front that Peter had first noticed the cracks in the fence and thought of the plan for Jerry's escape. The cracks were places where the soldiers of the Jap work battalion had run into underground rocks when they had driven the posts. They weren't big cracks because the soldiers had avoided big rocks and run the stockade around them. But near the ground, before the posts sloped up toward each other and the signs of laziness had been spaced out and partly concealed, some of the cracks were almost big enough for a man to squeeze through on his side.

According to Peter's measurements Jerry needed a space twenty by eleven inches. The crack Peter had found hidden by the long grass out back near Donny Garver's workshop was nine inches wide at the ground and, at twenty inches above the ground, had narrowed to eight. The extra inches of width had to be added and Peter had to do it all with a knife. The knife, made with Donny's help in the workshop, was the only tool he had. Anyway, whittling, he told himself, didn't make so much noise as sawing. It was just slow. He had worked an hour every morning for the last two weeks—and sharpened his knife on Donny's whetstone every noon—and sometimes it seemed as if the knife were being worn away faster than the stockade posts. But this morning in the bright moonlight he could see that he was really accomplishing something and was about halfway finished.

As he lay down in the long grass and got into position to start work he could hear the guard who had been relieved and was on his way back to the guardhouse tramping up the hill toward him on the other side of the stockade. This was always one of the scary moments and this morning the guard was walking right beside the fence. When he came up opposite Peter, the sound of his boots churning through the grass seemed so close that Peter might have reached out through the crack and tripped him up. When he had finally gone by, Peter breathed deeply and began whittling. The guard on duty was a good forty feet away and couldn't look toward Peter without leaning perilously far out from the rim of the crow's-nest. Even if he did hear something and try leaning out, he wouldn't see anything but the top of the grass. The main thing was for Peter to be extra quiet when he changed position because that started the grass waving above him.

Some night, Peter thought, it would be Jerry lying there, not whittling but simply waiting. Of course, it wouldn't be four o'clock in the morning but eight in the evening. And as soon as the guard who had been relieved had gone away to his quarters and the new guard had settled into his droopy position facing in toward camp, Jerry would inch out through the long grass on the other side, reach the woods beyond and then stand up and keep going. He would have almost eleven hours to get away before the early-morning roll call showed he was gone. By then he could be down below the pine line in the lowland jungles or around the mountain to other mountains or wherever he thought best.

The only trouble with the plan was Jerry himself. Jerry didn't want to escape. He just wanted to drink *camote* brandy and play poker and wait for Colonel Kori to come for him and finish him off. At first, after answering all Peter's questions, he hadn't even wanted to talk any more. But Peter had hung around second meals and nights by the cook-shed chimney until he had had to talk more—and more and more. Now their conversations were a habit, and Jerry said he had even begun to feel responsible for Peter because of the bad example he had set him with Margo. He didn't believe in interfering in other people's lives but he was indulging himself, he said. At other times when he was feeling drunk and sentimental he would often end a conversation abruptly by telling Peter to go away and stop poisoning himself with bitter nonsense from a self-pitying cripple.

Perhaps he was bitter, but not about people so much as life in general. And Peter didn't think he was exactly self-pitying either; more just sad about Margo. Maybe drinking—now that the bandages were off his finger stubs and he no longer winced every time his useless arm got jostled or bumped—was a kind of self-pity, but it was also a kind of despair. He despaired because his body was wrecked and he could never be the sort of active photographer again that he had been. He despaired because he had always been a good husband and he didn't want to meet his wife again and disillusion her now that he loved someone else who was dead. He despaired because he had first approached Margo in lust and had never had a chance to express the kind of real love he came to feel for her. All in all, he despaired because he considered himself better off dead than alive. These were the reasons he suggested in the stories he told about himself, but Peter preferred to think on the basis of his own experience that the real reason was physical: Jerry hadn't recovered enough energy yet to take an interest in anything much besides Peter.

When Peter showed that he was making a conscious effort to broaden Jerry's interests, Jerry accused him of trying to feather his nest in heaven by being charitable. But Jerry knew it wasn't true. Peter had no other close friend and confidant and he enjoyed Jerry's company. Perhaps he didn't look up to him as much as he once had. Perhaps he didn't feel the same old whimsical charm in him any more. But he liked to hear him talk. He liked to hear even the world-weary philosophical things he said when he was drunk.

"What's philosophical mean?" Jerry had said. "I never met a philosopher in my whole life, only professors of philosophy. A real philosopher would have to be an adult thinker and no human being can be an adult anything. He hasn't got time. He hasn't got eternity. That's the dirty trick of being a human being. What commonly passes for philosophy is the codified notions of bright children now dead who spent their lives pretending to be baby gods and paring pretty patterns out of paper to paste on the night sky." When Jerry had said the last sentence he had let each *p* in it explode drunkenly, like a curse.

274

Although the things Jerry said often seemed blasphemous and even frightening, they also seemed more than mere drunken nonsense. They were directed at Peter and, feeling as fond of Jerry and responsible for him as he did, he listened to them with interest. "Dead is where I belong," Jerry said, but Peter still hoped that some night in a few more weeks when the rains had come and a typhoon was blinding the guards Jerry would squeeze through the hole Peter was whittling and go to find Bean and a submarine and a surgeon for his arm.

The main basis for Peter's hope was the increasing interest Jerry seemed to be taking in camp life. He said it was amazing that a hundred and twenty-odd people, packed into two two-story barracks measuring forty-five by eighteen feet each, and fenced in on a two-acre field, could evolve such a complicated society as the one in camp. In another few years, he said, the camp would develop a whole new culture and the internees would have to be kept interned after they were liberated so that anthropologists could be brought from the States to study it. Peter knew what Jerry meant. He had felt camp was a world apart when he had first come into it, too. Now he had grown used to it even if he still didn't feel like a part of it.

One thing in particular that made Jerry prick up his ears and take an interest in life lately was the cohabiting controversy. About a week before, Captain Hira had called together the Governing Committee and announced to them that the barracks were too crowded and that the enforced separation of married men and women was an unnecessary hardship which he didn't approve of. He could, he said, make available a thousand square feet of roofing iron and an adequate supply of nipa matting if the internees wanted to build additional shacks around the barracks for husbands and wives who wished to move out and live together.

The Governing Committee had thanked Captain Hira and told him they would consider the matter and find out how the camp electorate felt about it. They'd retired to the church shed and met. They'd met all afternoon and all evening, and the camp was rife with wild rumors about what it was Captain Hira had wanted. Some people said they were going to be moved to Japan. Some said rations were going to be doubled if the sugar men were willing to go out every day and run the mills. Some said rations were going to be halved unless everyone in camp signed a declaration that could be posted in the barrios pleading with the guerrillas to turn themselves in. Still other people said it was a repatriation and Camp Dewey had been assigned fifty berths on a Swedish liner sailing for the States on the fifteenth of October and that the Governing Committee was trying to agree on a list of the people who were sick enough or strategically important enough to go.

When the real subject of the meeting was finally announced it caused as much excitement as any of the rumors would have if they'd turned out to be true. Within half an hour of the announcement the first fight took place. A Mrs. Garnett in the women's barracks, the wife of a sugar man, called pretty little Mrs. Bax "a pious slut" because she'd said she wanted to cohabit with her husband. Mrs. Bax was Californian Spanish and rather secular and fiery for someone who had married a Lutheran missionary. So she told Mrs. Garnett that it was no business of hers how other women who were attractive and had attractive husbands might feel about marriage. Mrs. Garnett wasn't particularly attractive and there were rumors that Mr. Garnett had been seen out walking with Bonny Illingdon. Naturally there was a fight. And it ended—in hair pulling and scratching—only when lights went out and they couldn't see to fight any more.

The next morning in the men's barracks the stories about the fight were being passed around and laughed at after breakfast as the men changed into their G-strings and got ready for work. It seemed as if all the men were agreed that the fight was silly and just-like-women when Reverend Fisher could suddenly be heard through the top floor speaking much too distinctly.

"Yes, it *is* a moral question, Ray. It's a moral question whether anyone should be given the opportunity to bring a child into our world of hunger and imprisonment."

"You mean to stand there and tell me, Fisher," said Ray Henry, drawling but with equal distinctness, "that you or someone else on some goddamn committee ought to be able to tell me what kind of a place is right for *me* to have *my* kids in? Why, I thought this war was against that kind of dictation."

"It's not a question of dictation," said Reverend Fisher, "just of mutual consent determined by the majority. And I say this: that I'd be willing to share my ration with the illegitimate child of some poor teen-age girl a lot sooner than I'd be willing to share it with any child a grown man like you produces."

"Well, why don't you just leave that up to me, Reverend? I ain't heard the old lady bitching about being pregnant yet."

Peter noticed that Ray's southern accent was becoming thicker and that Reverend Fisher's Philadelphia accent was becoming thinner all the time.

"That may be amusing but it's no answer. There's also the question of decency," continued Reverend Fisher intently, "whether or not half a dozen couples can decently live together under one roof when they're only separated by nipa matting and when we obviously haven't got enough materials to build separate little sheds for every one of them."

"I'm surprised you have such a dirty mind, Reverend. How do you know Betsy and me don't just want to be around where we can pinch each other when we feel like it without gettin' an invite and makin' a special trip for it? But just supposin' that there are six other couples in this shack of ours all wantin' to shack up. Well, then, Monday evenin' when the wash is done, that's our evenin' and those six other couples, they'll just damn well go out and walk or play bridge or somethin', because they'll get their turn later in the week."

The bystanders all chuckled and Peter could see Ray had scored a good point.

"Oh, stop clowning, Ray. It doesn't make it decent to have a schedule so that every envious bachelor and prankster can listen at the walls and know what couple he's gossiping about when he tells tales later. We're too small a community, I say, to jeopardize our morale by separating men with women from men without women."

"I'd like to see my Betsy catch any snoopers outside our wall. I surely would," said Ray with a large, intimidating laugh. "But say some brave feller does come through the barracks one night announcin' that Betsy and I are havin' ourselves a time and say this makes all the bachelors feel downhearted and discouraged, why, then, Reverend, I suggest you get out your prayer book and do some matchmakin' and hitch 'em up due and proper."

"Wood gang, on your feet," bawled Mark Price to break it up.

"I declare I never saw so much bull shit from a horse's ass

277

in all my life," drawled Ray as he started for the stairs in his G-string.

"Then besides everything else, there's the aesthetic question of whether we want a shanty town all over the parade ground," announced Reverend Fisher to his dwindling audience.

Poor Reverend Fisher, thought Peter as he followed Ray down the stairs. He really argued more logically than Ray even if he seemed silly doing it.

That night the camp newspaper, posted on the bulletin board next to the chimney corner, had a large, carefully inked headline:

### SEX REARS HEAD IN DEWEY

When Peter told Jerry about the controversy, Jerry smiled more broadly and looked more like his old self than he had since coming into camp.

"There you are, Peter," he said, "that's life in a nut shell. Fisher thinks he's grown up and sensible, so naturally he can't see disturbing the delicate make-believe peace of the camp for a children's game like sex. But your big dopey muscle-bound friend Ray Henry thinks this silly itch, as Donny Garver calls it, is the foundation of life. And of course they're both right. It is the foundation and it is a childish game. That's why none of us can ever be more than children. But Fisher's a phony. He wants to pretend he's an adult. Ray knows damn well he's just a lovable boy and needs his Betsy."

"You make it sound too cosmic," said Peter. "They just don't like each other. They never have."

"Wait and see how cosmic it is. I bet it's the biggest controversy yet. I bet this camp will never be the same again."

And Jerry seemed to be right. The arguments became so hot and numerous that the camp divided into what Donny Garver called the *cohabiters* and the *out-of-the-habiters*. The division was so complete—and so completely new, with missionaries and sugar men, marrieds and unmarrieds, old maids and mothers aligned unpredictably on one side or another—that the Governing Committee finally decided the only way to resolve it was by a full camp referendum. This in itself was a problem because, whenever a camp-wide vote came up, Mrs. Page and her Committee for Worker's Suffrage got busy and insisted that there be a referendum first

on whether Jimmy Page and the other kids under eighteen
who worked a man's day shouldn't also have a man's vote.
This time Mrs. Page seemed to be swinging a lot of new
support, including Mrs. Kahn and Peter's mother, and Peter
began to think he might have to vote. The idea embarrassed
him. What business of his was it if Ray and Betsy wanted to
live together? It was just as Ray suggested when he kidded
him about it: "When you-all get to be a full-fledged voter,
Pete," he drawled, "who you goin' to vote in as your personal
cohabiter? Now Norman here's goin' to vote himself Candy
Kulhausen. But who you goin' to take when we pass out the
spoils?"

The first referendum had been held yesterday and to
Peter's relief—in spite of the fact that Jerry had teasingly
gone and added his vote to Mrs. Kahn's and Peter's mother's
—Worker's Suffrage had been defeated 58 to 33. Today was
the day of the second referendum, the important one on cohabitation, and Peter couldn't help but feel a little excited
about it as he worked at the fence posts.

It was a big day in another way, too, because Peter was going to have his first date. Jerry had insisted that he wouldn't
even consider Peter's escape plan and would inform the
camp committee about his dangerous, pigheaded whittling
operations unless he too made an effort to get out of his rut
and stop feeling guilty about sex and shy around girls. To
help him, Jerry had been teaching him how to play bridge.
A day or two before, Jerry had apparently decided that the
time had come to get him a partner. The first Peter knew
about it was yesterday afternoon as school was letting out
when Maggie Higgins caught him by the arm and said, in
a way that was unlike her, "I was talking to Mark Price,
Peter, and he was telling me you've been learning to play
bridge. Would you play with me tomorrow night if I could
get Candy and Norm to play with us?"

Peter had muttered yes, of course he would, and escaped
to his bunk and his geometry book. He hadn't gone near
Jerry and the Staff Room all evening. The idea that the men
didn't think he could do things for himself angered him and
hurt his pride. And the idea that Maggie should know it and
go along with it out of pity shamed him so much that he
found himself later blushing over his geometry in the privacy of his bunk. By today the shame had abated somewhat
and turned to sad reasonableness. After all, he *was* miserably

shy and they *had* only meant to be kind. Jerry was only treating him the way Peter treated Jerry.

Peter heard the steps of the tea guard coming up along the other side of the stockade. He was either early or Peter had been daydreaming. Peter jumped up fearfully, unbent the grass he had been lying on, sprinkled a little of the goat manure on it to help it recover strength and listened tensely. The Jap outside had already called to the Jap on top to come down for his tea, but Peter hadn't yet heard the creaking sound which the sentry made getting out of the crow's-nest. That was what he didn't like about this moment of his daily routine: he had to rely all on his ears to be sure that the guard had stopped watching and the coast of camp was clear.

The faint splashing of liquid as the tea guard poured out a cup for the lookout told Peter that he had waited long enough and perhaps too long. Moving silently with as much speed as he could, he crossed Bufferland. It was an uneasy feeling to know that, with the tea all poured, one of the guards might glimpse his retreating back through a crack in the stockade and stop him with a shout or a bullet. But nothing happened. He reached the pine grove and waited in its shadows until the sentry had climbed back into his lookout. Everything was all right. He hid the pouch of manure under a rock and hurried up the hill toward the church shed where he had to serve for Father Gibney at early service.

"You play bridge very well," said Maggie as Peter walked her home across the parade ground toward the women's barracks.

"Candy doesn't pay any attention," said Peter. "And Norm doesn't pay attention except to what Candy does."

"Anyway, I'm glad we won," said Maggie.

"You won," said Peter politely. After the surly way he had accepted Maggie's invitation to play, he had resolved to be as polite as he knew how. "You left 'em in your prop wash," he added.

"Funny you remember that," said Maggie. "It seems like centuries ago that Dad was teaching me to fly."

"Have you heard anything more from your folks?"

"Nothing but that one letter Captain Hira brought. I guess they're still all right in the camp in Manila."

"How did they happen to leave you behind?" asked Peter. "I've been curious about it."

280

"Dad's plane could only take three on such a long flight and there were four of us: Mother and Dad, my brother Franky and I. Dad didn't trust me to fly that far alone and come back for *him*, so he said he'd come back for *me*. He tried. I was waiting at what was left of the airport. He made three approaches and then went up and circled. After a while he came down low again and dropped a note wrapped around a monkey wrench. I've still got it."

"What did it say?" asked Peter.

"Hold tight, baby, I'll be back with a skyhook."

"I'm awfully sorry," said Peter.

"No need to be. I'm old enough to be away from my parents and I guess one camp's as good as another."

"Just the same," said Peter, "I hadn't realized."

"Well, you've had a hard time, too. When are we going to play bridge again?"

"I expect you've already got a date for tomorrow night," he said.

"No, tomorrow's fine. Will you hold a table or shall I?"

"Oh, I'll hold it this time. I'm sorry I didn't think of it today."

"It's all right. I had some homework to do anyway. Good night."

Maggie reached out across the sympathetic distance that separated them, squeezed his hand and turned up the steps into the women's barracks.

"Good night," called Peter.

He returned to the men's barracks full of excitement. Being older and beautiful and troubled herself, Maggie certainly was nice to him. He was a baby, really a selfish baby the way he let himself be so taken up in his own problems.

As he came to the men's barracks he heard shouts on the ground floor. He went in to see what it was all about and found that it was the ballot counters. Cohabitation had won 63 to 40. Peter ran upstairs to tell Jerry and the others in the Staff Room. He told Donny, but Jerry wasn't there so he ran out back by the cook-shed chimney. Jerry wasn't at the chimney either. A moment later Peter came up on him in the darkness, sitting on the edge of one of the laundry tables. He was swinging his legs slightly and gasping in a way that frightened Peter.

"What's the matter, Jerry?"

At first Jerry didn't answer, but after a while he said,

281

"Drunk tears." His voice was hoarse. "Just drunk tears."

Peter had never seen a man cry before except Mayor Ziegler on the first day of internment. It embarrassed him and he started away from the table to leave Jerry alone.

"Don't go away," muttered Jerry. "It's a human thing to do," he added after a pause. "Most human goddamn thing I've done in months."

"Were you thinking about Margo?" asked Peter.

"I don't know. Yes, I guess so. One of the old men was talking about his daughter—said she was an enticer, just had an air about her that made men want to touch her. Stupid sentimental thing to crack up on but that was how Margo was in her quiet way, only I never met her father."

"She was awfully beautiful. Even I could tell that."

"Even you, huh. She said you had eyes too big for your britches."

Peter blushed and remembered Margo pouring coffee for him the first time he'd met her at the hotel.

"She was fond of you, Peter."

"She was nice to me, too," said Peter. "I'd have done anything for her."

"So would I if I could have. . . . You know, when that patrol plane came over our boat, I could see the pilot like the broad side of a barn. Did I tell you that? I could see him like a sitting duck, but I couldn't hit him. Me, the sharpshooter, the best sniper Bean had. I was shaking so much with the chill between fevers that I couldn't even find the safety catch. He knocked Margo clean out of the boat before I got off one shot. By the time I could swim that little distance the water had turned red around her, so I swam back to the boat and waited for the sharks. Margo drifted away and the sharks followed her. That was her last act of enticement. She led the sharks away from me, off into the sea."

Peter thought Jerry was going to weep again. "I wish you wouldn't cry again," he said.

"I won't," said Jerry. "It's only a game anyway. *Play the game.* That was one of Margo's favorite truisms. But she was right in a way. It's a sensible answer and it lets you get some fun out of life. You have to make some rules, of course, and abide by them, but you also have to hold part of yourself in reserve, separate and not too scrupulous, so that you know it *is* only a game and the rules *are* only formal and the other players can have different rules. You have to remember that there might be such a thing as real life if you had an infinite playground and everlasting energy."

"Isn't that like wishing you were God?" said Peter.

"No, it's just realizing how you were created. Don't ever accept the game as real life. If you do, you die. You lose the power to imagine all the other possible games and playgrounds and players. You lose the vision of real life. And the style and grace you can bring from it to your own game. You stop being a baby god and become just a baby."

"I don't think you know much about theology," said Peter.

"I knew more theology when I was ten than you'll ever know in that half-baked Protestant church of yours," said Jerry, slurring the words.

"You're a fine one to talk. You're not even a Catholic."

"No, that's right, I'm not."

Peter could see that he had said the wrong thing, so he quickly told Jerry about the victory of the cohabiters.

"That's good," said Jerry. "That's playing the game. They're dear people. They're good people."

"It's almost lights-out," said Peter.

"Time you led the old drunk back to pasture."

As Peter walked to the barracks with Jerry he told him about his bridge game and how he and Maggie had won.

"And how's your hole coming?" asked Jerry at the foot of the stairs.

"It's pretty nearly half done. I'd finish it up in short order if I thought you'd ever use it."

"Maybe I will," said Jerry.

"Do you mean it?"

"Well, I have to get myself off your back somehow. You're wasting too much time on me. You're not doing well at school. You're not taking advantage of Donny's shop. You haven't got any girl friends."

"You know that's not because of you. It would be the same if you weren't here, except that I wouldn't have any kind of a good friend at all."

"You think I've got a prayer of finding Bean out in those hills in my condition?"

"You know the hills better than the Japs and your legs aren't in bad condition. I mean, they wouldn't be if you walked a bit and didn't drink so much."

"Well, we'll see. Maybe I'll go after I see how the cohabiting scheme works out. Or maybe after I've seen you win a bridge tournament. I don't know why I'd leave, but maybe I will. They're good people here."

Jerry started slowly up the stairs. By the time he had reached the top, the guards pulled the switch, the lights went out and Peter said good night. He had to sleep well and work hard on the hole in the morning.

## CHAPTER 20

The old school shed was a snare drum to the rain. It beat on the tin roof with an endless even roll, which ten thousand crack bandsmen couldn't have matched. Inside the drum fourteen people sat at tables. They seemed to Peter like naked minds swimming in a sea of sound. One by one they sank to think and then bobbed up to communicate their conclusions with unearthly brevity and clearness.

"One club," said Peter loudly.

"Pass," said Mrs. Newcombe.

"A heart," said Maggie.

"Pass," said Mr. Newcombe.

"Two no trump," said Peter.

"Four hearts," said Maggie after the next pass.

"Four no trump?" said Peter.

"Five diamonds," said Maggie.

"Double," said Mr. Newcombe unpleasantly.

"Five no trump?"

"Six clubs."

"Six hearts," said Peter.

"Double," said Mr. Newcombe again, when it came around to him.

"Redouble," said Peter.

Mr. Newcombe opened the jack of spades and Peter laid down the dummy with hands trembling. He had the ace and queen of spades in it, and since Maggie had shown no kings, that gave her the problem of deciding at the first trick whether to play the ace or finesse the queen. Maggie really took her time about it. Mr. Newcombe began drumming his fingers on the table, but Maggie looked at him coolly and went back to thinking. That was one of the nice things about

284

her. She was always self-possessed. Perhaps coming from a rich family before the war and being used to lots of parties had something to do with it; anyway she never let any of the grown-up bridge players ruffle her or stampede her.

Tonight was the last night of the tournament and she and Peter were tied with the Newcombes for third place. The first- and second-place teams were so far ahead that they were out of reach, but Peter dearly wanted to beat the Newcombes. Take your time, Maggie, he thought. Take all the time you want. Jerry says what you do with the opening lead often makes all the difference.

Jerry would be standing somewhere behind Peter, leaning against the wall. That son-of-a-bitch Mr. Newcombe had asked Jerry to keep away from the table during play because he was Maggie's and Peter's coach. Peter mentally rolled the profanity around on his tongue and liked the feel of it. It was only recently that he had allowed himself to think and use any swear words and the pleasure was still new.

Mr. Newcombe was tapping once more and Peter began to think Maggie was delaying just to annoy him. The Newcombes took their bridge seriously and acrimoniously. Jerry said that not cohabiting together they couldn't find anything else to fight about.

Cohabitation so far had been a great success. The three new two-story shacks out back beyond the laundry tables housed forty cohabiters and their children. The buildings were rather crowded together and the people inside were more crowded together, but the buildings had been dressed up with walks and flower gardens and none of the people inside had asked to return to the half-empty barracks yet. As a matter of fact, life and gossip in the barracks had become a lot more dull and Peter spent less time, if he could help it, in his six-by-seven-foot space than he ever had in his three-by-seven-foot space back in the dark old days three or four months ago.

It was sad to think that none of it might last. Liberal Captain Hira had been replaced by a new commandant, Captain Shijugi. Donny Garver, who had been hauled in and personally slapped by Shijugi twice for working after lights-out in the Fake-It Shop, had written a song about him which compared his disposition to that of a parrot with a stutter or a burro starved for burrs, a yak without its butter or a bitch without her curs. In his first two weeks of vicious moods as commandant, Shijugi had decreased the daily rice ration from fourteen to ten ounces a person, closed up the school because he found it was teaching American history, destroyed Donny Garver's still, and most recently threatened to stop cohabitation and to prohibit recreational activities in the former school shed. The one hope, Peter thought, was Mark Price. Mark was good at being firm with the Japs and now that things were tough again he had been elected camp chairman to replace Mr. Catlow, who had come down with dysentery. The rest of Mark's old corrupt administration hadn't come back into power with him and Peter hoped that Mark would prove himself this time by keeping a clean house and telling Shijugi where to get off.

Maggie played the ace of spades and then quickly did the rest.* When her final gamble worked and she laid down the nine of diamonds to make a 400-point overtrick and an almost sure top score on the hand, she dropped her head between her arms and sprawled out across the table, sighing with relief. Peter gave her trembling hands, thrust toward him, a quick pat, and Mr. Newcombe rudely pushed the next board to be played up against her cascade of black hair, nudging her head with it.

"Nice going, Maggie," said Peter. "That should be a high on the board."

"Why did you discard the eight of diamonds on that first diamond lead, Emily?" asked Mr. Newcombe. "It tipped her off to making the finesse."

"It was the only one I had," said Mrs. Newcombe. "Why did you double the five-diamond call? That's what tipped her off."

Peter looked around to give Jerry a smile of triumph, but he wasn't there.

"Well, let's get on with it," said Mr. Newcombe, seeing that his wife was right.

"Did you see Jerry go out?" Peter asked Maggie as they

* She cashed the ace of clubs on the table and ruffed three clubs in her hand, taking out three of the four outstanding trumps on her returns to the dummy. She drew Mrs. Newcombe's last trump and overtook the jack of diamonds with the ace to make her third re-entry to the table. Sloughing her last spade on the good fifth club, she got back to her hand by trumping a spade with her last heart. Then, with sheer bravado, she finessed the ten of diamonds from her hand under the dummy's king.

picked up their cards.

"I'm afraid I was too busy thinking about the hand," she replied.

"I'm glad he's gone," said Newcombe. "I never do feel safe when that fellow's eavesdropping."

Peter flushed with anger.

"I didn't realize you'd ever done anything anti-Japanese," said Maggie innocently.

"Who said I had?"

"Well, if you've never done anything patriotic," burst in Peter angrily, "you've got nothing to worry about and no reason to spread lies about Jerry being an informer."

"Are you calling me a liar?" asked Mr. Newcombe.

"Go feel an eel," muttered Peter.

"I'm going to call the tournament director," said Mrs. Newcombe shrilly. "There's no reason why we have to play with a couple of foul-mouthed gutter brats."

"Go ahead," said Maggie calmly, "but I don't think you'll get far calling us gutter brats."

Peter wanted to say something about the Newcombes trying to break up the tournament because they were losing, but Maggie put her finger to her lips, asking him to be quiet.

"Calm down, Emily," said Mr. Newcombe. "We only have one more hand with them. I'll bid a no trump."

As the Newcombes bid and made what seemed to Peter a routine game in no trump, he calmed himself after the fight and returned to wondering about Jerry. The rain hammering on the roof was the first big typhoon of the season. Earlier in the day, when it had started, Peter had asked Jerry whether this wasn't the night and Jerry had said no, not until the end of the tournament. He was proud of the way Maggie and Peter were playing and Peter couldn't understand why he would stop watching and go out into the rain. Surely he wouldn't escape from camp without saying good-by. He knew where the hole was and when the guards changed, but Peter had expected to go down to the pine grove with him and give him a silent send-off. It would be bad enough having him gone. Jerry knew that. He surely wouldn't make it so sudden and casual.

Peter concentrated on the hands and told himself that Jerry would be back soon. But when the sit-out round came, and Maggie and he were the odd couple who had to talk and twiddle their thumbs for three hands, Jerry still hadn't returned.

"Maybe I ought to go look for him," said Peter.

"Oh, it's raining too hard," said Maggie. "It would soak through your rain cape and make you wet and miserable for the rest of the evening. We've got to really whip those two deadbeats now, you know."

"I can't help worrying about him," said Peter.

"Whatever for? Mark and Donny have probably smuggled in a bottle and they're having a party. The way you baby that guy, you'd think you were running him in the derby."

Peter smiled. It was the kind of expression she remembered and treasured from her father.

"I guess it does seem pretty funny when I'm so much younger than he is," he said. All the same, he hoped Jerry wasn't at a party. Destroying Donny's still was the one good thing Shijugi had ever done, he thought. It was too bad for Mark and Donny, but it was one of the reasons Jerry had finally faced up to the fact that he had to escape. It was high time, too. He'd been in camp for four months now and one of these days, if he didn't go while the going was good, Colonel Kori might come for him and all Peter's efforts would be wasted.

"You're quiet tonight," said Maggie.

"That was beautiful the way you played the slam," said Peter.

"I almost collapsed afterward. And I think I'd have slapped that jerk Newcombe if you hadn't patted my hands just when you did."

"Oh, come on," said Peter.

"No, really, you took me by surprise. I don't think you've ever touched me before except by accident."

Peter blushed. Of course he hadn't ever touched her, but he hadn't realized that she'd noticed it.

"It hasn't been on purpose," he said.

"Did you ever see anything of that Enid Larsen when you were on the outside?" asked Maggie.

"Oh, a little," said Peter.

"You don't still think you're in love with her, do you?"

"I don't know," he muttered.

"It seems silly at our age," she said. "You just tell me if I'm being rude, won't you?"

"You're not being rude."

"You're the only person I know shyer than I am, so I take advantage of you," she said.

"You, shy?" said Peter, grateful for the slight change of subject. "After the way you told off old Newcombe?"

"Oh, I don't mean with deadbeats like him. I mean with people I like."

Maggie blushed, and fortunately the tournament director, Mr. Barsini, stopped the conversation by ringing the bell for the next round.

When the evening was over, Jerry still hadn't come back and Peter couldn't wait for the results to be tabulated before going to look for him.

"If we beat the Newcombes and come in third, we'll win a *camote*," said Maggie. "I may just eat your share."

"To heck with you," he said, grinning. "I'll sign up for the next tournament with Bonny Illingdon."

"Hah," said Maggie.

"Jerry's probably only sick or something and I'll be back fast," said Peter. "But if it's anything more serious, you don't mind running home alone in the rain, do you?"

"No, I'll be fine. I'll see you tomorrow noon."

After extras Maggie and Peter studied together in the closed-down school shed. He was helping her with trigonometry and she was helping him with everything else. In the evenings—almost every evening now—they played bridge and then, if it was fine, walked back and forth along the embankment until lights-out, looking at the stars over the China Sea and talking restlessly about what they were going to do with life after the war.

Peter ducked into his straw rain cape and out the door into the furious rain. It had been an exciting evening. He was sure they had done well. Not that they had played such good bridge—not by Jerry's standards—but everything had worked and somehow they had made all the right guesses. If it weren't for Jerry's disappearance, Peter felt he would be wildly happy. No one had seen Jerry in the Staff Room or at the Chimney Corner. He hunted fruitlessly in the dark of the laundry tables and then headed for his mother's shack. That was where Mrs. Gibney lived and, being camp interpreter, she would know if anything awful had happened. He stamped up onto his mother's porch, lifting his dripping cape off him as he went.

"Peter, come here."

It was his mother sitting in the darkness at the other end of the porch. Her voice sounded unusual. As Peter started toward her, he saw that someone was with her. A strong masculine hand gripped him and drew him, wet as he was, into an awkward embrace.

"Dad!"

"Let's have a look at you, big fellow." His father drew him toward one of the lighted windows. "Why, you're almost as tall as I am."

"Only an inch to go. Gee, Dad, isn't this something? What happened? How did you get here?" To control the confusion of his excitement, affection and embarrassment—the sudden irresponsible relaxation and almost jealousy that he felt at being demoted from his position as man of the family—Peter pulled away from his father and sat down at the porch table. His mother poured him a cup of hot *garvee*, the coffee substitute invented by Donny Garver from burned chicken corn, and while he drank it, his father told about his experiences. Lights-out arrived and he talked on in the darkness. He was making a tremendous effort to sound like his old self, Peter thought, but all the same, his voice was tired and almost old. He had been locked up for months, first in the Enao jail, then in the Banong jail, and finally, for the last two weeks, at Kempeitai headquarters at Abanao. He had been fed little but not tortured.

"I didn't start to worry until your friend Kori got ahold of me. He'd have tortured me when all his other tricks ran out—I'll bet my bottom dollar on it—but three days ago he didn't show up for our morning chat. The soldiers came in and searched my cell as if they thought I'd hidden him under the mattress or hung him up from the meat hooks on the ceiling. What a ruckus! My guess is one of his old girl friends or a relative of one of his victims caught him out on a dark night and stuck a knife in him. Anyway, they didn't find his body right away, because first they had his geisha in for questioning and then they tortured his mistress from the casino."

"Rainha?" exclaimed Peter.

"That's right. I don't think even Wong would have wished her the beating she got. Her screams were awful. The guard who cleaned my cell and brought me my food—a nice little fellow from a farm near Kobe—told me that they disfigured her and beat her senseless before they finally carted her off to a hospital. After that, things quieted down until this morning when a new police chief arrived. A fellow called Fukawa. Altogether a different type of individual from Kori. Much less twisted and Westernized. Almost Chinese, he's so smooth and soft spoken. Come to think of it, I wouldn't be surprised if there was some Chinese blood there somewhere. He questioned me for about an hour this afternoon, trying to tie me in with Jerry Costeau. Then he apologized for the way I'd been treated and sent me to camp."

"I forgot all about Jerry," said Peter. "I was looking for him when I came over here before lights-out."

"You won't find him, Peter. They had him sitting in the office at the guardhouse when Fukawa brought me in from town. Renny says they sent Mrs. Gibney to fetch him from your bridge game several hours ago. I suppose Fukawa wanted to see if we showed any sign of recognizing each other. Well, we didn't. We didn't bat an eye, either one of us. But they turned me loose and kept Jerry prisoner. I'm afraid he's in for a bad time of it. Fukawa asked me two or three times in different ways if I'd ever read *Man* Magazine before the war and if I'd ever heard reports of a guerrilla who took photographs. Well, that can only mean one thing: he's connected Costeau the magazine photographer with Costeau the internee and with the guerrilla who took pictures. You may as well face it, Peter: Jerry's chances are pretty slim. I think the only reason Fukawa asked me about him was a last effort to incriminate me, not Jerry."

"We have to do something," said Peter.

"There's nothing we can do. What worries me is you, big fellow. After the unwise way Renny says you've been associating with Jerry here in camp, I'm afraid they may haul you in for questioning again."

"What about bribing Fukawa?" said Peter intently. "You said he was kind of Chinese."

"Be reasonable, darling," said his mother. "What could we bribe him with? We hardly have enough to feed ourselves now that they've cut the rations."

"I can get money," said Peter. "A lot of it."

"Peter, I've never had to bribe anyone in my life," said his father. "Once you start there's no end to it. It would take hundreds of dollars to bribe a man in Fukawa's position and even if we could raise that much and find a way of getting it to him, there'd be no assurance that he wouldn't pocket it and kill Jerry anyway."

"I can *get* hundreds of dollars," said Peter. "And the money's Jerry's anyway. He pretended it was mine but it's really his."

"Wait a minute! You don't mean you've got all that money he had in the hills hidden here somewhere, do you?" asked his father.

"Not all of it, but more than a thousand prewar pesos, I think."

"That's a lot. That might do it," said his father slowly. "We'd have to find someone else to make the offer. Either one of us, and Fukawa would have a good excuse to shoot us. But if someone in authority here in camp could get to him and broach it in the right sort of way, he might take it. And I guess on second thought he'd stick to his bargain on a thing like this. He's no fool. He doesn't want it bouncing back at him after the war."

"Give me your watch, Mother," said Peter.

"Don't do anything foolish, please," she begged. "I've just got my family together again." She thrust the watch at him in the darkness.

"Don't worry, Renny," said his father. "Where have you got the money, Peter?"

"A place I know," he said, strapping the watch to his wrist.

"Now hold on, young fellow, I'm coming with you, you know."

"You can't, Dad," said Peter. "It's not in camp and I'm the only person who can get out and bring it back."

"No, no," said his father. "You're not going to try any fool stunt like that." He groped out in the dark and caught Peter's arm and held it in a grip like the grip of a skeleton. "I thought you meant the money was right here."

"I can get it easily. I made the hole in the fence myself. I know just when the guard changes. I can be back with it by four in the morning."

"I'm sorry, big fellow, I can't let you do that."

"You can't stop me," said Peter. "You can't hold me like this all evening."

"No, but you're my son. You'll obey me."

"We've gotten along for two years without you," blurted Peter savagely. "I won't obey you now, not about this."

For a moment his father relaxed his grip as if he had been hit, and Peter, realizing what a cruel thing he had said, did

292

nothing to tear his arm free. Then the fingers tightened again and Peter thought they would slip right through his skin until his father's skeleton bone met his bone.

"You *will* obey me about this," said his father. "You're goldarn right you will, even if I have to hold you here all night."

Peter's mother was crying. "Are you sure, Tim?" she sobbed as Peter and his father stood silent, glaring through the darkness. "Peter has done a lot of things, and this Frenchman Costeau, he's a good man, isn't he? If Peter thinks it's safe, maybe we should take the chance."

"That money we lived on the year out of camp," said Peter, "when Dad was in the hills, it all came from Jerry. The letters from Dad, they came through Jerry. All the friendship and help I've had for months have come from Jerry." His voice had been trembling and now he too began to weep.

"We owe this man something, Tim," said his mother. "I didn't know it was so much."

"So does his country," said Dr. Baldwin, "but that doesn't make any difference. Costeau's ready to take his medicine. He certainly doesn't want any teen-age boy throwing away his life on a wild gamble like this. Why, look at those stockades and lights, Renny! You don't really think a boy his age has a chance of getting through them, do you?"

"I *can* get through them," said Peter. "I've been through them every night for four weeks." He was exaggerating, but it was true that parts of him had been through while he was working on the hole.

Before anyone could answer, a flashlight beam came around the corner of the shack and flashed briefly in their faces. It was Mrs. Gibney.

"Fukawa is staying overnight and keeping Costeau with him in the guardhouse," she said. "They're going to execute him in front of all of us at roll call in the morning. An example, Shijugi calls it."

Peter felt his father's grip relax. He tore away and jumped off the porch. His father chased him quietly and desperately through the dark, driving rain. Peter led him along the front of the women's barracks, around back past the cook shed and out among the laundry tables. By then he was far enough ahead of his father to hide under one of the cohabiting shacks and lose him.

Peter glanced at the radium dial of his mother's watch. It was ten to twelve. He heard his father stumble over the stoop of the next shack and he moved out from under the foundation. When he reached the edge of the pine grove his heart was making more noise than the rain. It wasn't the exertion, but the pain and happiness and freedom. If only he hadn't said such lousy things to his father on his first night home. Still, he had said them now, when he had some reason. And he would make up for them later.

The guard in the crow's-nest wasn't slumped on the railing tonight. He was standing upright under the center of his little conical tin roof trying to get as far away from the splashing raindrops as he could. He had on a raincoat, and as well as Peter could tell in the blurry lights of the stockade it didn't look glistening. That meant probably that it wasn't wet and the guard hadn't just come on duty but was still waiting for his relief.

*What a night.* It seemed to be increasing in violence. Peter wished he'd had time to snatch up his rain cape. The drops which fell on him from the pine boughs as he waited for the change of guard seemed less like drops than whole buckets of lukewarm water.

It's all a game, he thought, echoing a phrase of Jerry's. I don't give a damn what happens to me. I'm a child and I'll never be anything else. The only thing that's real and really counts is thinking. If I don't think about fear, I won't have it.

The guard was already facing away from the camp, looking for his replacement.

He wants to be home to bed, thought Peter. He can't see anything out into the darkness in this rain and he certainly can't hear anything with the pounding on that piece of tin over his head.

Peter moved out toward the stockade, watching the guard intently and ready to flatten himself in the beaten-down grass if the guard should start to turn around. He reached the cover of the fence and crawled along it until he came to the hole. He had never measured the hole against himself or squeezed all the way through it. One of his shoulders was in the mud and the other was pinched by the narrowing gap between the posts. He forced his way through, to make sure he could do it, and then pulled back again. It was a stupid thing to do because the new guard came past a moment later and stepped where he had been.

When the old guard had gone and Peter had waited five minutes by the watch, he crawled out through the grass and muck and backed, crawling, toward the trees on the Outside. The new guard was restless. He stamped about in the crow's-nest, half turning his face and making Peter flatten himself in the mud. Peter backed farther and flattened again. He backed against a pine trunk, got to his feet and ran into the forest.

He was free. Free to cross mountains like the howling of a dog or the wind itself. Free for four hours, or free even to escape to the guerrillas in the hills. The knowledge that he could do it if he wanted beat down on him and washed away like the rain. He laughed out loud at it and scarcely heard himself above the storm.

What's so free about being a guerrilla and killing people, he thought. That's all nostalgia now, just a sentimental idea, like self-pity or superstition or fear of death. The real freedom is the beautiful wildness of the night. Maybe I have only four hours to be out in it, but I can have the idea and feeling of it again any time I want. And that's the same as being free forever.

Stopping to catch his breath, he turned up his face and reveled in the water which streamed down on it from the black, tossing branches overhead.

It's like being young, and I *am* young, he exulted, young, free and guiltless. O God in the rain, he prayed, God in the sunshine, he chanted to the wind. O God in the moonlight and God most of all in the life that's in me, thank you for turning me loose these four hours in the woods. And thank you even more for setting me free forever to pick my own path and be a child and not mind admitting it. Now please help me, also, not to be too frightened to make the most of it.

What a chucklehead, he thought. I've got four hours to be free and do anything I want after I get the money, and instead I stand in the rain like a drunk, with a lot of ideas that I could just as well think out tomorrow or the next day or any time when Jerry's been ransomed. All the same, his feeling of elation and discovery didn't leave him and, as he dashed down the hill, he caught himself yelling recklessly with the wind. It was so long since he had run! In fact, it was the first time since his broken leg had healed. And he didn't limp at all—he seemed to flow down the hill like a torrent of water. He passed the spot where he had bumped into Colonel Fleer's houseboy, running away the day the war had started, and soon he was north of the golf course and starting uphill again, up his own hill toward his former home. The cottage stood deserted and derelict in the lights from the hotel. The shutter on the kitchen window was hanging by one hinge. But it was only a thing, a toy to be broken and fixed if possible—even a microscope was only a toy.

He pressed on to the road, crossed it, circled the water tower and went up the short cut to the school. There were lights in Father Gibney's cottage—probably Japs who had overflowed from the houses around the country club. He made a sweeping detour around the dormitories, climbing the ridge beyond on a bias and descending in the same way toward the gully on the other side. The rain seemed to be slackening and there was a hint of light which said that the moon was up there in the sky somewhere riding out the storm.

The gully was roaring with flood water and ducked him twice before he made the shore of the island. The shore was halfway up to the clearing now. Not a chance of finding the outer tunnel. He burst his way in through the undergrowth, straining angrily at the clinging vines and oblivious to the slashing sword grass. The confusion of boughs and leaves and water had changed everything. Even the clearing seemed different and he wondered if the Inner Keep was still above stream level.

He groped about wildly to find the entrance of the inner tunnel. Then the moon flashed out garish and ghostly and he saw where the tunnel had been. It was almost choked now with plants. He crawled into it, forcing them aside. When he came out at the edge of the rocky overhang which formed the cave, he found he was at the tip of the island. The flood water raced at his feet and fed on the bank of red clay which supported him. The path around the jutting end of the rock had caved in and been washed away. He took off his shoes and left them in the tunnel. Then, clinging to the rock face and worming out his own toeholds in what was left of the slippery bank below, he edged his way around the point. On the other side the bank under his feet broadened but the rock in his hands smoothed out and became more perpendicular. Finally there were no more hand-

296

holds. He spread his arms, pressed himself flat against the surface of the stone and squatted unsurely. Little by little, rolling his haunches and toeing with one foot while he heeled with the other, he sidled under the end of the ledge and into the cave.

Boy, there's never been any darkness darker than this, he thought. The stockade was easy. I wonder if I can find the money or ever get back around the point with it if I do.

There was an odd musty smell under the vine-curtained ledge.

An animal. A pig or a wild cat, he thought, and drew back toward the entrance. But I've got to, he thought. It's just spooky. Anyway, I'd see glowing eyes if there was anything in there. He unsheathed the whittling knife on his belt and crawled slowly into the blackness. I have plenty of time, he thought. If I jab around enough with my knife, I'm sure to hit on the box eventually.

The smell grew stronger. Funny, it was almost as if he had heard a noise nearer to him than the noise of the storm. He came up against something hard that pushed into his stomach. He reached for it and felt steel. A gun barrel. He jerked it aside and lunged forward with his knife outstretched ahead of him. It sank into something soft. Only clay. As he wrenched it free, he heard a clear gasping sound on his left, back in the direction from which he had come. He whirled and crouched to jump at it. The moon, like a damp match, flickered briefly through the churning turmoil of the vines which overhung the ledge and formed one side of the cave. Peter sank backward, sick and lazy with horror. He thought that he had seen—sitting almost beside him and staring at him with the eyes of a corpse—Enid.

## CHAPTER 21

All thought of living and all thought of any kind gasped out of Peter and he pressed himself away from the thing he had seen until he was against the rear wall of the cave and could go no farther. The moon shone again and longer, and the apparition was still there. It *was* Enid, in a way, but so ragged

297

and wild and filthy that really it could only be some horrid leftover of lust and shame. It was huddled against the clay bank near the entrance of the cave. A shotgun lay out in the middle of the floor. It wasn't seeing the gun or Peter now but hiding its face in a pile of crumpled newspapers. Then the moon went out and Peter sat empty and shivering.

After a while he noticed that it was sobbing, poor tortured ghost—sobbing in a way that was more ugly and inhuman than any crying he had ever heard. The sound of it, like a metronome in his brain, slowly collected the half-thoughts which flickered there and marshaled them into rhythms of live speech. Odd ends of ideas which he had begun to finish weeks and months ago started up and brought themselves to bear in a kind of cold otherworldly coherence.

It's not a damned soul sent to punish me and drag me back to hell because it *is* Enid, and commixing isn't allowed in hell. That's a crazy idea. I don't believe in that kind of hell any more. Hell's for the living, and when you give in to it and despair, like Jerry was trying to do for a while, you die forever right then and there. When you give in in a different way and decide to be purposely evil, like Kori, you can't ever be evil enough. You always have some soft spots left where you can be gotten at and tortured and enraged. The only way to escape hell is to become one of the harmless living dead and feel proud about being a grown-up sheep in a little concentration camp. But if you're not scared of hell, there *is* a way to have heaven. You have to open yourself up to good and bad both and take heaven and hell together. That way there's more elation than misery and more beauty than boredom. And as long as you're a live, adventurous child and remember it's mostly a game, nothing can hurt you beyond recovery.

"Enid," he called above the storm. "Enid," he called, and his voice sounded stronger. "You don't need to be scared. I'm just Peter, your friend. I sneaked out of camp for a few hours to get some things I left here."

He crawled over toward the spot where he had seen her and reached out and touched her skin. It was as cold and neuter as the time he had saved her from her leg cramp at the beach. He found his way closer to her head and stroked her hair.

"Enid? You remember me, Enid?"

She said nothing, but her sobbing began to sound more

like real wet tears and less like dry terror. He bent over her and put his mouth against her cheek and, yes, it was wet with true living tears. And also, it was she that had smelled like a wild animal.

"How long have you been here, Enid?"

"Days," she sobbed.

Peter searched his mind for what could have happened. The shotgun. That was what her father left her for protection against the Japs when he went off overnight to the mills.

"Where's your father?"

"In Manila buying machinery."

"You didn't shoot a Jap, did you?" exclaimed Peter.

"I bet it was four nights ago. . . . That means Papa will be back tomorrow."

"Four nights ago!" Peter's hand jumped back from her hair and he moved away from her. *She looks like a million dollars, that girl friend of yours.* That was what Colonel Kori had said in the hospital, and now Kori had disappeared. Three days ago. That was what Peter's father had said.

"You killed Colonel Kori!" he whispered.

"It is you, Peter? You are still my best friend?"

"You shot him with the shotgun."

"Uh-huh. . . . Half his neck I blew away. It seemed only a big piece of white skin until the blood started to come out."

"You were his mistress so as to get to Sweden," he said.

"No! No, I wasn't, Peter. I told him I had to see the tickets first. But he kept taking me out. Especially after Papa left, he took me out every night. Then on the night four days ago he brought me home from a dance at the club and tried to undress me."

"So you shot him?"

"No, I didn't make much fuss at first. I was a little drunk and it seemed as if he had been talking cleverly. But when he got close to me with his shirt off, I didn't like the way he smelled."

"I know. Sort of sweet and unhealthy. You must have told him so, the same way I did."

"All I did was giggle and tell him to go home and take a bath."

"That was enough. I'll bet he had a temper tantrum."

"He hit me with his riding crop and chased me all over the house. At first I thought it was impossible, so I stopped

299

to laugh at him. But he still came after me trying to hit me with the whip. He kept yanking off more of his clothes and looking uglier and redder and crazier each time I looked back. I got scared. I ran to the hall closet."

"Is that where you kept the gun?"

"Yes. He thought he had me trapped there and by the time he saw the gun, he had no chance to get out of the way. A while later I realized how awful it was, so I ran to the kitchen and wrapped some food in newspapers and came here to hide."

"It seems funny you came here where we taught each other to play the Game," said Peter.

"It didn't have anything to do with that. It was the only good hiding place I could think of. I thought I could figure out what to do here. I thought I had plenty to eat, too, but I ran out of food ages ago. And I still don't know what to do. Whether they'll arrest Papa at the airport or let him live at home so he can help me or they can trap me through him or what. Can't you think of something? You are my friend still, aren't you?"

She crawled toward Peter and he let her cradle her head in his arms. Even if it was only in self-defense and legal under American law, she was a murderess, he thought. She'd done what he had once wished he'd done. She'd murdered the devil, but it wasn't the devil: only Colonel Kori, a wretched dead soul trying to clamber aboard any raft he thought might be life again.

"Aren't you going to help me?" asked Enid again.

"I'm trying to think. Why don't you go out by the edge and rinse off a bit in the rain water?"

"I'm sorry," she murmured. "I'm not so clean, I guess." She got up obediently, and against the dark sky he could see her darker silhouette trying to catch the rain water in her hands and scrub her face with it. Peter felt touched and ashamed.

She's more of a child and more honest than I am, he thought. She's alive and she killed Kori for trying to drag her down among the dead. She tried to shoot me, too, and I tried to stab her with a knife. Well, that's what we already tried to do, playing the Game and being grown up. I guess killing's one of the games too, with just as silly rules as most. If you're a guerrilla you can shoot Japs. And if you're assaulted even by someone you know well, you can kill him.

He glanced at his mother's watch and jumped up. It was

two-thirty. When Enid came back from the entrance of the cave, Peter was stabbing his knife repeatedly into the floor of the cave.

"I'm not so stinky any more," she said.

The knife struck one of the tin boxes and he dug it up.

"You can't think of any way to help me, can you?" she said challengingly. But she didn't sound as if she believed it. She was still counting on him.

"I'm going to take you back to camp with me. Mother and the other people there will take care of you until your father comes. Maybe we can even get word to your father when he arrives at the airport tomorrow."

She began crying again and stood over him crying while he dug up the second box. When he rose to his feet, she put her arms around his neck and pressed against him.

"Thank you. I do love you, Peter. I really do."

He pushed her away from him and carried the boxes out to the entrance of the cave.

"But you don't love me," she said. "You think I'm dirty."

"It isn't that. We don't have time. Besides, you killed a Jap, and God only knows what else you did. I wish I had a light."

"I have some matches somewhere."

He heard the rustling of newspapers and in a moment she touched his back and found his hand and put some matches in it. They were damp, but the third one he tried blazed in their faces and blinded them. He pried open the money box. It was a good tight cooky tin and rusted under the edges. The money inside was wrapped in oilskin. And then the match went out.

"Have you got a bit of string, too?" he asked.

"I have a hair ribbon."

He took it and tied it tightly around the package of hundred-peso notes. Then he tied it again to his belt and strapped the bundle firmly against his waist.

"I didn't go to bed with anyone but you," she said.

"But you would have to get to Sweden." He took the box of receipts and put them back in the hole.

"I suppose so," she said simply.

"Well, what does it matter?" he said. "I still love you. I love a lot of things now."

He kissed her on the cheek and tried to laugh. He snorted with laughter. But when she held on to him, as if asking forgiveness, he kissed her again, as well he remembered. Her

301

hand felt the features of his face, making absolutely sure they were real. She was kind, he thought, because she needed him and he was treating her roughly. She couldn't care anything about kisses as frightened, dirty, hungry and like a wild animal as she was. But when the moon showed her to him briefly, she was staring at him with the same intent, unbelieving look of experiment and discovery as he had once seen on her face before. The rain was pouring down again in earnest, cascading over the ledge beyond her shoulder and spattering their chilled legs.

"We have to get out of here before the stream rises above the cave floor," he said.

"Did you really fall off a table at Kempeitai headquarters?" she asked, holding on to him still.

"Oh, of course not. Kori beat me up with a rifle."

"I thought he probably did," she said. "I'm glad I killed the son-of-a-gun."

He took her hand from his waist and moved toward the entrance. "Follow me exactly and don't make a sound. Don't talk unless I talk to you. Oh, and take your shoes off. Put them down the back of your dress."

He sidled out above the whirling water and along the face of the cliff to the place where he could get up off his haunches without being bowled over backward by the overhang. When she had caught up to him and he felt the tips of her fingers outstretched against the flat of the rock, he stood up and shouted to tell her what he was doing. He sidled on farther to give her room and a moment later he felt her finger tips again as she stood precariously beside him. Inch by inch, panting into the stone and patting hands where the going was easiest, they rounded the point and reached the inner tunnel.

It was three-fifteen now. They put on their shoes and hurried out through the tunnel and the tangle of bushes to the edge of the stream. Peter went over alone holding the oilskin of money high above his head and reeling and weaving as the current bore down on him and the rocks rolled under his feet. When he had made the shore, he left the money behind, went back and helped Enid across. He led her out of the water and up the ridge, making her scramble and run to stay with him. He kept on that way around the dormitories to the head of the short cut. There she sat down on the pine needles shaking her head and sobbing for breath.

It was twenty to four. The noises she was making sounded loud even above the storm.

"I'm sorry," she gasped in his ear. "I can't."

"Okay, rest," he said angrily.

He sat down with her and gave up all hope of reaching the stockade before the guards changed. When she was able to go on, he walked with her slowly and silently, surrounded by the storm, across the rest of the valley. The four hours of freedom were over and his parents would have to sit through a fifth. He was wondering what he had done with the four hours except slide back down the wet clay bank into the river of his past. But coming to the place in the woods where he had felt such elation earlier, he found that a little of the elation was still there. He was stronger and freer than he had been. He could swim in his river and if Enid had leg cramps he felt he could keep her afloat too.

"We'll rest here," he whispered in her ear. There was no point in crawling up to the stockade and lying in the mud before they had to. They couldn't cross the bufferland inside without a distraction to help them. And the tea guard wasn't due for half an hour.

Enid subsided on the wet pine needles and the rain water poured over her. He lay down beside her trying to share his warmth with her and she huddled against him trustingly.

Poor Enid, he thought. I can't help feeling ashamed of her. It's going to be hard presenting her to Mother and Maggie. She looks awfully dirty and ragged. And even when she's washed up and changed, she'll still be a million miles behind in school, and she'll still have a lot of silly, bitchy ideas and cheap dreams in her head. But so what if she isn't perfect? And if I don't love her perfectly? Even if it was all lust and I made up the rest, there's still a kind of fondness which grew out of it. What I feel about Maggie, that's probably just admiration for her cool sense and calmness around grownups. I suppose no love is perfect. Even the slavish way Mother loves me is partly enslaving and selfish. Even God's love has to suffer children to swell with beriberi in the Chinese slums.

He looked out through the tossing branches to the black sky. In the sky was freedom and a wonderful mixture of universal sadness and buoyancy. He felt numb and detached and excited.

You have to be in the center of the cone of fire, he

thought, and think it's all geometry in order to ignore the ragged edges of the flame. You have to suffer the baby gods and goddesses even if they smell like wild animals. You have to suffer Enid when she's obedient and loves you and you have to love her imperfectly when she's her old self again. You have to suffer all the children, yourself most of all.

"I'm cold," murmured Enid, shivering. He hugged her tighter. It was lucky she had said something. He'd been getting cold too and rambling dopily. It was quarter to five. They had to start soon.

"I wonder what they'll do to me," she whispered.

"You'll be all right," he said. "You're a neutral and they don't dare hurt you when you only did it in self-defense. The camp committee will get word to your father and he'll get word to the Swedish consul. It'll work out."

He made it sound easy and she pressed against him, too exhausted to do anything but believe him.

"We have to go through the stockade in a minute," he said. "Would you mind kissing me one last time in the new way, as wide awakely and as much like the old days as you can?"

She smiled and closed her eyes. He kissed her cold lips and found that her tongue and the inside of her mouth were cold too. It wasn't like the old days. It probably never would be again. She tensed slightly and her tongue flickered through his mouth as dry and desperate as a moth which had once flown into it during a hymn in church.

Funny how we've both changed, he thought. I've lost my guilt and she's lost her guiltlessness. He pushed her away gently, jumped up and pulled her up after him. When they reached the free bufferland on the outside of the fence, it was not raining so hard as it had been earlier. The guard was back in his usual position, slumped away from them on the rim of the crow's-nest facing camp.

"Watch the guard," he whispered. "If he starts to turn around, fall flat in the grass."

They walked slowly and erect across the open strip of weeds and grass. Peter squeezed through the hole and pulled Enid after him. He sat her down in the mud where she could lean against the stockade while he kept watch back out the hole. When the tea guard slogged past with the big can of tea on his back, Peter realized that he would never hear the creak of the ladder or the slosh of the tea tonight. He counted slowly to a hundred, pulled Enid to her feet and tugged her along out into the bufferland. When he could look back and see the top of the fence, the guard had only just begun to climb out of the crow's-nest and was still facing them. Peter stood rigid and held back Enid. But the guard went on over the edge, so they walked slowly up the hill through the pines and the rain to the barracks. Freedom was over.

As they rounded the corner of his mother's shack, a man stepped out of the graying darkness and grabbed Peter roughly by the arm. It wasn't his father but Mr. Garnett.

"So you did come back," said Mr. Garnett unpleasantly. "If I'd been you I'd have kept on going into the hills. You're in plenty of trouble. They're having a meeting about you at the hospital."

Peter remembered dimly that Mr. Garnett, as well as being a member of the garbage crew, was the elected camp policeman. He hadn't had many cases. Fritz Laski had stolen a camp chicken once and been locked up for two days in the cobbler's shop. Old man Barnaby had been tried and acquitted of milking the goats early in the morning before the goatherds were up. Why should Mr. Garnett grab Peter?

"Who's that with you?" asked Mr. Garnett. "So! It was just a girl all the time. And *they're* worried because they think you've gone over the fence. Hah! What's your name, tramp? Come here so I can see you."

"That's Miss Larsen," said Peter wearily. He felt no protective anger and the *Miss* sounded as foolish as it had the time he'd used it on Colonel Kori. "I found her in the woods. She asked for sanctuary so I brought her here."

Mr. Garnett lighted a match in Enid's face.

"Take it easy," said Peter. "She's had a god-awful time."

"I'll be damned," growled Garnett. "You are from out of camp. You better both of you come and see the committee."

He marched them along the back of the two barracks to where the infirmary stood on the edge of the embankment. There were lights inside. The infirmary lights were on their own circuit and allowed to be kept lighted all night if necessary. Inside, within the whitewashed walls of matting, Peter blinked at a roomful of people. It was the room known as the outpatients' clinic and the people were sitting on the benches around the walls. They blinked back at him as if they had been out in the dark too. His mother and father were there, and also Mark Price. Seeing Mark, Peter went straight to

305

him and handed him the oilskin of money.

"That's for Jerry's ransom," he said proudly. He turned and went to his mother and father, leaving Enid alone beside Mr. Garnett at the door. His mother's face was scrunched up tight from weeping and his father's neck looked thin and jerky. The whole Governing Committee was present: Dr. Sharp, the dentist, and Dr. Dyson, the surgeon, Mr. Kulhausen, Mr. Fincher, Reverend Bax, Reverend Fisher and Jonathan Mercer, the head of the Seventh-Day Adventists. Mrs. Gibney was there too, because she was the interpreter.

Peter's father gripped Peter's arm reassuringly. "It's all right, big fellow. You got back; that's what matters."

Everyone was staring at Enid. Poor Enid. She stood blinking in the light, just like Peter. But she looked awful. She had on what was left of her rust-colored, gold-flecked birthday dress. It was smeared with mud and dripping with water and it gapped in front where half the buttons had been torn away. Her hair hung in snarls and twig-filled mats. Her face was streaked with tears and dirt. And a band of shredded silk stocking clung to one of her scratched, bleeding legs.

"They arrived at Mrs. Gibney's shack together," announced Mr. Garnett, breaking the silence.

"Well," said Mark, "we were discussing how to save you from the Kempeitai or whoever had you, Peter. Now I guess we can get back to Jerry."

"Come on, Enid," said Mrs. Gibney cheerfully. "Let's wash you up and feed you and perhaps later you can help us."

She took Enid by the arm and led her out across the dark porch toward the infirmary kitchen.

Thank you, thought Peter.

"There's twenty-three hundred prewar pesos here, Peter," said Mark, "and a note from Jerry certifying that you earned it. Is that right?"

"I didn't know how much it was," said Peter. "He called it my Christmas bonus, but I think really it was just what he had left over when he got ready to go to Australia."

"May I see that?" asked Peter's father.

"Sure, Doc," said Mark, tossing it across the room to him. "Now, am I right in understanding, Peter, that you want me to use part or all this money of yours toward getting Jerry released from Colonel Fukawa?"

"Yes," said Peter. "Do it the best way you can."

"Okay. I'm to use my discretion. It's a deal between me and Fukawa and the devil. No vote necessary. What's the Larsen girl doing here?"

"Colonel Kori tried to rape her so she killed him with a shotgun."

Peter was interrupted by gasps and curses from the men around the walls, and Mark Price had to shout for order before Peter could go on.

"She hid in the same place where the money was," he said. "She thinks she's been there for three days. It's a small cave we both knew in the woods back of school. I was surprised to find her there. That's why it took me so long to get back."

"Kori *is* dead," said Peter's father. "That's why Fukawa replaced him."

"Where the devil was her father during all this?" asked Dr. Dyson.

"In Manila buying machinery for Mananok," said Peter. "He's due back tomorrow, or today, I mean. He left her the shotgun for protection."

"I'll say!" said Reverend Fisher. "I don't see what we can do but turn her over to the police."

"How did you get in and out of camp?" asked Mark. "Over the fence, under the fence, through the gate or what?"

"Under the fence."

"Did you bribe any guards?"

"No."

"Did any guards see you?"

"No."

"Did you drop anything or leave any traces between here and the cave?"

"I don't think so. There's the gun and some newspapers and tin cans on the cave floor. But if the rain keeps up that will get flooded anyway."

"He's probably left footprints," said Peter's father. "But the rain ought to take care of them too."

"Yes," said Mark, and paused thoughtfully. Peter glanced around quickly at the other members of the committee. They all looked worried and unfriendly. "Okay, then," resumed Mark decisively, "this is our story: the Larsen girl simply climbed over the stockade during the typhoon and was found wandering around in the dark by Doc Dyson. Naturally, Doc, you brought her to the infirmary. As for

Peter, he never left camp. He sat up half the night on his mother's porch talking to his father. Anyone who doesn't agree with this story, please say so."

No one said anything.

"That's fine," said Mark. "Now I better get over to the guardhouse and start talking. I've got an hour before the execution and a couple of hours before Larsen arrives on the morning plane from Manila."

"I think we should hear what line you plan to take," said Reverend Fisher, "so we can vote on it."

"I'm going to bribe Fukawa with money and Shijugi with fear for his job. I don't know what kind of a bargain I can make any better than you do. But I'm damn sure that a neutral girl who's been assaulted by a Kempeitai colonel and then just walks into a well-guarded prison camp is a pretty good talking point. It may talk louder than the money. I may not even mention the money."

"It's practically an international incident!" exclaimed Mr. Fincher in his high voice.

"Damn right," said Mark at the door. "Mrs. Gibney!" he shouted.

"We should have a show of hands giving you discretion, Mark," said Mr. Kulhausen. "After all, if the Japs are embarrassed enough, they can always keep us quiet. This thing could get too big to handle."

"It certainly could," said Reverend Fisher. "I personally think it needs more discussion."

"All right, discuss it, then," said Mark. "If you decide to fire me or impeach me or whatever it is you do, you can find me at the guardhouse."

Mrs. Gibney appeared in the doorway. Mark took her elbow and they went out. Peter ducked past Mr. Garnett and caught up with them on the edge of the infirmary porch.

"What did you do with Enid?" he asked.

"She's eating some soft rice in the kitchen," said Mrs. Gibney.

"Don't worry about her, Peter," said Mark. "Go to your bunk. Perhaps you can get there before the old men wake up. The less people who know you were out all night the better."

"All right," said Peter.

Mark and Mrs. Gibney hurried off in their raincoats down the infirmary steps and out along the embankment. Peter felt a hand on his shoulder. It was his father.

"It's good to feel you and make sure you're really here, big fellow," he said. "Your mother and I had quite a night of it."

"I'm sorry I spoke to you the way I did earlier," said Peter.

"It's all right," said his father. "It was partly my own fault for putting Jerry in touch with you in the first place. I had no idea he would use you to do messenger work. He had no right."

"Mark says I should sneak back to my bunk," said Peter, trying to avoid discussion.

"Yes, run along, darling," said his mother in a drained, expressionless voice. "I'll have some breakfast ready for you on the porch. Your raincoat is on the porch, too," she called after him. "Put on something dry and clean even if it's only a G-string."

He looked back in the gray light and saw that his parents were standing on the porch holding hands and watching him go. If they hadn't been there, he would have liked to go to the kitchen and have a word with Enid. Now he dismissed the idea and returned straight to his bunk as Mark had told him to do.

The barracks was still asleep, but at six the lights would be switched on from the guardhouse and a new day would begin. He looked at his mother's watch, which was still ticking in spite of the soaking it had had. It said ten to six. He stripped hurriedly and crawled into his bed. The sheets, which Mrs. Kahn had made for him out of flour sacking, seemed almost as chill and damp as his clothes. Afraid of dozing off, he propped his head up against the wall and tried to imagine how Mark would be dealing with Shijugi and Fukawa. But he couldn't get far at forming a mental picture. The only clear detail in it was the expressionless glare on Mark's face, the same glare of impartial ill-temper that he wore in a poker game. The lights went on and Peter let his head fall sideways onto the sheet, so he would look as if he were asleep.

"Another day, another dollar," yawned Illingdon as usual "A million days, a millionaire."

For once the urge to throw a jar of Illingdon's own tomato pickles at Illingdon's head and silence once and for all that jeering greeting to each fresh day hardly stirred Peter at all. The main thing was that Illingdon was awake and would prod Peter in a moment so that he could get up before he fell asleep.

Illingdon picked up the piece of liana he used for a cane and dug it into Peter's ribs.

"Rise and shine, boy. Never get rich that way."

Peter opened his eyes, and there—almost as if it was as usual—was Illingdon, trying to look spry and lean and industrious in his cane and pajamas. Following the usual formula for the days when Jimmy Page served at Communion and Peter was still in bed to greet Illingdon, Peter muttered, "Go catch a train or something, Pop."

"That's what I think I will do: be on the platform when the six-fifty-seven comes roarin' in. Only way to make a dollar in Jew York is to get in there before *they* make it all."

"I thought the Scotch were the twelfth tribe," said Peter, slipping out of bed. He stood naked, wondering what to wear. His new canvas shorts, made for him by Mrs. Kahn, looked pretty bad now that he could see them. Even when they dried, the mud would be too soaked in to brush off. He would have to wash them and wear his old patched khaki ones for a day or two.

"Scots, lad. The word's Scots. Scotch is something you drink."

"My Jap grandmother married a Scotchman," said Peter.

"You poor stooly kid," said Illingdon. "You just say your grandmother was a Jap as sort of an excuse for yourself."

Peter hurried out of the cubicle, buttoning his shirt, while Mr. Illingdon denounced him to the other old men as "a poor disconnected mind that had broken under Jap torture." In a way, perhaps Mr. Illingdon wasn't so bad. Peter enjoyed the fight with him each morning—the *flyting*, as Illingdon called it. It was something outrageous which had nothing to do with anything else. Of course, this morning nothing seemed to have much to do with anything else. As Peter passed down the front of the barracks every scene and face he saw in his sleepless, excited state seemed a separate crevice into which his mind darted like a puppy on a walk. Nothing held his attention for long and nothing seemed to have any special importance over other things.

On the porch of his mother's shack he found his parents waiting to eat the morning rice and sirup with him. The rain had subsided to a tired drizzle. His father, he noticed, was concerned about something and was telling him what it was.

"I'm afraid you may be in hot water for leaving camp the way you did, Peter," he said. "People seem to feel that if the Japanese had found you gone, they'd have considered it an escape and taken reprisals."

"A kid like me?" said Peter with surprise.

"You're not such a kid any more," said his father somewhat irritably. "Anyway, the camp committee doesn't seem to think so. When that meeting broke up at the infirmary, I was waiting at the door. As the men came out, I could see they were trying to avoid me. So finally I collared Dr. Dyson—you know I used to work with him at Abanaoa General —and he told me that you're going to be tried this afternoon for endangering the public welfare."

"Gosh!" said Peter politely. He didn't understand or believe what his father was saying but he didn't want to show it. "What about Jerry and Enid?" he asked. "Are they all settled?"

"No, Price is still out there talking. After the highhanded way he dealt with the other men on the committee, they're just waiting for him to make a slip. In fact, I'd say you and Mark Price have both done a pretty good job of antagonizing certain people around here."

"They must be crazy, Tim," said Peter's mother. "He's just a child, after all."

"No, you take a fresh look at him, Renny: he's big for a child. And I don't want him acting like one either. If they decide to discipline you, Peter, I want to see you stand up and take your medicine like a man. Whatever they do and however unjust it may seem, coming right now, it won't amount to much. Besides, from what I hear you probably deserve to be lined up a bit. Isn't that right?"

Peter's father was looking at him with good humor and Peter smiled back wanly.

"I guess so. But not for leaving camp and trying to save Jerry's life."

"Well, I don't think that's entirely what they're after you for. There seems to be a feeling roundabout that you're big for your britches, that's all."

"Oh," said Peter.

"They have their gall," said his mother. "He does the same work as the men and he's a lot more polite. By the way, whatever was it you said to Mrs. Newcombe last night, Peter?"

"Mrs. Newcombe? Well—" Peter laughed unsurely—"I called Mr. Newcombe a liar for saying Jerry was a spy."

"You shouldn't do that sort of thing, *mon fils*. You only give him an excuse for thinking he was right."

"Well, I don't know," said his father. "Doing anything always makes someone mad. What time is that roll call you have?"

## CHAPTER 22

Peter stood restlessly between his father and Mr. Barsini. Usually roll call was over before seven o'clock, but today the order to dismiss hadn't been given. A detachment of guards came out at eight and dug a grave just inside the stockade. The officer in charge held the detachment there, standing and waiting like the internees.

Why was Mark taking so long? It was a good sign that they hadn't brought Jerry out to stand by the grave. It was a good sign that they hadn't dragged Enid across the parade ground from the infirmary, where she had been left with the patients who couldn't get up. But what was Mark doing? The longer the wait continued, the more Peter found himself thinking morbidly of the five guerrillas he had seen executed in the market place. The last three had writhed wretchedly as the machine-gun bullets fanned across their chests. The man before had gurgled as the bayonet pierced his belly. Only the first man had shown no sign of fear. That was because his head was bowed under the sword and his face couldn't be seen. Perhaps the old-fashioned way with the sword—even though it was a Jap way and the Jap might be a butcher with a blunt sword—was still the best way, and more dignified and ceremonious than bayonets and machine guns. But no, no. Peter shook his head vehemently. Jerry was not to be killed.

The separated ranks of men and women had been standing on the wet grass for more than two hours now. Even Mr. Kono, who called the roll, appeared to be fidgety and puzzled. The men around Peter seemed triumphant that something had gone wrong with the Jap execution plans. But

Mark was still out there talking.

A green Packard was parked on the road in front of the guardhouse. Someone whispered, "Isn't that Mr. Kulhausen's old car? Which of the Japs does it belong to now?" Until recently, Peter knew, it had belonged to Colonel Kori. Now perhaps it was Fukawa's.

Occasionally a few raindrops fell. Occasionally a fragment of cloud bowled in over the embankment from the cloud-filled valley beyond and transformed itself into a brief white mist.

At nine-thirty another car came grinding up the driveway and a Japanese got out of it with two white men. One was a stranger, but the other looked like Enid's father, Mr. Larsen.

The internees shuffled their feet, but it was remarkably quiet. It was not the atmosphere of a funeral: there was more hope for the dead and fear for the living in the air than there would have been at a funeral.

At two minutes after ten, Mark Price came out of the guardhouse. He was followed by Shijugi and another Japanese. Behind them walked the two white men who had just arrived by car. Mark marched, and almost strutted, through the gate, bringing his delegation behind him. Not that he really strutted. That might be what some people thought. But really he had short, bandy legs, a barrel chest and a lot of energy.

He rolled to a stop in front of the halfway between the rectangles of men and women. "I've got a lot of good news for you," he shouted, "and some bad news, too. Rice rations have been reincreased to fourteen ounces a day. The school will be reopened tomorrow. All rumors about stopping co-habitation and prohibiting card playing or visiting at the school shed in the evening are false. For this we have to thank the generosity of Captain Shijugi."

Mark turned and bowed to Shijugi. Shijugi bowed back and turned and bowed curtly to the assembled internees. The internees bowed in their turn to the commandant.

"For this we have also to thank Colonel Fukawa, senior officer in charge of police and prison camps on Panoc, who has been kind enough to pay us a visit today."

Colonel Fukawa went through the same mummery of bowing that Shijugi had performed, but he did it in a per-functory way, smiling blandly.

"The Imperial Japanese Military Government also permits

313

me to hand on to you," said Mark, "this piece of news." He pulled a sheet of paper from his pocket and, shrugging his shoulders, crumpled it up and put it back. "Yesterday the Italians surrendered to General Eisenhower."

"That's the beginning of the end," whispered Mr. Barsini excitedly. "No wonder they're so generous."

"It sure sounds that way," muttered Peter without much interest. Why wasn't Jerry with them, ready to be released?

"The most important news, at least to me, is bad," said Mark quickly. "Last night our fellow internee Jerry Costeau, a patriot and a damn fine news photographer, made sure of his own tongue by taking poison."

Mark turned away toward the gate and Peter saw that the guards had brought in a stretcher and were carrying it toward the grave that they had dug. Peter dashed out from the ranks and sprinted toward the grave. Mr. Kono shouted at him. One of the guards came running toward him. Peter stopped and stood waiting for the guard. Then Mark Price came up from behind and grabbed him by the shoulder and led him in front of Captain Shijugi.

"Request permission for this boy to break formation and go to the guardhouse with me."

Mrs. Gibney stepped forward and Mark whispered in her ear. Shijugi started making angry noises in his throat, but Mrs. Gibney went to him quickly and took him apart with Colonel Fukawa to tell them something in Japanese.

"Ah, so," said Fukawa, turning and nodding at Peter. "Boy and girrul of opposite sides. Rike Romeo and Juriet."

Mark gripped Peter firmly by the arm and marched him toward the guardhouse. As he looked back he saw the sheet on the stretcher tumble into the grave. The soldiers began piling dirt on Jerry. Peter shuddered and struggled weakly to get loose. Out of the ranks of the internees grew the sound of humming. Donny Garver must have started it. They weren't singing words but they didn't need to because the words sang themselves: *What a beautiful thought I am thinking concerning the great speckled bird.* Above the humming Peter could hear Mr. Kono shouting angrily to dismiss the roll call. Peter shook Mark's hand from his arm and walked on, dry-eyed, across the unscythed grass outside the stockade.

"If it hadn't been for the bridge tournament, I could have gotten Jerry to escape last night," he said bitterly. "I wanted him to go at the eight o'clock change of guard. That would have been just in time."

"I don't think he'd have gone," said Mark. "He asked me once about escaping. I told him to go ahead, but he knew there would have been reprisals. They'd have probably tortured everyone they suspected of helping him, and that would have meant the whole Staff Room, Peter."

"I never thought of that," said Peter. "All the same, why did he have to kill himself? Why couldn't he wait and see if it was necessary?"

"Perhaps he knew there was nothing we could do to help. I didn't realize what a lot they had on him. Fukawa had a bill of particulars longer than your arm. It would have been as tricky for him to tear it up as for a police chief to destroy the record of a criminal in the States."

"He should still have waited," insisted Peter.

"What for? When a man feels he's lost his style and his luck, he has to be allowed to cut his losses and toss in his hand. You know as well as I do that that's how Jerry felt. He just didn't want to live any more."

"That's crazy. He still enjoyed a lot of things."

"Maybe so, but don't forget five minutes ago you almost died for some pretty crazy reasons yourself."

Peter said nothing. It seemed as if Mark had arranged everything but what was most important and least arrangeable. Peter tried to remember the last thing Jerry had said to him. "Don't lead from an ace unless you have to, and if you have to, then lead the ace."

Jerry had said a lot of helpful things. Perhaps the last one was about cohabiting. "There's a lot to be said for having these dopey women around, Peter. The men act better and not so many of them get dirty and sick. I wish I'd been a cohabitor. In here, you can really get to love social institutions. Like the family, I mean, and the state and the morning shower and all the rest of that crap."

At the guardhouse Mark made Peter wash his face in the dirty bathroom. When Peter returned to the guardhouse office, Mark was talking to the other white man who had come from the airport with Mr. Larsen. He was the Swedish consul. He had come with Mr. Larsen, not knowing anything about the murder of Colonel Kori, to take Enid back to Manila with him and fit her in on a ship to Sweden if Mr. Larsen could ever send him the passage money. At least in Manila

Enid would have a chance to go to a good convent school and catch up on her education.

Peter shook hands with the consul and thanked him, because he would be taking care of Enid. And even as he realized that Enid was going away, she came into the guardhouse herself, along with her father. She was dressed in a cotton frock that someone had found for her and she looked clean and normal, except, like Peter, a little sleepy perhaps. There weren't any Japs in the room and Mr. Larsen thanked Peter and shook his hand for helping Enid come into camp. Feeling how wet and trembling his hand was, Peter felt sorry for him. He wasn't much of a father for Enid to have, but he was fond of her and he did try to take care of her in his way. The consul thanked Peter on behalf of Sweden, and Mark handed Peter the oilskin of money saying that he hadn't needed to use any of it. Then Enid shook Peter's hand too and said that she wished he was going to Manila with her.

"Could I talk to you a moment before you leave?" he asked.

"Yes, gentlemen," said Mark. "Let's go out on the porch and leave the kids alone."

"I guess Mark fixed up everything for you," said Peter when they had gone.

"Well, Papa says the Japanese were embarrassed by having me escape into camp and having that man they buried commit suicide. When Papa brought the Swedish consul with him, that settled matters, you bet."

"The man they buried was Jerry. He was my best friend. I guess Donny Garver must have made the poison for him."

"I'm sorry," said Enid. "I didn't know about it."

"I'll write to you if I ever get to Sweden or anywhere," she added after a silence.

"We don't get any mail. Besides, it doesn't matter. One of the things Jerry used to say was 'Children run high fevers but they get over them quickly.'"

"That's a high-flown way of saying you don't love me any more."

"Yes," he admitted. "But I feel fond of you. You look nice in that clean dress. How much money must your father send the consul to buy you a passage to Sweden?"

"Oh, he won't really be able to do it," said Enid.

"How much?" persisted Peter.

"Pretty near two thousand krona, I think."

"How much is a krona?"

"It used to be fifty centavos before the war."

"Here," said Peter. He unwrapped the oilskin and counted off ten of the musty one-hundred-peso notes.

She put out her hand excitedly and then pulled it back. "I can't take it," she said. "You're my best friend and it's kind of as if you were paying me for something you don't need to."

"That's not why I'm doing it. It's because I want you to go to Sweden, and because I do love you in a way."

She hesitated a little longer and then took the money and kissed him, trying hard to be exciting.

"Enid!" exclaimed her father. He had just opened the door to come and take her to the car. She made no effort to stop the kiss, but Peter pushed her away.

"Good-by," he said.

"Good-by, Peter."

She went out through the door and Peter grabbed her father's arm.

"How much does a passage to Sweden cost in prewar pesos?" he demanded.

"Nine hundred and twenty," said Mr. Larsen irritably.

"Have you got that much?" asked Peter.

"Of course not. Otherwise my daughter would be home now."

"What about you? What are you going to do when the war's over?"

"I'll get along, thank you," said Mr. Larsen.

"But none of the Americans will ever buy machinery from you again. How will you earn a living?"

"This is very impertinent," said Mr. Larsen. "Thank you for helping Enid." He tried to go out the door, but Peter still held on to his arm.

"I'm sorry, sir. What I mean is, don't you want to go back to Sweden with Enid?"

"Nothing I'd like better."

"How much money do you need to do it?"

"You can add, *Yugend*. Nine twenty times two is eighteen forty."

"Don't you have any money already?" asked Peter, shocked.

"You little son-of-a-gun. Of course I have money. I have about four hundred and I'll get the rest. She *will* go back to

Sweden. You can be sure of that."

"If I give you five hundred as well as the thousand I've already given to Enid, will you promise to go back at once?" asked Peter, peeling off the bills.

"You will, won't you, Papa?" This time it was Enid at the door. She had been listening outside and now she came in showing off the money Peter had given her. She ran to Peter, took the second wad of bills from his hand and, holding on to him, leaned her head against his shoulder.

"Thank you, Peter," she said. "That was the nicest of all the nice things you ever did." She looked up and lightly kissed him. "I know you don't like Papa much, but he is my family and we will send the money back to you. We really will."

"What is the address?" asked Mr. Larsen mechanically.

"Oh, I dunno," said Peter. "Care of the Episcopalian Church, New York, will always reach me, I guess."

"Come on, Papa, we're going home," said Enid in a soothing, singsong way. She let go of Peter and pulled her father outside after her. As she jumped into the car where the Swedish consul was waiting, Peter could see that she was taut with happy excitement and eager to be going.

"Good-by," called Mr. Larsen stiffly as the engine started.

"Thank you, you son-of-a-gun," shouted Enid.

The wheels spun in the mud and with a spatter the car shot off down the hill toward the afternoon plane.

"I heard you throwing your money around," said Mark Price as he took Peter by the shoulder and escorted him back toward the stockade. "One of these days you're going to wake up from being a dreamy kid and find that you're just about the biggest grown-up sucker ever born."

"I suppose so," said Peter, "but it suddenly seemed to me as if trying to scorn grownups who act dead like Mr. Larsen is just the same as trying to scorn Jews or Frenchmen, or kids or old men. . . . Or even Japs. I don't think if you're alive yourself you can scorn anyone, can you?"

"A lot of people manage."

Peter said nothing.

"Besides, you can die of being too alive, you know," said Mark.

"I don't think that's true," said Peter. "You have a switch that turns you off before you get that alive. And I think you

318

ought to let it. You shouldn't switch it off on purpose ahead of time."

They came to the gate. Inside, Mr. Garnett fell in beside them.

"I'm supposed to take the boy into custody, Mark," said Mr. Garnett. "They want to try him for endangering the public safety."

"What!" said Mark. "Who wants to try him?"

"The committee."

"Why, those goddamn frightened old women!" Mark cut off across the parade ground toward the infirmary. "Don't worry, kid," he shouted back. "It's a load of crap."

"I wish they'd wait until tomorrow," said Peter. "I'd be a lot more wide awake then." Mr. Garnett only grunted in reply. He had a hard hold on Peter's arm and was leading him toward the cobbler's shed which served as a jail. At the wood shack, Father Gibney was splitting logs into kindling. Peter had to serve for him tomorrow at early service. They passed the school shed. School would be back in session tomorrow too, he thought. He glanced down the front of the barracks. His mother and father were on the porch. They were back together again. In their hopeful, uncritical way he had seen that they were proud of him. Peter sighed and felt the long tension of sleepless excitement loosening its hold on his mind.

Mr. Garnett shoved him into the little shed of nipa and corrugated iron, and locked the door. Peter wondered what good the lock was when he could always break through the walls if he wanted to. He cleared a place for himself to sit on the cobbler's table and tried to think. Jerry was dead. All the old crowd of guerrillas were dead except for General Sam, and he had a new bunch now. Even Enid was gone. Poor pretty Enid. He and she had become so fond of each other at the last minute. In a way it was sad to think of her laughing and recovering her teasing good looks and gestures back there in the Swedish playgrounds.

With a crash on the tin roof, the rain began to pour again. His footsteps and Enid's were being obliterated so that the guards would never find them. Why was it that the committee wanted to punish him? For being big for his britches? Funny.

That's a funny game, that governing, he thought. It's probably lucky people were created children and can enjoy so

319

many pastimes. Otherwise there'd be nothing worth doing except love and war. There must be a real game, though—beyond bridge and kissing, and war and governing and geometry. If there weren't, Jerry would have told on the guerrillas instead of giving up the little games—all the games he enjoyed himself and taught me to play. It's hard to imagine a real game, without rules or boundaries or limits to pleasure and excitement. Of course, you have to be a grownup to play —and that's impossible. But you can keep it in mind. I guess that's the best you *can* do.

"Peter?"

The rain had slackened again and he thought he'd heard someone whispering through the matting wall.

"Peter?"

It was Maggie.

"Hi," he said.

"Hold tight, baby. Here comes a skyhook."

The matting thudded twice and then a rock arced in through a slit between the top of the wall and the bottom of the tin roof. The rock was wrapped in string.

"Pull her in," whispered Maggie.

Peter pulled on the string until a package of newspaper fell over the top of the wall onto the cobbler's table. Peter unwrapped half a baked sweet potato.

"That's your share of third prize," she said. "The Newcombes fell all the way to fifth place."

"That'll learn 'em," said Peter, eating. "It's a damn good *camote*."

"I know. I had the other half."

"I'm sorry we couldn't bake it together and go out and eat it in the woodshed and kick down the fence and swim away into the China Sea," he muttered. "That's the way I feel."

"Let's do it tonight. I can arrange a bridge date with Norm and Candy and I'll borrow a *camote* from Mark's pot at the poker game."

"I may still be in the jug," said Peter.

"Are you kidding? I saw Mark on the way to the infirmary and from the look on his face I'll bet the committee will wish they'd put themselves in jail. Heck, you didn't do anything wrong. Why, there are some people, like me, who think you're a hero."

"What for?"

320

"Because you went out of camp and risked your neck to try to save Jerry."

"Who says I did?"

"Who usually says? It's the rumor that was going around this morning on the parade ground."

"I'd like to know who started it."

"I suppose one of the committee men told his wife at breakfast and she got bored during the long wait and passed it on. It's true, isn't it?"

"What does it say I did exactly?"

"Went over the fence into the woods and dug up a hundred thousand pesos some place."

"A hundred thousand! Two thousand three hundred. And if the Japs find out I was gone, I'll be cooked."

"Oh, not even Mr. Newcombe would be that much of a deadbeat—to tell the Japs, I mean. Besides, I'll bet they wouldn't listen if someone did tell them. They've lost enough face already having Enid break into camp without having you break out and in again the same night. Did you know, by the way, that Shijugi is out in the rain with a bunch of the guards making an inspection of the fence?"

"No," said Peter, smiling.

"Sure, half the camp's laughing at him."

"What about the other half?"

"Oh, well, you know how the worriers are. Can I set up that bridge game now? It's starting to rain again."

"Okay. I guess you're not sore about Enid, huh?"

"Why should I be sore? She's gone to Manila. Mark told me you even paid her off and sent her to Sweden."

"I guess I did. I *was* fond of her, though."

"I know you were. Look, I'm getting spattered. Let's talk about it after bridge tonight."

"Okay."

The bulge where Maggie had been huddling in against the outside of the matting wall disappeared and Peter heard her footsteps as she dashed out from under the eaves toward the barracks. Peter cleared a couch for himself on the cobbler's table and lay down. He suddenly felt that he was really alone without even his own presence as a reason for keeping up appearances. What he had done and hadn't done were both of them inadequate and unending to think about. Now that Jerry would never wake up again, Peter wondered if *he* would ever go to sleep again—and break the bleak nightmare of seeing things go past him, on and on in unimportant gray. He tried to weep, first for Jerry and then for himself. But he couldn't find tears for either one. He lay twitching meaninglessly on the cobbler's table, without wanting to or even resenting it.

## CHAPTER 23

When Peter awoke, the sun was shining in through the west wall of the shed and Mr. Garnett was standing over him shaking him.

"On your feet, kid. The hour of reckoning's come."

Peter looked up at him with a foolish smile. He was a strange man, Mr. Garnett: awfully hard-working and hot-tempered for anyone so small, and awfully gloomy and bossy for anyone so fiery. Probably the trouble was that he always felt he was in the right but usually got the worst of things.

"Come on, on your feet," repeated Mr. Garnett.

Peter jumped up, still half asleep, and stumbled through the door of the cobbler's shed. Outside, the sun struck him full in the face and brought him reeling to a stop. When he lowered his forearm and squinted at the world, he wondered if he had ever seen the sky so hard or the lowering sun so naked and drab. It seemed as if the typhoon had passed without leaving a trace of moisture in the air to soften things.

"Don't I get any dinner?" he asked self-pityingly.

"Now what do you think? Your old lady came around with it about an hour ago, and I told her you were asleep, so she said not to wake you, she'd keep it for you until later."

"Oh," said Peter. "I guess Mark didn't get the charges against me dismissed, huh?"

"You're damn right he didn't," said Mr. Garnett. "If Shijugi hadn't found a hole in the fence and called him away to the guardhouse to explain it, I think the committee would have put him on trial too—for contempt."

Peter had forgotten about the hole. But it didn't matter. Mark wouldn't admit to knowing anything about it and the hole itself was so black with fungus and damp that no one could tell when it had been made. It might have been axed when the fence was built.

"I'm sure glad I'm not in your shoes," continued Mr. Garnett. "They're going to throw the book at you, boy. And a damn good thing, too! Maybe you kids will start giving us a little peace and quiet around here now."

Peter stared at Mr. Garnett and tried to think of some reason why he should be so hostile. Mr. Garnett stared back balefully, his face twitching.

He's crazy, thought Peter. There's no point arguing with him. He turned away from Mr. Garnett in hardhearted silence and led the way toward the infirmary. As he walked along the embankment, he gazed at the shining view over the China Sea and shuffled his feet.

Italy down and two to go, he thought. To heck with Mr. Garnett and the committee. To heck with the Japs—if they don't like the hole in the fence, they can block it up. To heck with Mark, too, for not being here to defend me. No matter what any of them do, the war will still come to an end and someday I'll be free.

Defiantly Peter looked up from the shining ocean and saw with a shock that the porch of the infirmary ahead of him was crowded with people. He flushed, fixed his eyes on the porch steps and hurried forward. The people had gathered to eavesdrop on his trial through the matting walls. He ran past them up the steps and into the building. Inside, there were more spectators. They filled the benches on both sides of the door and their eyes stung his back as he passed through them. The members of the committee sat at the long table opposite the door. Peter came to rigid attention before them. He had the impression that their faces were all either unsure or unfriendly, but he made no effort to verify it. The weary, sleepless feeling of a world gone gray and unimportant came back to him with new disgust. He found a dark spot in the matting over the heads of his judges and fixed his eyes on it.

"Thank you, Mr. Garnett," said Reverend Fisher, who seemed to be presiding in Mark's absence. "Now if you'll please go outside and clear away all those extra spectators on the porch we can get started. The ones inside here are enough to witness that it's a fair trial and the ones outside are only an added gossip hazard. In fact, if you could stay out there and keep off the eavesdroppers all the way through, it would be most helpful."

"Will do," said Mr. Garnett. He hovered for a moment at Peter's elbow—almost as if he'd stopped to salute. Then he was gone and only his voice was left, booming in through the partitions in a fierce, officious monotone. "No other witnesses needed. Go on about your business, please. Clear the porch of the court and keep moving, please. Absolutely no other witnesses needed."

A chicken ran cackling among the pilings underneath the floor and Peter felt himself relax a little. The feeling vanished at once. Reverend Fisher pounded on the table with a split of firewood which served him as a gavel.

"Court is now in session," he announced sharply. "As court recorder, will you please read the oath for the spectators, Mr. Fincher."

They were taking the trial altogether seriously and Peter realized that if it didn't go that way they would only be harder on him. The oath which Mr. Fincher read was long and complicated and formal. It pledged the spectators to keep quiet about what they heard at the trial unless they were specifically authorized by the committee to tell about it later on.

"Good," said Reverend Fisher when the oath had been read. "Now, Mr. Fincher, please pass among the people here present and have them put their hands on this Bible and repeat the words *I do so solemnly swear*."

As Mr. Fincher carried out his instructions, Peter stared at the spot on the wall and tried to recognize the voices of the oath takers behind him. But the voices muttered and Peter began to think—half grateful and half hurt—that there was no one in the room he knew well.

Then Mr. Fincher came to an unmistakable exception: "So all right, I swear. But swearing or not swearing, it better be the right verdict or I'm telling you respectfully that everyone in camp will hear about it."

It was Mrs. Kahn. Peter smiled with pleasure to hear her. She probably wouldn't do him any good, but it was nice to know that someone was on his side. After all, even his father had called Mark Price highhanded and said that Peter probably deserved to be lined up a bit.

"Mrs. Kahn," rasped Reverend Fisher, banging his gavel of firewood to stop the tittering among the other spectators,

"I'm afraid that's an inadequate response. I must ask you either to take the oath properly or leave the courtroom."

"Oh, all right," said Mrs. Kahn. "I do so solemnly swear."

As Mr. Fincher finished administering the oath, Peter tried to prepare himself for the worst—and to feel scornful about it.

So what if they keep me in the cobbler's shed for a few days? That's nothing compared to being put in prison by the Japs. And I guess I do deserve something, if only for what I did to Enid. Maggie says I paid her off. It was conscience money. I thought I was being generous but I guess I was really only looking after my new freedom, and trying to feel better about the way I treated her last night, when she said she loved me and I kept thinking of her being dirty. Maybe I was even dishonest when I crawled under the fence last night. It did seem exciting. And I never did think how I might be endangering everyone else. Still, that doesn't make it wrong. Jerry being dead means I should have done it no matter what motives I had. In fact, I should have done more—if I could have thought of more to do. Well, what the heck. The sheep can walk past the cobbler's shed and say I stole a chicken or something. It doesn't matter. At least they won't think Jerry had anything to do with it and blame him.

"Peter Baldwin," intoned Reverend Fisher, "you are accused of willfully endangering the public welfare. The facts are not in dispute: you escaped from camp last night without the approval of the committee or of any committee member or of any adult of any kind. If the guards had caught you they'd not only have beaten you up, they'd have questioned and probably beaten all your closest friends and perhaps have cut rations for the entire camp. Very well, then, the question at issue is not one of fact but of intent: whether you knew you were doing something wrong at the time, whether you know it now and whether you're sorry for it. As soon as you satisfy us on those three points, we can decide whether to punish you with a term in the cobbler's shed or let you off with a lecture in civics. Which is it to be : guilty or not guilty? How do you plead?"

"I guess I'm guilty," muttered Peter sullenly. "I didn't think I was doing anything wrong and I still don't."

"Now wait a minute, Peter," said Dr. Dyson, who was sitting beside Reverend Fisher. "Have you any idea why we have an elected government here in camp?"

"To deal with the Japs, I guess, and make rules," said Peter.

"Oh, much more than that," said Dr. Dyson. "We're elected to *represent* the camp. That means if someone like you does something against the Japs we have to protect him. We punish him ourselves and if the Japs aren't satisfied, they can punish all of us by cutting rations or advancing lights-out, but in theory, according to our agreement with them, they're not supposed to take further action against the individual. Does that help you understand why what you did was wrong?"

"You didn't keep the Japs from taking Jerry to the guardhouse and making him think he had to die," said Peter bitterly. "I bet you couldn't have protected me either. Anyway, I didn't expect you could. I expected the Japs to treat me the same if they caught me as they did before, when we were living on the Outside."

"Defendant is appealing to a record of which the court has no knowledge," said Reverend Fisher. "What happened to you before, Peter, we don't know. To be brutally frank, the people who see the most of you rate your previous performance all the way from that of a hero to that of an informer."

Peter clenched his fists. He hadn't thought that even Mr. Illingdon really believed he was an informer.

"I wasn't," he muttered. "I didn't tell on anyone. I swear I didn't."

Jonathan Mercer, the head of the Seventh-Day Adventists, laughed and stroked the underside of his long curly black concentration-camp beard.

"You're attacking the boy unnecessarily, Fisher," he said. "Let's grant that he *was* a hero outside of camp. It's irrelevant. What we have to consider is: suppose the Japanese come around this evening and say they've found tracks leading both ways, to and from that hole in the fence. Then what? Are we going to turn the boy over to them or not?"

"The tracks ought to have washed away," said Peter, trying not to feel frightened. "And the parts of the hole that I made by whittling are already so black no one can tell *when* they were cut."

"Holy mackerel!" said Dr. Sharp. "You mean you enlarged that hole yourself?"

Peter heard grunts and gasps of surprise behind him. He had confessed to something new. As he realized it, his nervousness increased. He sensed the whole atmosphere of the room changing and the minds of the judges growing stern against him.

"Would you mind telling us how you did it?" demanded Jonathan Mercer.

"By whittling early in the mornings," he said.

"Are you sure you're not exaggerating, Peter?" asked Reverend Bax, trying to help him. "How does one cross Bufferland to whittle in the mornings?"

"You go out at four when the guard changes and come back at five when the tea guard makes his rounds."

"Well, for heaven's sake," said Mr. Fincher indignantly. "How many mornings did you do this?"

"Twenty or thirty."

"Whatever for?" asked Reverend Bax unhappily.

"So Jerry could escape."

"My God!" said Dr. Sharp, settling his head into his hands. "Did Jerry know you were doing it?"

"I told him when I was about half done. He threatened to tell the committee."

"Then you knew we would disapprove," said Reverend Fisher.

"I guess I did."

"But you went ahead anyway?" asked Dr. Sharp.

"Yes," said Peter.

"I guess Fisher's right," said Dr. Dyson. "It *is* time you were taught a lesson, Peter. You've been taking the law into your own hands long enough."

"Aren't you sorry, Peter?" asked Reverend Bax.

"Not when I really think about it," said Peter quietly.

There was a silence and Reverend Fisher stood up, making the table creak ominously. "I move we retire to pass sentence," he said.

"Now hold on, Fisher!"

Peter started and turned unbelieving toward the voice which had spoken.

"I've heard just about enough," said the voice tautly. It was Peter's father, his face stiff and white with anger—Peter's father, and he was on Peter's side.

"I'm new here, so I've tried to keep quiet," his father said, "but goldarn it, this thing has gone too far. What the merry heck do you people think you're doing? If you're conducting a trial, where's the defense lawyer, where are the rules of evidence, where are the restraints on leading questions and hearsay and opinion? On the other hand, if you're just having a hearing to determine what's fair, why hasn't anyone asked Peter to tell his story from start to finish? I like to believe I taught this boy of mine to think clearly and stand on his own two feet, but you haven't given him a chance. Well, from now on you can deal with me. You can hold me responsible, too, because I'm proud of Peter and proud of what he's done."

Some of the spectators in the back of the room began to clap and stamp their feet. Peter closed his eyes hard, overcome with pleasure and embarrassment. He had never heard his father speak so warmly of him before. It was a long time since he'd counted on hearing his father at all. Reverend Fisher was pounding his makeshift gavel and the room fell silent.

"Dr. Baldwin," said Reverend Fisher loudly, "you're not on trial here and we can't allow you to pretend you are. If you have something to say in your son's defense, say it."

"I have plenty to say," said the doctor. "To begin with, I tried just as hard as any of *you* would have done to stop Peter from leaving camp last night. But I was wrong. Peter knew what he was doing and he did right. It'll be a strange day when a sound conscience—even a young one—isn't more reliable in a tight spot than a debating society like this one."

Reverend Fisher pounded his gavel again. "That's out of order, Doctor," he said angrily. "If you go on simply abusing the competence and integrity of this court, I'll find you in contempt and have you jailed with your son."

"Oh, come down off your high horse, Fisher," snapped his father. "I've already expressed my contempt for this court and I think I've already indicated that if my son goes to jail I'm going along to keep him company. How the deuce do you expect me to feel about this court anyway? I've been in Jap jails for the last year and for almost a year before that I was out in the hills doctoring for the guerrillas. All those months—though I didn't realize it at the time—the medicines I was using were being smuggled out of town and given to the natives who brought them to me by my own thirteen- and fourteen-year-old son. Apparently he did more than that, too. He took photographs for Costeau to document the guerrilla effort, he picked up useful information about Jap troop movements and in the end he withstood a Jap interrogation and beating without telling what he knew. If he hadn't I wouldn't be alive today. That's why I can't stand by and watch you persecuting him with legal trivialities he doesn't understand. If he needs any other defense I can only repeat what I said before: I wouldn't have advised him to do all the things he has done, but he's done them alone, and he's done them well and he's done them as he thought right."

"Does his cleverness and his rectitude extend to that embarrassing Swedish girl he brought home with him last night?" asked Reverend Fisher sarcastically.

Peter blushed. He felt ashamed not only for himself but also for his father, put in the position of trying to defend him where Enid was concerned. Yet for some reason his father didn't even grow angry again.

"Peter's girl friends are strictly between him and me and the hairbrush," he said.

The spectators laughed and Peter blushed more deeply than ever.

"Even when they may be Nazis?" asked Reverend Fisher venomously—and Peter saw now that the venom was because he was losing the argument.

"I've treated too many Japanese wounded to take that question seriously," said his father. "I've also become more lenient than I once was about what you people here call commixing," he added earnestly. "The various romantic ways I was taught to love my wife, my God and my country haven't been easy to reconcile in these years of the war. I can see that a boy, who gives his loyalties wholeheartedly and literally like Peter, must have found them even more difficult. Love is a hard thing to fit into a war and a hard thing to leave out. I understand you've had your share of trouble with it right here in camp. But now that you've organized a society and got it to work, please don't be blinded by your local rules. Mind you, under the same circumstances I'd be doing exactly what you are: preserving the safety of family and community. But I've been forced by other circumstances and my oath as a doctor to act differently. And before you cast stones at Peter I ask you to remember that no court, including this one, can try a man or a boy without trying itself and the society it represents at the same time."

"I didn't realize the boy's father was here," said Jonathan Mercer, standing up. "A man's home is his castle. We have no jurisdiction."

"I agree," said Mr. Kulhausen.

"He jeopardizes the entire camp," began Reverend Fisher.

"So does the war and the beliefs we're fighting for," said Reverend Bax.

"We can't let him go scot free!" exclaimed Mr. Fincher. "It's in his interest as well as ours that we have something to point to which might save Shijugi's face if he ever finds out what Peter's done."

"Let's give him a week's suspended sentence," said Dr. Dyson.

"Good idea," said Dr. Sharp.

"I'll vote for it," said Reverend Bax.

"So will I if the boy's father will accept it," said Jonathan Mercer.

"What do you think, Peter?" asked his father. "Guilty but not guilty. That seems human enough to me."

"Case dismissed," said Reverend Fisher brusquely. He got up and walked quickly to the door.

"I should damn well think so!" It was Mark Price. He was standing in the doorway eying Reverend Fisher angrily. The minister went by him without speaking a word.

"The Japs have accepted the fact that the hole in the fence has always been there," announced Mark.

"Whoop-pee," enunciated Maggie distinctly from the back of the room.

"And how it is!" said Mrs. Kahn belligerently, as if she thought Maggie hadn't said it loud enough.

"Congratulations," said Peter's father.

"Thanks, Dad," said Peter hoarsely. "It sure was good to hear your voice."

"You're so big," said his father. "I'll have my work cut out for me if I try to use that hairbrush."

"Oh, come on," said Peter, embarrassed.

"How about your window in the Staff Room?" asked Mark. "You want it back again, so you can still see that American fleet?"

"I don't know," said Peter. "Where are *you*, Dad?"

"I've been put in Father Gibney's cubicle," said his father. "But we'll be seeing lots of each other now. You go and bunk with your friends."

"Good," said Mark, and turned to the door.

"I've got your dinner waiting," said Peter's mother huskily. "You think Norm and Candy would mind waiting that long?" asked Peter of Maggie, who had come up and was standing nearby, shy of his father.

"Well, we saved our dinners to eat with you between hands," said Maggie.

Peter looked at his mother.

"Stove five," she said. "Mrs. Barsini is watching it for you."

"Thanks," he muttered, kissing her. He looked at his father, who smiled and nodded.

"I feel like running," Peter said as he neared the door with Maggie.

"Let's run, then."

They collided with Mr. Garnett coming in from the outside. He grabbed Peter's arm.

"Okay, kid, you're free," he said, squeezing the arm and releasing it with an emphatic jerk of his head.

Maggie had taken advantage of the delay to get a head start across the porch and down the steps.

"Thank you," mumbled Peter. "I hope I really am." He started after Maggie and caught up with her halfway to the barracks. His leg felt better than new. He could still climb trees. He could still be a half miler. He ran ahead of her and touched the corner of the barracks.

"I do feel freer," he breathed, turning and catching her before she crashed into the corner piling of the foundations.

"So do I," she panted, hugging him.

They separated at once and then both of them laughed at their own shyness.

"It's a funny way to feel in a prison," he said.

Maggie nodded happily. They linked arms and walked across the parade ground toward the school shed. The sun was setting in the China Sea.

"Look," said Maggie, pointing. "It's all smeared and broken."

"A Jap fried egg," said Peter with relish.

"Your father's terrific," said Maggie.

"You'll be seeing *your* father soon. It's only a question of waiting now."

"We don't have to wait for anything," she said. "We've got bridge games and schoolbooks and things to do at once."

"I guess that's right," said Peter. "Boy, am I hungry!"

# Clip and Mail This Special Shipping Label and...

SHIP TO:

_____

PRINT YOUR NAME HERE

_____

YOUR ADDRESS

CITY

STATE          ZIP #

CONTENTS: 6 INDISPENSABLE PAPERBACKS

## We will send you all six of these widely-acclaimed reference paperbacks for only $370

A $26.30 HARD-COVER VALUE

FASTER READING MADE EASY

BETTER ENGLISH MADE EASY

A NEW GUIDE TO BETTER WRITING

A DICTIONARY OF SYNONYMS AND ANTONYMS

WEBSTER'S NEW WORLD DICTIONARY

**PERFECT FOR HOME, SCHOOL OR BUSINESS OFFICE!**

SEE OTHER SIDE ▶

# Let these Get-Ahead books help you write better, read faster, speak more effectively!

Here's an unusual opportunity for everyone who is determined to get-ahead in business, socially or at school. Just print your name and address on the special shipping label printed on the opposite page. Clip it out and mail it together with the coupon below. We will paste your label on a package containing six valuable get-ahead books jam-packed with the powerful ideas, practical helps and short-cut steps you need for improving your writing, reading and speaking skills right now. These books cost $26.30 in their original hard-covers. Now, they're yours for only $3.70 in practical paperbacks. Here's a brief glimpse of what you get:

### (1) Better Writing

Shows how to get your thoughts on paper easily, quickly, more clearly and forcefully.

### (2) Faster Reading

Proven-successful ways to increase your reading speed and help you understand and remember more.

### (3) Speaking Effectively

Tested ways to improve your English, sharpen your speaking skills, sway an audience, add power to talks.

### (4) Synonyms & Antonyms Dictionary

Provides exact words you need to express your written and spoken thoughts. Easy to use.

### (5) Increase Your Vocabulary

How to expand your vocabulary quickly. 30-day new-word-mastery technique.

### (6) Desk Dictionary

632 pages of clear, complete, up-to-date definitions, pronunciations, usages, origins of words. Illustrated.

## MAIL THIS COUPON WITH SHIPPING LABEL NOW

### FREE TRIAL OFFER

Popular Library, Dept. 95–185
355 Lexington Avenue,
New York, N.Y. 10017

Send me postpaid, all six get-ahead books, in handy desk-top slip case. I'm enclosing $3.70 and, if not fully satisfied, I may return the books in good condition within 10 days for a full refund.

Name_____

Address_____

City_____

State_____ Zip_____

Be sure to enclose shipping label with coupon